THE
FIFTH FAVOR

Titles by Shelby Reed

GAMES PEOPLE PLAY

THE FIFTH FAVOR

THE
FIFTH FAVOR

Shelby Reed

HEAT | NEW YORK

THE BERKLEY PUBLISHING GROUP
Published by the Penguin Group
Penguin Group (USA) LLC
375 Hudson Street, New York, New York 10014, USA

USA I Canada I UK I Ireland I Australia I New Zealand I India I South Africa I China

Penguin Books Ltd., Registered Offices: 80 Strand, London WC2R 0RL, England
For more information about the Penguin Group, visit penguin.com.

HEAT and the HEAT design are trademarks of Penguin Group (USA) LLC.

Library of Congress Cataloging-in-Publication Data

Reed, Shelby.
The fifth favor / Shelby Reed.—Heat trade paperback edition.
pages cm
ISBN 978-0-425-26511-6
1. Erotic fiction.   I. Title.
PS3618.E4358F54 2013
813'.6—dc23
2013006080

PUBLISHING HISTORY
Ellora's Cave edition / 2008
Heat trade paperback edition / November 2013

PRINTED IN THE UNITED STATES OF AMERICA

10   9   8   7   6   5   4   3   2   1

Cover photo: Shutterstock.
Cover design by Jason Gill.
Text design by Laura K. Corless.

THE
FIFTH FAVOR

CHAPTER ONE

B illie could see the heading now: *An Afternoon with a Real-Life Gigolo*. No, too tabloid. *Face-to-Face with Fantasy.* That was better.

She'd never been assigned an article like this one. She'd never met a male prostitute, or visited a private club catering to women's sexual fantasies. And what surprised her most of all was that she liked the idea. Its lurid excitement. The thought that a woman could walk into this elegant space and choose her type of man for her type of pleasure.

Shifting her briefcase to her other hand, she glanced at a plush sofa in the lobby's sitting area, thought about making herself comfortable, and decided against it. The weirdness of the situation wobbled her usual confidence. She felt restless and self-conscious, the same squirrelly discomfort she'd experienced the first time she went to bed with a man.

She felt like a virgin.

A few feet away, the owner of Avalon stood at a reception desk with a phone tucked between her ear and shoulder, speaking French into the receiver, her passionate delivery sprinkled with bursts of husky laughter. In the short, introductory conversation Billie had shared with her before the phone interrupted them, Azure Elan had divulged that her clientele spanned the globe. She understood what women wanted, and she delivered . . . at a thousand dollars an hour. But a reporter like Billie Cort could wait, apparently, and all morning too. The phone conversation showed absolutely no sign of drawing to a close, and now Billie wished she hadn't killed herself to get to Avalon so early. *Be on time*, her editor had ordered when she made Billie's appointment a week before. Avalon didn't invite back visitors who weren't prompt.

Repressing a sigh, Billie let her gaze sweep the lobby while she waited. It was a study in neoclassic elegance, monochromatic shades of sedate ecru and ivory. Trompe l'oeil cherubs smiled benignly from the ornate plaster ceiling, their fat arms embracing lush, naked nymphs. Somewhere beyond the fresco, in the rooms lining four floors of a century-old town house, people had sex. Regularly. All night long, engaged in the most expensive, erotic pleasures imaginable. The club's clientele consisted of the wealthiest women in the world. Its "companions" were rumored to be the most exquisite male specimens, representing every country, every culture, every female's ideal.

Outside the heavily draped windows, traffic sailed by, a silent film of Monday morning rush hour in Washington, D.C. Inside Avalon, the absence of noise draped the perfumed air, rent only by the faint, tinkling notes of Mozart. Billie felt as though she'd stepped into a different dimension, where only beauty and ecstasy and fantasy existed.

A far cry from the black hole her own personal life had become.

Restive, she moved away from the window, briefcase clutched against her thighs.

A door squeaked open somewhere nearby, followed by a resounding click. Curious at a new sign of life in the hushed building, Billie wandered across the marble tile to peer down the long, chandeliered passage that led off the lobby. A man in a white Nike T-shirt, shorts, and running shoes had slipped through a back door marked *Fire Exit* and started in her direction. He used the towel around his neck to wipe the perspiration from his face as he approached the lobby.

Billie squinted at him. An employee, maybe? Azure said the club employed over twenty male escorts, all young and extraordinarily attractive.

The man approaching her was more than attractive. Tall, muscular, he moved with the liquid ease of someone totally confident within his body. He drew closer, and when his dark eyes met hers, he smiled and let the towel fall against his shoulder.

She politely returned his smile and cast a look over her shoulder at Azure. The slender club owner gave her an encouraging nod as if again bidding her to wait, all the while murmuring into the receiver.

When the man reached the lobby, he paused and glanced at Azure, who snapped her fingers, pointed to Billie, and mouthed, "That's her."

"Good morning." He continued toward her, still breathless from exertion. "You're the reporter from the women's magazine?"

Billie nodded, disconcerted. He couldn't be her interview, could he? Nora Richmond, her editor at *Illicit*, had purportedly retained the services of the infamous Adrian once, and described him as sleek, polished. Billie had pictured elegance and suave sophistication, three-piece suit and expensive Italian shoes. But this man, twenty-something with a healthy, glowing charisma, could have been a student jogging around one of the nearby college campuses.

"I'm Billie Cort." She extended her hand when he reached her. His fingers wrapped around hers and squeezed gently, sending a frisson of warmth up her arm.

"I'm Adrian," he said. "Please excuse my appearance, Ms. Cort. I run to work most mornings. If you have a few minutes, I'll catch a quick shower before our interview."

"That's fine." Billie's voice sounded brisk and confident, but inside, she quivered. In thirty-three years on the planet, she'd never come face-to-face with a man quite like this exquisite creature. His olive complexion and black gaze spoke of an exotic heritage. His ragged attire did little to disguise his raw male beauty. The cotton shirt clung to his chest, damp with perspiration. Sweat slicked his strong thighs, wetted his black, short-cropped hair, sparkled on his upper lip.

It wasn't until she looked into his eyes at such close proximity that she understood. Promises of ecstasy glittered there, diamonds in an obsidian sea. In that instant, all his youthful exuberance slid away and exposed the wild, worldly creature she'd expected. He was Avalon's favorite son for a reason, and the reason was written in that black, black gaze.

He hadn't yet released her hand. His fingers burned her knuckles. If he tugged even a little, she'd collide against his hard, damp body.

"Forgive me, Ms. Cort," Azure said as she hung up the phone and walked around the reception desk. "I see you two are getting acquainted."

Glancing past Billie's shoulder, Adrian exchanged some sort of silent communication with the raven-haired proprietor and relinquished Billie's hand. "Give me fifteen minutes to get ready."

"Of course," Billie said, her attention volleying between the dark demigod and his employer. "Take all the time you need."

He backed away and disappeared up the stairs that curved behind the reception desk, taking two at a time with effortless grace.

"He cleans up beautifully," the club owner said wryly, stopping beside Billie to gaze up the staircase. "Normally, I wouldn't introduce you to a companion in such an indisposed state. But it's my understanding you're only interested in an interview?"

"That's right." Billie clutched her briefcase like a shield. She knew Azure's kind. The woman's blue eyes were cold, discerning, framed in an ivory, angular face that spoke of shrewd determination. No doubt she could sum up a person's character in a single glance. Right now Billie was the subject of Azure's laser scrutiny, and she didn't like it. As a reporter she was accustomed to being the observer, to detecting vulnerability and ulterior motives in body language, facial expression, the steadiness of a gaze. But Azure stripped her down with those chilled blue eyes, touching vulnerable places Billie had thought well defended.

Never let them see you sweat. Shaking her hair back from her face, she straightened her shoulders and returned the club owner's unwavering look.

After a tense moment, Azure glanced away. "I'm so sorry for the telephone's interruption." She spoke with just a hint of an unidentifiable accent, laying one slender, manicured hand on Billie's forearm to lead her to the sitting area. "Tell me about the article while we wait for Adrian. What do you think your readers want to know?"

Billie chose the nearest damask sofa and sat, posture arrowstraight. "The usual things to begin with. What exactly does a companion at Avalon do? Besides the obvious, of course. Many women have no idea such clubs exist."

"Many women can't afford such a club."

"I know I couldn't."

"Then you're most fortunate to have this assignment, aren't you?" Azure smiled as she seated herself on a Queen Anne settee. "I'm sure you'll find the experience enriching."

"No doubt." Billie bit her lip, then ventured, "I'd like to know how Adrian got into this business."

"He was born for this business." Azure's hand mindlessly caressed a bronzed sculpture that graced the table beside her. Two lovers entwined, their limbs meshed like vines. "He's not just a pretty face. The average Avalon client seeks intelligent conversation, companionship, culture. For some, sex isn't a necessity—although few turn aside the chance with a man like him." Her incisive gaze drilled into Billie. "In a million years, I never thought I'd spare him—albeit anonymously—for a magazine article, nor trust a complete stranger to paint a picture of my beloved Avalon for women everywhere without sparing a single detail that could endanger the club, Adrian, myself . . . " Her long fingers gripped the material of her ivory dress in white-knuckled fists, then released it. "But as I'm sure you're well aware, your editor, Nora Richmond, is one of our best business referrals. So you see, we treat our contacts well, Ms. Cort. And Adrian will treat you well if you keep your questions harmless enough to protect us all."

She paused again, glanced down at her nails. "Besides, exposing Avalon for its true magnificent purpose would bring about some very unpleasant consequences for you, so keep that in mind if you and Nora want to maintain your jobs, hmm? Now tell me," her husky voice lightened at last, "how long will it take you to get what you need?"

Billie swallowed. "It depends on how he answers my questions."

"And that depends on how you pose them, Ms. Cort. Adrian

will tell you everything you need to know about his position here at Avalon. He'll tell you about the life of an escort in excruciating detail . . . he has no shame. But he won't divulge the names of his clients, so don't bother to ask. He's sworn to secrecy on anything that could flag us to the authorities. And he won't answer questions about his personal life. He protects his privacy most fiercely."

"I can be persuasive," Billie said evenly. If she couldn't get personal details about the man, details that marked him as human and attainable, it wouldn't be much of an article.

"Adrian has a will of granite." Azure's finger drifted along the sculpted buttock of the statue's male figure. "Push him too far, and he'll show you the door."

"But it's my job to push for information."

"He won't have it. There are others here who'd be happy to tell you their personal stories."

"No—it has to be Adrian." Billie frowned at her own declaration. Where had that come from? Technically the article didn't have to be solely about him. Nora Richmond may have sampled him and found him the crème de la crème, but Billie didn't have to limit her research to him. And now that the club owner had given her free rein to speak with more than one of the escorts . . .

Ah, hell. It didn't matter. She already knew the article belonged to Adrian. She'd seen his face, heard his quiet voice, looked into his seductive eyes. The unexpected yearning he'd instantly stirred in her deepest femininity would pack her article with the punch that promised to make her one of the most successful writers in *Illicit*'s history.

"Let me rephrase. I'd like to start with Adrian," she said firmly, "and if I hit a brick wall, I'll shift gears."

"As you see fit." Azure's feline smile didn't quite reach her eyes as she rose to her feet. "He's all yours until one o'clock this after-noon, and then you must let him go. His schedule is full, as is his waiting list."

Billie hesitated. "What if I need more than one day?"

Azure moved toward the hall, her attention clearly elsewhere now. "Talk with my secretary, Maria, and we'll see what we can ar-range."

"I don't have to monopolize his working hours," Billie said quickly. "Maybe I could meet with him on his day off."

Azure's laughter floated across the lobby like low-pitched chimes. "Ms. Cort, it won't take you long to find out just how many brick walls you'll hit with Adrian even here, in the place where he feels most anonymous. He would never agree to meet with a reporter on his personal time. Besides, I can't imagine you'll need him longer than a few hours. He'll be very cooperative with the questions he's prepared to answer, but I don't want him pushed beyond that. He works long nights, and I won't have you exhausting him. He needs to be on his toes, tonight especially."

Billie nodded, squelching the urge to ask what was so important about a Monday night in mid-August, when even the leaves on the trees wilted from the heat. Perhaps a visiting celebrity held an ap-pointment? Or royalty, for that matter. Anything was possible. Whatever it was, Azure Elan held a tight rein on her property, and Adrian had obviously helped to make her a wealthy woman. Billie jotted a mental note to question him on his relationship with the proprietor.

"Good luck, Ms. Cort." Azure paused at the edge of the corridor and glanced back, her pale gaze lingering on Billie. "Enjoy yourself. Adrian has a wonderful way of sliding beneath a woman's skin. I'd be prepared for anything if I were you." With a parting wave, she glided down the hall, her white, silky tunic floating like diaphanous wings around her willowy figure, leaving the scent of Chanel No. 5 in her wake.

Ten heartbeats passed—inexplicably rapid heartbeats—and Adrian reappeared, this time at the foot of the winding staircase, so silent in his descent that Billie was caught unaware. She jumped up from the sofa.

"I startled you," he said.

"Yes." She rested a damp palm against her pounding heart and leaned to retrieve the notebook that had slipped from the outside pocket of her attaché. "I think I've been in a state of surprise since I walked into this place."

Her bald admission brought a smile to his mouth. "You don't frequent private women's clubs?"

"Not on Mondays," she said with a wry grin. "Bear with me, Mister . . ."

"Just Adrian." He regarded her with open curiosity without moving from the foot of the stairs, and Billie returned the look, holding his gaze even as tiny currents of sexual awareness threaded down her spine.

His hair, damp from the shower, was brushed away from his patrician features. The white cotton shirt he wore was unbuttoned at the throat, sleeves rolled to the elbows, exposing dark, corded forearms that spoke of sun and strength. His khaki pants fit him smoothly, creased perfectly down the front, cuffs breaking just right at the top of his gleaming loafers. Casual elegance.

The faint, herbal scent of shampoo and expensive cologne tickled her senses from all the way across the room.

Extending a hand to her, palm up, he said, "Come upstairs."

She grabbed her briefcase and took a step toward him. "You don't have a last name?"

"Everyone has a last name." His hand hovered in the air, waiting.

He was forcing her to cross the marble floor to meet him, and like a luna moth drawn to a midnight moon, she drifted toward him.

When she reached him, she took his hand and looked up into his face. "Is it Jones? Smith? Or Brown?"

His lips twitched. "None of the above."

"And you won't tell me?"

"It's not necessary information."

She tilted her head, studying his angular features. "You don't look like an Adrian."

His smile broadened. "Imagine that."

"More like a Carlos, or a Juan, or a Diego."

"Those are Hispanic names."

"Aren't you Hispanic?"

"I'm anything you want me to be." His gaze flickered beyond Billie's shoulder for an instant, then returned to her face. "But for the record, Azure names all the companions."

As if on cue, a door at the end of the hall clicked open, but from where she stood, Billie saw no one in the narrow passageway.

Adrian's eyes burned into hers. "Are you ready to begin?"

What a question. How many other ladies had he asked in that very same way, for very different reasons?

She nodded mutely and followed him away from the hall, up the elegant, sweeping staircase that led to a woman's deepest secrets.

CHAPTER TWO

It took me three months to get an appointment with you," Billie said from a plaid wingback chair, watching Adrian as he knelt in front of a small refrigerator. "Azure told me your schedule stays full."

"But I'm free now." He withdrew a pitcher of orange juice and straightened to his full height. Six feet or so, she guessed. He looked as well suited to the elegant bedroom as the handsome, ecru-striped comforter and matching draperies. "Have you had breakfast?" he asked over the splash of juice filling the glass. "How about a croissant? A bagel?"

"I don't eat breakfast."

"Then you should drink something." He returned to the sitting area in front of the fireplace and handed her a crystal glass.

She eyed its orange, pulpy contents. "This looks too healthy for the likes of me. I'm fairly sure coffee runs through my veins."

"Is that why your hands are shaking?"

Embarrassed, Billie shrugged and took a sip of the chilled juice.

"Let's start with basic information." She set the glass on a tiny round table and reached into her attaché for a handheld recorder. "How old are you?"

Cradling his own glass in his hands, he sat on an identical chair across from her. "Twenty-eight."

Ageless to a hungry woman's eyes. "And your background . . . do you have a degree?"

"An undergraduate degree in sociology. Further educational pursuits were interrupted by all this . . . opportunity." He gestured to the plush surroundings.

To her left, a marble-mantel fireplace spanned half the wall. Reproduction paintings in ornate frames flanked what appeared to be a bathroom door across the room. The damask curtains were drawn on all four windows, with only a sliver of morning sun peeking through the heavy silk material.

No personal touches anywhere. Nothing to mark the surroundings as Adrian's, just cool elegance. Billie's gaze darted back to his face. "Is this your personal room?"

"Yes."

"But you don't live here."

"I have another residence in the city."

"I see." She withdrew a pen from her briefcase and scrawled notes across a tiny, spiral-bound pad. His answers stirred new questions. "Do you live with anyone?"

At his silence, she looked up and found him smiling.

"I live with Rudy," he said.

Billie's eyebrows rose. "Your . . . lover?"

"My Labrador."

She returned her attention to her notepad. "Azure said you wouldn't answer personal questions."

"It depends on what they are." He took another swallow of orange juice and ran a thumb across his bottom lip, his dark gaze steady on her face. "I'll let you know if you cross the line."

Without directly meeting his eyes, Billie said, "Are you bisexual?"

He didn't seem surprised by the question. "That's a loose term nowadays, Ms. Cort."

"But do you have sex with men?"

"No."

"Have you ever?"

"I could be very wealthy if I did things differently, but the answer is no."

"You must be doing something right," Billie pointed out. "Your clothes, your style, everything about you speaks of money."

"I'm comfortable. I buy what I need, and I want for nothing material."

"So what *do* you want for, Adrian?"

Their eyes locked, and her heart stuttered just once before it thundered into a reckless dance behind her breast. She burned all over, as though her entire being had passed through a flame.

He leaned forward and rested his forearms on his knees. "What does any man want?" he asked softly, searching her face as though the answer could be found there. "Or any woman?"

Billie breathed in his cologne. Soft musk, a hint of patchouli. "A home. Nice things. A family. Someone to love."

"Three out of four isn't bad." His lashes dropped as he considered the glass in his hands. "What else, Ms. Cort?"

"Will you tell me about your family?"

His gaze returned to her face, shuttered. "No."

"Do you love anyone?"

"My family," he said, and the slight narrowing of his eyes warned her away from the topic.

After several more minutes of stop and go, Billie landed on the subject of Azure Elan, and some of the tension left his broad shoulders as he sat back in the chair's winged embrace, his long legs stretched out before him.

"I met Azure at a party when I was a college student. By working for her, I was able to pay for my undergrad education."

"And you went to work for her, knowing fully what a companion at Avalon does?"

"Yes. But I began here as a bartender, not sure if I wanted the lifestyle. Gradually, thanks to the generous attention and support of some of the patrons . . ." He arched a brow and left the thought hanging.

Billie made a note on her pad. "The clients suggested that Azure promote you?"

"A few weeks into my employment, yes."

"That didn't take long."

A smile tugged at his mouth. "No. The vote of confidence was quite flattering."

She moved the recorder to the table by her elbow. "What's your relationship with Azure?"

"She's my employer," he said. "The boss."

Billie raised her brows. "And nothing more?"

"Nothing more."

"What about before? When she first hired you?" When he stared back at her without responding, she added, "Adrian, I need to capture as much of your world as possible in a few short hours. In your line of work, doesn't a club owner like Azure sample what she offers her customers?"

"Maybe you should ask Azure."

It was too soon to plumb that particular shadowy corner. She could come back to it. Her next question would probably meet with the same stony dead end, but it was worth a shot. "You sleep with a lot of women," she began, drawing aimless scrolls on her notepad. "Do you ever find yourself . . . personally involved?"

Adrian shifted to set his glass on a nearby table. "Ms. Cort, every woman I've ever touched has elicited some sort of response from me. Sometimes it's romantic. Sometimes companionable. Other times it's passionate, because what male with blood running through his veins could help it? Despite the unique and misunderstood nature of my position, I'm a man like any other. Women move me. All women, in one way or another."

Yet he seemed so detached. She couldn't picture him riled or moved or emotional, despite his eloquent claims. She scribbled a few words, clicked her pen twice, then sat back to study him. Her attention wandered lower, to the triangle of skin at his open collar, to the fine, dark hair that sprinkled his forearms, to his fingers, skilled in pleasure, which had touched a thousand women. For an instant she imagined them on her. Pulling away her beige linen suit jacket, tugging the silk shell from her skirt, sliding beneath to soothe her burning skin. Every nerve in her body danced.

Clearing her throat, she crossed one knee over the other and subtly squeezed to ease the ache building between her thighs. "I think I'll take you up on that bagel now," she said.

An hour later, Billie clicked off the digital recorder and tucked a wave of hair behind her ear. "Let's take a break."

He stood, laced his fingers behind his head, and gave a shuddering stretch. He reminded her of a panther, glossy and primal. Darkness lingered beneath his elegant surface, made Billie acutely aware of herself, her surroundings, her words. Almost as though she should protect herself, and yet she couldn't identify the danger.

"Are you getting the information you're after?" he asked as she stood and roamed the perimeter of the room.

"Most of it, anyway." She kept her tone light, even as she sensed his regard moving over her like a warm current. "You're not an easy subject."

"What haven't I told you, besides a few personal details?"

"Your life story."

"Hmm." His lips curved in a smile. "What else?"

"A client's experience. I mean minute by minute. Since the members here guard their privacy like the crown jewels, maybe you could fill me in on the more graphic details when we resume."

"I thought you'd never ask."

She purposely avoided his eyes and studied the fine furnishings as she wandered, trailing her fingers along gilded edges and sleek, polished wood. The king-sized four-poster bed held a feather mattress so thick, it rose two feet from the box springs.

At the bathroom door, she paused. "May I?"

"Go ahead."

Cautiously, she peeked inside the room and caught her breath. Her reflection leaped back at her from every angle, surrounded by travertine marble.

"This is incredible." She stepped inside and turned a slow circle, taking in the twin marble washbasins, granite-topped vanities, gleaming gold-leafed fixtures. The walls were covered entirely in mirrors. A bathtub, large enough for six adults, sat catty-cornered in an alcove, engulfed in exotic plants.

In the corner of the tub, rising from the foliage, a three-foot Kouros statue stood ready to spout water from its palms with a turn of the gilded fixtures at its foot.

"I've never seen anything like this," Billie said when a hundred reflections of Adrian appeared behind her. "Where do those doors lead?"

He crossed to three knobs jutting unobtrusively from the mirrors. "One holds a toilet and bidet. This one's a closet. And this one—" He flung open the door. "This is a shower."

Billie moved beside him and peered into the dim chamber. The entire space was tiled in alabaster, with double showerheads extending from each of three sides. "My God. You could throw a party in here."

"Perceptive." When her gaze flew to his, he smiled. "How old are you, Billie?"

"Thirty-three."

"With such innocent eyes for a cutthroat *Illicit* reporter."

She studied his expression, found it sincere. "Despite rumors to the contrary, not all of us fit the hard-hitting mold."

"I see that." He reached up and brushed an errant strand of hair from her cheek, a tender gesture that caught her completely off guard. "And I like it."

She couldn't quite catch her breath. They stood too close in the shower doorway. His presence, his delicious heat, stole her oxygen. "Don't tell anyone you figured me out," she said abruptly, using wry humor to defuse her own shaken response. "It's a sign of weakness in this business to let anyone know you have a heart."

"Of course it is." Frown lines creased his brow as his thumb lingered at the curve of her cheek. "Our industries share more than a few stray similarities."

They stared at each other a moment longer, then Billie swallowed and looked away from his dark gaze. "That tub looks wonderful." She moved toward it as an excuse to break the thick, too-intimate moment. "Do your clients like it?"

"I've never entertained a woman who didn't." A note of mild amusement edged his words as he followed and stopped beside her. "It has special jets. Take a look."

Billie stepped up on the marble platform, her hand gliding over the plush stack of Egyptian cotton towels nearby. "I haven't seen a whirlpool tub like this before."

"Only six exist in the world. Specially designed for Avalon." Stepping up behind her, Adrian leaned to twist a gold knob. Instantly, steaming water splashed into the tub.

Billie's lips curved into a smile. No ten-minute wait for the tap to run warm. Within seconds, four inches of water undulated beneath her hand. "This is heavenly." She fluttered her fingers through the steady, massaging waves.

"And this," Adrian said as he pressed a button hidden behind the Kouros, "is ecstasy."

Plumes of water shot from myriad jets placed strategically at the back, sides, and bottom of the tub. Rhythmic spurts. Billie stared at it, illicit images dancing through her mind. "The special jets, I presume?"

Adrian merely smiled and led her hand back to the water, turning it so that a spray pulsed against her palm.

The vibration hammered through her veins, down low in her stomach. Lower. Her knees weakened, and the most obtuse question of all time slid from her lips. "What's . . . so special about them?"

His mouth brushed her ear. "Why don't you take off your clothes and find out?"

She already felt naked, standing there with her hand shoved against the undulating jet and Adrian's hot, hard body a narrow inch behind hers. "Because this is an interview."

"All right. Let me see if I can put it into words." It sounded like a threat. Before she could reply, his free hand swept around to gently hold her abdomen as he eased her forward, closer to the tub.

"The jets are positioned to accommodate the varying statures of our clients," he murmured, his cheek against hers, his warm, spicy scent filling her senses. "They pulse and massage and caress in ways a man's tongue cannot. The little railing here, and the niches for the feet, hold the woman in place while the jets stimulate her, and of course her companion is always her attendant, so she doesn't even need to stand on her own if she chooses. All she has to concentrate on is how many orgasms she can achieve."

Tightening his hold on her waist to keep her from slipping over the edge, he guided Billie's hand from jet to jet beneath the water, sampling each one, his voice growing husky over the gentle hum of the hidden motor. "This one provides direct stimulation and brings a quick, intense orgasm. This one has a timed delay. A tease, if you like. But the resulting climax is worth the wait." He shifted her hand to a dual jet with a softer pressure that sprayed higher, over the surface of the water. "And this one stimulates the breasts, while below . . ."

They dipped beneath the water again, where a tiny, sharp stream greeted Billie's tingling palm, flickering up and down, up and down. The sensation on her palm echoed a phantom caress between her legs, and she felt herself go damp and quivery there, as though she floated in that roiling tub, spread open to that flickering stream of silken heat, anchored in buoyant water against the hard, hungry body of her waiting companion.

Adrian.

His fingers burned her waist through the silk of her blouse, and perspiration beaded her skin, between her breasts, the nape of her neck, the small of her back, as his tone dropped impossibly lower. "Are you making note of all this, Ms. Cort?"

Oh God, was the response that welled on her lips, and even though she withheld it, he seemed to hear her as if she'd groaned aloud.

"The tub is almost filled." He nuzzled her cheek, his slick fingers trailing beads of water up her wrist when he drew her hand from the tub. "Last chance."

Her eyelids slid closed. "But I have so little time to get what I need from you."

The faltering statement rang out in the bathroom, vulnerable and raw and needful.

Humiliated, Billie straightened in his embrace and turned to glare at him. "We're wasting time. Let's get back to the interview."

"I wasn't aware that we'd digressed." Adrian stepped down from the tub, handed her a towel, and reached for another to dry his own hands. "You asked me to tell you about the jets."

"Adrian, please." Billie squelched the frustration rising within her. She didn't want this man to group her with the clients and conquests and hungry-eyed females passing him on the street, yet how was she different? She was one of the few who'd sought him not for his lovemaking, but for his story, his truths. And now all she could think about was the sensation of his lips against her ear, his breath warm, his words like fingers stroking her nerves, stroking her skin . . .

Get it together, Billie.

"Let's go back to the other room," she said, a light suggestion to banish the tension choking the air.

He didn't speak, and for an alarming moment, she thought he would end the interview, show her to the door. Perhaps she'd breached some boundary after all, simply by telling him *no*.

Rejection for such a man wasn't food for power.

With a half glance in her direction, Adrian finally tossed the towels on the counter and motioned brusquely toward the doorway. Once again seated in the bedroom, he waited in silent observation while Billie activated the recorder with trembling fingers.

Pressing the record button, she looked up at him. His steady regard bathed her in heat. He wasn't finished toying with her. A carnal shiver worked its way up her spine and her nipples hardened beneath the linen jacket.

As if he knew, Adrian said, "Why don't you take off your jacket and get comfortable?"

Billie opened her mouth to decline, but found herself sliding the material off her shoulders. Painfully aware of his observation, she wriggled out of the jacket, folded it, and laid it across the arm of her chair. When she turned back to him, he said, "Now your shoes."

"Oh, I'm—"

"You've got until one o'clock to interview me." He rose from the chair, knelt in front of her, and lifted her foot against his crotch. "That's a whole morning in these torture devices," he said, slipping the shoe off and setting it beside the marble hearth. His palm caressed her bare sole. "Now the other."

Speechless, Billie let him remove her other shoe and closed her eyes at the desire that sizzled through her. The simple touch at her foot left her aroused and aching. How could any woman survive making love with this man? Just the flashing image brought a groan to her lips, one she barely suppressed.

"That's better." He considered her face for a moment before he straightened and seated himself again.

Billie glanced blindly at the notes in her lap. "Uh . . . where was I? Tell me about your clients."

The topic sent a bevy of emotions skittering across his features: amusement, aversion, interest, resignation. He folded his hands across his lean stomach as he searched for the answer. "They range in age from twenty-one to fifty, with most in their forties. Accomplished businesswomen. Doctors, diplomats, attorneys, politicians. Rich, lonely housewives."

"Married women," Billie said.

"Many of them, yes. So alone in their marriages they have to seek intimacy from a total stranger."

"And pay for it too."

"Yes."

She stared at her notepad again and closed it with a sigh, knowing she couldn't concentrate on the questions she'd scribbled there earlier. "Tell me about a typical visit with a client."

Adrian rested his head against the back of the wingback chair, his features shadowed. "First the client has to present a clean bill of health. Blood test, the whole nine yards."

"And you?"

"Every six weeks I see a physician, have a complete blood workup. It's all in my file downstairs, which you're welcome to examine. Every companion has a file for the clientele's reference."

"Okay." She made a mental note to stop by Azure's office after the interview. "So when the client arrives for her appointment, how does she choose you?"

"She looks at pictures during a preliminary meeting with Azure or her secretary, Maria. She reads files, bios, asks questions. Then she makes her appointment."

"And then what?"

Adrian shifted and the candlelight glow from the brass chandelier touched his profile. "I meet her at the time and place she specifies. Parties, gallery openings, the opera. Sometimes here at Avalon, and sometimes in a restaurant or bar. Whatever she wants."

Billie tried to picture such a rendezvous and a current of forbidden excitement surged through her. "Do you ever travel to meet these women?"

"As far as Prague. Once a year I meet a particular client there. And recently, twice to London." His thumb rubbed at an errant thread on the arm of the chair. "You do understand that not all of these women seek sex. Some want a companion for business and social events. Some just want male company."

"I see."

He glanced at her. "Do you? You look doubtful."

"That's because . . ." Billie shook her head and laughed. "To be completely frank, Adrian, I can't understand a woman hiring you and spending hours in your company without entertaining sexual thoughts."

"Is that what you're doing, Billie?" His lashes shielded the expression in his gaze as it dropped to her mouth. "The conditions are different, but the potential is there. Although it's through your work, you've hired me. And although it's for the sake of an article, you're spending hours in my company. Are you entertaining sexual thoughts?"

No answer she could summon would save her pride. "That bathtub number you pulled on me was pretty potent."

His brow quirked. "You liked that, did you?"

Cheeks flaming, she changed the subject. "Once you meet the client, what happens?"

"That's a broad question. I'd rather walk you through it." His voice was soft, his features hidden again in shadow as he let his head drop back. "We could leave no stone unturned, if you'd allow it."

Billie lowered her gaze, heart hammering. "I'd rather stay on track."

He was silent for a long time, watching her from the shadowed

depths of the wingback chair. Then he said, "The course of the evening all depends on the client. Let's say you've made the appointment, Billie. What would you want to do, the very first thing?"

She swallowed and searched for an honest answer. "I guess I
would want to get acquainted with you."

"So we'd go out to dinner. Have a drink. Or if you seemed particularly tense, like you do right now—"

"I'm not tense," she protested.

"But we're speaking hypothetically, aren't we?" His knowing
smile silenced her. "If I sensed you were uptight, I would suggest we
have a drink here, in this room, without any distractions. We would
talk, just like we're doing now. Then . . ." With one graceful movement, he got to his feet and gazed down at her. "Do you like to
dance, Billie?"

"Sometimes." Inside she quaked, but damned if she didn't sound
positively cool.

With that same mild humor playing around his mouth, Adrian
crossed to the armoire and pulled open the doors. "Before anything
happens between us," he said, reaching inside to switch on a stereo,
"may I have this dance?"

Tony Bennett's mellow croon floated from invisible speakers
buried in the ceiling. Adrian returned to her, took her hand, and
tugged her to her feet. "In a typical scenario, the client would probably say yes."

"I have two left feet," she said huskily.

"It's just a dance, Billie. Say yes."

Tony Bennett's voice slid around the notes of the ballad. Adrian's regard slid around her desires, the inhibitions that kept them
firmly imprisoned, and set them free.

"Yes," she whispered.

Leading her to the middle of the room, he tucked her hands

against his chest and drew her against him, and Billie discovered her nose fit perfectly in the curve of his neck.

They danced. As the ballad faded and another, sultrier refrain painted the room with notes of seduction, she clung to him and let him lead. Her former fiancé, Ted, had always complained that she didn't know how to follow. Time and again at social functions he'd stalk off the dance floor, leaving her marooned and embarrassed. And all because of her natural propensity to lead.

The humiliation seemed like a distant dream now, and Ted, a wispy phantom. Following Adrian's slow, swaying movements was suddenly the easiest thing she'd ever done. Playacting, she told herself. He was allowing her to stand in a client's shoes. But how far would he take this? How far would she let him?

Her lashes fluttered open when his chin moved against her hair. "Ask me what happens next, Billie."

Separate of her will, her fingertips slid beneath his arms to surround his back, across cotton-covered muscle, drawing him closer. "What happens next?"

"Nothing." His whisper brushed her forehead, his embrace gentle, nonthreatening. "You're too frightened. But I know what you want, how much you want it. I can take one look at you and know what you need."

"How?" She drew back to meet his gaze. "How can you know what a woman needs with just a look?"

"Your eyes are a dead giveaway. You're starving, Billie. For love. For sex. For attention. Who denied you all these things?" The truth exploded against her unguarded heart and she tried to pull away, but he held tight. "You wanted to know what a client experiences."

"I came here to research an article. I didn't come for this."

"Maybe not, but it's what you want now that you're here. A woman never leaves here unsatisfied."

"But I'm not looking for sex. I'm not," she repeated, needing to convince him. Needing to convince herself.

"You should be." His fingers brushed the stubborn wave of hair from her cheek, tender, comforting. Then he grasped her arms and brought them up around his neck, looped his own around her waist, and swayed her to the music again, pelvis to pelvis, his gaze locked on hers. "Have you ever asked for it?"

She made a scornful sound. "I'm a woman in her thirties. What do you think?"

"I think you don't know how."

Her silence was her confession.

Moving with a suddenness that alarmed her, Adrian caught her chin in his fingers and forced her gaze to meet his. "All you have to do is say three little words, Billie. *I want you.* You can whisper them in my ear, and nobody has to know but you and me. Nobody will know what we do in this room. You can have anything, everything. The way you like it, over and over. Just say it."

Mesmerized, she stared up at him, her throat dry with desire.

"Say it," he whispered, his ferocity softening, melting into sinuous intent. His fingers crept through her hair and cradled the back of her head as he leaned to kiss her chin, her jaw. "I can give you anything."

Desperation and carnal need rose in a huge wave and shoved the words into her throat. "I want . . ." She tried to swallow and failed. "I don't know. I just want."

His hand left her hair and slid down her neck, her spine, down, down, to rest on the curve of her buttock. Then he pulled her tight against him, tighter than before, and for the first time Billie was aware of something more than her own desire. The quickened rush of his breath, his heartbeat thundering beneath his muscled chest, the hard press of his erection through linen and khaki and skin. Adrian wanted too. He wanted her. Or any woman. He could have anyone.

"No—" She cupped her hand against his mouth to halt its descent. It brushed against her palm, warm and soft, before he grasped her wrist and drew her thumb between his lips, let his tongue slide over it once, twice, then sucked it deeper into silken, wet heat . . .

Frantic, she jerked away and found herself by the fireplace again with six safe feet between them. She tried to berate him for invading her desires, probing her mind, *sucking on her thumb like that, for God's sake* . . . but she couldn't form the words.

Nor did Adrian speak. Tony Bennett was the only one with something to say, and he crooned unobtrusively from the ceiling speakers as Billie gathered her attaché, jacket, and the recorder and slipped into her shoes.

"I'm not comfortable with the route this interview has taken," she said without looking at Adrian.

"You're not comfortable with the truth," he replied.

The tape recorder slipped from her trembling fingers and cracked against the hearth. She swiped it from the floor to examine it, jabbing the buttons to no avail. It was a cheap model. Something had broken. Inside the recorder. Inside her. "That's an hour of interviewing down the toilet," she muttered.

"Then you'll come back."

She turned to look at him and found his black gaze watchful, unreadable. "This article could make my career. I have to come back."

He retrieved a pad and pen from the bedside table and scribbled something, then tore off a sheet and handed it to her. "My private cell phone number, Billie. Call me and I'll be more than happy to schedule another meeting with you."

Disarmed, she stared at the paper. "You can do that? Even with your busy agenda?"

"For you, I would."

She folded the paper and slipped it into her attaché, her indignation defused. "And the next time we meet, we'll conduct our appointment with utter professionalism, right?"

His smile was grim. "Speak for yourself, Ms. Cort."

She opened her mouth to reply, then shut it and turned away to put on her jacket. Nothing she could say would restore her defenses. When he showed her downstairs to the door, all courtesy and civility again, she emerged into the too-bright afternoon sun on shaky legs, no doubt like the numerous other clients leaving Adrian's seductive embrace.

CHAPTER THREE

Adrian held aside the lobby window's drapery, his attention focused on the slightly stiff posture of the slender woman retreating from Avalon. Even the soft fall of footsteps on the marble tile behind him failed to draw his attention, and he didn't move until a soft male voice brushed his ear.

"Who is she?" Lucien murmured, staring over Adrian's shoulder at Billie Cort's departing figure.

"No one. A reporter." Adrian's gaze followed her as she crossed the street and disappeared around the corner, then he sighed, let the sheer panel fall, and glanced at his friend. "You're here early."

"Boss's orders. I'm on probation these days." Lucien scraped a hand through his tousled dark hair and offered a wry smile, but Adrian noted the tremble of his fingers, the shadows beneath his red-rimmed eyes.

"You're hung over." A flat, disapproving observation.

Lucien's gaze darted away. "Hot date last night." He moved across the deserted lobby and busied himself flipping through the old-fashioned appointment book Azure had left on the desk. His white knit shirt was untucked and rumpled, hanging off his lean frame. He was too thin, the result of living off recreational drugs instead of food.

"I want to know when you plan to recover between clients, Ad. The way Azure's booked you, you'll be going all night. And it's only Monday." He offered Adrian a crooked grin. "You ought to double up with some of these ladies. Bet they wouldn't object."

Adrian didn't respond, just watched him, his brows drawn down as he focused on the faint, bluish shadow that marred Lucien's unshaven jaw. He knew better than to ask about the bruise; Lucien would inevitably react in ferocious defense, as he did whenever Adrian questioned him about his ever-growing proclivity toward drugs, alcohol, and danger. Especially danger. Whoever Lucien was spending his free nights with had a combustible temper. It wasn't the first time Adrian had noticed bruising on his friend's face.

"So why was a reporter here?" Lucien asked, finally meeting Adrian's eyes.

Adrian sauntered toward the reception desk. "She's doing an article on a day in the life of a male escort. She writes for *Illicit*."

Lucien's dark brows shot up. "Juicy magazine. Even juicier reporter. I caught a good view of her shapely little ass when she hightailed it out of here. Plan on giving her a sample of what it's all about to be you?"

A sudden vision of Billie Cort's big green eyes flashed across Adrian's mind and he sucked in a soft breath. He'd wanted her, and the attraction had caught him completely off guard. She wasn't an extraordinary beauty. She wasn't refined and elite and willow-thin. No plastic surgeon had touched the laugh lines around her eyes, or the small breasts curving gently beneath her tailored blouse.

She was real. A glimpse of the past, when life was simpler, cleaner, and more truthful. She was vulnerable and pretty.

She was dangerous.

Adrian offered his friend a rueful smile. "I tried to give her a freebie, but she wouldn't have me."

Lucien laughed. "Now *that's* refreshing. Maybe you should've gotten her number."

"I'll see her again. The interview's not finished." He hesitated, his humor fading. "You should rest before you go to work, Luke."

"Now, now. Don't let Azure hear you calling me by my good Christian name."

"I'm serious. You look like hell."

Lucien shrugged. "I've got a couple hours. I'll suck down some of Consuela's Brazilian blend and take a cool shower. Joe's got some stuff too that'll wake me up in a hurry."

Reproach tightened the muscles in Adrian's jaw. "Couldn't work better than a decent night's sleep and a good hot meal, and you know it."

"Yeah, but it's faster and a hell of a lot more fun."

Adrian stared at him, speechless with a sick, confused disgust, and for a moment the two men stood with gazes locked, the air between them heavy with a nameless provocation.

Then Lucien looked away, rubbing his arms as though he were chilled. "You really ought to relax, Ad. Join the party once in a while. This is a lifestyle most men would kill for."

"I sure as hell wouldn't covet yours."

"How would you know when you've never tasted the real thing?"

The heavy innuendo was all Adrian needed to push him past tolerance. He started toward the staircase, too incensed by his friend's flippant disregard for his own well-being to stand another minute of it.

"So I take it you don't want to grab some lunch with me?" Lucien called after him, the question heavy with sarcasm.

"No," Adrian said without looking back. "I seem to have lost my appetite."

Upstairs, he closed himself in his room, fixed a drink, and sank down on one of the wingback chairs. In a matter of hours, his first client of the night would arrive. Sandra Rochaille, wife of a French envoy, visited Avalon every six months like clockwork. Lush, blonde, and insatiable, she had initially captivated Adrian with her long limbs and lack of inhibition. But Sophie's predilections rode the edge between adventurous and aberrant, and the last time she'd left Adrian's bed, he'd felt . . . dirty.

Faint discomfort ran through him. Too close to shame. A black shadow he never allowed to seep into his conscience.

Of course, the whole morning had been one of failed defenses. Again he thought of the reporter, at the wonder in her green gaze when she'd slowly circled the luxurious bathroom. Despite a hint of cynicism that spoke of a broken heart, she'd exuded a sort of inno-cence that Adrian found utterly provocative. If she'd let him, he would have stripped her down to see what dwelled beneath. Sweet-ness, something told him. Vulnerability. She'd struggled with her own desire standing in the circle of his arms.

He ran a hand over his face and inhaled. Her scent, soap and faded flowers, still lingered on his skin. Instinctively his body stirred and he shifted on the chair, knees falling wide as he tried to force his thoughts to the night ahead. And failed.

I just want, she said when he'd finally broken down her defenses. And so had he. He'd wanted her to desire him, but truthfully, whether she knew it or not, any man's tender arms would do. The woman was wounded and aching for love. Her posture, her eyes, the vulnerability of her features screamed it. It didn't matter who Adrian was, or that he was the one who held her.

But it had mattered to him. His eyelids slid closed as he envisioned all the pleasure he could have shown her, if she hadn't had the decency to decline. No toys or tricks needed for this one; just deep, primal fucking. Stripping away her inhibitions alone would have been erotic enough to test his endurance.

In response to the sultry thoughts sliding through his mind, his cock stirred and swelled to hardness. What was wrong with him today? He rarely thought about sex when he wasn't working. With an ironic smile, he set aside his drink, loosened his belt, and slid down on the chair, fingers slipping inside the placket of his pants to ease the pressure building inside him. Not as gratifying as the soft touch of a woman's hand, but enough to quicken his pulse until it pounded in hot, strategic places.

The pressure increased to a relentless throb. He unfastened his fly, freed his erection, let his fingers trail over it until it jerked in demand of a firmer touch. A shudder of need went through him. God—when was the last time he'd needed this? It wasn't the right way to start the work night, but suddenly his body demanded relief so desperately, he couldn't think past the moment.

His fingers curled around his shaft and stroked base to tip. Again. Again. Faster, driven by a wild, rising urgency. Billie Cort had awakened something hot and hungry within him, and a moment's relief, unfortunately, would be just that.

It didn't matter, he told himself as pleasure stole the breath from his lungs. If this didn't solve the problem, he'd work it off tonight. In a matter of hours he'd have all the satisfaction a man could want.

Arching his head against the back of the chair, he gripped the armrest and braced himself against the coiling rapture while his other palm quickened its steady stroke. He had all night to exorcise his inexplicable desire for Billie. And when he saw her again, he'd do his damnedest to shield himself against the seductive, innocent appeal that made her such a rare objet d'art in his world.

They met again a week later, this time at a small café in the Adams Morgan section of Washington, where Billie would feel safe, buffered by the public's presence.

"I can't afford to pay you for more than an hour this time," she told him, skirting her gaze from his dark, piercing regard as he sat across from her. "The magazine's footing the bill, and I've been allotted—"

"This is my day off," Adrian said, fingertips caressing the lip of his water goblet.

Billie grimaced. "Does that mean you're charging me time and a half?"

"It means this hour is on me. No charge."

Billie sat in surprised silence before she spoke. "Azure said you'd never meet me on your day off."

"Azure was wrong." A smile tugged at his mouth. "I enjoyed talking to you at Avalon, Ms. Cort, but things could have gone more smoothly if I'd understood how uncomfortable you were there."

"I wasn't uncomfortable there."

Adrian's smile widened. He didn't need to point out the screaming falsity of that declaration.

She shifted on her chair and murmured thanks to the busboy as he leaned to refresh their glasses of water. When they were alone again, she reached into her purse and withdrew a small notebook and pen. A strange tension constricted her throat, a mixture of dread and anticipation of the conversation to follow.

Lying awake last night, envisioning this new exchange, she'd decided to come straight out and ask him the juicy stuff. He couldn't twist the sexual tension between them and put her on the spot this time, not in such a public place. All he had were words, and Billie could deflect anything in the hustle-and-bustle, brightly lit environment of the café.

"So how's business?" she began, flipping open the notebook.

"Lucrative." He leaned back in his chair, propped his elbows on the armrests, and laced his fingers across his stomach. "How about you?"

Humor quirked Billie's mouth. "Definitely stimulating."

Adrian smiled, genuinely this time. Something about him seemed different. More relaxed and casual, although he was flawlessly attired.

"Is your shirt custom-tailored?" she asked, noticing how it stretched across his broad shoulders and accentuated the tanned tone of his complexion. "It looks quite expensive."

"Is that question part of the interview?"

"People want to know what a man like you wears on his day off."

"The shirt was a gift," he said. "The Levi's I purchased myself. Want to check the label in my shorts too?"

Heat burned Billie's cheeks, but she jotted down the information as though she hadn't heard that last part. She was delaying the inevitable, just as she'd promised herself she wouldn't, and the humor in his features told her he knew it.

Straightening her shoulders, she met his gaze squarely. "I'm just going to ask you this flat-out. There's no painless way to word it."

"I'm not easily offended, Ms. Cort. Especially by the kinds of questions I know you want to ask me. Fire away."

She nodded, took a sip of water, and carefully arranged her flatware. Fork on the left, knife and spoon on the right. *Fire away.*

"Are you a sexual addict, Adrian? Is that why you're in this business?"

To her surprise, he seemed to consider the question, his dark brows furrowed. Then he sat forward and said, "The business swarms with sexual addicts, to be sure. For some of the companions at Avalon, the answer to your question would be a resounding yes. As for me, I simply enjoy sex, enjoy giving pleasure, especially when the woman appears to have known so little in her life." His black gaze dropped to her lips. "The sound of her cry at climax, the astonishment, the shatter of every pretense at that instant of ecstasy . . . it's nearly as satisfying to me as the experience of orgasm itself." He waited, attention unwavering on her face.

Billie scribbled a couple of words in the notebook, nothing that made any sense because an uninvited image was dancing across her mind's eye, one of herself arched beneath him, every muscle straining as she crested that elusive peak. Oh, to make love with this man, to know the touch of his graceful hands on her flesh, the soft brush of his hair against her throat as he kissed her breasts . . .

She took another sip of water to hide her illicit thoughts, then inquired, "Who taught you the art of lovemaking?"

Adrian squinted, as though the answer was not easily retrieved.

"I'm guessing it wasn't Mary Jo Johnson in the back of your dad's station wagon," she added dryly.

"No." His smile, usually so practiced and smooth, crept across his mouth unbidden. "I was an athlete in high school, didn't have much time for dating. There were a couple of girlfriends in college. But overall I think sexual prowess is innate. A matter of knowing what the woman wants, and when you don't, being unafraid to ask."

His gaze drifted back to her face. "A skilled lover is also a skilled listener. Despite the fact that I pride myself on sensing a woman's needs, the occasion does arise when I have to stop and simply . . . ask."

No one had ever asked Billie what she wanted in bed. Not even Ted, the man she once thought to spend the rest of her life with. Throat dry, she scribbled a few disjointed words across the page.

"How do you perform so tirelessly when you have multiple clients in one night?"

As soon as the question was out of her mouth, the waiter appeared with pad in hand. Adrian's attention never left Billie's face as they ordered their lunches, nor did the mild smile on his lips falter. He regarded her with what appeared to be enjoyment.

She hadn't perceived herself as particularly amusing before now. Laughter didn't come easily to her. Ted often had alluded to the fact that she was too solemn.

She bit her lip and waited until the waiter disappeared again before she met Adrian's eyes. "Maybe I should paraphrase that with, how many times do you have sex in a night?"

"It varies," he said with a shrug. "Sometimes once. Sometimes several times. Sometimes I don't keep count."

Her brows shot up. "How is that possible? I mean, men can't . . . How can you—"

"Think, Ms. Cort."

Unbidden pictures flitted through her mind and sent warmth creeping up her neck. "I could see being able to control your own response once or twice, but more than that? I don't believe it."

"Is that a challenge?" he asked softly. Before she could stumble through a response, he continued. "Haven't you ever had a man withhold his orgasm for your pleasure, Billie? It's a privilege to me. A test of strength and generosity and self-control. It offers its own kind of pleasure. The pleasure of giving."

"It sounds supremely difficult," she said huskily.

He sat back. "It is. But as with everything at Avalon, the level of challenge depends on the client. Some are more enticing than others. For example, if you were the client—"

"Don't use me as an example," she said quickly. "Remember what happened last time?"

His gaze wandered over her hair and settled on her lips. "Tell me, Billie. What happened last time?"

She closed her eyes briefly, drew a breath for strength. "I want to get through this interview without feeling mortified."

"Talking about sex mortifies you?"

"With you it does. When it concerns my own experience."

"And why is that?"

"Because this interview isn't about me," she declared. "It's about you. I'm not here as your client."

He sat watching her, as though he knew the presence of unspoken truths that clamored for release within her.

She straightened and took a sip of water, determined to reclaim her decorum. "How many women do you think you've been with?"

"Don't change the subject just yet," he said gently. "Would you like to know why I think addressing your own sexuality is hard for you?"

The answer was a firm no, because he obviously already knew the real reason; it was stamped in the dark depths of his eyes even before he spoke. This man's talents were only partially comprised of sexual skill. Somehow he could read a woman's turmoil, *Billie's* turmoil, her innermost insecurities, as though they were printed across her forehead. He would strip her to the bone if she allowed it.

"It's because you haven't explored sexual boundaries of any sort, Billie," he went on. "I'd venture to say you're virginal in every aspect except the physical. Pleasure could become so familiar to you, so certain and reaffirming, if you felt safe and loved and sure about what you were doing. But you don't feel safe when you're giving yourself to a man, do you? It terrifies you."

"Oh, so they teach you psychology at Avalon too?" Her response came bitterly, blatant evidence of her exposure at his hands. "If you keep redirecting this interview toward me, Adrian, I'll walk out of here right now, the article be damned."

He merely waited, expression placid, while she sucked in angry breaths and squelched the inexplicable indignation he'd stirred with his probing.

In a moment, emotions once again reined in, she clicked her pen and said, "So let me get this straight. You go all night withholding your own release—"

"Not all night." He leaned closer, lashes concealing the heat in his eyes. "Sometimes at the end, with the very last client, when I'm tired and hard and aching, I let myself go. And that kind of climax is worth every moment of pent-up frustration, all night long."

Billie's lips parted, but no words would come. All she could do was stare at him while the sultry picture wove around her. How was it possible to go from sheer indignation to shivering arousal within the course of a few sentences? He wielded his words like weapons and sex toys. He was some kind of sorcerer. And dangerous to a woman like her, because he'd pinpointed vulnerabilities she didn't even know she had.

He glanced down, fingered the handle of the spoon beside his plate. "But it takes a special kind of client to push me over that edge."

"What kind?" she asked foggily, while molten heat collected low in her belly, between her thighs.

His attention drifted to the low-buttoned collar of her blouse. "Someone soft. Someone tender and real." He paused. "She doesn't come along very often."

Billie cleared her throat. "Anyone lately?"

Adrian sat in silence for so long, she wondered if he'd heard her. Then he said, "No client presently fits that bill."

Their food arrived, effectively shattering the tension.

Eventually they talked on, with Billie shooting questions at him and Adrian answering them in his unruffled, restrained manner. No personal details, of course, beyond the explicit ones he provided her, without blinking, of what a woman could expect in a companion's bed at Avalon. Fantasies fulfilled, every wayward desire granted, everything short of inflicted pain, and even some of that if the client desired it.

As he spoke, Billie's gaze wandered over the fine lines of his features, the aristocratic arch of his brow, the stubborn chin and sensual lips. He was so controlled and decorous. What did he become in the heat of passion, when primal need stripped away all civility and nothing remained but the drive to possess and take and spill oneself, over and over? Did his smooth voice become terse, guttural, desperate? Did he cry out at climax, muscles tightened, skin slick from exertion, hair fallen over his brow and dripping with perspiration? Did he ever abandon his mind and all sense of politesse in trade for rapture?

The women's club cloaked him in some sort of armor. Not once in the conversation did she ever catch a glimpse of his heart, of vulnerability, of the true person who dwelled beneath the trappings of the polished icon he presented.

All too soon the time slipped away, fruitless, frustrating moments lost with the truth just out of reach. When the waiter brought out a discreet leather folder and handed it to Adrian, he took it and waved away Billie's insistence that she pay for her own meal.

"Please," he said, slipping a credit card inside the folder. "Allow me this one genuine pleasure."

Such a simple one for a man who had seen pleasure in its most excruciating and exalted forms.

They emerged into the thick humidity of the summer afternoon and paused in front of the restaurant. Adrian didn't depart right away; he stood and waited while Billie withdrew car keys from her purse and slung the strap over her shoulder.

"You've given me a great deal of information," she said, "but Adrian, what I have is not enough to write a well-rounded article."

He slid a pair of expensive sunglasses over his eyes and effectively cloaked his expression. "What do you want?"

"I don't know, but this isn't it." Too snappy. Layers of frustration piled one upon the other, all there for his examination.

They stared at each other in silence. Then he sighed. "What more could I tell you?"

She weighed her response, knowing she tread in a precarious place. "You could tell me something about the man you are. Not your deepest, darkest secrets, of course—"

"That *is* my deepest, darkest secret."

"But with the material I have, I can only describe a robotic, two-dimensional figure." Her words quickened, pushed forth by some nameless urgency. "You need to tell me something personal about yourself. Something about your past, or . . . or what's in your heart. What do you love? What do you hate? Are you an insomniac? Do you like ice cream? Ever had your heart broken? Republican or Democrat? Boxers or briefs? Something besides just . . . the shadowy figure in these notes."

The reporter in her had drifted away, and God, how gauche the woman sounded who pleaded with him in her place. Certainly now he would wave her off and depart, and she'd never see him again.

Adrian, who'd been listening with a frown of mild confusion, shifted his weight and folded his arms across his chest. "I'll have to think it through," he said, all traces of humor gone from his lips. "What I want to tell you, how I want to say it. I'm private, Billie. My privacy is my most valued possession."

She nodded, face hot with relief and anticipation. "I wouldn't strip you of it, no matter what kind of reputation reporters carry. As someone who has come to like what I know of you, I wouldn't twist your truths or try to expose you."

He watched her, emotions hidden behind the dark lenses. Then, simply, "I believe you."

"Good." Her breath drained from her, taking a modicum of tension with it. "When can I meet with you again?"

"It has to be at Avalon this time." His jaw hardened almost imperceptibly. "And if an hour is all your magazine can afford, I'm afraid we'll have to make do."

"I understand."

"Also, you'll have to go through Azure to schedule this last appointment. And don't mention that you met with me today."

She didn't ask why, only extended her hand, willing it to be steady. "I'll see you soon, then."

His warm fingers enclosed hers, sealing some sort of pact she didn't yet understand. "I'll look forward to it, Ms. Cort."

CHAPTER FOUR

Adrian paused in the doorway of his condominium's kitchen and considered the black Labrador gazing mournfully back at him. "Why are you looking at me like that?"

The dog, Rudy, blinked and huffed.

"Where's your banana?" Adrian patted him on the head as he moved past to grab a bottle of beer from the refrigerator.

At the mention of his favorite stuffed toy, Rudy whined and leaped up as quickly as his ninety pounds would allow, then circled and stared at his master, ears perked.

Adrian bumped the refrigerator door shut with his hip and frowned as he twisted the bottle cap off a Heineken. "You threw it off the balcony again, didn't you? Damn it, Rudy."

With the dog anxiously leading the way, Adrian crossed the spacious living room to the French doors and stepped between the filmy sheers fluttering in the night breeze. The balcony overlooked the city's lush tree canopy, a carpet of blackness punctuated by sparkling lights.

Grasping the balustrade, he leaned forward and squinted at the sidewalk fourteen floors below. There it was. The faded, thoroughly chewed and well-loved stuffed banana, lying forlorn on the concrete in front of the building.

"I'm not going down to get it this time," he told the dog, who sat at his feet and gazed back with an eerily human plea in his brown eyes.

Five excruciating minutes passed while Rudy followed him around the apartment in silent protest of his master's decision. Finally, with a weary sigh, Adrian set aside his beer, stepped into a pair of running shoes, and grabbed his apartment keys.

"I'll get the banana," he said, eyeing the dog, "but this is the last time. And you're losing your balcony privileges."

Tail wagging, Rudy settled on the cool teak floor of the foyer and watched him flip open the locks. As Adrian started to twist the knob, a low sound emitted from the dog's throat, a warning, soft and urgent.

Adrian glanced back at him. The dog was staring past him, as though he could see through the door to something ominous on the other side.

From the hallway came a dull thud, as though a weighty object collided with the wall by Adrian's apartment.

"Stay," he muttered, easing open the door. Initially he saw no one, but when he stepped into the hall, his stomach nose-dived.

Lucien clung to the wall, bloodied and beaten and reeking of alcohol. He was barefoot. His grimy T-shirt hung off one shoulder, hair matted with filth, eyes so swollen and bruised, Adrian hardly recognized him. "Christ! Luke—"

"Ad," he choked, grabbing at Adrian's shirt with desperate hands. "Help me." Then he tilted back against the wall and slid to the carpet, his fingers leaving streaks of red on the pristine white plaster.

D rink this." Adrian forced Lucien's shaking hands around a cup of coffee and directed it to his friend's mouth.

When the hot liquid hit Lucien's busted bottom lip, he cursed and sloshed it down the front of his chest.

"Jesus!" He glared at Adrian through one partially swollen eye. "How about a little salt to go with my wounds?"

"I'm sorry." Adrian took the cup and set it on the night table, then handed him a napkin. He studied his friend in abject silence, too disturbed to conjure words. Then, for the hundredth time in three hours, he asked, "Who did this to you?"

"If I tell you, will you beat him up for me?" Lucien's bruised mouth twisted into a rueful smile. "Come on, Ad. You know I'm not going to tell you. I can handle it myself."

"Bullshit," Adrian said quietly. "You're going to die if you keep this up. Don't you care?"

"I care. But it's like being on a train with no brakes, you know?" He shrugged and winced at the pain caused by the subtle motion. "I can't give up my fun and games. I tried. It's got such a hold on me."

"Sounds like addiction, and you know it."

Lucien closed his eyes. "Oh, I don't know. You've got a hold on me too, Ad. But I hadn't considered myself addicted to you. Not till now, anyway."

Adrian clenched his jaw and looked away. "Say the word and I'll take you to a rehab clinic."

"On the off chance that the third time's the charm? I can already tell you, three times in rehab will end in three failures. Just what my shattered self-worth doesn't need. Come on, Ad." His hand enfolded Adrian's and squeezed gently. "You're a smart guy. Don't you know a lost cause when you see one?"

A surge of anger, kindled by grief and helplessness, seized Adrian's stomach and twisted. "God damn it, Luke. What do you expect me to do? If the situation were reversed, if I were in your shoes, burned out, beaten, and dying a slow death, wouldn't you pull out all the stops and help me? I'm your friend!"

"And therein lies the problem." With a sigh, Lucien lay back against the pillows and lifted a trembling hand to gingerly examine the abrasion high on his cheek. "All you have to do is love me back, you know, and the problem will be solved. No more abusive boyfriends. No more drugs. I'll be so good—"

Adrian shot to his feet, face hot. "Jesus Christ—don't. *Don't!* I'll put you out of here, Luke. I don't care if you die in the hallway, or curled up in some gutter with a thousand dollars crammed up your nose. You will not manipulate me in my home. You will not lay that burden on my shoulders."

"Sorry." He held up his hands, palms out in a gesture of contrition. "You know how wasted I am, how maudlin I get when I'm stoned. I'm kidding, Ad. Really."

But under all that sarcasm, under the flippant excuses, lay an ultimatum. *Love me like I love you, or I'll die.*

Adrian stared at him, his throat knotted with a mixture of agony and outrage. "I can't help you. It's beyond me now. You need to be hospitalized. You need therapy and medication and constant supervision. I'm not your man. I can't help you."

Tears spilled over Lucien's lashes and rolled down his mottled cheeks, even as he laughed and folded his hands across his stomach as though nothing were truly amiss. "Just let me crash here for tonight. I'll sleep it off and be out of here in the morning. Really. You know I don't mean that crap. I'm sorry."

Adrian swallowed his despair and bent to turn out the lamp. When he reached the door, he paused and glanced back at his friend.

Lucien looked small and broken in the middle of the double bed, a skeleton of the big, vibrant eighteen-year-old Adrian had met in the dorms a decade ago. Luke DeChambeau was an old man at twenty-eight, riding the slick rails of drugs and alcohol to certain destruction.

It occurred to Adrian then: he'd been grieving the death of his friend for at least a year, struggling against the current of its inevitability, and still Lucien hung on, driving the knife in deeper with each destructive day.

Lucien's family in upstate New York was so proud of him. After eight years, they still believed their only son was a physics professor at a community college in Virginia. He was as skillful a liar as he was an Avalon companion. He even had Azure fooled.

"Does Azure know why you didn't show up for work tonight?" Adrian asked, his voice low as weariness stole his indignation.

The faint glow rising off the city beyond the window flooded the sparse guest room with a purple hue, slashing across the foot of the bed, across Lucien's hollow features. "No. I figured silence was better than her wrath when she heard the truth. I was already walking on thin ice with her. She'll fire me when she finds out about this."

"I'll call her and tell her you're sick."

Lucien shifted his dark head on the pillow. "She'll believe you too. She takes you so damn seriously."

"You'll stay here tomorrow, and as long as you need, to get back on your feet."

"If your doorman sees me, he'll kick me out," Lucien said with a trace of humor. "Last time he caught me, he thought I was homeless."

Adrian's lack of response spoke volumes about how homeless Lucien really was.

"One night is all I need," Lucien added. "I don't mean to put you out."

"It's putting me out because I know you're going to do nothing to change things."

For a moment Lucien didn't reply. "I might surprise you," he said finally, his voice thick with unshed tears. "One of these days I'm going to pack up, leave the hell Avalon's made of our lives, and start over. One of these days, Ad, I'm going to fly." He shifted to meet his friend's eyes. "Will you miss me then?"

"My God, Luke," Adrian said softly. "I already do."

The apartment was silent when Adrian rose at daybreak. He threw on his running clothes, then gently opened Lucien's door, watching the slow rise and fall of his friend's chest with an anxiety he didn't want to feel.

Lucien's love was too big a burden to carry. How the hell had it started? How had their friendship become fodder for a passion Adrian hadn't invited or entertained?

Avalon held the key, as with everything in their lives confusing and turbulent. At Avalon, straight sex bled so easily into fantasy; fantasy into lost inhibitions, and for Luke DeChambeau, into loss of self. Drugs, alcohol, money, sex . . . all had proved inadequate for the boy who couldn't get enough. Except his friendship with Adrian. The one truthful, untainted thing in both their lives had somehow gotten mixed up in Luke's tormented mind, and Adrian had been oblivious to his friend's developing feelings until it was too late.

Faced with the granite obstacle standing between them, he'd tried so damned hard to accept it, to brush it off as sheer misunderstanding, even as he felt himself recoiling from the shock of Lucien's unsolicited affection.

In their world, in Avalon's twisted, surreal existence, sex was interchangeable with friendship, with mere acquaintance, with money, with drugs. Lucien couldn't understand why Adrian didn't desire him, and Adrian had run out of ways to explain it to someone who'd long ago been sucked into the Avalon miasma.

Half buried beneath the blankets, Lucien stirred, grimaced in his sleep, and Adrian silently pulled the door closed again. He grabbed a bottle of water from the refrigerator and retrieved Rudy's leash and Frisbee from the foyer closet. Then man and dog headed out of the condominium building and toward the park, into a place of escape and physical exertion and play, enough to wipe the agony from Adrian's reality for a blessed few hours.

He came home at noon, fed Rudy, and looked in on Lucien, who was watching the small television situated in the guest room's narrow armoire.

"Reality TV," Lucien said with a wan smile, both eyes so swollen and bruised, Adrian didn't know how he could see the screen. "Gay rednecks."

"How fascinating for young minds everywhere."

"They should throw in a few of Azure's companions. No one would ever believe a word we had to say."

Adrian smiled but didn't respond, just watched his friend with speculative concern. "Did you get something to eat?" he asked finally.

"Cereal. I also borrowed the Advil I found in the bathroom cabinet."

"The bottle's yours." Adrian tilted his head to study him. "So what do you think? Anything broken? Ribs? Nose?"

"Just heart," Lucien said, and after a meaningful pause, looked back at the television.

Adrian shifted his weight, at a loss for words of comfort. Their growing estrangement sapped even the most generic phrases from his mind.

"By the way," he said, when the silence between them stretched to agony, "I called Azure for you. Told her you had a raging fever."

"Did she believe you?"

"Of course."

"Of course." Lucien rolled his eyes. "You can do no wrong."

Flashing him a mild grin, Adrian rubbed a hand through his sweat-slicked hair. "I'm going to jump in the shower. I have to be at the club at two."

He started to withdraw, but then Lucien said, "Ad?"

"What?"

For a moment, Lucien didn't reply, and the tension between them blazed, brimming with unspoken emotion and frustration and hopelessness. His hands clutched the blanket pooled in his lap, his expression unreadable beneath the myriad bruises and abrasions. "I remember saying some things last night that were pretty tasteless."

"It's okay, Luke. Don't worry about it."

"I was stoned out of my mind."

"It's okay," Adrian repeated, tension crawling through his muscles. He wanted to forget it, to move on. He wanted to forget that his best friend was no longer his best friend.

"But I wasn't so stoned that I didn't know what I was saying." Lucien looked up, his throat moving as he swallowed an obvious surge of emotion. "I don't know why I came here. I shouldn't be here, I shouldn't be around you, and we both know it. I can't do this anymore, Ad. I thought I could get past it, thought I could put you back into that safe friend place where you've always been. But my heart won't listen. And I just can't do it anymore."

Adrian's pulse picked up speed, kindled by dread. "What are you saying?"

"I'm saying . . . you don't need me in your life. And Ad," he added, when Adrian opened his mouth to argue, "I don't need you in mine."

Adrian threw his hands in the air. "Here we go again. Fine, Luke. You want out of this friendship? Great. Crawl back to your real friends, the ones who feed you drugs and booze, the ones who beat the crap out of you and don't care if you live or die. You're right. There's nothing here that can't be swapped for a bigger, more satisfying return."

"You don't understand." Lucien's voice thickened. "It's tearing me up. I see revulsion in your eyes, know what my feelings have done to our friendship, and it's killing me. I can't do this anymore."

"Yeah? Me neither." Adrian stepped into the room, thought better, and backed up again to the safety of the threshold, anger and unbidden guilt vibrating through him. "Incidentally, I do understand. I understand what a manipulative, lying junkie you are. You forget that I know you better than anyone, Luke. You'll do anything to get what you want, even if it's me. But now you're all played out. The guilt card's gone, overused a million times. You just threw down the friendship card. And you're right. I don't want you back. Your friendship was all I ever wanted, but that's over."

He paused, every muscle in his body thrumming with ire and disappointment. "I'm going to get ready for work. When you're done feeling sorry for yourself, do us both a favor and go home."

Lucien stared at the ceiling and listened to the sound of running water coming from Adrian's bathroom on the other side of the wall. Adrian was preparing for a night at Avalon, donning the princely disguise that would earn Azure thousands of dollars in one weekend alone. His good looks and charisma weren't the only reasons the club owner was in love with him.

There were so many reasons to love Adrian.

Easing himself into a sitting position, Lucien fought back a wave of nausea brought on by pain and the lingering effects of too much cocaine and Jim Beam. He considered, for an instant, doing what Adrian wanted and checking himself into a local rehab clinic. Like a good dose of chemotherapy, it would buy a few more months. Prolong what had become unbearable, a life wasted on drugs and sex and empty promises. A love-free existence. It most certainly would buy a taste of Adrian's approval, and what Lucien wouldn't give for just a brief glimpse of the old warmth, the old acceptance in his friend's face.

His fists clenched against the sheet. No. He wouldn't do it anymore. Weariness crashed down on his head, forced tears between his lashes. God, he was tired.

It was the look of derision in Adrian's eyes a few minutes ago that had sealed his decision. Not a decision, actually—more of a knowing. A knowing that it all had to end, that the time was now, and the means to do it a few feet from where he sat listening to the grandfather clock in the hallway tick off the seconds of his torment, while his pulse thudded in tandem.

Down the hall Adrian's bedroom door opened, and the scent of shampoo and aftershave floated to Lucien's senses. He closed his eyes and breathed in, missing such a small pleasure even before it was gone.

Soft footsteps approached his door, then Adrian passed by, dressed in the requisite khakis and white oxford Azure preferred for all the companions. Lucien sat in utter stillness and listened to the sounds of his friend moving about the apartment: the low murmur of his voice as he spoke to the dog, the gentle clink of a coffee cup or plate being set in the sink, then footsteps with a sharper ring, indicating Adrian had put on his shoes.

The sounds of a man living a life that would flourish without Lucien in it.

The jangle of keys reached his ears and he drew a shuddering breath, wanting to cry out, to reach out, to offer the farewell and thanks Adrian so deserved from him, but grief paralyzed him. Cowardice. He never could give back an ounce of what Adrian had given him all these years.

So he sat in the tiny guest room and waited for his friend to depart his life, waited with pulse vibrating as though he stood in the wings, ready to dance across the stage as yet another soapy tragedy from Avalon's den of iniquity.

The apartment door swished open and Lucien braced himself for the final click that would forever part him from the one person in the world who held his heart.

Adrian's voice called, "I'm leaving."

Lucien closed his eyes. "Okay. Have a good night."

Silence. Then, "Eat something, Luke. There's food in the refrigerator."

"Thanks," he said softly, knowing his friend couldn't hear his response. Then the door closed, and into the dearth of sound, he whispered, "Night, Ad."

Five minutes later, he pulled on the jeans and T-shirt Adrian had loaned him, rummaged through the living room desk for stationery and a stamp, and sat down to compose what he hoped was a reasonable, decorous letter of resignation from Avalon and life in general. It would be better, more merciful to send it directly to Azure instead of leaving it for Adrian to stumble across, so he left the apartment door cracked and rode the elevator down to the lobby, where he stuck the addressed envelope in the building's outgoing mailbox.

The doorman squinted at him in instant suspicion when he padded back to the elevator, and Lucien offered him a crooked smile as the brass-paneled doors closed between them again.

He rode up with a beautiful teenage girl in low-slung jeans and a belly shirt, who stared at him from beneath her lashes and said, "Wow. What happened to your face?"

"Train wreck," Lucien said. The doors slid open on the fourteenth floor. He started to exit the elevator, then stepped back and pressed a kiss against her astonished, open lips. "To live well is the best revenge," he told her, smiling into her eyes. "Take it from a dead man."

Back in Adrian's apartment, he tucked his driver's license in his back pocket, turned off the lamp that sat on the entry table, and crossed the living room to the balcony doors. Night hadn't fallen yet, and the smog mingled with clouds over the setting sun, casting a strange pink iridescence across the city's tree canopy.

"Stay," he told Rudy, who waited anxiously at the French doors with a threadbare stuffed banana in his mouth, as though he too had business on the balcony. Then Lucien stepped into the warm summer wind and closed the glass doors behind him.

It took him an eternity to hoist himself onto the concrete ledge, partly due to terror, but mostly because he was still sore from having the hell kicked out of him yesterday. He straddled the balustrade and stared down at the traffic snaking along Connecticut Avenue as far as the eye could see.

Too many pedestrians crossed the sidewalk fourteen stories down, so Lucien waited. He waited until the sun rested like a fat neon orb on the treetops, until the sidewalk below was clear, until no cars were parked in the building's circular driveway. He waited until the wind dried the tears on his lashes and his body quit shaking, and he had no more excuses.

"Adrian," he whispered. A prayer.

And then he flew.

At Avalon, Adrian left a message with Maria that Lucien was still sick, then flipped through his file to check the night's clientele.

Helen Feinstein had booked three hours of his time. The fifty-year-old socialite was hell-bent on clinging to her youth, so full of plastic and saline Adrian often pictured a blow-up doll when he watched her undress.

Mary Ellen Frazier came at seven, a new customer he hadn't met before. She wanted to go to dinner, and then back to the club for intimacies. She liked a dominant lover. She liked bondage.

Gwendolyn Campbell came after that, lightly penciled onto the schedule as always, in the untimely event the authorities ever got hold of the records. Gwendolyn was a U.S. senator, a member of the president's cabinet. Her membership was utterly secret, and despite the tension her hush-hush presence brought with it whenever she visited Avalon, she was a respite of sorts to Adrian. Conservative, intelligent, easy to please. No weird stuff, just straight screwing, and usually once was all it took.

Adrian sighed and rubbed at the tension between his brows.

Inexplicably he thought of the reporter, of her wide, green eyes and pointed chin and the tenderness in her expression, a permanent disadvantage for someone working in the slick world of media. He pushed her image aside, confused by its appearance.

Later that night, as his second client shuddered beneath the slow, circular thrusts he'd learned she favored, Billie Cort crept back before his mind's eye. Her reluctant smile, the stubborn wave of dark hair that fell against her cheek, the softness of her breasts pressed against him when they danced . . .

The way she said his name.

Adrian buried his face in Mary Ellen Frazier's damp, perfumed neck, unprepared for the fierce climax that coiled in his groin and struck, wrenching a groan from his throat.

When Mary Ellen left, a thousand dollars lighter and sweetly deluded that she'd brought him more ecstasy than he'd known in a lifetime, he showered, dressed again, greeted the senator, his final client, and mustered the energy to wrap up this day he'd thought would never end.

At midnight he climbed into his BMW and took the long way home, through side streets slick and glossy with rain, where he could pass row houses with glowing windows and wonder at the families that gathered behind them, living everyday lives with everyday desires. The back roads reminded him of home. Reminded him of his family, and the past he'd so ignobly discarded.

Approaching his condominium building from the rear, he parked in the back lot, then realized he'd left the security card on the entry table for Lucien's benefit, and God only knew if his friend had pocketed it, gone out, and never returned.

The doorman would have to let him in.

Annoyed and weary, he strolled, head down, in the tepid misting rain, up the sidewalk and around the corner toward the main entrance, only to be greeted with the blue and red flash of five different police squad cars. A fire engine. Two ambulances. All parked in the circular drive and lining Connecticut Avenue.

Ahead on the sidewalk, a figure lay sprawled beneath a paramedic's sheet.

Adrian's heart quickened and he knew instinctively that some-one had fallen from one of the balconies. He stopped, stared up at the jigsaw puzzle of black and illuminated windows checkering the mammoth building. His gaze narrowed on his own balcony, found the windows dark, then darted back to the figure again. Uneasiness coiled in the pit of his stomach; a film of perspiration broke out on his skin and sent a shiver through him.

But his mind wouldn't translate the dread into one solid real-ization.

Although the flurry of activity focused around the victim, the authorities all but stepped over the covered body as they talked and moved around, as though that person hadn't been a person at all, but always splattered on the concrete, always lifeless, always a tragic, run-of-the-mill statistic.

"Sir?" A police officer in a yellow slicker approached Adrian, features dogged with weariness and disgust. "You'll have to cross the street and use the other sidewalk."

"I live here," Adrian said absently, his attention riveted on the shapeless lump covered by the sheet. Another, harder shiver ran through him, and in its wake, the dark suspicion he hadn't con-sciously grasped until now. It stole the breath from his lungs.

He took another step closer to the corpse, and the officer moved in front of him, clipboard in hand.

"Your name, please, sir."

"Antoli. Apartment fourteen-oh-one."

He stood in dull silence while the policeman scanned the sheet of residences, then the officer peered up at him. "Can I see some identification, Mr. Antoli?"

He handed the man his driver's license, waited while he studied it, then took it back and tucked his wallet into the rear pocket of his pants.

Instead of stepping aside to let Adrian pass, the officer cleared his throat and motioned to another official, a stout, bald man in a black raincoat.

"Mr. Antoli," said the grim-faced detective as he approached. "You were acquainted with Luke DeChambeau?"

CHAPTER FIVE

B ut if he'll agree to see me, why can't I go back?" Billie paced the office, too restless to sit after her editor had motioned to the love seat for a third time. "You still haven't given me a solid reason."

Nora Richmond leaned back in her desk chair, rubbed a weary hand across her well-plucked brows, and exhaled. "Oh, for Christ's sake. Fine, Billie. I'll tell you the truth, and then will you drop it?"

"It depends on what it is."

The editor jolted forward and met Billie's gaze, her brown eyes dark with concern. "You're a real pain in the ass, you know that? You can't finish the interview because one of the escorts died last night. Fell off a fourteenth-floor balcony."

Billie's heartbeat hitched and stumbled. "Not Adrian."

"No, Adrian's alive and well . . . and being thoroughly questioned by authorities. It was his condo balcony the guy fell from."

Stunned, Billie could only sit there. Then she shook her head. "They think Adrian had something to do with it? As in, he *helped* the guy over the balcony?"

Nora's pen tapped a restless rhythm on the desk. "Did he mention someone named Lucien during your interview?"

Billie couldn't think. "I don't know—maybe. He talked about a few of the other escorts, but I'd have to go back through my notes to give you names."

The chair squeaked under the editor's lanky weight as she swiveled toward the window and stared out over H Street's bumper-to-bumper, midday traffic. "Apparently, Adrian was tangled up with this Lucien guy. Rumors bounced around the club over the nature of their friendship, although Azure claims they were good friends—nothing more."

"Adrian's heterosexual," Billie said flatly. The warmth of his embrace, the steel press of his arousal against her stomach as they danced had been too certain. She straightened from her slumped position against the wall. "He told me he was."

Nora's snort of laughter was her only comment, to which Billie replied, "Damn it! I have no reason to doubt him! I asked him point-blank if he was bisexual, and he said he doesn't sleep with men."

"Hmm. Sounds noncommittal to me."

"You should know for yourself, Nora." It came out more bitter than she'd intended, but suddenly the thought of her editor—her friend—paying Adrian for sex twisted her stomach in funny little knots.

Nora had once said his lofty fee was a small price to pay for heaven. Billie hadn't exactly asked how Nora knew heaven could be found with Adrian. She didn't need to. The forty-year-old senior editor of *Illicit* magazine was a true hedonist, joyful and unashamed in her pursuit of ecstasy. And Adrian was certainly the man to provide it.

Nora swiveled back and gave her a hard look. "Why are we even having this conversation? Azure's shut the door in our faces. You're done with Adrian and Avalon, Billie. There are other escort services to pinpoint. Plenty of hungry boy-toys waiting to spill their stories for print. You're not desperate."

But desperation was a good description for the tightness that constricted Billie's chest. The half-written story throbbed for more. More Adrian, more of his darkness, his sensuality, his raw, carnal effect on her. It would bleed through the paper and into the reader's senses if she could only finish the article. It was Adrian's story, and she was in over her head, too deep to pull out now.

She mentally waved aside the additional realization that she actually liked him.

"Billie?" Nora's voice held a warning edge. "The idea was to write a titillating piece about a man all women would desire—not a suicide, not a murder mystery. Don't you leave this office until you agree to stay away from Avalon."

"I promise to do the right thing," she said, willing her expression to remain blank. "The right thing for *Illicit* and for myself. Same as always."

Nora got to her feet and came around the desk. "Listen to me. I know you're hungry for a good story, and yes, Adrian's is certainly fascinating. But for all you know he could be some kind of nut, and you're no Lois Lane, honey. I'm your boss, damn it. You have to follow orders."

With a halfhearted salute, Billie smiled at Nora and backed out of the office. She wasn't about to give up on Adrian. The man was no murderer. And every time she thought about the article and the publicity it would bring the women's magazine, a spark of excitement flared within her. Some of it was lingering desire from her tumultuous few hours with the escort. But mostly it was her intuitive taste for surefire success, and this article, with its provocative premise, would turn heads all over the country.

One more hour of Adrian's time would be all she'd need.

The low hum of male voices rose and fell in the dining room, flatware clinking against china, the haunted strains of Debussy floating over all. No one laughed. Just hushed conversation. The scene was a somber shadow of the usual camaraderie that infused Avalon's monthly employee luncheon.

Like a high-price funeral parlor, Adrian thought dully. How appropriate, days after Lucien's swan dive into oblivion. His family had buried him somewhere in upstate New York, and Adrian hadn't driven up for the interment. The thought of lying to Luke's parents, who stubbornly clung to the belief that their youngest son had been a college teacher, threatened to destroy the last bit of restraint Adrian held over his roiling emotions.

It was unbearable to picture himself standing at his friend's graveside, scrambling for words of apology that wouldn't form because he was sorry about so many things. So many brush-offs and moments of insensitivity . . . and what had he offered Luke in the last desperate minutes of his life?

He hadn't even looked his friend in the eye at the very end. He should have known what Luke was thinking; should have read the shattered pieces of the man's spirit in the wild look about him. In the way Luke laughed and cried at the same time. In the slump of his shoulders, the pallor of his skin.

Hell, Luke had shown up at Adrian's door already dead.

"Coffee, Mr. Adrian?" A young, accented voice permeated his dark musings and he stirred to find an aproned server waiting to pour him a cup.

"Please." He offered the Hispanic boy a distracted smile. The teenager obliged him, then continued around the table of twenty. When the server reached Azure at the head, she touched his cheek. "*Gracias*, Jorge. That will be all."

Watching her with wide, star-struck eyes, Jorge nodded and backed into the kitchen. No doubt Azure had tested the waters with the kid for future employment. She had a penchant for dark-haired men of all ages.

When the door swung shut, Azure stood and tapped a knife against her crystal water goblet. Instantly the room fell silent.

"I'm so pleased to see everyone here." Her silky voice was just loud enough to reach her audience's ears. She glanced at Adrian, then at the empty seat beside him. Lucien's chair. A place setting had been laid out in macabre tribute to the missing companion, china and crystal sparkling in the chandelier's diffused glow.

"There is little I can say to ease the heavy sense of grief and shock over what happened last week. We've lost a member of our family, and no one can ever take Lucien's place." She paused, her blue gaze sweeping the handsome faces of the nineteen men surrounding the long table. "The detectives say it appears Lucien chose to end his own life, but as you know, they're conducting a thorough investigation and will leave no stone unturned."

Adrian stared at his plate, all too aware of the instant attention focused on him. The authorities had done more than interrogate and humiliate him in the last few days, more than break valuables in his condominium during a brief, careless search "for the suicide note." When they found none, they'd dragged Adrian through the mud, concurrently inserting suspicion into the minds of his fellow companions.

A spear of indignation lodged in his center, shoved aside his grief, twisted. He was innocent, and yet he was not.

"As a result," Azure went on as she circled the table, "I trust that each and every one of you will be as helpful and forthcoming as the detectives demand."

Her fingers fluttered down on Adrian's shoulder as she spoke, more accusation than comfort, and his fists clenched against the urge to shove aside her condescending touch. Burning under the stares of his coworkers, he reached instead for his cup. The tremble in his hand sloshed the coffee in brown splotches on the pristine table linen.

Joe, the tall, blond companion sitting across from Adrian, and one of Lucien's drug buddies, stood and held up his wine goblet. "I propose that from now on, we leave Lucien's place at our table empty, so we can be reminded of what we've lost, what *Lucien* lost, every time we gather here." His pale blue eyes were despicably mournful, mouth turned down at the corners.

What we lost . . . what Lucien lost . . .

It was all Adrian could stand. Something inside him snapped, like bones splintering in his soul, and he shot to his feet, the chair legs screeching on the marble floor behind him.

"You self-righteous bastard! Stand here and own up to shame, to regret, to your guilt. But don't you dare add to his disgrace with your so-called anguish."

"How would you know the level of my grief?" Joe said calmly. "Or anyone's here? You make no effort to know any of us, Adrian. How do you know I'm not torn up over Lucien's death?"

Adrian's fists clenched at his sides, a mirror of the frustration and outrage knotted in his throat. "You have no idea what anguish is, you son of a bitch! All you had to do was ask Lucien. He knew it forward and backward, no thanks to you."

"That sounds like an accusation." A chilled smile twisted Joe's lips. "Exactly what are you getting at?"

Azure caught Adrian's sleeve to restrain his rebuttal, but he jerked free from her grasp. "You know what I'm talking about. You—all of you who shot up and coked up and partied him right into his grave—this is on your heads too. You helped push him off my balcony. Hell, you gave him the wings to fly. Pat yourself on the back, Joe. He wouldn't have jumped without you."

The feigned humor fled the blond companion's features, and he lunged at Adrian over the table's expanse. His fist caught Adrian's collar, shaking the dishes hard enough to overturn a goblet of wine. "Fighting words, Ad. You have proof to back that up? Seems to me you're the only one around here the cops are looking at."

Rage swept through Adrian anew, sizzling through his veins and blocking out everyone around them as he dislodged the other man's grip and grabbed at Joe's shirt to close fingers like a vise around his throat.

"Gentlemen—please!" Azure again laid a hand on Adrian's shoulder, and for a moment, no one moved. Then Adrian relaxed his hold, stepped back. With a snarl, Joe seated himself, brushing off placations from the men on either side of him.

"Take a look at yourself, Adrian," he spat, smoothing his hair back from his reddened face. "It wasn't *my* balcony Lucien jumped from."

"Be quiet, Joe," Azure said tightly. "Adrian, go upstairs and gather yourself. Take this no further. There's no sense to it."

No sense to any of it. Her words arrowed through Adrian. She was right. There was no power, no effect in an outburst of aimless fury.

Still he shook, tears of rage scalding his eyes. No words would come from his throat that weren't choked with agony and vehemence and bewilderment. Wiping a hand across his face, he backed away from the table and left the dining room.

Behind him, Joe resumed his toast as though there'd never been an interruption.

". . . And I propose a toast to honor Lucien's memory. May he rest in peace."

"Hear, hear," someone said, followed by the soft clink of crystal.

In the end, everyone drank to the dead man's peace, except the one Luke DeChambeau had called his best friend.

A soft tap at the door of his private quarters brought Adrian out of the bathroom, clad in boxers and wiping foam from his half-shaven jaw with a hand towel. The tepid shower had helped cool his anger and provided a modicum of control over his grief. To show anything except his usual poise was to relinquish power, and he'd left the luncheon downstairs vowing it would be the first—and last—time any of the stones crumbled from his fortress.

Azure stepped into the room and closed the door quietly behind her, her ice-chip eyes trained on his face. "You don't have to work tonight, you know."

Oh, but he did. Anything to escape the haunted confines of his condominium, the stillness of the sheer curtains covering his balcony doors, through which he saw Lucien's final departure with every morbid glance in their direction.

"I know," he said, his voice carefully emotionless. "Are you sending me home?"

She studied him in thoughtful silence. "No. I think perhaps you need the distraction. But after tonight, I want you to take a few days off."

He folded the towel into a neat square to give his hands an occupation, aware of her discerning gaze moving over his half-naked body.

What did she want? Surely not to offer comfort. Azure's brand would have them sweaty and writhing between the sheets in a matter of minutes, not exactly his idea of mollification tonight.

He'd only slept with her a handful of times in the eight years he'd known her. It had happened early in his employment, a rite of passage for new companions, and at the time he'd been more than happy to oblige tradition, shell-shocked with pleasure and compliant under her throaty instruction.

Eventually, though, his passion for her became the distant fascination of a child with a high-maintenance toy, and when he'd tried to withdraw, she'd clung and become insecure and possessive of him. Not so very mysterious after all. The proprietor of the most prestigious brothel in the world was, at the core, just a woman.

Maybe Azure had never forgiven him for not falling under her spell. Their relationship remained remote, full of unspoken sentiments. Azure's, not Adrian's. He liked her well enough, but she was a cat, one with a luxurious pelt and claws concealed beneath all that silk.

Now she stood in his room, clad in a glossy white robe, black hair hanging like a sheath behind her shoulders, eyes as clear as crystal. Waiting.

Adrian, who could read the average woman's thoughts just by examining the tension in her facial muscles, couldn't decipher the intent that lurked behind Azure's smooth façade.

She finally spoke. "You look tired, Ad."

"I am tired." He sighed and ran a hand through his shower-damp hair. "I haven't slept much these past few days."

"The police have nothing on you, you know."

A grim smile crossed his lips. "I hope not, considering I didn't kill Lucien."

She stepped away from the door and moved toward him. "If I ask why he chose your balcony to leap from, would you have an answer?"

He'd thought scar tissue had formed over the wounds accusation and indignation had inflicted within him. Now her implication ripped through him, and he bled anew.

"We've already been through this, Azure. He was staying at my place, drying out. I wasn't there when it happened. You know where I was. In this room. With Gwendolyn Campbell. You *know* what I was doing. You saw the comments Senator Campbell left for my file. Or did you erase that lightly penciled evidence to preserve her esteem?"

Ire licked at his temper, tightened the muscles in his neck and jaw. A relentless throbbing began behind his eyes, and he sensed his control slipping, slipping. "Tell me you know I didn't push Lucien off that balcony, Azure."

"I know you didn't push Lucien off that balcony," she recited, with just a hint of a smile on her beautiful lips, as though she recognized his anguish and fed from it. "And while I never saw hide nor hair of you here the night Lucien died, I did see the card Senator Campbell left regarding your attributes. A stellar performance, my love. Bravo. She's absolutely enamored of you. And oh, such a powerful woman."

Reaching out to brush his hair from his forehead with maternal tenderness, she added, "It's excruciatingly erotic, is it not? To have such an important political figure melt to thrashing, raw, needful female under your touch? These hands . . ." She grasped his fingers, held them to her cool ivory cheek. "These hands could hold more power than all the forces of Capitol Hill combined. The senator's good mood will stretch far into the next week, I'm certain. Does it ever occur to you how your talents might just influence the state of our nation?"

Adrian looked at her in astonishment and laughed, a short, humorless sound. "It might if I were fucking all of Capitol Hill. Something I'm sure you wouldn't hesitate to arrange for the right price." He withdrew from her grasp and headed back to the bathroom to finish shaving.

Azure appeared in the doorway behind him, her ethereal image reflected in every corner of the mirrored room. "You've grown distant," she said, using the sharp tone she saved for miscreant companions. "Your outburst at lunch was totally unprovoked and uncharacteristic of you. I know you're grieving. But don't burn your bridges here at Avalon, Adrian. It's your home, and we're your family."

He relathered his face, dipped the razor beneath the faucet, and stroked it along his jaw, meeting her gaze squarely in the mirror. "What family would condemn its own son? I sat at that table today and realized . . . if you're my family, I'm a stray. If this is my home, I have nowhere to live."

She started to speak, anger flickering like hot blue flames in her eyes, but he shook his head. "I've helped to make you an extraordinarily wealthy woman, Azure. Don't burn your bridges with *me*, because I'll walk. There's nothing to hold me here now that Lucien's gone. Nothing."

He stared at her in the mirror and read the conflict in her face, a mixture of fury and regret, then a gradual, dawning recognition that his threat was real.

A mask of conciliatory mildness dropped over her features, and she approached him from behind, sliding her slender arms around his waist.

"Dear Adrian," she whispered, the brush of her words like a feather stroked over his naked back. "How I miss you. Your smile, your gentleness. Won't we be friends again?"

He closed his eyes and dropped his head, drained of anger and drowning in sadness. "When you finally realize Lucien only wanted to fly," he said hollowly.

Billie waited two weeks before she ventured to contact Azure Elan. She knew the final appointment she'd scheduled with Adrian had been canceled, but it was amazing what a little persistence could accomplish.

She left four messages with the woman's secretary, each more urgent than the last, before Azure finally returned her call.

"I'm sorry, Ms. Cort," the club owner said, her voice as smooth and sweet as buttercream, "but Avalon is already receiving too much peripheral publicity from this situation. Your research has met a dead end, I'm afraid. Adrian's no longer available."

Disappointment crushed the last vestiges of Billie's hope. "Did you fire him?"

Azure's hesitation reverberated with surprise. "He's taking some time off while this tragedy is settled. Of course I can't tell you where to find him, and he wouldn't want to talk to you anyway. Not with all the chaos. I told you he's intensely private."

Billie ignored the discouragement. "Is he in custody, Ms. Elan?"

"No," Azure said, sharply enough to serve as a warning. "Now I really must say good-bye. Good luck to you, Ms. Cort."

"Wait—"

A muffled click, followed by the drone of the dial tone, told Billie she had as much a chance of touching Adrian again as she did the face of the moon.

CHAPTER SIX

Nothing soothed a case of supreme frustration quite like a banana cream cheesecake from Nirvana gourmet market. Billie had to drive five miles out of her way in rush hour traffic to reach the nearest store, and she always had to wait for the bakers to put one of the creamy, luscious concoctions together, but it was worth it. Better than sex, she thought as she sat in gridlocked traffic. At least better than sex with her ex-fiancé had been.

Normally she hated shopping. Grocery stores everywhere were inevitably filled with married couples, families, or young mothers pushing squalling kids in rickety metal carts.

It wasn't the sound of crying babies that bothered Billie. It was the dearth of a child's sounds in her own life, and the constant lack of opportunity to experience a real family.

Billie's father had left when she was a baby; her mother, while hardworking and kind, hadn't known what to do with her singular, precocious daughter. Silence reigned in every apartment they'd lived in. Her mother hadn't liked to be bothered in the evenings when she got home from a ruthlessly demanding job as a brokerage secretary, and often Billie had tucked herself into bed without exchanging more than a handful of words with her. In the end, the damage to Billie's heart came not from being broken too many times, but from lack of contact, stimulation, and challenge.

Until Ted Chadwick, brilliant law professor, handsome, witty, sophisticated. Who, with his false promises of love and security, had made up for all the romantic rejections her heart had never suffered with one single, supreme infidelity.

It was hard to believe only a handful of months had passed since he'd left. Billie wondered if he and his socialite princess were living in newlywed bliss in some sterile, gated community around the Beltway. She wondered if Vickie St. Claire of Potomac had trouble sleeping when Ted shook the house with his snoring every night, or if his penchant for throwing his dirty socks at the foot of the bed had yet to get under her skin.

She wondered if the new Mrs. Chadwick liked to share the comics section with him on Sunday mornings over a cup of his famous coffee, thick as gravy and strong enough to curl the toes, or if she enjoyed lazy, hand-in-hand walks with him in Rock Creek Park every Saturday afternoon as much as Billie had.

Bitterness sat like an aching knot in her sternum.

Up ahead in the creeping line of traffic, a horn sounded, followed by screeching brakes and angry voices floating on the air. A fender bender—a surefire way to spend one's evening stuck bumper-to-bumper.

Billie had nothing better to do. She sighed and turned on the radio.

The sun was sinking behind the tree canopy when she finally parked her car in the crowded grocery store lot and headed straight for the bakery inside the cavernous brick building.

She stood in line, placed her order over the wide glass showcase, then wandered down a nearby aisle while she waited. She had all the time in the world . . . and an empty, sterile apartment waiting at the other end of the night.

Every item on the shelves appealed to her rumbling appetite, even the healthy stuff. As she wound through the fresh produce, inhaling the snappy scent of bell peppers and citrus, an eerily familiar male voice floated over the fruit stands.

"So young, and already such a flirt."

Billie stopped. Clinging to a wisp of breathless hope, she backed up behind a pyramid of oranges and stared at the man talking to a woman with a toddler on her hip.

Impossible.

Her pulse kicked up dust and she silently muttered thanks to Mother Fate for her infinite lack of predictability. Adrian, the mysterious, now-somewhat-sinister object of her musings, stood in the middle of Nirvana Market, his forearms braced on a shopping cart handle, smiling at a baby who held a handful of his sleeve in her tight little fist.

He looked nearly inconspicuous, a handsome man in faded Levi's and tennis shoes. A Yankees baseball cap covered his dark hair, the bill shadowing his features. Casual. Beautiful. A day's growth of beard on his jaw did little to detract from his excruciating attractiveness.

"She's eight months old, but she does know how to flirt," the baby's mother said. "Let go of the nice man's shirt, Gabbi." She dislodged the child's hand, then told Adrian, "I'm sorry. She must like the colors on your T-shirt."

Eight-month-old Gabbi's big blue eyes were fixed on Adrian's face, not on his T-shirt. Billie released a shaky breath. Good God. Even babies weren't immune.

Adrian smiled at the toddler. "She's beautiful."

So are you, the young mother's tremulous laughter said. She tilted her head and asked him in a mildly flirtatious tone, "You wouldn't happen to know what kind of apples are right for baking pies, would you?"

Hidden behind the stack of oranges, Billie rolled her eyes.

"My mother uses the green ones," Adrian said, but the woman appeared to have already forgotten about apples, or pies, or even the restless baby on her hip. She smiled back, as suckered by his good looks as any of the jet-setting heiresses floating nightly through his bedroom.

Crouching there with the sweet, tangy scent of citrus filling her senses, Billie imagined a storewide announcement blaring overhead. *Special in the produce aisle. Every woman's fantasy can be yours for the low, low price of a thousand bucks an hour.*

But the fantasy was human after all. He had a mother. One who baked pies, no less. And it appeared he liked children.

He chatted with the woman for a few seconds, then stroked the baby's soft, downy hair and bid mother and child good-bye.

Besieged by curiosity, Billie crept around the fruit kiosk behind him and watched as he sauntered down a nearby aisle, leaning on his mostly empty cart.

He liked thirty-dollar wine, she soon discovered, and pasta. Steaks. Skim milk. Frosted Flakes? The world's most desirable male escort ate kids' cereal for breakfast? The realization did little to take the edge off her surge of sexual awareness when he stopped to examine laundry soaps and she had a chance to study his sculpted backside in faded jeans.

Billie forgot about the banana cream cheesecake, the protests of her empty stomach, everything except Adrian as he strolled through the market, disguised as Every Man.

When he went through the checkout line and toted his two plastic grocery bags through the automatic doors, she followed, vaguely aware of a tugging in her center, as though he led her by an invisible string knotted around her heart.

She paused and hung back behind a concrete column, waiting to see where he'd parked. He crossed the lot on foot, though, slipped between a Mercedes and a Dodge pickup, and headed down the sidewalk toward the suburb of Chevy Chase.

Billie had to run to keep him in sight, not an easy feat in four-inch strappy sandals.

God, she thought, hobbling half a block behind him. *Doesn't the man own a car?* But he obviously enjoyed the evening stroll. At one point, he stopped by a crumpled mass of army blankets and newspaper that turned out to be a homeless man. Transferring his groceries to one hand, he withdrew his wallet from his back pocket and pulled out a few bills.

The homeless man took the offering, they exchanged a few words, and then Adrian kept walking, his stride graceful and brisk.

Billie trailed him past two apartment buildings, a shopping center, three gas stations. Twenty minutes later, just when she was seriously considering abandoning the chase, he veered off to a driveway that circled in front of an exclusive, high-rise condominium building.

Billie forgot her cramped toes and ran, panicked she'd lose him inside the building. Ducking behind a limousine parked in the drive, she heard the red-coated doorman say, "Evening, Mr. Antoli," as he swung the door wide for Adrian. "Need help with those groceries?"

"I've got it, Marvin." Adrian's low voice floated on the night air before he passed inside and headed up a shallow marble staircase.

Antoli. Antoli. It rang in her mind as she hunkered by the limousine's rear bumper. His last name was Antoli. Italian. Dark good looks. Darker eyes. Of course.

The limousine driver peered through his side mirror at her. She straightened and returned his annoyed stare, then slid around the back of the stretch Mercedes and cautiously trailed an elderly man with a Saks Fifth Avenue shopping bag who approached the glass doors from the sidewalk.

Marvin the Doorman stood in the lobby with his back turned to the entrance, having stepped inside to answer the phone on the reception desk.

"Mind if I slip in behind you?" Billie asked the pedestrian. "I'm staying with a friend here and I seem to have lost my—er, entry card."

The man offered a tentative smile, nodded, and stuck his access card into the electronic lock.

Billie waited with one eye on the doorman's red-coated back. This was too easy. There had to be some sort of stumbling block, but she hadn't encountered it yet. She murmured thanks when the elderly man held the door for her, and followed him inside as though she had every right to step into the affluent building where Adrian Antoli lived his very private life.

The doorman didn't so much as glance at them. Holding her breath, Billie followed the elderly resident up the shallow marble stairs, where he continued toward a hallway to the right.

While she paused, trying to decide which route to take, the doorman hung up the phone. On impulse she dashed left, down a chandelier-lit corridor that intersected the central hall where Adrian had disappeared. She might be on the wrong path, but she was in. Now what?

Someone was baking with cinnamon. The warm scent drifted in

the hall as she took a few steps down the plush ruby runner and found herself staring at an alcove filled with rows of brass mailboxes, their little glass windows glistening in the dim light.

Stepping into the niche, Billie held her breath. *L-1, Francois*, read the label on the first box. *L-3, Thompson.* The residents' surnames were listed with the apartment numbers.

She skimmed mailbox labels for a good five minutes before her eyes passed over *1401, Antoli.* Rising on tiptoe, she peered into the tiny glass window. Adrian Antoli, or whoever he was, hadn't yet retrieved his mail. She couldn't quite make out the printed name on the envelopes, and damn it, she had to know his real first name. She slid to the left a little, her eye against the window, breath fogging the glass . . .

A dark, male hand flattened against the box next to her head. With a startled screech, Billie whirled around.

Adrian's face looked lethal. It was her only thought before he hauled her by the arm into the hall, tried the knob on a nearby janitor's closet door, and, finding it unlocked, yanked it open and shoved her inside.

"I'm certain you have a reason for invading my privacy," he gritted as he pulled the door closed behind them and pinned her against it. "Make me understand, Ms. Cort. Quickly."

It was pitch-black inside the tiny space. Billie had stopped breathing somewhere between the mailboxes and the janitor's closet. Now she gulped oxygen like a marathon runner, her heart stumbling to keep up with her thoughts. The acrid scent of Pine-Sol filled her nostrils. Where was the doorknob?

Her hand brushed it before his fingers dug into the tender flesh of her upper arms. With an indignant grunt, she tried to jerk free of his steely grasp and found it futile. His face was close to hers. His breath rushed against her lips, his hard chest pressed to her breasts.

"I'm waiting. What do you have to say for yourself?"

"What do you want me to say?" she shot back.

"Someone at Avalon gave you my address. A complete breach of privacy. Who was it?"

"No one. I—"

One hand left her arm and groped by her head. They both blinked in the sudden, naked glare of the overhead bulb. "Are you a cop, Ms. Cort?"

"No." She squirmed against the grip he kept on one arm and avoided his probing stare.

"A private investigator?"

"I'm a reporter, you know that. I followed you home from the grocery store."

His dark brows drew down. "You followed me? On foot?"

Too flustered to give further voice to the humiliating truth, Billie nodded.

"Why?"

Heat seeped into her cheeks. "Curiosity."

He squinted at her. "I think you're a cop."

"If I were a cop, Adrian, I'd have you in a self-defense chokehold by now. Would you please let go of me?"

He released her so abruptly, her heels slid against the glossy linoleum. "This is inexcusable. Did Nora Richmond put you up to this?"

"Nora has nothing to do with it," Billie said, trembling with a wild mix of adrenaline and misplaced excitement. "She told me to stay away from you, to forget about the article."

"You should have listened."

"I did listen. But then I saw you at Nirvana Market."

His eyes narrowed. "How did you get into this building? The doorman let you in?"

"No. I got by him while he was on the phone." She shouldered her purse and drew a shaky breath to regain her composure. "Look, Adrian, or whoever you are . . . I started a story. Your story. It had the potential to pull *Illicit* up by the bootstraps, but when I called to arrange another interview with you, Azure said . . ." She peered at his stony expression and chose tact. "Circumstances threw a wrench in my research, and I'm tenacious. I can't help it. I'm sorry for invading your privacy. I won't bother you again."

He didn't reply right away, but gradually the silky mask of composure dropped over his features again. Cool, collected, in control of his passions.

"You want to finish the interview?" he said skeptically. "That's why you followed me?"

She nodded, watching his face for a sign of surrender. After a moment, he sighed and opened the door.

"Come on." He recaptured her elbow, gently this time.

"Where are we going?" Visions of him tossing her out on the street darted through her mind.

"Upstairs, to my place. You'll get your damned interview."

They rode the elevator in terse silence, separated by a striking Asian couple dressed in haute couture. When the couple stepped off at the tenth floor and the doors slid closed, Adrian punched the Fourteen button again and turned to Billie. His mouth was a firm, furious slash. But his eyes, like black opals, glittered, and slowly, unexpectedly, slid down to the fitted bustline on her navy sleeveless dress. Lingered. Then lower. She couldn't read his expression anymore. His ungodly lashes were in the way.

Uneasy, she said, "What kind of an interview will this be if you're angry with me?"

"Maybe one you'll never forget." A humorless smile lifted the corners of his mouth. "You should've thought about that before you followed me home."

Heart hammering, Billie eyed the control panel. She could dive for the emergency button, but he stood too close to it.

A sigh escaped her, shaky and uncertain. Although he was obviously angry, he didn't look as if he harbored violent intentions anymore. And if she thought hard about it, she didn't want to miss this chance. She wanted, as he'd so delicately put it, her damned interview.

The elevator slowed to a stop and the doors slid open.

"After you." Adrian gestured toward the dimly lit hall.

Squaring her shoulders, Billie moved ahead of him and paused while he drew a set of keys from the pocket of his jeans. His apartment was the first door on the left, across from a Chippendale console that showcased an opulent floral arrangement. Fresh flowers. Signs of affluence in every corner.

Inside, he laid his keys on a glass console beneath a black-framed mirror and switched on a lamp. His groceries, still bagged, sat beside it. "I went back downstairs to get my mail," he said in wry explanation, "and somehow got distracted."

Billie hovered by the door. "Tell me you don't want to give me this interview and I'll go. My conscience is catching up with me."

"Why listen to it now?" He motioned toward a wide, warmly lit living room, but she hesitated when her gaze fell on a dog's purple chew toy, half hidden behind a floor lamp.

"Where's your dog?" He'd said it was a Labrador, a friendly breed, but nothing would surprise her at this point.

Adrian seemed to weigh his response before he said, "I'm having new carpet installed. Rudy's staying at my sister's."

Billie nodded, rubbing her arms against a sudden chill. "Your sister lives nearby?"

"In Bethesda."

So he had a sibling, and a mother. And Frosted Flakes in his grocery bag. Details she suddenly felt guilty for knowing.

He directed her into the living room, where she gingerly seated herself on a tan leather sofa.

"Your home is beautiful," she said, her gaze skimming the surprisingly traditional furnishings. She'd pegged him for a chrome and contemporary type, but warmth and comfort pervaded every inch of the room, down to the new, creamy Berber carpet beneath her feet. Most of the furniture, an eclectic collection, appeared antique. An impressive compilation of books lined the shelves that swallowed an entire wall to her right. Dostoyevsky, Ayn Rand, Leon Uris. He liked mysteries. History. Art.

"You didn't bring your digital recorder or notebook," he said, watching her from the entry.

"I didn't count on trailing you home."

He crossed to a walnut credenza and opened the cabinet to display a fully stocked bar. "What's your pleasure?"

"Nothing," she said. "Thank you."

He withdrew a bottle of Jim Beam, splashed a finger of whiskey in the bottom of a glass, and turned to rest his backside against the cabinet's edge. It took him three swallows to drain the amber liquid. He replaced the bottle, slammed the cabinet doors a little too firmly, and moved to sit beside her. "Let's go, then."

Billie was unprepared for the effect of his nearness. The scent of whiskey, faded aftershave, and warm exertion floated to her senses, sped up her pulse. Even angry, he was astonishing.

"Well?" he prompted.

"I'm drawing a blank." Up close, his features weren't just beautiful. They had character. Laugh lines etched the corners of his eyes, hinted at a quick sense of humor. A tiny scar marked the bow of his upper lip. She hadn't expected to find vulnerability in his face, but there it was. Just a glimpse, before he looked down at her hands clutched in her lap.

"You're shaking."

"I've made a mistake by coming here." She started to rise, but he caught her wrist.

"This isn't just about the interview, is it? You want something more." The realization dawning on his face stripped her, left her feeling exposed.

Billie hesitated, her heart stampeding in her chest. "I couldn't stand the thought of losing this article. But the way I ended up here, sitting in your apartment . . . it feels wrong. I'm sorry for following you, for invading your privacy." She glanced at his fingers, strong, tanned, curled around her pale wrist. "I'm leaving now."

He released her. She reached the door and opened it just in time for him to say, "Wait, Billie."

Her palm went damp on the doorknob, her gaze fixed on the floral arrangement across the hall. It filled the air with the sweet scent of roses, cloying, *eau de funeral home*. Maybe fresh flowers in stuffy apartment hallways weren't such a luxury.

"Don't go." His voice grew closer, his tennis shoes thudding softly on the teak entry behind her.

"Why not?" A sudden, irrational urge to cry choked her. "My job is on the line here. Maybe I'll just anger you more and you'll call Nora. She'd have my head if she knew about this, believe me. So why risk it?"

The heat from his body soaked her back. "I can't think of a single reason," he said against her hair. "Just . . . stay." One hand crept around her waist, fingers splayed across her stomach, a needful, plaintive gesture. "One of the companions at Avalon died."

"I know." She found herself leaning back against his hard body as heat coiled tightly in her middle. "Your friend."

"Azure called him Lucien, so that's how the world knew him. But his real name was Luke." He paused, his fingers flexing against her stomach. "He killed himself."

"It's terrible. I'm so sorry."

His body tensed behind her. "The police thought I had something to do with it."

Billie turned to look at him. "Did you?"

"No." His troubled gaze wandered over her face. Then he dipped his head and caught her lips in a soft, clinging kiss. One of the sweetest Billie had ever been offered. One of the most erotic.

When he withdrew, she swallowed and said, "Why did you do that?"

"Because you looked like you believed me when I told you I had nothing to do with Luke's death." He stepped back. "Will you stay for a while? I'd like your company."

An odd and earnest request, one she couldn't deny. Wordlessly she stepped into the foyer and waited while he closed the door again. He retrieved the grocery bags from the console, handed her one, and led the way to a galley kitchen with granite countertops and sleek, brushed-steel appliances.

"There's a wine rack in the pantry," he said, unpacking groceries as she withdrew the bottle of Chardonnay from the bag.

Billie opened the folding door he'd indicated and slid the bottle into the iron rack, her heart trip-hammering in her chest. She hadn't stood in a man's kitchen and helped put away groceries in a long, long time. There was something excruciatingly intimate about it.

They worked in silence. Billie opened a few cabinets before she found where he kept the canned goods, put away the rest of the items in the bag, and then turned to watch him. He looked different than the sleek, seductive figure she'd met at Avalon. Maybe it was his casual attire; maybe it was the unhappiness that lined his face. But he seemed younger. Less formidable.

He closed the pantry and gazed at her. "Thanks for your help." Then he motioned toward the living room, and she followed him to the sofa, where they sat as before. The tension between them stretched taut and painful, having nothing to do with anger anymore.

"Tell me about Lucien," she said.

CHAPTER SEVEN

We were college roommates," Adrian said, his dark head resting against the back of the beige leather sofa. "He was a physics major, brilliant but lawless. He could sniff out excitement, pursued it like a full-time job. When he started working at Avalon and dropped out of school, I thought he was crazy. Then things went wrong for me. I ran into financial trouble. He introduced me to Azure, and she wasn't what I'd envisioned. You know what she's like."

"Very beautiful," Billie said, taking in the subtle darkening of his frown. "Exotic and sexy."

"Persuasive. Like Luke, I fell into the business headfirst." His hand rubbed restless circles on the soft expanse between them. "He and I both changed after that."

"How?" she asked.

He sighed, his gaze fixed somewhere beyond her shoulder. "Avalon's one of the finest pleasure clubs in existence. But it doesn't matter whether you're working on the street or under a crystal chandelier. The business—prostitution—opens the doors to heaven and hell. Drugs, money, iniquity. It's all there if you want it. I never knew pleasure could be twisted in a million different ways until I found Avalon."

He glanced at her, his dark eyes troubled. "Imagine the wildest possible sexual experience, Billie, and then intensify it fifty times. That's what it was like for us those first couple of years. Every night. Days too. After a while your enthusiasm starts to wear. You settle down, work your hours, go home to live your life the best you can. But not Luke. He tried it all and went back for seconds."

"Adrian," Billie said carefully, "there are rumors about you and Lucien. That you were more than friends."

"We *were* more than friends. We were like brothers. And they think I'd hurt him. It's insane."

"But doesn't it make sense the police would want to question you first? He chose your balcony to jump from."

Pain creased the space between his brows. "Yes, he chose my balcony. I don't know his reason, but I do know why people talked about Luke and me. They talk about things they can't put a name to . . . in this case, a friendship between men that seemed to surpass normal boundaries. But what's normal? Certainly not a life at Avalon. We forged a friendship within a lifestyle most people condemn."

Intrigued, Billie braced an arm against the back of the sofa and peered at his face. This was the man she'd wanted to meet that first interview at Avalon, and now she understood why he stayed so carefully hidden away. "So you didn't deny the rumors? They didn't bother you?"

He shrugged. "I've never given a damn what people say or think. I know what I am, and I don't need people to tell me. As for Luke, he was uninhibited, passionate in all his relationships. He cared for his friends and lovers with equal fervor. The truth is I didn't even know he slept with men by choice until this past year. Sure, he'd done it occasionally for extra cash, for drugs. But then it became apparent that he preferred men over women, and when he claimed to have feelings for me, I brushed it off.

"The night before he died, he came to me, beaten up, stoned, scraping the bottom. I took care of him, just like always. Cleaned him up. That's when he swore to those feelings, and I knew he was serious." He closed his eyes. "I wasn't comfortable with it. I couldn't accept it."

"But you couldn't have been surprised," she said gently.

"He was my best friend. I wasn't truly surprised, just unprepared for the intensity of it. We had an argument about it. I left for work angry—with him for manipulating me, with myself for feeling guilty. When I got home, the police were here, and Luke was a corpse on the sidewalk."

Abruptly he sat up and shoved his hands through his hair, ruffling it like a raven's feathers. "If I'm really honest with myself, I know I was only part of his problem. So much was wrong in his life. He started coming to work with bruises. I figured he was being abused, maybe by a lover, but he shut me out. And Azure didn't want the outside world brought into Avalon. She turned a blind eye."

"Did you tell all this to the police?"

"Of course. They have Lucien's address book, but nothing in it points to his lovers' identities. He was careless in every aspect of his life except when it came to protecting his sexual partners. In that one way, he was painfully discreet."

His wry tone countered the despair in his eyes. "So Lucien dies, chooses my balcony to leap from, leaves no note that they can find. And who do the authorities look at? Me. The only person who gave a damn about him. The only one who . . ."

He shook his head and pressed his fingertips against his brow. "I feel like I've been dragged to hell and back. Like I'm being punished for caring about him. What they can't see is that I didn't care enough. I could have gone beyond Azure and contacted the authorities with my concerns when I saw someone was physically hurting him, when I saw how bad his drug abuse had gotten. But I didn't, and the next thing I knew, Luke was dead."

Sympathy tightened Billie's throat. Her instincts told her he was innocent, racked with guilt and grief on top of insult and indignation at being suspected, but the stoniness in his demeanor proclaimed nothing would comfort him.

"Will Azure vouch for your innocence during the investigation?"

A rueful smile lifted the corners of his mouth. "She doesn't need to. Like I said, I have an alibi for that night. I was working. On the surface, Avalon is a premier escort service, so the activities of my client and me should technically be considered above-board."

Relief, followed by a surge of irrational jealousy, clenched her stomach. "Well, good," she said firmly. "Then it's over for you."

His black gaze shifted back to hers. "But it isn't. Our work is still highly confidential. During questioning I had to break the confidentiality clause in my Avalon contract, and the investigators on this case have all the integrity of a watering can, even though Azure pays them off. And the high-profile client I was with . . . hell. Everyone suffers on this one. My days at Avalon are numbered."

Billie waited for him to say more. When he only looked at her in silence, she said, "I won't put any of this into the article. I'll respect your privacy, Adrian."

"I'm past caring what you do with this information," he retorted. "Tell it all. Nothing's sacred in this world. If you want to know more, I'll tell you. No, I'll do better than that. I'll show you."

The drop in his tone shivered along her nerves, and she stiffened. "What?"

"I want to show you what I do." He slid a hand along the back of the sofa and inched toward her. "I want you to know why women pay for me."

Billie recovered just in time to flatten a palm against his chest. "Adrian, no."

He paused. "I'm sorry—*no*?"

"Right. That's what I said." She swallowed and felt like a child bypassing a jar labeled *Free Candy*.

Beneath her hand his heart thundered, his cool words belying the frantic rhythm that matched her own pulse. "Our track record is beginning to worry me."

The dry comment brought a reluctant smile to her lips. "You don't hear 'no' very often, do you?"

"I can't remember the last time."

"Don't get me wrong . . . I find you incredibly attractive," she said, knowing honesty was her only defense with a man who made his living by peeling away female inhibitions. "What woman wouldn't be aroused by you?"

"What woman would follow me home, two miles on foot, in the dark? You're not just any woman, Ms. Cort, although you work damn hard at blending in with your tailored, conservative persona. You'd like people to think that the wildness right under your surface is tightly reined. But it's not. It radiates from you in waves."

"Thank you, I think." Her words trembled.

"It's not a compliment. I'm not a nice person." His hand cupped her jaw, his thumb brushing her cheek. Then his palm slid down to her neck, and the slight pressure he applied snagged her breath in her throat. "You're awfully trusting to assume I'm telling you the truth about Lucien."

She swallowed. "I pride myself on my ability to read people. And what purpose would it serve to lie to me?"

"Maybe I do it for sport." He slid closer, his provocative scent following him like an errant shadow. "Look around you, Billie. We're alone. What would stop me from wrapping my hands around your lovely neck?"

Billie's pulse went wild. Fear laced with excitement made it hard to speak, but she straightened her spine and returned his piercing stare. "I'm going on instinct with you, Adrian. I don't think you pushed your friend off that balcony, and I don't think you'd hurt me."

His black eyes narrowed, then his lashes dropped like a privacy shade, shuttering his emotions. "I wouldn't hurt you. I'd pleasure you, if you'd let me." His fingertips slid over the curve of her breast, gently stroking, gently promising. "Will you let me?"

Billie closed her eyes and heat flooded her face, prickling her skin, pooling between her thighs. So many months without a man's touch, and this man had a touch a woman could only dream of. "I won't have sex with you."

"It's not required." A somnolent mask dropped over his features as he caught the zipper at the back of her neck and slowly drew it down, exposing her flesh to the room's coolness. "I can touch you right here on this sofa, in a million different ways. Taste you. Take you to heaven and back again. I'm offering you the ultimate research for your article, Billie. You can say you don't want what I have to give, but I'll know you're lying."

Desire, hot and heavy, seeped through her veins, her limbs, fed by the certainty that she'd run out of reasons to say no.

"Why are you doing this?" Her breath came in broken rushes as as the zipper reached its end and her sleeveless dress began to sag off her shoulders. "I already know what you can do. You don't have to prove anything to me."

He shifted toward her in increments, as though she might flee if he moved too abruptly. When he had her cornered against the arm of the sofa, he twined a hand in her hair and tugged her head back, his mouth hovering an inch above hers. Gone was the smooth, silky-toned son of Avalon. In his place dwelled a man barely in control of his emotions.

"Maybe I need this." The fierce words rushed between her lips, flavored with sudden desperation. "Maybe I need it with you, right here, tonight. You're so damn innocent, Billie. It sets me on fire."

Oh God.

"And what if I say no again?" she whispered, even as she fumbled for a handful of his T-shirt and tugged it free from his jeans. "That I don't want you?"

"You're a lousy liar. Don't you want to know what it's like?"

"I don't know," she lied, then turned her mouth against his palm and kissed it. With gratitude for all the ecstasy he would bring her in a few short moments, with sympathy for the turmoil within him that he could only mollify in this one way.

A single swipe of her tongue against his skin left his salty, clean taste imprinted on her memory. She wanted to taste all of him, his solemn, beautiful lips, the column of his neck, the muscled planes of his body. The power of his arousal beneath her tongue.

He was a stranger, an alien creature, impossible to reach or understand. And still she wanted to try. "Tell me what you need."

"This," he whispered, watching her lips move against his palm. "Just this." He rose over her, pinning her against the cushions, and stroked her hair with a tenderness that seemed misplaced among the sultry sensations it awakened in her.

"Do your clients pleasure you?" she asked hoarsely, her head tilting and following his fingers as they massaged her neck.

"If that's what they want. You pleasure me, Billie. The sight of you. The sound of your voice. I want to hear it all sorts of ways. Laughing. Whispering. Moaning. Crying out." He caught her mouth in a lush, hungry kiss, and there was nothing sweet or grateful about it this time. Erotic delight arrowed through her with each sleek thrust of his tongue between her lips, a sultry promise of what he would do to her if she let him.

She wouldn't survive it. His mouth was hot, wet, ravenous on hers. His fingers drew the bodice of her dress around her waist, pulled her arms free, then enclosed her breast through her bra, where its tip tightened beneath his cupping caress. He leaned down and bit her gently through the lace, tugged and sucked and worried her nipple with his teeth until her back arched off the cushions and a helpless sound of delight escaped her throat.

"Oh, yes." She reached to embrace him, to touch his dark, silky hair, but he caught her wrists in one strong hand and anchored them above her head.

His eyes, black and liquid, stripped her naked before he cupped her other breast and drew its tip into his mouth. An electric current ran from her breast to the wet, wanting place between her legs, so that every tug of his mouth echoed down low, as though his lips touched her there too.

When he lifted his head, her bra was damp, her nipples hard and aching. Her chest rose and fell in small, rapid waves as his gaze lingered there on the results of his seduction.

"Adrian . . ." She struggled to find the words to express her desires, knowing he had heard it all, wishing there was a way to make it sound new and honest and real to his ears. "Will you take off your shirt? I want to look at you."

He released her hands and stood. While she watched, breathless, he crossed his arms in front of him, caught the hem of his T-shirt and drew it up and over his head.

Instantly Billie's throat constricted with the need that surged through her body. Naked to the waist, every muscle taut, he was sculpted like the Kouros statue in the whirlpool tub at Avalon. A work of art. Sleek, hard, contemporary art. Pleasure for the senses.

Without moving his gaze from her face, he slid a hand down to his straining fly and stroked himself through the denim. "What else?"

"Your jeans."

He released the first button. "Tell me something."

"What?" It came out a croak. She cleared her throat. "What?"

"When was the last time you had sex?"

"Six months ago." It felt like a century. Another lifetime. The Billie Cort of last March would never have dreamed she'd be here, drenched in desire, watching Adrian strip while her pulse crashed in her ears.

He stepped on the heel of his left tennis shoe, withdrew his foot, then did the same with the right. "Was it making love? Or fucking?"

The harsh term pierced her pleasured haze. She forced herself to picture Ted's face, to recall the touch of his fingers on her skin . . . too fast, too rough and impatient. The memory left her empty. "I thought it was making love. But maybe it wasn't."

"And did you . . ." One last button, and his jeans gaped open. "Have an orgasm?"

Oh God. "Maybe. I don't know." He was naked beneath the jeans, hard, and big. He would fill her hands, her mouth, her body.

She tore her gaze away from the faded fly of his Levi's, from his straining penis and the seductive play of his fingers over its tip. "When was the last time *you* had sex, Adrian?"

"A few nights ago. Love had nothing to do with it. I gave my client two thousand dollars' worth of orgasms."

"And what about you? Did you . . . ?"

"It was inconsequential, and had nothing to do with her." His lashes lowered. "Right now I can't remember what an orgasm feels like."

Billie said nothing, just watched the shift of emotions darken his brow. Anger, confusion, sadness. Then his features smoothed over, replaced by a mask of poised command and hotter intent. In a moment, if he wanted to claim her, he would. With his hands, his mouth. He would fulfill fantasies she didn't even know she had.

The sensations zinging through her were foreign, misplaced, frightening. She was glad he hadn't found true pleasure with his last client, as though she had some sort of claim to him now that she'd broken down his walls of privacy.

He peeled off his socks and set them aside with his tennis shoes, then straightened again. "When was the last time a man made you come with his tongue?"

A threat. A promise. She felt like she could climax simply from the touch of his gaze on her body. "A long time ago."

His chest was smooth, carved from stone, his nipples hard and brown like the rest of him. His erection, a powerful, formidable presence, pushed free from the confines of his jeans. His hand closed around it, stroked it fully now, base to straining head. Billie had never seen a man touch himself, and the erotic sight of it tore the breath from her lungs.

"How long?" he demanded.

She licked her lips, tried to remember. "Graduate school, maybe. Eight or nine years ago."

"Eight or nine years. A travesty." He nodded at the sofa. "Lie down for me, Billie."

Mesmerized, she shifted and stretched out, found a beige-striped pillow and tucked it beneath her head so she could watch him. Though she was wild and aching with desire, a tiny frisson of apprehension shivered through her. The unknown. She might come apart in his talented hands.

"Take off your jeans," she entreated, gathering another cushion against her chest to hide behind. "Let me touch you."

He didn't do as she asked. He knelt by the sofa and brushed the hair back from her eyes, and his gentleness surprised her.

"What are you going to do?" she whispered.

"I'm going to make you come." He pulled the cushion away from her grasp. "More than once." Discarding the pillow, he tugged the dress down her hips and off, folded it and set it aside, building block upon block of sexual anticipation. "You're a beautiful woman, Billie. Your hair. Your skin." He slipped a hand beneath her back and unhooked her bra, then sat back on his heels to consider what he'd uncovered.

Even just half-exposed, Billie had never felt more naked. She held her breath, spellbound, as his warm hand slid beneath the loose bra cup and closed over her bare breast. She had small breasts, ultrasensitive. She hardly thought about them, or what it would do to every wild, pulsing nerve in her body to have a man's hands on them as though they were precious, fragile, inherent to his pleasure.

God, she'd been so empty. And now she was so unprepared.

Her eyelids slid closed as Adrian's thumb whisked back and forth over her nipple, enticing it again and again, until she bit her lip to keep from crying out. Galvanized frissons of sensation shot from her breasts to her womb. Tiny, rhythmic shivers, shades of the orgasm to come.

He leaned forward and his lips traced the valley of her cleavage, paused to fasten on the inside curve of her breast, gently suckled as though to leave a faint tattoo marking his presence. Then he shifted and licked her nipple in quick, flickering laps until it puckered hard enough to hurt.

Another pre-orgasmic shudder trembled through her. "Oh God."

Lifting his head, he caught a lock of her hair and brushed it against his lips, his chin. "More?"

Billie shook her head, fingertips digging into the smooth, buttery leather beneath her. "I don't know what I want. I don't know what I'm doing." Agitated by uncertainty and impatience, she caught his hand. "Do what you said." She guided his touch to her stomach, quivering under the pressure of his palm.

He considered her mismatched lace panties with a faint smile before his fingers slid inside the low elastic to find the trimmed curls there wet with desire. To find her secrets. Just a teasing, tickling touch, a whisper against her, then away again, yet it brought her back off the sofa.

"So responsive," Adrian murmured. "I knew you would be."

"Please . . ." Billie's palm slid over his smooth, naked shoulder while the other grabbed at the sofa for something, anything to anchor her to the earth. "Please."

His lips, hot, damp, brushed her navel. His tongue traced it, dipped within and retreated, plunged and withdrew, the way he'd made love to her mouth when he kissed her. The way his shaft would slide into the yearning core of her body. Then he turned his bristly cheek against her tender skin to watch his own hand burrow between her thighs and find the wet, sensitive flesh that craved his touch. One finger glided over her, parting the folds of her sex, tracing the swollen pearl of her desire, around and around until she nearly sobbed from the intense pleasure-pain of it.

"Billie," he said, nuzzling his nose against her stomach as he slid a single fingertip lower to find the entrance to her body, "you're so wet."

Mortified, tormented by his gentle probing, she sank her fingers in his hair and let her head drop back against the cushion. Part of her wanted the torture to go on and on. Another part of her wanted it over and done with, braced for humiliation over her blatant and easily won surrender. "Don't do this. Don't make me wait. Do what you promised."

His tongue circled her navel. "Remind me." He turned his cheek to stare up the length of her body at her, eyes gleaming with lust. His fingers teased between her legs, played in her wetness without entering. "What did I promise?"

"Oh God." In anguish, she closed her eyes and tugged at his hair, her hips moving restlessly against the sofa cushions, against his evasive hand, straining for fulfillment. "Adrian, please, just do it."

"This?" Two strong fingers pushed into her wetness, deep and firm, and she bit her lip to keep from screaming, first with pleasure, then with frustration when he withdrew to tease again. "Or this?" His thumb rubbed her in light circles, sending electric shocks through her limbs.

"Oh, yes. That. All of it. Put your fingers inside me. Please."

He spread her knees wide and exposed her to the heat of his perusal, his expression impassive save for the dark fire in his eyes. "I'm going to taste you. Inside and out." His fingertip traced her sensitized skin, taunting, driving her to a level of need that obliterated pride and propriety and everything except the driving urge to be filled. By his fingers. His tongue. His cock. Anything.

"Adrian . . ." She squirmed, but he held her spread wide.

"If I make you come, you'll owe me," he said, darkly enough for Billie's lashes to flutter open.

She lifted her head to stare at him. His dark hair was tousled from her desperate clutching, his lean cheeks flushed, lips reddened from exploring her skin. The sight of his hand buried between her legs sent a fresh surge of arousal burning every nerve. "I can't afford you. You know that."

"This isn't about money." His finger probed her opening, delved inside her again, just enough to make her shudder while her inner muscles contracted in a bid to hold him. "You'll owe me your time."

She didn't know what he was asking. She didn't care. "Yes," she choked, thrusting against his hand. "Yes."

He eased back and drew her panties down her legs and off with methodical ease, and cool air brushed her burning flesh, followed by the intense heat of his words uttered close. "A favor for a favor, Billie. What do you say?"

Her answer came in a soft, surrendering whimper when he pressed her thighs apart again, ducked his head and found her with his flickering caress. Then he did what he promised, he made love to her with suckling lips and grazing teeth and plunging tongue, relentlessly, ravenously, and Billie shattered, over and over, knowing somewhere in the back of her mind that she'd made a deal she didn't understand.

A favor for a favor.

And then she couldn't think anymore.

She watched Adrian covertly as he fastened his jeans and leaned to swipe his T-shirt from the rug. His muscles moved like fluid beneath his tanned skin.

Why had he bothered to undress when, in the end, he didn't let her touch him? More than once she'd reached for him, wanting to touch his erection, to feel its silken throb in her grip, but he'd held her hand aside. Despite the thrum of liquid satisfaction that still pulsed between her legs, she felt strangely bereft. This was a man who could go all night, but she'd wanted him to be as wildly excited as she felt with each calculated thrust of his fingers and tongue inside her. To see him lose total control was the one desire he hadn't fulfilled for her tonight. After two powerful orgasms, though, she'd finally quit worrying about it. And now she was terribly confused.

When he glanced at her, she flushed and finished zipping her dress. She didn't know what to say in the aftermath. Shame and wicked delight bickered in her conscience.

A scrap of lace hanging from a dark finger floated into view. "You forgot this."

Jesus. Her bra. She didn't remember taking it off. Snatching it from his hand, she wadded it beside her to put it in her purse. She could go home without wearing it. Sometimes small breasts were convenient.

Glancing around her feet, she frowned. There was one sandal. Where was the other? "I'm missing a key article of clothing," she said without meeting his eyes.

Adrian pulled his T-shirt over his head and shoved his arms into the sleeves before leaning over the back of the sofa to look. "Here's a shoe."

"Thanks." She took the proffered item and sat down to put it on. While she was occupied, he left the room. His voice, low, polished, came from the foyer. He was calling her a cab for the two-mile journey back to the grocery store and her car.

So this was what it was like to feel cheap. It burned in the back of her mind until he reentered the room and stopped in front of her. His feet were bare. He had perfect feet. A perfect body. What must it be like to be trapped inside such a flawless shell?

His hand settled on the crown of her head and caressed her hair, letting the strands sift through his fingers. When she looked up at him, he traced the curve of her bottom lip with his thumb, tested the edge of her teeth, glided across the tip of her tongue until, with a fresh surge of lust, she closed her lips around his thumb and drew on it, hungry for more than this mere taste. She would fantasize about taking more from him. His cock in her mouth. The hard thrust of his hips as she drew on his pulsing flesh. The scalding jettison of his release on her tongue. But it would only be a fantasy.

He watched her through lowered lashes, his hot gaze fastened to the sinuous workings of her mouth for a silent, electric moment. Then he drew her to her feet, held her face and kissed her. Gently at first, then hungrily. As though he couldn't get enough of her.

The last of her confused dismay dissolved. "You didn't let me touch you." She clung to the front of his T-shirt as his lips wandered over her brow. "I'm not like your clients. It matters to me."

He drew back to consider her, and for a long time he didn't speak. "Thank you for that," he said finally. "But now you have to go. Get your purse. I'll walk you downstairs."

When Billie climbed into the taxi, Adrian paid the cab driver, then braced his forearms on the back window. "Billie. Have you forgotten?"

"No." She watched the melting shift of shadows in his eyes, unable to read them. "A favor for a favor. I owe you."

"I need your phone number."

With a slightly trembling hand, she jotted down her cell number on the back of a receipt and passed it to him through the window.

"I'll call you." He leaned in to catch her lips one last time in a soft, lingering kiss. Then he stood back and the taxi rolled out of the drive. Billie took a single backward glance at him standing barefoot, hands buried in his pockets, where she'd left him. God help her. Whatever he wanted, she would gladly give.

The apartment seemed eerily deserted when Adrian returned. He closed the door, turned the locks, switched off the foyer chandelier. Then he moved through the living room, methodically straightening the rumpled sofa and the pillows that had been tossed askew, all without allowing himself to replay the torrid encounter that had transpired between him and Billie.

A glimmer of gold beside the coffee table caught his eye and he stooped to pick up a single, delicate hoop earring. The first sign of a woman's presence in his home in six years.

Her scent still drifted on the air, perfume and warm, wanting female. He followed the dissipating trail of floral desire back to the foyer, where he set the earring by the telephone. A reminder to not let her get away quite yet.

What did he want from a woman like Billie Cort?

His body had an obvious answer: to take her, over and over and relentlessly, until she begged him to stop, until she begged him for more. So what had prevented him? He'd tried to define a relationship with her by *his* standards tonight, tried to classify her as one of his clients, tried to turn her into a mercy fuck. And failed. His attempts at gaining control had backfired.

Pressing a palm against the hard, relentless throb beneath his jeans, he drew in a steadying breath and forced his mind to focus. He'd maintained the space between them with an iron will, without knowing why the hell he was holding back. He could have had her, could have screwed her senseless just like the other women who filled his schedule every week, all the while knowing Billie wasn't someone he could take to bed and then cast aside. The ultimate conquest, and yet he'd denied both of them.

A frown lowered his brow as he headed toward the shower, stripping as he went. She was untried. Virginal in mind and spirit. The innocence that hovered about her, disparate with her wily reporter persona, teased Adrian's senses like an aphrodisiac.

She wasn't the kind of woman who could give away sex without giving away her heart, and he liked that in her, that vulnerability. It was, at the very core, something new and different in his world. It also stood as a reminder of another time, when he believed in the wholesomeness, the rightness of desire. Desire earned and given freely, not bought, before he knew its worth could be meted out in paper currency.

She was hot-blooded and sensuous too, and didn't seem aware of it. It called to the primal male in him, made him restless and hungry to touch her. But tonight a deeper part of him had won out, preserved the strange wholesomeness between them and shielded it from the anomaly his lifestyle had become because of sex.

Maybe, at the very bottom of it, he knew a whore—even a high-priced one—didn't deserve a woman like Billie. She was reality, gritty and truthful and tangible. He . . . he was a phantom born out of Azure Elan's sensuous imagination.

Stepping beneath the steaming, relentless spray, he leaned against the shower wall and let the water beat on his head and the nape of his neck, washing Billie from his skin, but not from his thoughts.

A running reel of the last two weeks flashed before his mind. His life had changed irretrievably. He'd lost his best friend in the blink of an eye. He'd lost himself. And then he'd found Billie. To-night she had followed him home and slipped one foot in the door of his secret life, a place no woman had ventured in years. In her own fumbling way, she'd reminded him he was just a man, fallible, needful, a member of the supremely imperfect human race . . . and shamefully undeserving of what she had to offer.

Looking at Billie, touching her, tasting her, had filled him with a wanting fiercer than any he'd known. For the first time, he was faced with something he couldn't truly have, because of what he'd become.

He swallowed the inexplicable lump in his throat and reached for the soap. As he lathered his chest, suds sluiced down his torso, snowy white dripping sinuously between his thighs. Automatically his fingers skimmed down his stomach, ready to relieve the agonizing pressure, and then he hesitated. Watched in distant fascination at the way his turgid cock jerked toward his hand, like a desperate creature with a mind of its own.

Abruptly he turned and wrenched the cold water tap to full blast, forcing himself to stand beneath the spray's icy needles, teeth clenched against the frigid shock. Self-punishment for playing with fire. Billie couldn't be his client. She couldn't be his lover. She didn't fit in his world, or he in hers. Yet his desire to see her again raged, driving him to the sick realization that he would call her, he would talk to her and think about her, he would push the envelope until danger reared up before him and both their hearts were on the line.

Christ almighty—he didn't know what he wanted from her. The answers were too new, too startling, to even entertain.

CHAPTER EIGHT

What Adrian wanted in return for her pleasure, Billie found out Friday, was a date to Music under the Stars, the annual summer festival where a string quartet would pay homage to Mozart in Rock Creek Park.

Bewildered by the innocent-sounding invitation, she played his message on her voice mail again to make sure she'd heard it correctly, then a third time, just for the thrill of hearing his low, polished words asking for the pleasure of her company "in accordance with their arrangement."

Shivering with excitement and a shaky uncertainty, Billie dug through her purse, retrieved the only phone number he'd given her—his private cell phone number—and left a brief acceptance on his voice mail. Then she searched her closet for the perfect outfit and came out with a black, low-cut sleeveless dress. Casual but sexy. She soaked in a bubble bath in her cramped porcelain tub, letting her knees fall open and closed again so that the water's gentle current caressed the aching place between her legs. Visions of the whirlpool bath at Avalon floated through her mind. Her nerves jumped and danced. Was this a date? She wasn't even sure she and Adrian were friends. What the hell did he want from her?

Something more than she could imagine, her instincts told her, but the uneasiness it stirred only fed the fire burning low in her belly. Instead of fear, arousal gilded every scenario she conjured regarding what a date with Adrian Antoli would hold in store. She would brave any challenge he threw her way. Common sense had abandoned her and left Cousin Spontaneity in its place.

She climbed out of the tub and reached for a towel, the floral scent of bubble bath heavy in the thick, humid air. Tonight would only lead to more of Adrian's special brand of pleasure, no doubt. But why would he bestow it on her, when he, a glorified male prostitute, could have any woman he wanted and be paid for it? Confusion lodged like a pounding ache in the back of her mind.

Billie hit the drain release and watched the bubbles spiral down, taking her enthusiasm with them.

She was fooling herself to think he wanted her for *her*, and this sudden insight had little to do with low self-esteem. Billie understood ulterior motives, and Adrian Antoli had a lot to lose, the least of which was his exalted position at Avalon, if Lucien DeChambeau's death were pinned on him. *But get a reporter on your side, one with a big mouth . . .*

Then she remembered his lips on hers as they stood in the doorway of his apartment. Again, when he put her in the taxi. His touch had felt genuine, had tugged on the armored casing that protected her heart, and she'd left knowing without a doubt that he was capable of tenderness. He too deserved love, companionship. But the idea that he might want it from her alarmed some deep, nebulous place in her morality.

Anyway, the last thing she needed was a relationship so high-fire-fueled by sex her brain would turn to mush.

Nora called just as Billie was fastening a single strand of pearls around her neck. "You're on speaker phone," Billie told her, scrambling around her apartment in bare feet while she searched for her black low-heeled sandals. "I know you hate that, but I'm running late."

"Hot date?" Nora asked.

If you only knew. "Something like that." She dove into her closet and shoes flew in every direction. Every pair she owned except the sexy, ankle-strap sandals she sought. Damn it, where were they? She crawled toward the bed and found them under the dust ruffle.

"Why didn't you tell me about this earlier?" Nora sounded maligned. "You always tell me about your boyfriends."

"And you always list the reasons why I shouldn't be dating them." Nora would have a field day with this one, for sure. Especially since she'd alluded to sleeping with Adrian herself. An image of her friend's rail-thin body clasped in Adrian's strong arms stopped Billie in the middle of slipping a sandal on her foot. Supremely disturbed, she stumbled and hopped to catch herself. "Damn."

"So that's the reason you're keeping this one to yourself?" Nora demanded. "You think I'm going to tell you why you shouldn't be going out with this guy?"

"That's part of it." Billie grabbed her purse, glanced in the mirror and tried to imagine what Adrian would think when he saw her. It was futile. Guessing what went on in his enigmatic mind was impossible.

The reporter in Nora had been awakened by her friend's ambiguity. "What's the other part?"

"I'll tell you about it on Monday. Good night, nosy." Billie grabbed her cell phone to disconnect.

"Wait! Call me tomorrow. I heard some more details on the investigation at Avalon."

Billie's throat went dry. "What is it?"

"Your boy Adrian's still not out of the woods. Apparently his alibi didn't check out."

"Shit," Billie said. "Shit!"

"That's not the response I was expecting."

Billie squeezed her eyes closed. The last thing she wanted was to make Nora suspicious. "I'm just . . . surprised. How did you find this out?"

"I told you I had lunch with Rich Hales, one of the detectives on that case. I think he's interested in me. He's been telling me info the investigators shouldn't tell anyone."

"For crying out loud . . ." Billie pressed the heels of her hands against her eyes. "Nora, that's totally unethical. He could ruin the entire investigation by leaking details like that."

"No kidding. And he won't get a second date out of me unless he has more to tell." She snickered at Billie's sound of disgust. "Listen, I know that article's gathering dust, but don't pitch it just yet. If the Avalon investigation goes public, maybe we'll jump on the bandwagon after all. And I know you're dying to be *Illicit*'s circling hawk. Maybe I'll wave my magic wand and let the exposé drop into your hot little hands, since you were so peeved about losing the assignment on Adrian." When Billie didn't respond, she said, "You still there?"

"Yes." Heart pounding, Billie shook off a creeping nausea and slung her purse on her shoulder. "I've got to go, Nora. I'll call you tomorrow." She disconnected without waiting for a response.

Billie found Adrian waiting for her in the driveway in front of her apartment building. He leaned against the most exquisite navy blue BMW sedan she'd ever seen, arms crossed over his chest, studying the tips of his loafers.

It wasn't the car that caught her breath. She paused at the glass door and watched him for a moment, transfixed. The summer breeze ruffled his hair, shot through with chestnut highlights from the setting sun.

Her gaze took in the breadth of his shoulders beneath the white cotton shirt, the tanned hollow of his throat where his collar opened. He looked casual in khakis, elegant.

She wondered if he knew his alibi hadn't checked out. She wondered if he'd lied about his relationship with Lucien. She wondered if those hands that had penetrated and pleasured her body with such skilled, deliberate care had pushed another man to his death with the same concentration.

She searched deep within her reporter's intuition for the answers and found herself lost. Somewhere in the last few days her heart had swelled, taken over her chest, and strangled her common sense. She didn't just desire this man anymore. It threatened to swallow her, the need that pierced her as she stood there, watching him. But to define the emotions roiling within her would be too frightening this early in the game. And maybe that was all it was. A game.

As if sensing the turmoil on the other side of the doors, Adrian lifted his head and met her gaze through the glass. Billie's heart flipped wildly behind her breast.

"You look beautiful," he told her when she stepped into the balmy evening.

"Thanks," she said, battling shyness. "So do you."

He opened the passenger door for her, then walked around to the driver's side. When he climbed in, he glanced over at her and paused. "You're nervous."

She cleared her throat. "I don't know what you expect from me tonight."

"I expect nothing." He started the engine. "Except the pleasure of your company."

Muted jazz softened the tension in the sedan. Curled up on the tan leather seat, Billie couldn't take her gaze off his fingers as they rested on the polished wood steering wheel. She felt them on her breasts, between her legs, inside her, where even now she ached for him. She saw his hands on a million other women, and wondered yet again why she was here, inside his expensive car on the way to a beautiful moonlit concert, as though the police weren't breathing down his neck and she wasn't playing make-believe.

His aftershave scented the air inside the vehicle. Soap, mint, warm male. They didn't speak again until he merged onto the highway. Then he said, "Are you having second thoughts?"

She hesitated. "No. I'm glad to be here."

"You do like Mozart, I hope."

"Very much." She stared past him as a low-slung sports car tore by in the left lane. Fast, sexy, dangerous. Pale in comparison to the intense force beside her. "Why did you invite me tonight, Adrian?"

He glanced at her, then back at the road. "You remind me there's still a world out there," he said simply.

While Billie waited, Adrian retrieved a leather satchel and a plaid blanket from the trunk of the car.

"What's in there?" She eyed the expensive-looking case he slung over his shoulder.

"A bottle of Chardonnay. Two glasses. Do you drink white wine?"

"I do tonight." It would calm her jittery nerves, and the humor in his expression told her he understood.

The quartet sat on a performance platform at the base of a grassy hill. While the musicians tuned their instruments, the hollow, haunted notes of cello and violin rose into the August night, at once discordant and melodic.

Adrian found a secluded spot beneath a gnarled dogwood and spread out the blanket.

Accepting a glass of wine from him, Billie sat on the soft ground, her legs stretched out in front of her. Fireflies infused the fallen darkness with their iridescent glow, drifting like tiny neon dancers on the breeze. The wine, tart and heady, chilled her tongue. She held it in her mouth, savored it, and let it slide down her throat to cool her heated senses.

Adrian sat beside her, his back resting against the sturdy tree trunk. Bracing an elbow on his bent knee, he studied the wine in his glass. Then he studied her. His gaze dragged over her hair, which she had worn curly tonight. It was wilder than usual. She was wilder than usual.

"What are you thinking, Billie?"

The Chardonnay had loosened her tongue, her muscles, stolen the top layer of her inhibitions. "Hmm . . . that I enjoy listening to musicians tune their instruments as much as the actual concert." She turned her head to look at him more directly. "They offer these concerts every summer. Do you usually attend?"

"Once in a while. I like some of the indie bands that play here."

"Do you come here with your clients?"

"No," he said, his tone somber. "This place feels worlds away from Avalon." He edged down on the blanket, shifted on his side and propped an elbow beneath him. The breeze fingered through his sable hair. "When I was a child, my father used to bring me here. Every Fourth of July there'd be a concert, fireworks, cookouts. It was magic to me. It still is, to feel so removed from the city when high-rise buildings sit right over the hill."

Billie was still focused on the hint he'd dropped about his father. "So you grew up in Washington?"

"Nearby."

"And are your parents still around?"

Adrian's lashes lifted and he watched her, as though weighing whether to share the information. Then a smile tugged at his mouth and he looked away. "They live in Miami now. I come from a big Italian family. I have three very possessive sisters who think one day I'll settle down with a nice Catholic girl. I'm a Scorpio, I like mysteries, and Halloween is my favorite holiday. Anything else?"

"I have a million more questions," she stammered in astonishment. "Will you answer them?"

"We could work out an arrangement." He took a sip of his wine, his gaze lingering on the low dip of her neckline. "Try me."

"Do your sisters know what you do?"

"The one who lives in Bethesda thinks I'm involved in organized crime. Technically, she's right. Sex for money's illegal, and Azure runs the most organized women's club in existence."

"Don't you deny it?"

He shrugged. "She doesn't need to know what I do."

"And if she ever found out?"

"She won't," he said, darkly enough to make her abandon the subject.

She slid down beside him on her hip and faced him, propping herself on her forearm. Her fingers toyed with the stem of her wineglass. "I was an only child," she said, anxious to banish the sudden, inexplicable tension between them. "My parents divorced after I was born. My mother raised me."

"Does she know what you do for a living?" A thread of mockery laced his voice.

"She passed away two years ago. Cancer."

"I'm sorry," Adrian said gently. "This is what put the sadness in your eyes?"

"Some of it, anyway." Billie glanced away from his probing gaze, feeling exposed. "She was my only relative. I never knew my father. He left my mother when I was a baby."

"Have you looked for him?"

The question sent a shard of regret through her. "No. I've thought about it, but deep down I'm just too angry at him." She shrugged, as much to ward off her sadness as to show apathy. "He could be dead, for all I know."

He tilted his glass, letting the wine slosh dangerously close to the edge. "He's missed out on you."

A simple sentiment, but it soothed the raw truth.

"Ever been married, Billie?" he asked after a moment.

"I came close once. But it didn't work out."

A pinch of irritation tightened her muscles at the memory, but she couldn't think fast enough to change the subject before he said, "I hit a nerve. You don't want to talk about it?"

"I don't want to think about it."

He fell quiet. It was her serve again, and she swung with all her might. "Do you ever have relationships with women, Adrian? I mean real romances. Outside of Avalon."

"Once."

Her brows shot up. "Only once?"

"There was someone," he said without looking at her. "A few years ago."

"Tell me about her." Her heartbeat tripled as she waited for his reply.

He raised his wineglass and took a slow drink, then set it on the blanket, rolling its base in languid circles between them. "She was a business student, a bright girl from a wealthy family. I met her after I'd started working part-time for Azure. For a while I was able to keep her separate from my life at the club. But Avalon's a jealous mistress. Eventually the truth came out."

Billie's gaze clung to his features. "And she left you?"

"Yes, she left because I gave her no choice. I didn't think I cared that much. I thought I wanted Avalon more."

Troubled memories skittered across his face. Regret? Sadness? It was hard to tell. Misplaced resentment flared in the pit of Billie's stomach again. So he'd loved a woman at least once. She ought to be relieved. It rendered him more human, more fallible . . . more touchable.

"What was her name?" she asked, certain he wouldn't tell her.

For a long time he didn't answer. Then he stirred and met her eyes. "Noelle," he said. "Her name was Noelle."

"You loved her." It was more of an observation than a question.

To her amazement, Adrian smiled. "Does that surprise you?"

"Maybe a little," she admitted.

His attention returned, trancelike, to the glass in his fingers. "Of course I loved her. But not enough."

Billie studied him, taking in the curve of his brows, the play of falling darkness on his features, like strips of a mask across his face. "You know, you're much more open than I thought you'd be. Certainly more than you were when we first met at Avalon."

"I've had my fingers inside your body," he said, his gaze lifting to find hers with piercing acuity. "I've made you come. I think that merits our exchanging a few personal details, don't you?"

Desire stung her senses and stole her reply. Her lashes fluttered closed when he slipped his fingers through her hair and brushed it

back from her face. "That feels nice," she said, leaning into the caress. An understatement. Even just a casual touch from his hand
burned the nerve paths from her head to her toes.

"You're so receptive." His voice wound around her, seductive and
mesmerizing. "Your blood runs hot, doesn't it, Billie?"

She opened her eyes and tried to focus on him. "At certain enjoy-
able times."

His smile widened. "What else do you enjoy besides Mozart and
musicians tuning their instruments?"

She sat up, drained her wineglass and handed it to him for a re-
fill. "I enjoy summer nights like this. And nights like Monday night,
at your apartment."

When he recorked the wine and handed her back the glass, his
fingers brushed hers. "What else?"

"I enjoy the way you look at me. The way you touch me. I want
to return the favor, Adrian. Any chance of that happening tonight?"

"How about now?" he asked evenly.

Billie imagined doing just that, crawling over him and devour-
ing him while the surrounding audience turned to stare at them
with one simultaneous gasp of horror. "People are all around us," she
whispered, her heart dancing.

"All the better." He sat up against the tree again and his palm
rubbed the blanket beside him, his face utterly cloaked in shadow.
She could only make out the liquid glitter of his eyes. "Come here,
Ms. Cort."

Her body moved of its own accord, drawn to his heat and sensual
promise. When she scooted back next to him, he took her wineglass
and set it aside. Then he made a place for her between his thighs and
drew her against him, his hand beneath her breast, one long leg
flanking her outer thigh as she leaned back in the cradle of his body.

To anyone passing by, they looked like an affectionate couple settling down to listen to the concert.

But a different sort of concert was taking place in Billie's body. Every nerve rubbed and sang as he caught her hand, lifted it to his lips, kissed each knuckle, then led it behind her back and between his legs. Through the heavy material of his pants she felt his erection, thick and granite-hard. It surged in fervent response to her fingers as they curled awkwardly around him.

On the stage nestled at the base of the hill, the quartet commenced a delicate minuet.

Billie's gaze darted around at the other spectators, but no one seemed to notice the fire that ignited between her touch and Adrian's body. He was so silent behind her. The only evidence of his growing arousal was the uneven rush of his breath against her cheek, his lips at her ear, nipping, licking, nuzzling.

Chills crawled up the back of her neck. Her body melted beneath the dress, desire drizzled through shadowed, aching places. In the shelter of night, his hand shifted from her ribs to cup her left breast, thumb whisking over her nipple, back and forth in quick, frantic passes that spoke of his increasing urgency.

Somewhere in Billie's foggy conscience, Mozart spun his magic, a pristine backdrop to Adrian's sultry embrace.

She glanced down and discerned the outline of his fingers on the curve of her breast. How could she resign herself to the possibility that his wonderful hands might have helped Lucien DeChambeau over that balcony? Here in the night, brimming with need, it was easy to forget the possibility of danger, the realization that she didn't know him, not truly. Tomorrow might bring a more unsightly truth than the one she'd come to accept, that she was vulnerable where Adrian was concerned. For now, she could forget that darkness hovered over this undefined, fledgling relationship, waiting to steal its promise.

Turning her head, she found the sharp line of his jaw and rubbed her nose against it, blindly seeking his mouth. He caught her chin in his fingers, sipped the breath from between her lips, and finally, finally settled his mouth on hers with slow, burning intent. And all the while she stroked him, reading the growing hardness of his erection, counting the heavy cadence of his heartbeat as blood rushed there, beneath the rhythmic pressure of her palm.

Mozart floated around them, gossamer wisps of song, incongruous with the pounding need that surged through Billie as her neck arched under his hand and their tongues parried and danced. No one had ever kissed her like Adrian. Billie hadn't known sexual intercourse could occur between mouths, and the sinuous mating of tongues and lips was hotter than any blatant caress.

Twisting against him, she inched her fingers into the thickness of his hair, ruffled through it, grasped with primal desperation as his mouth opened wider against hers, his tongue more insistent. With heart, soul, and body, she kissed him back and found triumph, and a woman's power, in the soft sound that rumbled in his throat.

Only need for oxygen broke apart the frantic coupling of their mouths.

"My God, Billie," Adrian said, his words breathless as he brushed kisses against the curve of her neck. "What are you doing to me?" For the first time in the few days she'd known him, he laughed, but it was a husky, disbelieving sound, void of humor.

Shifting to get a better look at him over her shoulder, she brushed the hair back from his forehead, traced the sculpted lines of his face. "Whatever it is, we're doing it to each other. I want to make love with you, Adrian. Will you take me home with you tonight?"

"No."

The air around them cooled.

"No?" She withdrew, stung by his unexpected reply. "But . . ."

"I'm sorry. I can't." He jaw hardened, the warmth in his eyes snuffed out. "I won't."

The music, like her dim pleasure, faded and died. Nearby, the spectators scattered on the curving hill applauded the end of the first composition.

Billie faced forward and clapped politely, but inside, his abrupt rejection had iced over her passion and left her chilled to the bone.

CHAPTER NINE

By the time the concert ended, she sat in stony silence beside him, huddled with knees clutched against her chest, as far away from him as she could get without leaving the blanket. Her wounds had healed into simmering indignation. What kind of game was this? Why the hell had Adrian lured her out to a concert, kissed her with every ounce of sexuality in his impressive stockpile, and turned her down flat when she reacted with enthusiasm?

Anger cleared the wine-induced fog from her mind, leaving her painfully lucid. She returned the two empty glasses to the leather carrier, walked the bottle to a nearby trash receptacle, and waited, arms crossed, heart protected, while Adrian shook out the blanket and folded it.

They walked in silence toward the parking lot lights.

"Billie," he said finally, "what do you want from me?"

"I'm certain it would put you immediately at ease if the answer was hot animal sex," she snapped.

"But I would know that's only part of it." He spoke calmly

enough to toss kindling on her anger. "So maybe I should say, what else do you want from me?"

She squinted at him. "The question should be, what do you want from *me*?"

"I wanted your company tonight. And now I want you to remember what I am, before we both forget." He caught her elbow to stop her. "Maybe I've misled you."

She flashed him a look of disbelief. "Truthfully? That thing you did with your tongue kind of threw me for a loop a few nights ago. Call me silly, but after that, I thought we had something going. It was stupid of me. I'd forgotten what you are, but suddenly it's come back to me with crystal clarity."

Directly ahead, an older couple meandered shoulder-to-shoulder, fingers entwined. All around the lawn lovers strolled together, dreamy from Mozart's lingering effect.

Billie started walking again with a quickened pace. She didn't feel dreamy. She felt like someone had doused her with a bucket of ice water.

"Why did you ask me here tonight?" she demanded, two steps ahead of him now. "You had to know how it would end up."

"I wasn't sure how it would end up. I wanted to see if I was right."

"About what?" She tried to quicken her pace, but he snagged her hand and halted her again.

"You've never had a one-night stand, have you, Billie? You've never taken your pleasure and ducked out into the sunrise."

"No. Hell, no," she added furiously, resisting the urge to twist from his grasp like a belligerent child. "I think more of myself than that."

"I don't have relationships. They blow apart before they're even off the ground. Sex gets mixed up in everything I do. It tarnishes everything. I won't have sex with you, no matter how much I want it."

She finally pulled her hand from his. "That's funny, considering where you had your mouth a few nights ago."

"You're right. A few nights ago, I thought—" He cleared his throat. "I felt differently."

"So what could've possibly happened in four days that makes me so untouchable?" To her horror, tears of frustration thickened her words. She cared too much for this man. And why? Only a glutton for punishment would fall for a gigolo.

"Maybe I should've been less direct in my response to you tonight," she added, a fresh wave of anger chafing her wounds. "I'll bet no one ever plays hard to get with you. You like games. Should I have played?"

"It's not any of that." The drop in his tone told her he was finally irritated. Good, damn it. She wanted to provoke him, force him to show something other than the silky, sexy remoteness Avalon had cultured in him.

"Then what?" She stepped toward him, shaky inside but forceful in her insistence. "Come on, you have nothing to lose here. Give it to me straight. What did I do?"

"You kissed me like you meant it," he said flatly, "and I liked it." Her jaw clicked shut.

The pale glow from the parking lot lights illuminated half of his face, not enough for her to read his expression as he continued, "I thought a lot about what happened between us in my apartment, and I won't lie. I wanted more. I knew seeing you again was risky, but I didn't expect this."

"This what?" She struggled to keep her voice low and steady. "What is this, Adrian?"

"It's starting to feel like a relationship."

Billie wanted to cling to her indignation, but it slipped from her grasp, replaced by soft confusion. "You say that like it's profane."

"In my line of work, it is."

"But I'm not one of your clients."

"Then there's no room for you in my life." He folded the blanket tightly against his chest. "I'm sorry if I misled you by inviting you here tonight. It was a mistake."

They began to walk again.

Instead of being insulted, Billie took a closer look at him as they passed through a puddle of light. Despite his careful tone, he looked . . . riled. Flushed. His hair was ruffled from her caress, his mouth still reddened from her kiss. He hugged the blanket to his heart like a shield.

"You coward," she said slowly, halting his progression. "You feel something for me, don't you? It's scaring the hell out of you."

"Jesus, Billie." A sad smile touched his lips, as though she sounded pathetic. It was what he wanted her to think, that she was the pitiful one. But suddenly she knew his truth. She recognized his vulnerability. How could he do what he did for a living and not be crippled when it came to intimacy?

At thirty-three, Billie didn't want to nurse any man back to emotional health. But this man . . . this man, she liked. Something deep inside her said he was worth the trouble, and tonight she wanted nothing more than to listen to that voice.

"Adrian." Heart pounding, she caught his hand. "It's been a wonderful evening. I don't want it to end like this."

"I won't take you home with me." His voice was unyielding, even as his fingers curled around hers.

"I understand that." She drew him unresisting off the dirt path, toward a small copse of trees, where she set down the wine carrier and took the blanket from him. Pale, purple light spilled through the branches from the parking lot nearby. She could see his face more clearly now, and the uncertainty there both astonished and touched her. "I want nothing from you."

"Good." A muscle jumped in his jaw, in direct opposition to the steely carelessness of his response.

"Except your arms around me." A few steps into the shadows, trees grew side-by-side like sentries, blocking out the world. There, she draped her arm around his neck and breathed a soft, tender kiss at the base of his throat, where his skin was warm and a little salty under the brief flick of her tongue. "And not the way you put them around your clients either."

"It's all I know."

"I don't believe you. And there's something else I don't believe."

"I'm afraid to ask what it is," he said aridly, his hands coming to rest at her waist.

"I don't think you want me to stop caring."

"I never asked you to start. This is a mistake." His tone was wooden. "You don't even know me, Billie."

"But I do." Her fingers slipped down the front of his shirt, over rigid muscle and smooth cotton, until she reached his belt. "I know your face, your smile, your scent. You smell wonderful," she whispered against his neck. "You feel . . . incredible."

His throat moved, his hands tightening on her waist. "What do you want to do, then? Drop right here in the leaves and go at it?"

"No." She slid her hands beneath his arms, down his sides, around to meet at the dip of his spine, reading the resilient muscle and strength and anger in his lean body. Her lips caressed the hollow at the base of his throat, soothing, placating with the truth. "I just want to taste you. To make you feel as good as you made me feel at your apartment."

"Jesus, Billie," he said again, but this time it was a groan of top-
pling resistance. She drew back slightly and slid a hand down the
placket of his pants, where his flesh had already stirred to life, at
once hard and demanding.

"Let me touch you," she said against his ear.

"You already have," he whispered.

She pressed a palm against his chest and backed him deeper into
the shadows, where darkness engulfed them completely. Knowing
he might come to his senses and push her away, Billie unbuckled his
belt with fumbling fingers, slid down his zipper, and reached inside
his briefs for the impressive proof of his desire. The rush of blood
and heat beneath her palm swelled his flesh, speeding his pulse until it surged against her fingers and kept time with the beat of her
own galloping heart.

"Adrian," she said, astonished and a little afraid as she measured
him in the dark, "you're so hard."

"All night long." His voice went husky. "I can't seem to control it
with you."

Pleasure curled through her, and though she couldn't see his
eyes, the labored rush of his breath confirmed his words.

"Do you like this?" she asked, knowing he'd demand the same
were their roles reversed. "Does it excite you, being touched like this
out here where anyone could stumble upon us?"

"Yes." He nudged aside her fingers momentarily to free his erection completely from his briefs. Then he led her touch back to his
burning flesh, which had grown impossibly harder, and a flood of
desire rushed through her own body in response.

She needed more of him. More taste. More touch. With her free
hand, she worked open the buttons on his shirt until it hung open,
his bare skin a slash of umber in the dimness. She scattered a path
of soft, lingering kisses down his throat to his chest, one hand

stroking his cock and the other sliding around his warm, sleek side to his back, reading the flex and tightening of muscles as he grew more aroused.

The scent of his skin filled her senses like ambrosia, sultry-hot and clean and sweet. He shivered; chills pebbled the hot skin stretched over ribs and lean musculature as she worshipped his bared chest with the brush of her lips and tongue. And all she could think was, *more*. He was a drug to her heated senses. A primal need, like food and water and air.

When she slid down his body, he caught her arm. "No. No, Billie."

"Yes." She knelt before him, dry leaves crackling beneath her weight. "I'm going to make you beg, the way you did to me."

Adrian stood like a statue, one hand still wrapped around her upper arm, the other in her hair. His fingers flexed convulsively, tangled in the curling strands as she took the tip of him in her mouth and gently tongued it, fearful he'd stop her from giving him the same pleasure he'd offered her four nights ago.

When she paused to look up at him, to read his reaction, he brushed an errant curl from her eyes and let his palm linger against her cheek. Reluctant gratitude, maybe. Permission to proceed. She closed her eyes and let him sink into her mouth again, as far as he would go.

The sharp sound of his inhalation rent the air, but he said nothing. He shifted like a restless charger, found the broad trunk of the tree behind him, and braced against it while she withdrew enough to slide her tongue along the sensitive ridge on the underside of his erection. His fingers tightened in her hair, his pulse throbbed against her fingers, inside her mouth.

She swirled around the tip, tasted a drop of his essence, a little salty and all male, drew his cock between her lips as far as she could, then out again in a teasing, seductive rhythm. He was big, steely, burning the tender skin inside her mouth. Blood rushed in cadence through his shaft; with every pull of her lips it surged more fiercely, indicating the wild stampede of sensation he was experiencing at her hands.

Billie had never thought herself particularly skilled at pleasuring a man this way, but he tasted so good, so exotic and delectable, she wanted to devour him. Acting on pure delight and instinct, she took him in again, played him with tongue and a light graze of teeth, savoring the shudder of his body above her.

"If you don't stop," he said, panting, "I'm going to come."

An exalted shiver ran through Billie and she wrapped her fingers more firmly around him, sliding them up and down in rhythm with her mouth. Steady, firm. Quickening as his breath quickened. Harder when he groaned, "Harder . . . yes, Billie."

"Beg me," she whispered, stopping long enough to let her hot breath tease the pulsing head of his erection. It jerked as if in protest.

"Please." His hand covered hers, tightened it around him, and slid it from base to tip and back, guiding her into a fiercer rhythm. "Put your mouth on me."

Adrian from Avalon wasn't there in the woods, under her mouth and hand. This Adrian, someone new, wanted like every man, shuddered like every man, responded like every man under a tender woman's ministrations.

The time for words passed, engulfed in grim silence. His fingers rubbed her hair in mindless, frantic circles, faster as she increased the speed with which she slid him in and out of her mouth. Her free hand moved around his smooth hip, shoved his khakis and briefs down to his thighs and gripped his bare buttock, where the muscle hollowed with every urgent thrust he made between her lips. Faster, faster.

Deeper.

Maybe she thought it. Maybe he said it. He didn't have to say anything. Instinctively she knew what he wanted, what would please him, and gave it with all her heart.

An unintelligible sound wrenched from his throat, a stifled cry, the sweet sound of pleasure too great to bear. A second later, when he pulsed into her mouth, she sank her fingers into his hips and held him in place, deep in the back of her throat, swallowing his essence. It was something she'd never done for any man, but she wanted to give Adrian everything. She wanted everything he could give.

As the last aftershock vibrated through his body, he slumped against the tree, caught her elbow and urged her back to her feet.

"Billie," he whispered.

Nothing more. But a million emotions crossed between them, riding on the back of that one breathless word, and then he pushed his fingers through her hair, sought her gaze in the darkness and lowered his mouth to hers, kissing her in desperate gratitude until she felt bruised. Until she held no thoughts except one: she would never be the same.

The atmosphere in the BMW vibrated with unspoken emotions. Billie didn't want to make meaningless conversation; she was drained, replete, and more than a little impressed with herself. Tonight she'd stepped over the line that restricted her day-to-day existence. She'd reached for what she wanted and taken it, taken *him*. Whatever price she'd pay, it was worth it.

Beside her, Adrian steered the sleek vehicle through sparse midnight traffic, the streetlights illuminating his features in rhythmic flashes.

Luther Vandross filled the silence with mellow, honey-sweet vo-

cals. Adrian had placed the CD in the stereo and offered another
hint of his persona. He liked the Rolling Stones too, she discovered
when he laid the CD holder on the console between them and it fell
open. Janis Joplin. Bruce Springsteen. The Red Hot Chili Peppers.
All classic stuff.

He steered the wheel with one lazy hand, the other resting on
his thigh. When he slowed the car at a stoplight, he glanced at her
and their eyes met. He was still thinking about what had happened
between them in the woods. She saw it in the drop of his lashes, in
the slight furrow between his brows. But she couldn't tell whether
he was pleased or disconcerted.

The answer came when he drove to her apartment building instead
of taking her home with him. He pulled the BMW through the circular drive and parked while she released her seat belt, gathered her
purse, and reached for the door handle without looking at him.

All her tipsy self-satisfaction had crashed to the ground. Out
with a bang, she thought, squelching the urge to cry.

"Well," she said, one foot out the door, "thanks for letting me
touch you. Believe it or not, I think I needed it more than you did."

"Billie." His fingers grazed her back, bare where the dress dipped
low, and she turned to find him watching her with dark, fathomless
eyes. "What are you going to write in your article?"

"The truth. Everything you've told me. Everything I've seen."

"What happened back at the park is intensely personal."

A rueful smile lifted her lips. "Maybe it'll give my article a nice,
snappy edge."

"Will you mention it?"

"I don't know." She studied the beaded purse on her lap. "Why
does it matter?"

"Put whatever you need to in that article," he said quietly. "But
there's a price."

Billie scowled at him. "The other night you told me you didn't care what I wrote. 'Tell it all,' you said."

"I changed my mind."

"That's not playing fair."

His mouth twitched. "Neither was performing oral sex on me in a public park."

Billie wanted to argue, but his particular brand of frankness, as usual, made her thoughts stumble. Staring through the windshield, she said haltingly, "You're saying I'll owe you if I write about what happened between us?"

"That's right."

"Jesus—" She clenched her fists, overcome with frustration and confusion. "What is it with you and debts? I gave you everything I knew how to give tonight, but obviously it wasn't enough. *I'm* not enough. I don't see why you'd want anything more from me."

"I'm a prostitute," he said in that same calm, infuriating tone. "Anything of value you take from me comes at a price."

Unexpectedly her pulse skipped a beat. "Does what happened between us tonight hold value to you, Adrian?"

"Should it?"

Her spine stiffened. "In my opinion, yes. I'm not some lonely, dissatisfied politician's wife. I don't need or want casual sex from you. I wasn't looking for anything from you except your story. And now see what's happening."

His brows lowered. "What exactly is happening, Billie?"

More games. She opened her mouth, then clicked it shut and started to climb out. "Thanks for the concert. I'm going now."

"Billie."

"No," she said, even as she swung her legs back into the car and swiveled to stare at him. "You're a real bastard, Adrian."

The confusion in his expression turned her angry resolve to

putty. "And you're not like the women I know. You're insecure and loving and honest with your emotions. What you want from me makes me uncomfortable."

She tried to swallow the lump in her throat and failed. "May I go now?"

"It makes me think I want it too."

Billie closed her eyes, counted to five in tandem with her thundering heart; opened them. "Damn you . . ." She lunged over the console to meet his waiting lips.

They kissed, long and ravenous and angry. Catching her hand, he folded it against his chest, where his own heart beat a quickened, steady rhythm. Instantly the kiss softened, became languid, a little contrite, laced with lingering desire.

"If you write about us," he said breathlessly, resting his forehead against hers, "you'll owe me."

"A favor for a favor?" She kissed him again, her lips clinging to his. No one had ever tasted as good as this man. "What will I give you this time, Adrian? My soul? My firstborn child?"

"Something," he said. "I'll call you when I know what it is."

CHAPTER TEN

Adrian shoved open the curtains in his Avalon bedroom and blinked at the explosion of morning sun. He'd overslept, ignored the soft, jangling call Azure's secretary, Maria, had placed to gently rouse him and help nudge his client out the door.

Overnight guests were a rarity at Avalon. The only reason Adrian had agreed to a last-minute slumber party with renowned criminal attorney Magda Himmelman was a self-serving one. He needed a good lawyer; the certainty of it had washed over him with dread and dismay yesterday when Detective Hales showed up at his door with the news.

Senator Gwendolyn Campbell had denied ever having been to Avalon even once in her pristine, upstanding life, much less the night Luke soared from Adrian's balcony. There was nothing in the club's records, either, to corroborate his insistence that he'd entertained that evening. Someone had erased it.

Even though he wasn't surprised, once again the surreal urgency of his situation shuddered through him. He had no alibi, only a clear understanding now that Azure wasn't willing to risk everything she'd accomplished to protect one of her escorts, especially not a high-powered client's privacy.

He startled when Magda slid languid arms around his waist from behind.

"What are you thinking?" Her tone was too lazy, her touch too proprietary as she pressed her cheek to his naked back.

"We overslept," he said.

It was time for her to go.

Sensing his aloofness, she released him and went to gather her clothes. While she showered and dressed, he pulled on a pair of drawstring bottoms and made her a cup of coffee. None of the other companions offered their overnight clients coffee upon rising. But for Adrian, it gave the morning's inevitable sense of ignominy a touch of civility for the client . . . and this time, for him too.

He'd performed like a well-oiled automaton last night, blocking out the reality of the woman taking her pleasure beneath him, banishing images of Billie that rushed time and again through his thoughts and threatened the steely control he maintained over his own orgasm. When at last he'd let himself go, one fevered word had pounded through his brain.

Billie.

Thirty-six hours had passed since he'd been with her, and he hadn't yet regained his equilibrium.

He had nothing left to give the customers rotating in and out his bedroom door. In that dreamlike, vacuous time since Billie knelt before him in the woods, ejaculation had become, inexplicably, an intensely private thing, a moment of weakness he wanted to share with no one.

But he had shared it, with Billie. *She* was a weakness, a chink in his carefully constructed armor. He'd given all.

He wanted more.

"I'm leaving my card," Magda said after she'd drained her coffee cup. She retrieved her purse and set a business card on the bedside table, then captured his gaze across the room, once again the cool, self-possessed, ball-busting criminal lawyer known far and wide. "I'd be happy to talk with you off the clock, Adrian. We could meet for drinks."

He shook his head and offered her a polite smile that said he had no interest in personal interaction outside Avalon. "Thank you, Magda, but I insist on paying for your services. After all, you pay for mine."

She nodded and paused at the door. "They don't have a case against you. You do know that."

"I didn't kill Lucien," he said, his façade slipping just a little. "But they don't seem to want to hear that."

She swept a lock of her frosted blond bob behind one ear and offered him a rueful smile. "Never a dull moment in this business, is there? Have you thought about leaving Avalon?"

"No," he said flatly.

One graceful eyebrow lifted. "Well, be careful who you run with. Be on your best behavior. For now, all the detectives can do is harass you . . . unless they find something, which I'm sure Azure has considered. But if this goes any further, call me immediately."

"Wait." Propelled by a sudden surge of gratitude, he approached her and leaned to brush his lips against hers.

Never kiss your clients good-bye, Azure always said, but Adrian was finished listening to her.

Deceitful, cold-hearted bitch. She had erased Gwendolyn Campbell and every other client from the books, and Adrian knew it. She had sacrificed him to the wolves, but he wouldn't take the fall without her. If it were the last thing he ever did, he'd hang tight to Azure Elan and drag her down with him until the darkness closed over both their heads.

* * *

Billie met Nora for lunch on Sunday and waited a safe, discreet hour before broaching the subject of Lucien DeChambeau's death. The two women sat at a shadowed corner table of Old Ebbitt Grill, hunched over plates of salade Niçoise, when Billie finally said, "So give me the update on the Avalon investigation."

Nora wiped her mouth on a linen napkin and sat back. "I only know a few details. Rich would tell me everything if I'd sleep with him."

"Don't," Billie said sharply. "He has the integrity of a barn rat."

"Worry not. The thought has barely crossed my mind." She picked at the salad with her fork. "All I know is that Avalon could be headed for a massive scandal, and I want you to write an exposé article on what you know about the club."

Billie's heart plummeted. Dabbing her lips with her napkin, she glanced up and caught Nora's gaze. It was now or never. "I won't write the article if a scandal breaks."

Nora's penciled brows drew down. "What do you mean?"

"I mean I'm not the right reporter for the job."

"That's ridiculous. You're easily the most tenacious and determined writer on staff, Billie. Why wouldn't you—?"

"A conflict of interest. Don't ask me to elaborate."

Nora watched her for a moment, suspicion and confusion dancing across her sharp features. Then she sighed and sat back again. "I don't know what you've been up to, but tread carefully, Billie. The woman Adrian claimed to be with on the night of Lucien De-Chambeau's death denies everything. Azure Elan asserts she's never even met her. No one saw her there, it seems, except Adrian."

"But they take guests all the time," Billie exclaimed. "She might have held a one-time pass."

"And I hear she's a politician of some kind, which wouldn't look good at all if her identity got out."

"So she's lying."

"Or Adrian's lying."

Billie shook her head, recalling the pain that tightened Adrian's features as he spoke of his friend only yards from where Lucien had jumped to his death. "He wouldn't lie. He cared deeply about Lucien. He'd never—" She cut herself off when she realized Nora was regarding her with narrowed eyes.

"Adrian spoke to you about Lucien?"

"Just briefly." She shrugged and lightened her tone. "I asked him about the other companions at Avalon. He mentioned Lucien was his closest friend at the club. He had no reason to kill the guy."

"That you know of," Nora said. "Don't be naïve, Billie. And for God's sake, don't let a useless fascination with the man get in the way of your common sense. For all you know, Adrian's a terrific actor who specifically fed you that information so he could have a character witness in his corner."

A sick sensation gripped Billie's stomach. She was more than a mere character witness. She wanted to believe Adrian was far, far away the night Lucien flew from that balcony, even if it meant him being tangled up in some client's arms like he'd claimed. But if he couldn't prove to the authorities that he'd been with the politician during those key hours . . . God help him. God help her, because her heart would suffer the brunt of the trauma.

Adrian called close to midnight. Billie had barely nodded off with a Michael Crichton novel propped against her breasts when the phone trilled and jolted every nerve in her body.

"I woke you," he said.

"Just barely." She shivered as his voice, husky-warm, wrapped around her senses. "But while we're on the subject, why are you calling so late?"

She held her breath, wondering if he would mention the collapse of his alibi. She didn't want to know the truth. She wanted to continue traipsing along, blinded by lust and infatuation, entangled in Adrian's shadows. Just for a little while longer. The pleasure he'd brought to her existence was too potent to abandon just yet.

"Did you write about us today?" he asked.

She hesitated. "I danced around the details, but yes, I did express a certain . . . semi-biblical knowledge . . . of an unnamed companion at an unnamed club."

"Read it to me."

As a rule, Billie never allowed anyone to see her rough drafts before she submitted them to Nora. But lately, every tenet in her stockpile seemed so easily undone by Adrian Antoli.

This was no different. She found herself padding across the carpet to her computer, where a first, unfinished draft of the article about him still protruded from the printer. "It's very rough," she told him, perching on the swivel chair. "I write first, then polish later."

"I'm listening."

Clearing her throat, she skimmed the first page, deemed it presentable, and began to recite what she'd written.

Adrian listened in silence. When she was done, he said, "It's very provocative."

"You're a provocative subject."

"And you're a talented writer. You're truthful."

"Yes," she said wryly. "It's not always a good thing."

"You wrote about what happened in the woods last week."

"Indirectly."

"Directly enough to turn me on all over again."

She drew a shaky breath. "Readers will want to know what it's like to be with you, and I think I answered that question in a tactful way. Don't you?"

"Tactful, yes. And I'm glad to know you enjoyed it as much as I did."

She took another deep breath to steady her racing pulse. "So now I guess I owe you."

"I've been lying here, thinking about what I want in exchange."

A current of excitement shivered through her. "And?"

"First I want you to tell me something. A secret."

"Fine," Billie said, her voice firm. "And then you tell me one. Play fair, Adrian."

He paused. "What if I don't like what you ask me?"

"That could go either way."

"You don't have to answer, then. You can just hang up."

Now that she had him, his low voice caressing her ear, she wouldn't dream of hanging up on him. Unless, of course, he made her angry, which was certainly in his power. "I'll just tell you no. Something I'm sure you never hear."

"Hmm," he said, and the humor in his tone told her he appreciated her acid response. "What happened in your life that makes you so wounded and skittish?"

She frowned, surprised. "What do you mean?"

"You had a lengthy relationship. I want to know about him."

Ted. The last person Billie wanted to remember in her state of hazy pleasure. She sighed and bid farewell to the slow, sexual burn Adrian had stirred within her. "Now?"

"Now. First get comfortable. Are you lying down?"

"Yes, Dr. Freud." She climbed beneath her covers and propped an extra pillow behind her head. "There's nothing to tell. I had a relationship that lasted five years, and then it ended." Bitterness crept into her tone. "It ended somewhat abruptly when Ted Chadwick, chief bastard of the universe, married someone else."

"I see." The even tone of his voice revealed nothing. "Did you want to marry him?"

"I don't know. Every time the subject came up, we'd agree to put it off. We were both so busy with our lives. He had his law professorship and I had my writing. I thought we were happy, but I guess I was the only one. I opened the newspaper one morning when he was away on a business trip and read about his engagement to 'Vickie St. Claire of Potomac.'"

Adrian's silence prompted her to continue. "When I confronted him, he immediately came clean. He'd been seeing her behind my back for months, trying to decide who he wanted more. Wholesome Billie, or affluent, old-money Vickie St. Claire."

"Did she know about you?"

"No. I was tempted to be the shrew, look her up and share the information, but it wouldn't have made him love me again."

"And now, Billie? Do you still want his love?"

It was a question Billie had asked herself a million times in the last six months, and always the answer was a predictable, undeniable yes. Until now. Now, with Adrian forcing her to search her heart for the truth, she felt brave enough to admit what had frightened her all along.

"I think," she said slowly, "that if I'd wanted Ted's love in the first place, I'd be married to him by now." Deep inside her, something broke off and floated away. Lingering grief. A thread of anger. She felt strangely free. Laughter bubbled to her lips. "I can't believe I just admitted that. You do this to all your clients?"

"If they merit it. But you're not a client."

"What exactly am I, Adrian?" Playing with the truth had frightened her, then empowered her. Now it was his turn to squirm.

The silence on his end made her wonder if he'd hung up. "You're in my dreams," he said finally. "I dreamt of you tonight. It woke me up."

Her pulse skittered. "And you called."

"Yes."

Hugging the phone closer to her ear, Billie rolled on her side, the silky sheets sliding against her bare legs as heat pooled between them. "What did you dream?"

"I dreamt about your mouth on me." His voice drizzled over her like warm, rich liquor. "Your tongue, stroking me. The softness of your hair in my hands. I woke up with a hard-on."

Billie's throat went dry.

"I can still feel your hands, Billie. The heat of your lips, the way it felt to come in your mouth. Even now."

Beneath the sheet, her hand slipped over her breast and found her nipple hard. "I feel your hands too, Adrian. Your mouth."

"Where?" He sounded breathless.

"On my breasts. My stomach. My thighs. Between them." A forbidden thrill quivered through her. This was foreplay, predecessor to phone sex. A pastime that hadn't appealed to her before now. So many firsts with this man. He peeled her inhibitions away like the skin from a peach, leaving her soft, wet, and ripe.

"Billie," he said, so quietly she had to press the phone against her ear, "what do you wear to bed?"

She glanced down at her bright pink Hello Kitty nightshirt and was tempted to lie. *A filmy negligee and nothing else.* "A T-shirt," she said, modifying the truth. "What do you wear?"

"When I sleep? Nothing."

"Of course. How silly of me to ask."

He laughed, and the rare sound brought a smile to her lips. He had a wonderful laugh, warm and gentle.

"So you're in bed now? Naked?" she prodded, titillated by the thought.

"Would you like me to be?"

"Of course."

"Then consider it done." A faint rustling indicated he was removing his clothing, and a shivery thrill snaked up Billie's spine.

After a moment, he continued. "Are you wearing panties?"

"Yes." White cotton with little blue flowers. Ted had abhorred them. Adrian probably wouldn't care. He'd rip them off her without looking at them. She squeezed her eyes closed, knowing what came next.

"Put your hand inside your panties, Billie."

She hesitated only a millisecond before she did as he ordered, and found herself already wet and sensitized. Her body shivered as she remembered the way his tongue had played her that night in his apartment. "How far are we taking this?"

"As far as we need to, to bring you pleasure."

"You too," she told him baldly. "I won't do this alone."

The desire in his voice slurred his words just slightly. "I'm right there with you."

She closed her eyes and imagined his hand moving like a smooth piston on his flesh, up and down . . .

Her breath snagged in her throat, her fingers faltering on her own aching flesh. She was shamefully wet. Shamefully needful. "Do you do this very often, Adrian?"

"Phone sex?"

"Touching yourself."

"Not too often."

"I guess you wouldn't need to." Embarrassment stung her cheeks.

"Everyone needs to, Billie."

"But in your business—well, if you wanted, you could probably have—you know, with your clients, at least three orgasms a day."

"But I don't."

"Even still, the last time you had to touch yourself, just for sheer relief, was probably when you were a teenager."

"How do you know?" Laughter edged his voice again.

Billie paused, guiltily withdrawing her fingers to toy with the elastic on her panties. "Name the last time."

"After our interview at Avalon."

He had such a way of knocking her breathless. "Liar," she said, flattered. "Why would you do that, knowing what kind of work night you had ahead of you?"

"Because you turned me down. Left in a huff before I could even kiss you. I couldn't get you out of my mind."

"Thank you, I think." She closed her eyes. She'd never perceived masturbation as a particularly sexy activity, but as usual, Adrian had a way of adjusting her thinking.

She shifted her hips, trying to ease the climbing tension that coiled low in her groin. "Okay, now you have to answer one of my questions."

"I'd rather not talk right now."

"You can always hang up," she said smartly.

His smile traveled the line between them. "I would never hang up on you, Billie."

"Good." She swallowed, forced herself to relax, her knees to fall open beneath the sheets. Every muscle in her body had tightened in anticipation of the pleasure to come. "Do you ever get lonely, Adrian?"

"Sometimes," he said, and she wondered if he knew how very solitary a picture he presented, despite his good looks, his sexual skill and charisma. That person was eye-catching in the moment.

But it was the human side of him, the one she now pictured on the other end of the phone line that captured her fascination.

"I don't want you to be lonely." She shifted back against the pillows, and her hand slid inside her panties again of its own accord, fingers caressing. Teasing, the way he would, if he were there.

"I want you to be here, with me." Everything ached. Her breasts. Her empty arms. The hollow place between her legs. The blood searing her veins. "If I told you my apartment number, would you come to me?"

"Not tonight."

"Then would you let me come to you?"

"No," he said gently.

Her temper spiked. "Why not?"

"Because I like the idea of hearing you climax over the phone."

That shut her up. When she recovered, she said, "But I want you to touch me."

"I am, Billie. It's my hand touching you. Tell me how it feels. I want to know everything."

Inside her panties, her fingers came to life. Awkward at first, then rhythmic, drawing tiny, ever-tightening and quickening circles as she searched her heated mind for snapshots of the night in the park, the way he sounded when he came in her hands and mouth, of lying open to him on his living room sofa with his mouth softly caressing between her legs.

Her excitement built to a feverish pitch. Brave with ten miles of phone signal between them, she told him in tight, husky words what he wanted to know, until her breath came too rapidly to form complete sentences, until her eyelashes fluttered closed, her muscles tensed, every nerve aroused, blood rushing to build, and build, and build . . .

"Oh," she whimpered, half mortified, half ecstatic as she shuddered once, twice, three times under her own fingers, which he controlled like the strings of a puppet with his low, steady voice.

"Tell me," he said, hoarse now. "How was it?"

"Shamefully good." No sense in lying. Tiny aftershocks of delight shook her body. "How about you?"

"I'm almost there. Talk to me, Billie. Make me come."

She sat up, straining to hear him, wild with desire for him. "I want to be back in the woods with you, Adrian. On my knees in front of you. I want to take you in my mouth. You taste so good, you're so hard and hot. You fill my mouth."

"Oh . . ." he whispered.

The words, so sexual and foreign to Billie's lips, spilled forth, breathy and fervent. "I can feel the blood racing through you, and I'm licking you, biting you, sucking you, until it feels too good, until you can't stop yourself . . ."

"Yes."

"Now?" she whispered.

"Oh, *now*—" His breath left him in a thunderous rush and she held the phone tight to her ear, her lips brushing the mouthpiece as she imagined his orgasm quivering through her too, through muscles already exhausted, nerves already strummed and sated.

For a long, wordless moment they listened to each other regain composure. Heartbeats slowed, breathing steadied. Then Billie collapsed against the pillows, and Adrian sighed.

"Billie."

"Adrian." She smiled, only a little stunned by the things she'd said to him. She didn't want to let him go. She wanted to ask when she'd see him again.

As if he could read her mind, he cleared his throat and said, "Ready to discuss the second favor?"

"You mean that wasn't it?"

He laughed, a soft, relaxed sound. "There's a dinner party on Friday night. I need a date. Someone discreet."

Billie rolled her eyes. "But I'm supposed to be a hard-hitting, I'll-do-anything-to-get-the-story reporter."

"I'd put money on your discretion, Billie."

She hesitated, oddly touched by his solemn declaration. He trusted her, it seemed. And something told her it was quite a stretch for him to admit it.

"This party isn't an Avalon party," he said. "It's being given in the suburbs, with people who don't know what I do for a living. It requires total prudence on your part, and I wouldn't trust another woman more than I trust you."

He wasn't joking. She sobered and sat up. "You want me to be your date?"

"You are still indebted to me, aren't you?"

Too easy. "A party in the suburbs? This sounds suspiciously wholesome, Adrian."

"Oh, but the possibilities are endless." His tone held a trace of humor. "I'll make it worth your while."

She narrowed her eyes, her mind flipping through his possible motives. What a strange request. "And there are no other strings attached? I won't have to strip naked and perform acrobatics or anything?"

"I always like to keep the options open," he said dryly, "but no. Nothing is required except your company."

An inexplicable reticence weighted her tongue. The more she saw of him, the more he invaded her thoughts, her dreams, her life. For the first time, she boldly identified the uneasy and electric sensation he stirred in her. Potential. Potential for falling in love, with a man who fought such sentiment with every atom of his being.

"Well . . ." She played with the elastic of her panties, thought about exchanging them for silk ones. "Okay."

"I'll pick you up at six on Friday. Wear jeans."

"Will we be roughing it?" she asked, digging for clues.

"No. I just want to see your perfect little ass in a pair of Levi's."

It was Billie's turn to laugh, and pleasure warmed her cheeks, a deceptive sense of well-being. "Hmm. You drive a hard bargain, but okay."

He sighed, a sound of repletion. "Go to sleep now, Billie."

Easier said than done. After they hung up, her eyes stayed open, attention fixed on the shadows of the ceiling, until the grayness of dawn crept across her apartment and banished the wild scenarios and warnings from her mind.

CHAPTER ELEVEN

She wore jeans, just like he'd instructed. Levi's. Snug, faded in all the right spots, and fitted beautifully to her delectable backside.

Adrian leaned against his car, his gaze wandering up her long legs as she walked out of the building and headed toward him. A smile born of sheer delight crept across his lips when he glanced at her face and found it fiery red with self-consciousness. For a reporter, she had a shy streak more intense than anything he'd seen from first-time clients.

It intoxicated him.

"I see you follow directions, Ms. Cort," he said, checking his pleasure behind a placid façade as he opened the BMW's passenger door for her.

Billie flashed him a smile and seated herself. "You offered such unarguable guidelines."

He handed her the strap of her seat belt, using the courtesy as an excuse to linger and watch her stretch it across high, tight breasts complimented by a long-sleeved, blue-striped top.

A wave of rich brown hair fell against her cheek as she leaned to buckle the metal clasp. Adrian only meant to brush the strands back, but when his fingers touched her cheek, she turned her head to look up at him, and something inside him dissolved, trickled sweetly through him and pooled low in his belly.

"I'm sorry," he said, bracing one hand on the hood of the car and leaning in, "but I have to do this."

His mouth settled on hers, soft, chaste, but then she parted her lips and touched her tongue to his, and he held back a groan that rose from the deepest part of him. If the lust pounding through him was any indication, it was going to be a long night.

He shut her door, rounded to the driver's side, and a moment later they pulled out of the apartment building driveway. He'd promised himself to get through the dinner party without becoming more deeply entangled with Billie. She was perfect for the image he needed to pull off tonight, for the cloying concerns of others he wanted to lay to rest. She looked wholesome and guileless enough to convince anyone that he had his life together, that he was just *fine*. He would have to be, to have a woman like her on his arm.

"Where are we going?" Billie asked as he merged the BMW onto Massachusetts Avenue.

"Bethesda." He glanced in his rearview mirror and caught sight of a stretch Rolls-Royce turning into the gated drive of a pricey town house they'd just passed. His attention flicked back to the road. He recognized that limousine, knew the voice and body and scent of the woman being chauffeured in its backseat.

Margery Cabot, wife of a diplomat.

A frown lowered his brows. He couldn't go anywhere without being reminded of the choices he'd made in his life. Choices that didn't suit the decency or vulnerability of the woman sitting beside him.

"Adrian?" Billie leaned to see his face.

He forced himself to smile and reached across the console to squeeze her hand.

She was silent. Then, "How's the investigation going?"

Wariness immediately corkscrewed in his gut, an end to the mindless fantasies he'd pinned on this night. He withdrew his fingers from hers. "Why? For the article?"

"For my own curiosity."

"I'm not under suspicion with you too, am I?" He meant the question to sound flippant, but it came out injured, angry.

"Of course not," she said, and looked away.

It sounded like a lie. An acid smile twisted his lips and he gripped the steering wheel. "Let's be truthful tonight, Ms. Cort. Nothing but honesty for the next few hours. Think we can manage that?"

She turned toward him, and the weight of her gaze warmed his face with self-awareness. She had a magical, disarming way of exposing him with her watchful green eyes.

"I don't know." Her tone was bruised. "I asked you about the investigation because you seem so distracted. Something's not right. I just thought . . ." She threw her hands up in an impatient gesture. "I don't know what I thought. It's none of my business."

She was hurt, and he'd made such quick work of ruining their night in the brief time they'd been together. He stared at the road, clenching and unclenching his fingers on the polished wood steering wheel. "I have nothing to hide. The detectives questioned me again this past week, but I've heard nothing from them since."

Like a pack of wolves retreating when their prey was only half dead, he wanted to add. A sick kind of blessing. He'd sat in the lobby at Avalon and answered their crude, pointed, insinuating questions as if by rote, never flinching, never allowing a single flicker of emotion to cross his features.

But the questioning left him so flayed, afterward he'd locked himself into his private quarters and spent the next hour with a shot glass and whiskey for company, until his vision swam, the world spun, and his stomach lurched in protest. Then he'd sprawled across the massive bed and slept, and suffered a night of phantom visitations from Luke, whose head was split open and skull exposed, blood glistening like red sequins on his bruised features.

The image had burned itself into Adrian's brain when the detective slipped back the sheet and asked him to identify his friend's sleeping face. Luke, lying on the sidewalk with a halo of puddled blood around his head. Still beautiful, even with the trauma and lingering bruises from someone's fists nights before. Luke had died as he'd lived—broken on the inside, with a beatific exterior.

Hopelessness expanded within Adrian, knotting the muscles in his shoulders. "I don't want to talk about the investigation. I don't want to think about Avalon or Luke or the detectives. I want to relax tonight, with you, in relative quiet. Is that asking too much, Billie? Because if it is, I'll turn around and take you home." His voice wavered, the words stilted. Christ, he was losing control in front of the one person whose opinion mattered to him.

"It's not asking too much," Billie said, her voice quiet. "I've written nothing about the investigation, and I only asked because I care. A mistake, obviously."

"What—asking, or caring?" He glanced in his rearview mirror, changed lanes, his chest inexplicably hollow. "Are you claiming to care about me?"

"What do you think?" He sensed her drawing herself erect, chin lifted, gaze straight ahead, and tone imperious. "You've had your fingers inside my body," she said, gently mocking his words from the night at Rock Creek Park. "You've tasted me. I'm not one of your clients—I'm allowed to care."

Adrian was at once surprised and impressed, followed by a gentle, disturbing curl of some warm emotion he couldn't—*wouldn't*—identify.

"Says who?" He flashed her a quick, repentant smile meant to soothe the friction between them.

"Says me," she replied without humor. "Telling me what I can and can't feel is not a part of our deal, is it?"

"Never." Another glance at Billie's face showed the troubled thoughts still darting behind her eyes, and his regret doubled for having fed the tension now emanating from her, for drawing lines of concern and anxiety on her unguarded features.

When Adrian braked at a stoplight, he used the opportunity to reach for her. Trailing his fingers along the silky skin of her cheek, he drew her to him and pressed his lips against her forehead to erase the frown there.

"Thank you," he said, dredging up the words from some deep, skittish place inside him. A token statement of contrition, but it seemed to be enough.

The light turned green and they drove on in restored, if fragile, tranquility. Adrian turned the BMW onto a winding neighborhood road and soon pulled into the circular driveway of a midcentury, split-level brick house.

Two other cars were parked in front of his. A child's baseball bat and brightly colored book were shoved up in the rear window of the Honda Accord directly ahead.

Adrian came around to Billie's door and opened it for her, reading the astonishment and confusion in her face with a repressed grin.

She stared at him as they started up the flagstone sidewalk.

"What's wrong?" he asked, knowing full well what she was thinking.

"This is the dinner party you told me about?"

"This is it." They stopped before a set of red double doors, which heralded a handmade wreath adorned with silk magnolias. Rosalie had a creative streak a mile wide, the rooms of her home a mismatched collection of crafts rendered by her hands, as well as the children's.

"One last thing," Adrian said as he rang the doorbell, "don't address me as Adrian. These people don't know who Adrian is."

Her green eyes widened. "I can't call you by your name?"

"You can't call me by that name."

"Then what should I call you?"

"Anything but Adrian." He leaned to kiss the frown from her mouth, his lips clinging, reassuring, before he straightened and folded his hands in front of him.

"You're not going to tell me who lives here?" she demanded, her voice husky with what he hoped wasn't just indignation.

"Of course I'm going to tell you."

The door swung open, and a chubby, dark-haired woman in a bright red T-shirt and Capri pants threw herself into Adrian's arms.

"Kids!" she hollered. "Zio's here!"

"This," he told Billie over the woman's shoulder, "is my sister Rosalie."

D id Zio tell you this house has been in our family for almost fifty years?" Rosalie asked Billie as she handed her a basket of bread to carry to the kitchen table.

"That's amazing." Billie swerved around Rudy the dog and dutifully delivered the bread, then sidled up to Adrian, who was setting flatware by the plates. "No offense," she whispered, "but tough luck going through childhood with the name 'Zio.'"

"Actually, it's a family nickname that sprang up in my old age," he explained. "Compliments of Sophie, my oldest niece. It means 'uncle.'" He glanced at his sister. "And no, Rosalie, I haven't told Billie anything about the house or our family because I can't get a word in edgewise around here."

"You should tell her more about you," Rosalie said firmly. "My God . . . stop being so secretive." Then to her husband, David, "Did you put the beer in the fridge downstairs? I completely forgot. And grab an extra bottle of wine while you're down there. The Mahaffeys are coming over."

David, a lanky man with thinning sandy hair, a warm grin, and a quiet tolerance, saluted his resolute wife and headed off to perform the assigned duties.

"Does Billie know you grew up in this very house?" Rosalie prompted her brother, as though the conversation had never left off.

Adrian, who had knelt to embrace the well-fed black Labrador after their long separation, offered Billie a dry smile. "Billie, do you know I grew up in this very house?"

She flashed him a look of mock surprise.

"When our parents retired and moved to Miami, they sold it to David and me." Rosalie nudged him with her foot and when he rose, promptly set a stack of dinner plates in his hands. "If you had any wits about you, you'd have bought this house and started a family of your own. You'd make such a good father. I don't understand why you—"

"Rosalie." Adrian spoke the quiet warning beneath his breath, and instantly a conciliatory grin spread across her chubby face.

"It's a wonderful home." Billie glanced wistfully around the mismatched, eighties-style kitchen. Despite its outdated floral décor, it was warm and cozy and *lived-in*, the kind of house she used to stare at from her mother's car window, wondering what kind of family such a home would hold. And now she knew. The big and noisy and loving kind, like the Antolis.

She moved to the big window over the sink and gazed out at Rosalie's four children, ages six to fourteen, who had barreled outside to romp in the lush, sprawling yard after dutifully greeting Adrian and Billie. All dark-haired and dark-eyed and olive-skinned, like their mother. Like Adrian. "What a great yard. There's so much room for them to play."

"We turned that grass to dust when we were kids." Adrian sounded reflective as he rested a hand at her waist and looked over her shoulder. "This home was a great place to grow up."

"And we all went to school up the street at the little public elementary," Rosalie added as she stirred something fragrant and spicy on the stove. "Except the prince, of course. He went to parochial school."

Adrian brushed his lips against Billie's ear. "My mother thought my morals would be warped in the public education system."

Billie bit her lip to keep from laughing.

The doorbell rang, Rudy went barreling and barking toward the foyer, and the Mahaffeys from across the street let themselves in bearing a pie, with blond-headed twin boys in tow.

"Kids are out in the back," Rosalie said as the boys headed for the kitchen door. "Tell them thirty minutes until we eat."

Then she introduced Billie to the couple as 'Zio's girlfriend,' and Adrian didn't argue, just kept his fingertips resting lightly on Billie's back, as if in reassurance.

Billie waited with shallow breath for someone to address him by his given name—one of Adrian's secrets she was determined to breach—but no one called him anything but Zio, even David. She couldn't very well demand Adrian's real name. They would think she was nuts.

Maybe she was. Her relationship with Adrian definitely was. But God, she couldn't get enough of his smile and laughter and gentle, solicitous touch. For tonight, she could pretend she was Zio's girlfriend, that she was as welcome and adored as his dark gaze made her feel every time it strayed to her face.

A humble, solicitous host, David kept the adults' wineglasses filled, and they stood around the kitchen and chatted while waiting on the food.

Warm alcohol and even warmer contentment soaked through Billie as she basked in the laughter and camaraderie around her. Part of her, though, wanted to step back and observe Adrian in such natural, nurturing circumstances. He seemed so different here, surrounded by people who knew and obviously loved him. The tension that had masked his features in the car had melted away, and his smile was genuine, relaxed, entrancing.

She learned he spoke fluent Italian, that he tolerated his older sister's henpecking with the patience of an adoring sibling, that Avalon had honed in him the ability to talk about anything and everything, from politics to child rearing to the Washington Redskins' upcoming season.

Eavesdropping on his conversation with Rosalie's husband, Billie discovered that Adrian knew something about mechanics too. David was restoring a 1968 Mustang and had a million questions, all of which Adrian seemed able and eager to answer. Billie lost him for a good ten minutes when the men headed downstairs to the garage to dabble.

When Myra Mahaffey went outside to check on a squalling child, Billie found herself alone with Adrian's sister.

"So how did you two meet?" Rosalie asked her in a conspiratorial whisper, leaning her elbows on the Formica island in the center of the kitchen. "He hasn't brought a girlfriend home in years."

Billie used the excuse of petting Rudy's velvety ears to avoid the other woman's shrewd gaze. "Well, it's funny, really. I'm a reporter for *Illicit* magazine—"

"Oh, my God! I've subscribed to that magazine since the beginning of time. I have stacks of it in the garage—I can't bring myself to throw away a single issue. You meet celebrities in your work, huh?"

"Sometimes."

Rosalie turned to peek at the lasagna in the oven. "Thrilling. And how did your path cross my brother's?"

Think, Billie. "It's a strange story. I happened to be reporting on this—this suicide—a tragedy, really. The man was a friend of your brother's—"

"It was Luke. Right?" Rosalie's tendency to bulldoze the conversation rescued Billie from having to grope for falsities. "You were covering that story, huh? What would a women's magazine like *Illicit* want with Luke DeChambeau?"

Billie gave a weak shrug, ashamed at herself for using Lucien's misfortune as an escape. "He . . . he moved in certain social circles, from what I understand. Washington elite. I don't normally cover such a—"

"Drugs and alcohol did him in, I'm sure. Same old story for him. And such a beautiful boy too. It's a terrible thing about Luke." Sadness filled Rosalie's chocolate eyes as she folded a dishtowel on the counter. "We knew him for years, and he had so many skeletons. I'm just glad he didn't drag my brother into any of it."

Billie exhaled, sickened by the web of deception Adrian had spun around himself. It was so expansive, it even draped its silky skeins over this warm home and the people within it.

"So how's he handling it?" Rosalie went on, deep furrows appearing between her dark brows.

Billie swallowed. "You mean Adri—" *God, Billie.* "Uh, you want to know how your brother's—"

"He's so hush-hush. He won't tell us anything. I didn't even know Luke had killed himself until a couple of days ago when my mother called. She found out from Luke's family, of all things. Zio never even told me about it, so I guess he thinks we still don't know."

Billie studied Rosalie's round, animated face. She obviously didn't know Adrian was under suspicion with the authorities. How could he come from an adoring family and maintain the icy shield that seemed to be such an integral part of his persona? Did *anyone* get close to him?

"I think he's deeply saddened by what happened," she said finally. "And it's hard for him to talk about it. But we've only known each other a little while. He doesn't tell me much, either."

Rosalie scratched absently at a burn mark on the countertop. "Billie, do you know what he does for a living?"

Billie's heart jolted and her palms went damp. "Oh . . . he's in sales."

God.

The other woman's eyebrows shot up. "He tells you that too?"

"That's what he says."

"And you don't ply him for details?"

She shrugged, anxiety coiling in her middle like an agitated rattler. "I have no reason to doubt him."

"But he's always been so vague about it. I worry. He's too secretive, always has been. It makes my mother and sisters crazy. It makes *me* crazy, especially if a month goes by and I don't hear from him. Sometimes I think we might as well live on opposite sides of the continent, you know?"

Billie had to scramble for a judicious reply. "He's not an easy person to know, Rosalie. But he enjoys spending time with his family, that I do know, because he's told me how important you are to him."

Rosalie patted Billie's hand. "And now he's got you, yes? And he looks so happy."

Billie blinked. "He does?"

"More than I've seen him in a long time. You're a nice, wholesome girl, Billie. You're good for him."

Billie tried not to think about the decidedly unwholesome touch of Adrian's hands on her body, or the way he could make her go all soft and quivering with just a slow, searching look.

And here she sat, in his family's home, surrounded by people who'd known him for years, and yet knew nothing about his life. Everywhere, hints leading to the truth. It only confused her more.

When she snapped out of her bemused reverie, Rosalie had crossed to open the back door.

"Kids! Dinner! Somebody get Daddy and Frank and Zio from the garage and tell them it's time to eat."

Dinner was a noisy, stimulating blur until the six kids—with Rosalie's hard-won permission—dashed from the table to return to their outside play. Then the adults lingered and slid into easy conversation over pie and cups of Rosalie's flavorful espresso.

Billie wasn't sure whether it was the potent shot of caffeine or the way Adrian laced his fingers with hers beneath the table that kept her heartbeat at an uneven tempo. His thumb drew slow lazy circles on her palm that made her stomach go light and funny. Countless times she felt his steady regard on her profile, and somehow knew she was being weighed and measured. In return she compared the weight of his secrets with the warm, loving man sitting beside her,

and decided she could pretend for one night that Avalon didn't exist
for either of them.

By the time they cleared the dishes it was nearly eight o'clock.
Dusk fell in that slow, bluing manner so characteristic of summer
evenings, heralded by the appearance of drifting fireflies. A few at
first, then enough to give the creeping night the appearance of flickering, falling stars.

A sultry, grass-scented breeze lifted Billie's hair from her face as
she let Adrian lead her down the sloping yard toward the woods,
through a throng of nieces and nephews who leapt and laughed in
their uninhibited bid to capture the glowing insects.

"Where are we going?" she asked him, sensing the purpose in his
stride as the grass crunched softly beneath their feet.

He slowed and drew her into the cradle of his arm. "There's
something I want to show you before it gets too dark."

He led her through the verdant, scattered trees, across a carpet
of decomposing leaves, and stopped only when the lights from the
house twinkled like distant luminaries through the woods.

"It's so quiet here," Billie said in a hushed voice.

"Yes. This was my secret world when I was a kid." He released
her hand to move ahead of her and gently nudged the toe of his
leather loafer against the crumbled ruins of a child's clubhouse.
"This used to be a fort. My dad and I built it twenty years ago, and
it stood forever, until last winter's blizzard finally knocked it down.
In high school, I used to come out here to get away."

She glanced around and her gaze fell on a large, rectangular
hammock stretched between two massive maples, its woven ropes
weathered and inviting. "This place has the distinct feel of a bach-
elor pad. Sure you didn't come here to make time with the girls?"

His smile flashed in the gloom. "On the rare occasion."

"Ah-ha. I thought you might be entertaining unwholesome

intentions, whisking me off into the deep, dark woods." She wandered over to the hammock and picked off the leaves and branches gathered in its cradle. "Let's swing."

Stretching out on its buoyant expanse, she made room for him and Adrian climbed into place beside her. He laid an arm above her head, then beneath it when she lifted her neck and snuggled closer to him. Their bodies melded and settled together, and after a moment of staring at the stars through the boughs overhead, he let one denim-covered leg drop over the side of the hammock and gently swayed them into a lulling rhythm.

Billie was enchanted. Cicadas and crickets performed a maracas symphony in the trees, punctuated by the low timpani of bullfrogs nearby. Adrian's scent, faded aftershave and soap, filled her senses as she closed her eyes and floated on pure, sensory pleasure. A velvet breeze blew across them and his arm tightened around her shoulder as though to warm her, a tender, unconscious reaction that made her feel safe, and somehow adored.

"Thank you for coming." His quiet words stirred the tendrils of hair against her forehead. "I'm sorry I snapped at you in the car."

Surprised by the quiet apology, she struggled to find an even reply, and settled on a simple, "You're forgiven." Her palm rubbed the soft material of his maroon jersey, reading the hard muscles of his abdomen beneath, while desire sparked and ignited between them. "I'm glad you asked me here. It's lovely."

"You're lovely. When I saw you tonight, you took my breath away."

Billie shifted to see his face, found it somber and watchful. Under the standard silky disguise of a courtesan lay an intensity and vulnerability far more exciting. His emotions ran deep, his sensitivity even deeper. Not so very different than herself, she realized with surprise. Something about the man under the mask was strikingly familiar.

She searched her mind for a way to bring the humor back to his features. "Say it in Italian, Zio."

A hint of a smile touched his lips. *"Lei sono bello,"* he whispered, a finger curling around a strand of her hair. *"Il mio amore."*

She shivered with giddy delight and kissed the spot where his heart thudded steadily beneath his shirt. "I bet you say that to all the girls."

"Just you. You're beautiful, Billie."

"Even in old jeans?" she asked, secretly pleased.

"Especially in old jeans. Unaffected. Real. You're the only thing around me that feels real anymore."

Before she could grasp the magnitude of the admission, before she could weigh its significance and what it meant in the constantly shifting tide of their odd relationship, his breath brushed the hair at her temple, followed by the warm pressure of his lips on her brow.

For a man whose life encompassed the raw, emotionless aspect of base human urges, he was unequivocally inclined toward gentleness. The tenderness of him, the dichotomy he was proving himself to be drove all rational thought from her mind, snagged her breath in her throat and filled her with longing. Deeper than sexual. Soul deep.

The world seemed to stand still as Adrian said with the touch of his lips what he couldn't put into words. He scattered soft, feathery kisses down her nose, over her cheek, evading her mouth, even when she turned her head and tracked the path of his caresses.

Cool air drifted over her stomach as he tugged her shirt free from her jeans and slipped his hand beneath, palm to her concave belly, and rested there.

"I've wanted to touch you all night." His lips were at her ear now, while her throat went dry with desire and other parts of her flooded with liquid need. "I watched you at dinner, talking and laughing with my family, and thought about putting my hands on you. How I would touch you later when I got you alone. How I would taste you. Your skin. Your warmth. All of you."

She closed her eyes and held his head in the crook of her neck, pulse thrumming as she realized something had happened to him tonight, a peeling away of disguises and defenses. Something that possibly had to do with her presence here, in this sacred place that no one else knew about. His secret world, he'd called it. And Billie knew, though he hadn't said it, that she too was his secret.

He shifted, his foot left the ground and he slid his hand higher, between her breasts, located the front clasp of her bra and freed it.

"We're out in the open," she said, half mortified, half titillated by the potential risk of his actions.

"Then we'll have to be silent." His palm swallowed her breast, circled her nipple until it tightened into a hard little knot beneath his touch.

"But your sister—"

"I told her we were going for a walk."

"Will the kids come back here?"

"No." He brushed teasing kisses across her mouth, his lips flavored with the warm remnants of coffee. "They think the woods are haunted."

She shivered and lifted her head to capture his elusive mouth, but he drew back, eyes even darker than the falling night.

"Ask me what I'm going to do to you," he whispered, "here, in the haunted woods, under the trees."

"What are you going to do to me?" A suspicious smile curved her lips, but his face was devoid of humor.

"I'm going to make you come."

The words, part threat, part promise, feathered across Billie's lips and stole her breath. "That's—that would be—"

"I want you to know more pleasure, here in this hammock, than you've ever known in your life."

She stared up at him, suddenly frightened by the promise, knowing how easy it would be to dissolve under his hands. Her common sense was slipping away. She grasped at it, shuddered at the sudden realization that she couldn't remember what her life was like before him, before this fluttering sentience. "Adrian . . ."

"Don't, Billie." He spoke fervently, surprising her into watchful silence. "Don't act modest with me, not now, when I want to touch you so much I ache from it. Not after everything we've shared." Beneath her shirt, his hand hovered above her breast, withholding contact, his fingers so close to her sensitive flesh that she felt their heat emanating through skin and muscle and bone, all the way to her hurtling heart.

It wasn't modesty that gave her pause, but rather a strange premonition that he would strip her, expose her, destroy her so easily. She was falling. Seduced. Spellbound. And because she had no choice, because she was so drunk on desire and the long-repressed need he'd awakened in her, she nodded.

"Tell me." He rubbed his nose against her cheek, one fingertip tracing the curve of her breast, circling her beaded nipple, raising goose bumps on her sensitive skin. "Say the words."

It was all he knew. Specifics. Flagrant demands, blatant expressions of want. She could give him this, what felt familiar to his worldliness. In return he would give her ecstasy, and these tiny glimpses of vulnerability she could so easily become addicted to.

"I want . . ." She licked her lips, closed her eyes, leaped. "Touch me, Adrian. Make me come. Right here. Like only you can."

CHAPTER TWELVE

Adrian dipped his head and captured her mouth, inhaling her breath and replenishing it with his own.

Instantly rapacious, Billie strained to meet the sweet hunger of his kiss, the gentle but determined caress of his fingers across her nipples, first left, then right, back and forth, distributing equal attention to both hard, aching tips until she moaned and arched into his touch.

Wedged between their bodies, her hand found freedom and curled into the material of his shirt, twisting in a spasm of delight as she drank him in. His passion, his tangible uncertainty, the mutual surrender to the sublime and wordless conversation of bodies in need.

Her pelvis shifted restlessly beneath him, one leg hooked over his hips to bring his heat and hardness closer, until the demanding ridge of his erection rubbed against her. And it was torture, torture with so much denim between them, when their bodies strained as closely as if he were already sheathed inside her.

He settled in the vee of her thighs and rocked against her, seeking to soothe the demand of his body, thrusting hard, relentlessly, the breath torn from his throat in harsh rasps. Her knees rode his hips, holding him there in that rhythmic dance. The hammock thrashed beneath them, the world spun.

For the first time in Billie's life, she thought she might orgasm simply from the press of a man's body against her own. Colors exploded behind her eyelids, her heartbeat a riotous, climbing thunder in her ears.

Then Adrian shifted himself next to her, eliciting a moan of frustration from her throat before his impatient tug came at her button fly.

The transition revived her. Her lashes fluttered open to the night and to his rapt, shadowed features above hers. Something about his intent, his sudden stillness, told her he wanted more than she could possibly give, here in the open, in the exposed gloom.

But she'd promised. She'd sworn to her need, and there was no turning back.

"What are you going to do?" She caught his face in her hands and found his cheeks feverish to the touch. "Adrian, we can't—"

"I know we can't. But you can." He curled himself around her, effectively shielding the movement of his hand inside her jeans from any unforeseen witnesses.

Billie tried to focus on his face in the dusky, fading light, found his eyes liquid and watchful, before lust weighted her lashes and she felt his fingers furrow between the wet, wanting folds of her sex.

Everything honed down to that one, electric sensation, and the world disappeared. He circled her slick flesh, teasing, slid one finger inside her, deep, curved upward to stroke and play an ultrasensitive spot she hadn't known existed in her own body . . . and opened his mouth over hers to swallow the whimper that shuddered forth from her throat.

Her body arched beneath him in surprised delight.

"You like that?" he whispered, retreating and offering a second's respite from the searing sensations.

"Oh, my God." She clung to him, gasping. Nothing had ever felt so good. He'd touched her before, sent her soaring to orgasmic heights, but this . . . *this* . . . "I've never . . . what are you doing?"

"Bringing you pleasure, and not nearly as much as you bring me." He sank his finger inside her again, and she felt her own body instantly draw him in, deep, deeper with the answering spasm that shook her frame.

"You're so soft." He shifted and penetrated her more deeply, taking in her harsh gasp with an indrawn breath as his lips hovered above hers. "So wet. Like drenched silk."

The promise of orgasm clamored within her, and in response her fingers dug convulsively into his back. "Oh no . . ."

He lifted his head to look at her and stilled the rhythmic stroke of his finger, all the while applying pressure to that magic place deep inside her, so rich with nerves and promise. "No? I should stop?"

Her eyes fluttered open at the teasing query, tried to focus. "No! Oh God. It's too much. Adrian . . . *yes*," she hissed when he plunged inside her again.

A smile drifted across his lips as he kissed the corner of her right eye, then her nose, her forehead. Chaste kisses, so incongruent to the sinuous invasion between her thighs.

"Take it," he whispered, inserting a second finger into her yielding, hungry flesh. "Take your pleasure, Billie."

Her body bowed beneath him, trapped against the stretchy give of weathered rope, her legs sprawling wide on the hammock, hips counterthrusting toward his cadenced penetration.

The lucid, rational part of Billie wanted to laugh. Here she was, out in the woods of middle-class suburbia, with a man's fingers inside her panties, inside *her*, a climax of unimaginable force trembling at the edge of her grasp. And the man who now plied her and played her . . . a prostitute. A gigolo. A beloved brother and son and uncle, and a suspect with too many secrets and too much sexual prowess.

A man she was falling in love with.

The impossibility of it, the crazy, twisted potential swept over her, then ebbed, lost in the surge of unbelievable pleasure that built and built within her like strings drawn too tightly across a fine-tuned instrument. She would die from this, die and scatter into a million fragments and drift like dust on the wind. The mounting tension frightened her, even as she strained toward its apex.

Brushing back the damp strands of hair that clung to her temple, Adrian nuzzled her cheek, found her mouth again with his velvety, sinuous tongue, and carefully slid a third finger inside her body, edging her closer to the ecstasy she craved . . . and feared.

"Open your eyes."

Someone spoke. A phantom. A satyr. Adrian.

"Billie." His lips moved over her chin, his words thick with lust and satisfaction. "Open your eyes and look at me."

When Billie did as he asked, he kissed her, breathed his need against her lips. "No, don't close them. Let me see you, just as you are, before it's too dark."

Sensing the telltale, fluttering constriction of the silky muscles surrounding his fingers, the mounting, soundless cry under his mouth, Adrian quickened the movement of his caress, never losing contact with that one place deep within her that made ecstasy so very accessible to her, a woman who'd had pleasure withheld from her enough to scar her heart.

She wound handfuls of his shirt in trembling fists, gaze wide and fixed on his until pleasure brought her head off the hammock and she buried her face against his neck, where she could shout out her climax only to have it muffled by his skin.

Her shudders of release went on and on, one spasm rolling into the next beneath him, shaking the hammock so violently, Adrian had to set one foot on the ground to keep them from flipping.

He closed his eyes and rode the wave with her, every nerve in his taut body singing in response, electrified by joy.

When had satisfying a woman become a treasure? When had the entire, sensual routine gone from mere product to something of value? He hadn't seen its potential, hadn't been aware of the gossamer threads that bound carnal fulfillment to pleasure of the heart.

It terrified him. It moved him. It dislodged his beliefs like a vast puzzle upended and falling into a million irretrievable pieces.

Gradually, Billie's body collapsed into the hammock's easy yield, and Adrian brushed a kiss against her open lips, a sentiment born of astonishment and exultation.

She tasted like coffee and passion, a flavor so luscious, he settled his mouth over hers and kissed her more fully, tongue sliding over hers and committing her essence to memory. Satiated woman. The sweetest flavor of all.

When he carefully withdrew and refastened her jeans, Billie snuggled against him, and he eased his arm beneath her again, their bodies settling together as though passion had never detonated between them, as though they'd never moved from the lazy, swaying position of two people reveling in the summer night.

It came to him then, permeated his disjointed thoughts. Billie was teaching him—*him*—how to make love. With a jolt of surprise at the crashing irony, Adrian realized he hadn't known how until now. He, the consummate lover, so renowned for his sexual skill, so proficient and controlled and practiced, had only played at making love, where Billie . . . *God*. Clearly, it was all she knew. Pretense just wasn't in her spectrum of capabilities.

Her breathing came light and even against his throat, fingertips resting, relaxed, over his heart. He laid his cheek on her hair and thought she might be drifting into sleep, but then her voice broke the night, languorous and hushed.

"Incredible."

He smiled at the one-worded declaration. "Was it?"

"Yes. And you're *terrible*." Her wry humor diluted the tension choking the air, a mild distraction from the low, driving need that still pulled insistently in Adrian's belly. "God, Adrian, I can't take you anywhere."

Laughter vibrated through him. He stroked her hair, pressed his lips against her damp forehead, submitting to the subtle liquidation of lust into tenderness.

After a moment she said, "So how many other girls did you say you've brought out here?"

"I didn't."

"Hmm" vibrated against his chest.

"No one as delectable as you." He caught her chin, lifted it to examine her eyes in the darkness and lost himself in the heat and acuity of her gaze. "No one but you in a decade."

The vulnerability of his own words etched in his mind, a flicker of warning that he'd gone too far. He started to shift away, but she drew him back with a gentle hand on his jaw. "I owe you."

His brow lifted. "Oh? And how will you pay me, Ms. Cort?"

Her fingers slid down his stomach to the front of his jeans, where his erection, still rigid and aching, instantly surged against the contact. For a moment he allowed it, closing his eyes, letting himself fall into the pleasure of her caress.

Then he caught her hand and lifted it to his lips, and she uttered a sound of protest. "Don't you ever let anyone return the favor without putting up a gallant fight?"

He kissed her fingers, one by one. "There are other things I want from you."

"Like what?"

"I'll have to think about it." What he wanted was to strip away her clothes, free himself, and drive into her moist, delicious heat until he exploded inside her, and her primal scream flew over the treetops. Instead he forced himself to relax beside her, into the gentle sway of the hammock and the fragrant warmth of her body.

They could have remained as they were, wrapped around each other in languid, sleepy pleasure, until the night passed and morning sun pierced the boughs overhead.

But Rosalie's strident admonishment, rounding up the children for the night, floated over the trees and roused Adrian at last. Extricating himself from the hammock, he helped Billie to her feet and waited while she refastened her bra, tucked in her shirt, and ran her hands through her tousled hair.

They walked together back toward the house, fingertips loosely laced, their steps slow, somnolent. Adrian set aside his unmet desire for another time, an excuse to see Billie again, to touch her, taste her.

Make love to her.

The thought lowered his brows. No. Not Billie. She would swallow him in impossibilities, enfold him in warmth and love and commitment. And realize, eventually, that she'd settled for a man whose only value lay in his ability to sexualize everything around him.

He searched his heated mind for a time before he knew her, before he wanted her, but the memories slipped like silken skeins through his fingers.

Cold reality washed away his newfound peace. He was fooling

himself, lost in this little suburban fantasy, where he could merely step from Avalon and into her life, arms open to take the bounty of emotion and domestic bliss she could offer.

The man within him who could love Billie Cort didn't exist.

A hollow sensation expanded in Adrian's chest as he released her hand and put a subtle distance of a few feet between them. For a little while, he'd nearly forgotten he had nothing to give anymore.

I n the bathroom, he washed her silky scent from his hands, splashed cool water on his face, braced his palms on the sink and let droplets run down the bridge of his nose and chin, refusing to look at himself in the mirror. Billie was downstairs saying good-bye to his family, ready to return to reality, innocent to the fact that he planned to drop her off at home and then set fire to the bridge that spanned their worlds.

He'd made mistakes before, but he'd never hated himself for it until now. He would hate himself for so many things after this night.

"Leftovers," Rosalie said when he came downstairs again, and placed a Tupperware container in his hands. "Feed your beautiful girlfriend. She's too skinny."

He leaned to kiss his sister's round cheek. "Thanks for having us, Rosie. And Rudy thanks you too."

"No, Zio, no! You can't take him!" Adrian's six-year-old niece, Tina, scampered through the living room in a pink Barbie night-gown, fresh from a bath, face frantic with dismay.

"Yes, he can," Rosalie told her firmly. "We don't need another mouth to feed in this house, especially one as picky as Rudy's." She squinted at Adrian. "You know he'll only eat beef and chicken. He turns his nose up at dog food. You've ruined him."

Adrian smiled and knelt to Tina's level. "You hear that? I've ruined Rudy. I guess that means I'm going to have to take him home."

She gazed back at him with wide eyes, confusion stamped across her dark features. "But I thought he was going to stay with us from now on."

"The dog was just visiting, Tina," Rosalie said in a gentler tone. "Tell your uncle to come visit more often so we can see Rudy."

"Will you bring him back, Zio? I love him." Tina's fingers buried themselves in the dog's soft fur and she hardly flinched when Rudy's tongue slurped a wet streak across her face.

Adrian regarded her with a grave expression. "Of course I'll bring him back. But tell me, *bella nipote*—is there anyone else you love besides Rudy?" He reached out and gently tugged her hair. "Say, maybe, me?"

She gave him a speculative look, weighing the options behind eyes as big and brown as chestnuts. "You're taking our dog," she said finally. "But I guess I love you."

Dutifully, she smacked her lips against his cheek, and he immediately wiped away her kiss with a sigh of mock disgust. "That was really wet."

Glee instantly melted the somberness from her features and she threw her arms around his neck.

Clasping his niece's thin little body for a sublime moment, Adrian breathed in the scent of bubble bath and a child's purity, and told himself he would come back to this lost place in his past. If only for the poignant reminders of what life was supposed to be.

Rosalie trailed him and Billie down the flagstone sidewalk with Rudy in tow. "You'll come back soon. The kids never see you. I swear I forget I even have a brother, much less one in the same town." She caught the front of his shirt and kissed both his cheeks. *"Ti amo."*

"Ti amo. I'll call." He hugged her, then watched, amused, as his

gregarious sister embraced Billie with rib-crushing fervor. Rosalie didn't always warm up to strangers so quickly, but his sister must have seen in Billie what so fascinated Adrian from the start. Her vulnerability. The warmth of her spirit.

"You'll come back too, Billie Cort, yes?"

"Yes," Billie said, laughing. "I'd love to."

"I'll look for your stories in next month's issue of *Illicit*. Take good care of yourself, both of you. And Rudy, the big *bambino*," she added, as Adrian opened the back door of the BMW and the dog clambered in.

She stood in the driveway and watched them depart, waving until they rounded the corner onto Massachusetts Avenue and her lone figure disappeared from Adrian's rearview mirror.

They drove in silence gilded by Sade's silky, mellow vocals.

Behind them, Rudy turned himself around three times and curled up to sleep on the backseat. Adrian didn't try to make conversation, and Billie seemed content to gaze out the window in wordless contemplation. He struggled not to look at her, but his gaze was drawn to her profile every time they stopped at a traffic light.

She was unaware of his troubled thoughts, of the dangerous path they'd started down tonight. The tranquility on her face, the sweet peace that marked her as a content woman, screamed at him. He would wipe it away with a few truths eventually, no matter how much he wanted to keep her in his life. Without wanting to, without being able to stop the inevitable, he'd add a new set of scars across her tender heart, and he detested himself for letting it go this far, to the point where they could both be hurt.

When he pulled into the driveway in front of her apartment building, she stirred and flashed him a look of surprise, one he understood too well. After the intimacy they'd shared tonight, it didn't make sense that he'd bring her back here and drop her off to her own world, when he could have easily taken her home to share his bed and seal their relationship.

But Billie said nothing, and the mild dismay marking her features smoothed into cool acceptance. She gathered her purse and leaned over the backseat to pat Rudy's head.

"Thanks for tonight," she said, pausing with her fingers on the door handle. "I had a good time."

Adrian searched his heart for the right response, for something that would preserve her feelings and his wall of defense simultaneously, but there was nothing. "Thank you for coming."

He made no move to kiss her, just sat watching her, while inside everything shifted once again to autopilot: feelings, desires, the wild yearning she'd stirred in him over and over in the last few hours.

Finally, hesitantly, she leaned toward him and paused, waiting for him to meet her halfway. Adrian acquiesced, lifted a hand to her hair, let it sift through his fingers as his lips brushed the soft, fragrant skin of her cheek. A fleeting indulgence.

In another time, another place, he could have loved this woman. He could have deserved her love. But the sentiment was as far removed from his grasp as reality was from Avalon. He'd forfeited it in exchange for life in a gilded cage, and his relationship with Billie was a casualty of that choice, plain and simple.

The leather seat squeaked a little as he withdrew, and they stared at each other, a million questions hanging in the air. Then Billie offered him a tremulous smile and climbed out of the car, and all Adrian could think was, *Thank you for caring.*

The shrill jangle of the phone jolted Billie from her dark ruminations and she glanced at the glowing clock. One a.m. Only

Adrian would call at this ridiculous hour. A shiver of relief went through her. He'd been so quiet on the ride home, preoccupied by something that darkened his features and stole the sweet remnants of pleasure between them.

"Were you sleeping?" he asked.

"No." She scooted beneath the covers and pulled them up to her chin, ignoring the slow simmer of need he stirred low in her belly. He wouldn't seduce her tonight, even though the mere sound of his voice had the same arousing effect of a physical caress.

Tension lay thick between them, something she didn't understand but dreaded with all her heart. "Just thinking," she told him.

"Me too."

"About?"

"Did you like my family, Billie?"

The question surprised her. She'd expected him to drop some sort of bomb. "Oh, yes. Rosalie was wonderful, warm and funny. And the kids, so cute. So bright."

"They liked you too."

"Will I get to see them again sometime?" It was out of her mouth before she could staunch the nervous flow of uncertainty.

Adrian paused, seemingly as taken off guard by her question as she was. "I don't know when I'll get out to Bethesda again."

Heat suffused her cheeks. "I'm not inviting myself. I just meant . . . they're great people."

He was quiet. Then he said, "Jesus, Billie. What are we doing?"

A question wrought with confusion and hopelessness and . . . fear. The bomb. Her heart leapt, charged with a surge of dismay.

"Well . . ." She fingered the edge of the sheet, dreading the loss of her fragile peace of mind. "We're seeing each other, I guess."

"It would appear so." The phone rustled as though he were

switching ears. Then his voice came stronger, firm with conviction. "I told you I don't have relationships."

Her heart slipped another notch toward her stomach.

"Do you remember, Billie?"

"Yes," she said tightly, mentally kicking her own behind. She knew this moment would come. She'd been so foolish. "I remember."

"You know why I don't . . . why I can't. But I'm making a liar of myself with you. I thought I could tell you good-bye tonight and end it. We're only a few weeks into this thing. It shouldn't be so difficult. I've been telling myself that all along, that I can stop it. That it's nothing."

She listened to his unsteady stream of words, her brows drawn down in confusion and dismay. He didn't sound like the Adrian she knew. He sounded . . . afraid.

". . . And I owe you an apology," he finished. "I'm sorry."

"For what?" She rubbed a hand over her face, pressed fingertips against her eyelids to staunch the mild burn of tears. Ridiculous to cry, really. There was nothing to cry over. Nothing to break between them. No promises made, only the guarantee of disaster for playing with fire, an inevitability that had been there all along, and now it was time to pay for dabbling.

"I shouldn't have taken you out to meet my family."

She opened her eyes. "So why did you?"

"I needed a date. To reassure them I'm living a normal life."

Billie sighed, exasperated with him, disgusted with herself. "Bull. Can we just be honest for a minute, Adrian? You may have started out with that reason, but you took me, you chose *me*, because you feel something for me. You can deny it, but then you really will be a liar."

"You give me too much credit for having a heart." He was recoiling, reining in his emotions, regaining control. "I feel nothing for anyone beyond a basic curiosity. It's the nature of my job, my lifestyle . . . it's *my* nature. You knew that about me from the beginning."

His voice grew more remote. She wondered if he was calling from his condominium, where he'd lost his best friend, or from Avalon, where he'd lost himself. "I like you, Billie. You're a nice person. Good company. But tonight was a mistake."

She flung an arm over her eyes and swallowed the lump of tears that had lodged in her throat. "Oh? Which part? The part where you introduced me to your family and exposed yourself as coming from a perfectly average, wholesome background? Or the part where you touched me and turned me inside-out while swaying in a hammock in the rich, beautiful woods—one of the most searing sexual experiences of my life? Which part do you regret, Adrian?"

"All of it. I can't have those things with you. You know what I am."

"Yes, Adrian, I know what you are. A gentle man. A likable one. Smart. Cultured. Sexy. I know what you are."

"But the other part—"

"What about the other part? You hide behind the other part." She yanked the pillow out from beneath her head and winged it across the bedroom, furious suddenly. "Did you call to tell me I'm not going to see you anymore? Because if that's the case, hurry up and say it. Then hang up and go back to work, and don't worry one bit about me. I've been on my own a long time, and I'm tougher than you think. I won't cling to any man who'd rather be a—a—" She stumbled, bit back the ugly words rushing to her lips.

"A what?" he countered softly. "A whore? A gigolo? Go ahead and say it, Billie. If you're going to waste your time caring about me, then you'd better get used to the idea, because I can't change. I won't. Not for you or anyone."

She bit back a sound of pure derision. "How about for *you*? Think you could walk the straight and narrow for yourself?"

He didn't reply. He didn't have to. Billie already knew the answer. "You're afraid." She sat up among the sheets as cold realization washed through her. "Afraid to live without women clambering to pay top dollar for you. All that money . . . it's a measure of your value, right? It's your self-esteem. What would happen if you were paid in love instead of cash? Would the world end? My God, Adrian. You're running scared."

The half-whispered accusation seemed to permeate his impassivity. "I was fine before you." His voice came low and furious. *Finally, finally.* True emotion. "Damn it, Billie. I want my life back."

"Then hang up and don't call me again, because I'm not going to pay you for sex, Adrian. What I offer is a worthless currency in your world."

The sound of their breathing, quick and angry, rushed in simultaneous cadence through the phone line.

And still he didn't hang up. He cursed, a bitten-off slew of Italian and English she couldn't grasp except for its elemental frustration. "I don't want what you're offering—you've mistaken my intent. I didn't ask for a relationship."

"What the hell *was* your intent? I don't think you even know. If you had, we wouldn't be having this conversation." She clenched the sheet between restless fingers. "This isn't just a favor for a favor anymore. It's gotten too messy for your taste, hasn't it? But it's what you've ended up with, Adrian, whether you wanted it or not. Things happen! You don't always get to choose. Life doesn't come knocking at your door as per scheduled appointment like at Avalon. This is what happens. Feelings. And—and conflict, and misery, and joy and—" She stumbled on "love" and bit her bottom lip to silence herself, quivering with a wild fusion of exhilaration and heartache.

"Every bit of it unwelcome and impossible." Desperation blurred his words, as though he spoke to himself instead of her. "All I want is my peace back. I want Luke back. I want everything to be like it was before you walked through Avalon's doors, Billie. You should know that."

Even as the declarations sliced through her, his turbulence pulled at her empathy, at her desire for him, at her penchant for giving love to a man who would only push her away.

No. A fresh wave of coldness soaked her to the bone. She could end it for both of them, damn it. *She would.*

Indignation and soul-deep abrasions spoke for her. "While we're being so honest with each other . . ." She swallowed and closed her eyes, knowing what she said next would ruin the intimacy between them far more than his words of frustration ever could. "What really happened the night of Lucien's death? Did you help him over that balcony, Adrian?"

For a long time he didn't speak. Astonishment crackled between them. Billie couldn't believe she'd been so callous and cruel. She couldn't believe he hadn't yet hung up on her, and now she wished he would. She wanted it to be over, for the hurt to stop before the damage was irreparable.

His reply finally broke the silence, soft, defeated. "He was my friend, Billie. My friend."

Anger drained away, leaving her empty and trembling with shame. She'd stooped so low. Yet she pushed again. Pushed him closer to the edge. Pushed him further from her heart. "But what about your alibi?"

"What about her?"

"I hear she denies being with you." She was hurting him. Maybe

more than he'd ever hurt her, and she couldn't stop the bruising accusation that propelled her words.

"She's a liar." His quiet voice held an edge now, rapier sharp and
unyielding. "She lied to the police, she lied to her husband . . . she
even lied to herself. They all do. It's part of the game."

"And Azure? What about her?"

"She's the biggest player of all. She lied about me, Billie. She
knows I was at Avalon. She erased the evidence to protect my
client."

Billie released a deep breath, her hand pressed to her pounding
heart.

He wasn't finished. "So you're not all blind faith and guilelessness after all. It's about time you question me. You know nothing
about me except what I choose to tell you. But consider this, Billie."
His tone evened out, all emotion suffocated. "How do you know I'm
not spinning tales around your pretty head?"

She swallowed. "I don't."

"No." Contempt crept into his words. "You make an easy target.
You're as lost as a babe in the woods. I can't believe you haven't been
plucked."

Sick regret roiled in her stomach. "You're wrong about me."

"And you're foolish to trust so quickly. But hey, anything for a
thrill, right? People sell their souls for a thrill. They die for it too.
How are you any different, keeping company with a man who
whores for a living?"

Despair trapped her answer in her throat.

"Thank you, Billie. You've done both of us an immense favor."

The phone disconnected with a muted click. Billie lay there, dry-
eyed, receiver clutched to her chest, and forced her illogical grief
back to a place of common sense. But it wasn't until much, much
later that it really sank in . . . the score was finally even. Pleasure for

pleasure. Truth for truth. Injury for injury. Equally given, equally received. No debt bound them. No emotion. No trust.

He'd sounded as if he never wanted to see her again, and that was fine with her.

But she cried anyway.

CHAPTER THIRTEEN

Azure stared at the handsome blond employee slouched so non-chalantly on the chair across from her desk and released a deep sigh.

"I hope this is important, Joe." She spared a glance at the gold Rolex on her wrist. "I've had a long day."

"This'll just take a minute." His blue eyes twinkled with glee. He was up to something, and she wasn't in the mood to play games.

"Make it short, please."

"Short and sweet, yes ma'am." He sobered, uncrossed his long legs. "When Catherine Barkley showed up for her appointment yesterday, she told me something I knew you'd want to hear."

"Oh?"

"Regarding one of your bright, shining stars and some woman he's been seeing outside of Avalon."

Azure's hands stilled in the midst of stroking the silken pearls around her throat, the only sign that his lackadaisical announcement had piqued her interest. Instant irritation snapped at the edge of her weariness. "Who?"

"Adrian."

Laughter bubbled in her throat. "What could Catherine Barkley possibly know about Adrian except that his schedule somehow stays too full to accommodate her?"

Joe's smile didn't quite reach his long-lashed gaze. "I reckon a little bitterness goes a long way with some women. She says she saw him with a girlfriend at a concert in Rock Creek Park the other night. 'All wound up in each other,' I believe was how she worded it." He paused and cocked a brow at his employer. "Far be it from me to interfere in anyone's love life 'round here, or even to give a damn what folks do in their free time, but I thought we were under strict instruction not to live our personal lives within a thirty-mile radius of Avalon."

Azure steepled her fingers beneath her chin and swiveled her chair away from Joe's probing regard. "Catherine Barkley must have been mistaken. Maybe she needs her eyes checked."

"Maybe she's tellin' a truth you don't want to hear."

"Adrian would never defy me," Azure snapped.

That earned a soft huff of laughter from the big blond cowboy, and she turned her head to meet his gaze with stony displeasure. "Joe, dear, are you tattling on Adrian? Getting him back for so ignobly pointing out your part in Lucien's moral undoing? Because if that's why you're here, you can run along and keep your dissatisfaction to yourself. I don't mediate snits and bickering between my boys. Nor do I tolerate cattiness. If you have a problem with Adrian, confront him like the man I know you are. He's a big boy too. I'm sure he'd be open to working out your differences."

His blue eyes narrowed slightly. "I like him just fine, Azure. I'm here out of loyalty to you. I don't set out to stir trouble, but I also don't turn my head when I see it coming. Know what I mean?" Then the tension in his ruddy features was gone like quicksilver, replaced by his customary, devil-may-care grin.

Azure blinked and let her gaze drift from his face. He was too cocky, too self-assured. How had she missed this objectionable element in him before?

She knew the men of Avalon as though they were her own children, and in many ways, they were. Each one hired for his magical combination of beauty, intelligence, amiability, malleability. They were rare individuals, jewels among the norm, and she rendered them priceless possessions by the time she was done with them, molded into seraphic creatures from every woman's fantasy. They could, in no way, be unyielding or singular-minded.

So how had Joe slipped beneath the wire? His skill with tongue and fingers and other impressive assets had certainly kept him in good stead before now, and he'd built an enthusiastic following in the two years he'd been a companion. But sexual prowess meant nothing if he couldn't be sculpted into a true Avalon entity down to his big, Kentucky-bred bones.

He'd never be an entity like Adrian. No one could be. But if what Joe said was true . . . She pressed her forefingers against her temples as a picture of Adrian's rare smile flashed across her mind's eye. He was, in every way, the quintessential prince of Avalon. Her finest hour. No one could supplant the dark swathe he carved through Avalon's halls.

As far as she knew, Adrian lived in complete devotion to her, with nearly no personal life to speak of. But she'd battled a constant, niggling suspicion that eventually he'd be taken by some purebred poodle who could afford to buy a semblance of his affection, because Adrian gave nothing of his true self to anyone. Azure herself only caught glimpses of the person he had been before Avalon, tiny tastes to entice and appetize, hints that the most human creature dwelled beneath that polished shell. No one had broken through to his core except perhaps Lucien, and even then, Adrian's penchant for keeping his friends at arm's length had helped drive the other man to destruction.

Azure had the suicide letter, scrawled in Lucien's premortem handwriting, to prove it.

While Joe drawled on about what he understood to be Avalon's creed of propriety, she slid open a desk drawer and regarded the envelope that had arrived at the club the day after Lucien's death.

Azure hadn't opened it right away. She'd held it hostage in her desk for a solid week, opening and closing the drawer to stare at it, while the hair stood at attention on the back of her neck and everything human within her clamored at her to release its truth.

Why Lucien had chosen her as the recipient of his swan song escaped her every imagining, but she felt gratified nonetheless. Nearly a month after her employee's death, it was the one fragile thread that bound Adrian to her. It was the key to Adrian's peace of mind, all she could have of him, because he so staunchly and foolishly refused to give her more.

Although she'd contacted Detective Rich Hales to clear Adrian's name last week—claiming the letter had, by a twist of fate, been lost in the paper shuffle between Maria's desk and her own—she'd paid the detective no small amount of hush money in order to keep the evidence of Adrian's innocence in her possession a little longer. Hell, she was hemorrhaging money to keep the detectives from digging into the true nature of Avalon, but it wouldn't last forever. She had a cozy relationship with the authorities, and neither side would endanger that mutual satisfaction.

She silently closed the drawer and gave a distracted nod as Joe prattled on. She wasn't ready to relinquish the suicide note to the authorities just yet and put Adrian's mind at ease over the true nature of his friend's death.

When she did, she would lose him. And after such a faultless track record. A yearly private investigation assured her of her prized companions' decorum outside the club, preserved her peace of mind for a few thousand dollars annually.

According to the reports, Adrian had never broken the rules . . . and yet something deep and chary within her, a businessperson's sense for smelling the potential for danger, now prodded her to engage Joe for more information on the unseemly rumor.

Tilting her head, she finally offered him a brief, chilled smile. "I'm thinking, darling. Trying to decide if I want to know more."

He raised his brows and stretched back against the seat, his self-satisfaction despicable. "You can always call Catherine and ask her about what she saw, but I doubt she'll repeat what she told me. We're real close," he added with a wink.

Azure closed her eyes to gather patience. "So she says she saw Adrian at a concert with a woman. Could it have been, perhaps, a client?"

"If it was, he must've really been pullin' out all the stops for her. Catherine said they were totally absorbed in each other."

Azure straightened and pinned Joe with a searching glance. "Did she describe this woman to you?"

"Yeah, let me see." He stroked his chin, his baby-blues rolling skyward. "She was dark-haired, pretty, not flashy. Thirty-ish. Catherine wasn't impressed."

"I see." Her brows drew down. "Not flashy, not a client . . ." A ridiculous notion teased her thoughts, and she pushed it aside as quickly as it had come. Adrian was much too bright and discriminating to settle for less than the most pristine mate. And why would he want a lover at all when he had everything a man could desire here?

She prided herself on knowing the warning signs of a companion's restlessness, and she'd seen no signs in him. Just grief over

Lucien's death. And grief did funny things to a man. Maybe what Catherine had witnessed was a simple dalliance for Adrian, a rebellious and badly timed step off the path.

Azure would rein him back in. And if she couldn't, she'd throw down the trump card, Lucien's suicide letter. A pathetic missive, tribute to his devotion for a man who'd refused to accept love at every turn—from women, from Lucien, and from Azure herself.

A sickened smile twisted her lips. The guilt alone would melt Adrian's icy veneer, render him vulnerable, needful. Tear him down to size. But even that small satisfaction wouldn't be worth the loss.

The letter had to wait.

Offering Joe a cool smile, she stood to indicate his dismissal. "Thank you for bringing your concerns to my attention, Joe. I do count on your discretion regarding this issue, of course."

"Of course." He stood, wide-shouldered and all healthy, hearty male. A beautiful specimen, Azure thought. Maybe she'd keep him a little longer. Work on his integrity.

"And Joe," she said, voice laced with sugary warning, "you're keeping your nose clean, aren't you, darling?"

His satisfaction dissolved. "If you're referring to that comment Adrian made about me doing drugs with Lucien, that was a damn lie. I don't mess with that stuff. Check the results from my last physical, Azure."

"Maybe it's time for a new physical, with a new doctor," she said thoughtfully. "Maybe it's time to start drug-testing at random. After all, we don't want another Lucien on our hands, do we?"

Joe's jaw tightened, but he said nothing except, "Thanks for hearin' me out, Azure."

"But of course, my darling."

When he was gone, she seated herself and buzzed Maria into her office. "Is Adrian here tonight?"

"Yes," the secretary said from the threshold, watching her employer with wide, dark eyes. "He's with that restaurateur who traveled from London to see him."

"Of course." Azure sat back and tapped her lip with one cadmium fingernail. "An overnight client?"

"I don't think so. I can check."

"Find out," Azure said tightly. "And the moment he comes up for air, send him to see me."

A drian sat in a wingback chair and stared at the aimless patterns swirled in the Turkish rug underfoot, counting the minutes while his client readied herself in the bathroom for an ecstasy he wasn't certain he could give.

Everything was wrong, but he hadn't been able to still himself long enough to examine the simple, searing fact that he'd hurt Billie, and regret was turning him inside out.

She'd struck back with claws bared, aiming at vulnerable places without hesitation. And ultimately she'd done what he couldn't bring himself to do—she'd cut the ties between them, by using the one weapon that would slice him to shreds: questioning his part in Luke's suicide.

More than likely he had hung up the phone in a worse state of pain and confusion than Billie. But now that the sting from her accusations had subsided, and he saw that she'd acted out of sheer insult, his remorse dug at his insides like an ulcer.

He'd inadvertently bruised feelings before. It was inevitable that clients would fall in love with their Avalon companions, and sensing danger, he'd blocked a few from his appointment book over the years. Feelings got stepped on. It was part of the job.

But innately he knew he hadn't cut a woman this deeply before.

So deeply that he felt it in his own heart, as though he himself had been rent by the careless words and actions and rejection.

Of course there was Noelle, his one attempt at a relationship after he'd gone to work for Azure. Noelle, with her almond-shaped eyes, high-wattage smile, and hunger for culture and travel. He hadn't intended to hurt her, either. She'd wanted to see the world with him at her side, accessing her father's endless coffers of money to keep Adrian more finely presented than a pricey accessory. He'd often felt more like a prostitute at her side than he ever did at Avalon.

He'd loved Noelle in a wild, foolish way, but not enough to endure the discreditable status she assigned him. When she found out about Avalon, he'd callously gone with the highest bidder, and his only regret was making her cry at the end. A note of strain had echoed in her good-bye, the sound of clotted emotion, of tears barely withheld—the same as Billie's voice last night before they'd hung up the phone.

It haunted him.

Hissing in a breath, Adrian shoved a hand through his hair and closed his eyes. Christ, what had he been thinking, taking Billie to his sister's house? What kind of sick, subconscious motive had driven him to drag her into his private, sacred world, only to shut the door in her face when she got too close?

Too close to what?

Behind him, Nina Weston emerged from the bathroom, her footsteps silent on the plush carpet, her approach announced only by the drifting, floral scent of her perfume. She stopped beside his chair, unashamedly naked. Her pink fingernails trailed across his chest, massaged him through his white cotton shirt, then dipped down into his lap.

When he caught her hand and gently urged it back to a safer

place, she knelt beside his chair and squinted at him. "What time is it?"

"Nine thirty." He squelched a restless sigh. "We lost a lot of time at the restaurant, I'm afraid."

"I was enjoying our conversation," she said with a shrug.

He attempted to pull a smile from his repertoire of meaningless sentiments and failed. "You still have another hour," he told her, using the low, polished tone that preceded seduction. Then he leaned toward her and kissed her with a gently probing tongue, the most sterile and disingenuous kiss he'd offered anyone in a long time.

When she didn't respond, he withdrew and angled his head to meet her eyes more directly. "What's wrong?"

"I don't know. You tell me." Her voice lost its sexy rasp. She stood, lean and lithe and golden. She wasn't pretty, but there was something strong and handsome about her features, though not enough to stir Adrian. He felt dead inside.

"Do you ever smile anymore, Adrian?"

Mild surprise stole his smooth reply. Rising to his feet, he affected a hint of curious humor. "Why? Do I not smile enough for your taste?"

"Not nearly enough." Dry amusement tilted her lips. "Remember, darling, I came all the way from London for these precious four hours. I expect perfection."

His brows crept up as his memory skimmed the handful of visits she'd made prior to this one. Nina never complained. He'd never given her a reason before now. "You don't think I can please you tonight?"

"Oh, I've no doubt. But let's just say . . ." Her fingers drifted down his stomach to play at the buckle on his woven belt, then lower, lingered, and found no response before drifting away. "Your heart won't be in it."

Agitated, he moved away from her and toward the bar to pour a drink as his troubled thoughts returned with breathtaking vehemence. "And how do you know where my heart will be?"

"I don't. But I can guess it's not with me. In fact," she said tartly, "it may be with someone else entirely. Look at me. I'm standing here naked in the middle of the room, having undressed *myself*, when always before you took my clothing off, piece by painstaking piece, and kissed every inch you uncovered."

He swallowed a bitter mouthful of whiskey and set aside the glass, then started toward her, but she put out a hand. "Something tells me that no matter what kind of consummate actor you are, you won't enjoy having sex with me tonight."

He stopped, kept his expression emotionless. "Whether that's true or not, technically it's not supposed to matter."

"But it does to me." She crossed her arms over her breasts, as though suddenly discomfited by her nudity. "I always enjoy my time with you, Adrian, but you're different tonight. You seem distant, pensive. I feel as though I paid four thousand dollars to be with a man who doesn't know I exist."

He searched his mind for a nonprovocative reply, and only felt desperation burn in his throat along with the traces of whiskey. If she hadn't called his bluff he would have rallied, would have taken her to bed and done his best to drive Billie Cort out of his system. He could easily perform, as long as he didn't think.

A rueful grin twisted his mouth. Ironic that he could control his body to the bitter end, but his mind stampeded of its own accord, entertaining flickering films of one woman, and one only, like an all-night movie marathon.

Forcing his body to relax, he moved closer and caught Nina around the waist. "I'm sorry. What can I do to make it up to you?"

She regarded him, pale eyes sleepy and shadowed. Christ, he thought. She'd come so far, and all for nothing.

"You could take your pleasure with me, right now. Act like a man instead of a highly skilled machine."

He shook his head. "You know I don't—"

"But you could. I remember once, Adrian"—her arms draped around his neck, the flowery scent of some expensive perfume filling his senses—"a most incredible mutual orgasm we shared. Last time I was in the States, as a matter of fact. The catalyst for this current jaunt across the pond. I thought if it happened once . . ."

He tried to respond with something even and glib, but no words would come. God, he couldn't do this. Not tonight. Not with Billie stalking his every move, every breath—

He pulled away, scrubbed his hands over his face, and searched for words. The rescue boat was passing him by while he opted to drown in silence, when it would have been so easy just to speak to his client, to say, *Come here, let me touch you, let me show you how good I am . . .*

"I'm getting dressed," Nina said quietly.

He glanced back at her and watched her retreat into the bathroom, a ridiculous thought yammering in his mind. Nina's neck wasn't as graceful as Billie's. Her shoulders weren't as sculpted, nor her skin as silky. He'd never had Nina's mouth on his cock, had never buried his fingers in her hair and lost himself in sweet, hot abandon between her lips.

Billie was a weakness. And now he had a dissatisfied client because of it. His whole world was endangered by what had started out as a mindless distraction, a mild amusement. He had only himself to blame.

A few minutes later his customer reappeared, fully clothed, her expression one of muted disillusionment.

Adrian forced himself to focus. "I'm sorry you came so far only to be disappointed, Nina. I'll speak to Maria, let her know your evening wasn't what you—"

"Your company alone gave me enormous pleasure, Adrian." She took a few tentative steps toward him and reached out to touch his cheek. "I'll at least pay for that. But I also want an answer. Between us. Something is wrong, isn't it? In your personal life?"

He closed his eyes and wished away her discerning touch, her probing questions, condemning his own marauding thoughts and emotions. "Yes. A private matter that has nothing to do with Avalon. Completely inappropriate behavior on my part."

She offered him a regretful smile. "I hoped you might be human. I wasn't certain until now."

The words hung in the air and mocked him. She was wrong. Somewhere along the way, his humanity had slipped from him. And awakening to it again was like struggling to the surface in an ocean of black, viscous matter.

He looked at her, his pulse thudding—echoing—his misery in his veins. "I'm sorry," he said, his first truthful moment in days. "I didn't realize until now—it's bigger than I know what to do with."

Downstairs, Adrian spoke quietly with Maria about reimbursing his client, then he said good-bye to Nina Weston, a loyal and long-time customer, for the last time. He knew it as he brushed his lips against her cheek and closed the door behind her. The sick sense of failure he experienced was one small indication of what lay in store for him if he didn't purge his mind of turmoil, if he didn't squelch the wild dissatisfaction that seemed to be overtaking his life.

He started back toward the staircase and found Azure waiting like a translucent ghost in the shadows. "Adrian."

He paused, then continued toward her, every muscle in his body instantly strung with tension.

"Your client left early," she said.

Adrian waited, knowing what came next.

"Why did she leave early, Adrian?"

"I couldn't perform," he said. It would end the discussion before it could flame into something disagreeable.

"Why not?" She moved toward him, footsteps silent on the tile. "You're taking care of yourself, aren't you?"

"Of course."

"Preoccupied, then?"

He conceded with a tilt of his head.

"I told you to take all the time you needed after Lucien died."

"I wanted to work. I needed to work. And this isn't about Lucien."

Before he could say more, another companion and his customer started down the stairs, and Azure motioned to Adrian to follow her to her office.

Once inside, she shut the door, her exotic perfume emanating spice and flowers through the room. "Sit down, darling."

He merely crossed his arms and waited while she rounded the desk and seated herself.

"You won't sit and talk?"

"I've been here since early this afternoon." He meted out the words with utter care. His emotions were so close to the surface. Azure could easily sense the unraveling of his defense and snag it, claw at it. "Is this a formal meeting?"

"Informal." Her brow rose just enough to imply danger. "Call it one of friendly concern."

"Azure—"

"Who was the woman you took to the concert at Rock Creek Park last week?"

Adrian stared at her. While he searched for a response, anything but openmouthed dismay, she went on.

"Is she responsible for your failure to perform? Are you spending yourself on her, Adrian?"

"No." He sucked in a breath and met her gaze with narrowed eyes. "I'm not spending myself on anyone."

"Not yet, maybe. Is this a fledgling romance? Are you courting? Playing a field you haven't stepped foot on in years for a change of scenery?"

"No." He forced his expression to remain impassive and stony.

"Hmm." She drummed her fingernails on the smooth Chippendale desk, studying his face like a chess player determining her next move. "Well, whoever she is, get rid of her. You're obviously distracted by her, and it's affecting your work."

He didn't argue, just stood in silent consternation, head throbbing. His silence shouted his guilt more vehemently than hasty words of denial ever could have.

"My God . . ." She rose and braced her hands on the desk, all pretense fleeing as she took a closer look at him. "You're haunted! Who is she?"

"It doesn't matter."

"But it does." Anxiety and anger marred the smooth countenance of her trademark expression. "It's stealing you from me— from Avalon. And she won't be worth it, Ad. I can promise you that."

He looked away, too tired to fight. "How, Azure? How can you promise me that? How can you possibly know what she's worth to me?"

"You have everything you need here." Her tone dropped, limned with outrage. "Don't you dare endanger it with some menial dalliance that in time will wear off and leave you with nothing! You'll regret it terribly, and once a companion leaves, that's it. You understand this."

"I understand." He clenched his jaw and forced himself to meet her eyes again. Cold eyes. Unyielding and reptilian. How could he ever have fooled himself into thinking she held his best interest at heart? "Anything else, Azure?"

Soft pleading dropped over her features, a skillfully donned mask. "I beg of you, break it off with her, whoever she is. And if I hear again that you've been seen with her in the city, your employment here will be terminated. No matter how much it grieves me to do so."

Adrian didn't trust himself to speak. He started for the door.

"Adrian."

"What," he gritted without turning around.

"Is it the reporter?" The question was desperate, quavering with equal amounts of disbelief and dismay.

His hand tightened on the knob. Christ, how could she possibly know?

In that instant, he felt as if he'd sold his soul, his identity, his every virtue to the devil, and she stood behind him, burning a twin set of holes in his back with her knowing blue gaze.

He wouldn't give her the satisfaction of seeing his face. Without reply, he stepped into the hall and closed the door behind him, his pulse trudging a sick beat of exhilaration and dread.

How's the romance survey coming?" Nora poked her head in the office door, a half-eaten soft pretzel in her hand.

"Slow but sure." Billie sat back and casually minimized her computer screen in case the editor decided to glance over her shoulder. She was supposed to be outlining her next assignment, an article about the dating world of thirty-somethings in Washington, a subject of which she was sorely ignorant. Instead she'd been scrolling through the piece about Adrian, too restless to type a single word.

Nora didn't know she hadn't abandoned the article about him, but Billie wasn't ready to share it and have her deepest truths exposed . . . and some of Adrian's too.

She pushed back from the desk and eyed the tall woman in the doorway. "I still have questions that need answering."

"About what?"

"About . . . about first-date experiences." Adrian was right. She was a terrible liar, and immediately Nora looked suspicious.

The editor chewed and swallowed, then gestured with the pretzel. "Billie, you already took the survey. You interviewed thirty women. How many more questions do you have about first-date experiences? Most of them aren't that exciting."

Billie smiled benignly.

"By the way, this came for you." Nora moved into the office and produced a cream-colored envelope addressed with sweeping, calligraphic handwriting. "A linen envelope. Who do we know that would write a letter on linen stationery?"

"There's no return address," Billie said after she'd studied it. It was postmarked from the District. A faint chime sounded in her head and her pulse picked up speed.

"Open it," Nora said as she finished off the rest of her pretzel.

"I will. Later." She casually set it aside and returned her attention to her monitor. "Go away and let me work."

Nora scowled. "Why can't you open it now?"

"Because I'm in the middle of something else."

"As your editor I could order you to open it."

"As a decent person you wouldn't be that nosy."

They exchanged sneers, and Nora dropped her pretzel wrapper in the Bugs Bunny trash can beside the desk. "Fine. But maybe you'll tell me later. It could be hate mail."

"When have I written an article with enough juice to merit hate mail?" Billie said. "You took the Adrian article away from me."

"And tried to give it back."

"No—you tried to sic me on Avalon during the investigation. But the article belonged to Adrian. It was about *Adrian*, not Avalon. I won't write an exposé for you. I don't have it in me."

The ferocity of the declaration sent Nora scurrying out the door. "Finish that survey," she barked as she disappeared.

Rising from her desk on shaky legs, Billie crossed to the door, checked the hallway to make sure Nora was truly gone, then shut herself in and locked the knob.

She perched on the edge of her desk and picked up the envelope, studying the graceful script. A week had passed since she'd heard from Adrian, and Nora hadn't seen Rich, the unsavory detective. It seemed as if, without a suicide note, without any evidence to further torture Adrian, the investigation was dead in the water.

Thank God.

Sitting there, staring at that envelope, she wanted to tell Adrian she'd never truly doubted his innocence, that all she wanted was to see him happy, and she wished like hell it could be with her. She wanted to ask him if he missed her at all, because her life had been on hold since the moment he hung up the phone last week.

The lucid side of her knew Adrian was truly finished with the whole mess, harbored no desire to speak to her again. He obviously had scads of common sense over her paltry supply and knew better than to contact her and feed the impossible relationship that had been flourishing between them. Part of Billie, the unwounded, sensible part, was relieved.

One last tie remained. The article was almost finished, yet a melancholy reluctance kept her from writing the final paragraphs that would close the door on Adrian Antoli forever. And when she was done, and turned it in, Nora would have her head. The editor might not even print the piece.

It didn't matter. Long ago, the assignment had ceased to be about getting published and had become a quest to discover the man so expertly masked beneath layers of pain and denial and enigma.

A quest to explore the foreign, uneasy, exhilarating emotions he stirred in her.

Holding the envelope up to the light, Billie squinted at it, but the linen paper revealed nothing. She slid a trembling thumb beneath the flap, gingerly opened it, and withdrew a card.

Dear Ms. Cort,

Please accept this informal invitation to attend an intimate gathering at Avalon on Friday, 1 September, at 8 o'clock in the evening. While the occasion is intended to entertain out-of-town clientele, consider it a social affair, or simply additional research for your article that has been so regretfully delayed.

As always, your discretion is most appreciated.

Yours sincerely,
Azure Elan

Billie returned the card to the envelope with shaking hands and slipped it inside her purse. Azure wouldn't invite her back to Avalon out of the goodness of her heart. Billie wasn't even sure the club owner had a heart. She had a reason, though, for issuing the invitation, and unquestionably it would benefit Avalon.

Anxiety coiled around her stomach and squeezed. She knew better than to step foot in the club again. Everything sensible in her screamed to steer clear. But if it meant seeing Adrian again, even across a crowded room with his dark attention focused on some high-paying client, she'd do it.

Her heart gave her no choice.

CHAPTER FOURTEEN

A young valet approached Billie's cab and helped her from the backseat without meeting her eyes. She wondered if the silent, red-coated parking attendants knew what went on behind the golden glow of Avalon's windows. It hardly seemed real, even to her.

Climbing the brick steps that led to the club's glossy red door, she paused on the landing, drew a deep, steadying breath, and rang the bell. The muted melody of Westminster chimes echoed from within.

"Welcome." The handsome, raven-haired butler in the black tails politely delayed her entrance while he examined the invitation she'd handed him. Then he examined her, his seductive gaze sliding down to her toes and up again in a visual caress. "Ms. Cort," he said as his smile widened. "Won't you come in?"

The elegant lobby shimmered with a thousand candles, the flames reflecting off gold and mahogany, diamond jewelry, polished smiles. Chopin floated in the background as women in cocktail attire milled around the intimate space, each the object of an Avalon companion's attention. To the side, observing her handiwork with a satisfied smile, stood Azure Elan in a white, floor-length gown as lacy as a spider's web.

Almost immediately she spotted Billie at the entrance and crossed the floor with fluid grace. "My dear Ms. Cort. Welcome back."

"Thank you," Billie said with an equally cool smile. "Whatever the reason for your invitation, I'm so glad you extended it."

"Take Ms. Cort's wrap," Azure told the butler, but Billie shook her head and tightened her grip on the silky material.

"That's not necessary."

"But you'll stay long enough to sample some of our chef's fine cuisine, won't you?" She took Billie's arm, gently removed the silk wrap, and handed it to the butler. "Look around you, Ms. Cort. You must stay just a little while. Pleasure abounds."

The club owner wasn't exaggerating. In every corner couples embraced, hands caressed, lips met and clung. A public display of affection like Billie had never seen. She turned a slow circle, taking in the carnal exhibit with fascination.

"There's someone I want you to meet," Azure said against her ear.

Billie allowed herself to be whisked across the room to where a solitary man leaned against a marble post, his sultry blue eyes fixed on the milling guests.

"Billie Cort," Azure said proudly, "this is Joe."

Instantly Joe straightened, the bored look disappearing from his handsome face. His blue gaze skimmed down Billie's copper, off-the-shoulder cocktail dress to her provocative high-heeled sandals and up again.

"Pleasure's all mine," he said, with just enough drawl to paint him a southern belle's delight.

Azure joined Billie's hand with his. "Joe will answer any and all of your questions. I know you want to finish your article, and he's more than prepared to tell you what you need to know." Her glittering eyes dared Billie to voice the question that leapt to her lips.

Where's Adrian?

Maybe, Billie thought, if she was as sweet as pecan pie, Joe might tell her. "I'm so happy to meet you, Joe," she cooed, mirroring his charm just short of mockery. "Call me Billie."

Azure glanced between them and seemed satisfied. "Eat, drink, and by all means, partake of any additional hospitalities we offer." As she floated away, she added, "And don't be shy, Ms. Cort. For tonight, you're an honorary member of Avalon."

Billie released a breath of relief in the woman's absence and turned to survey the crowded lobby. No sign of Adrian. She glanced at the blond companion standing next to her. "Well, Joe, I guess it's just you and me."

"I've been lookin' forward to this all day." He spoke with enough wholesome enthusiasm to make Billie wonder if the country-boy persona was an act at all. "Azure told me you were a knockout, but *mm–mm.*"

Two could play this game. She gave him a single, slow blink of lashes. "What exactly were you expecting, cowboy?"

"I don't know, sugar. But I'd like to unwrap you like a Tootsie Pop and find out what's in the center."

Billie laughed and shook her head. The companions of Avalon were skilled actors as well as gifted lovers, but this one could have easily time-traveled from *Hee Haw*, his hayseed charm was so outdated.

"Where are you from?" she asked as they strolled the perimeter of the crowded room.

"Anywhere you want, sugar. Dallas, Atlanta, New Orleans . . . you tell me." He winked at her, and she resisted the urge to roll her eyes.

Making conversation with Joe, it turned out, was more like listening to a recital of the world's worst sexual innuendos. But he was entertaining in his own hokey, down-home way, and for a little while Billie managed to keep her attention on the big blond cowboy and away from the far corners of the room, where Adrian might linger.

They stopped at a linen-draped table mounded with tiers of fruit and delicate canapés. A swan ice sculpture dominated the spread, glistening like wet glass in the flickering candlelight.

"Hungry?" Joe asked, and reached for a plate without waiting for her answer.

Billie's stomach gave a mild lurch of protest as she stood mutely beside him and watched him place three or four canapés on the crystal plate. When he handed it to her with a sexy smile, she took it and let her gaze wander the opulent lobby.

Everywhere her attention landed, lush bouquets sprang from priceless vases. Thousands of dollars spent for ambiance. Thousands more for pleasure. "Tell me about the women here tonight, Joe."

He glanced around with a bored sigh. "Most of them are from an annual business convention. Same faces every year."

"Are all the companions here?" she asked, keeping a carefully dispassionate expression.

"It's mandatory. This is one of the busiest nights of the year for Avalon."

Biting into a pastry filled with sherried mushroom, Billie let her gaze skim handsome faces, broad shoulders, and clinging, greedy-eyed females. Adrian would have jumped off the page with his piercing good looks. She didn't see him. "May I be blunt, Joe?"

"Of course."

"It looks as though there's one companion to every woman. How many clients are you scheduled to entertain tonight?"

He grabbed two glasses of champagne off a passing server's silver tray and handed one to her. "They arrive in timed segments. Six to nine, nine to midnight. Tonight my book's filled." His hand settled at the small of her back. "But I could make room for another, if she wanted."

She wanted nothing except to fool herself into thinking Adrian Antoli was nowhere near this party tonight. Setting her plate on a nearby service tray, she tipped the champagne to her lips and swallowed the flute's contents in one gulp.

When her throat stopped burning, she slanted her companion another look. He had the strong, bulky build of a football player. It was easy to picture him lounging in a barn loft, buck-naked with a piece of straw twirling in slow windmills between his teeth. He played the red-cheeked country boy to perfection. No doubt his schedule stayed full on a regular basis.

But Billie didn't want a ruddy, blond country boy. She wanted what she couldn't have . . .

And the object of her every desire had just started down the winding staircase.

The world stood still as disbelief and a dizzying rush of adrenaline made her take a second look, then a third. At first she wasn't certain the dark figure with the expressionless features was Adrian. God, what had happened to him in the days they'd been apart? He seemed so grave and remote. He wore a black jacket with a collarless, stark white shirt beneath it, his hair swept back from his aristocratic features, his dark eyes shuttered.

But his most striking accessory was the ivory-complexioned redhead clinging to his left arm.

"That's Adrian you've got your eye on," Joe murmured in her ear. "You can look all you want, but his dance card's filled."

"I see." Billie finally blinked. *Breathe in, breathe out.* "And the woman with him?"

"She's a staple when it comes to this convention, but no one's ever been with her except Adrian. She reserves him every time." He rocked back on his heels, eyes narrowed. "Cryin' shame. I always did have a weak spot for redheads."

The tightness in her throat threatened to choke her. No amount of self-convincing had prepared her for the sight of Adrian with another woman. And it didn't help that Joe now had his oversized paw resting at the small of her back, too close to her bottom for comfort.

"I'd like another glass of champagne," she told him with a praline smile.

"Anything for you, sugar," he said, and disappeared into the sea of bodies clustered near the bar.

Immediately her gaze darted around again, searching for Adrian and his russet-haired friend. It wasn't hard to find them; he shone like a solitary black pearl in a cultured strand. They stood near the ice sculpture, chatting with Azure, who embraced the woman like a long-lost sister.

When the club owner finally moved away from them, Adrian leaned to murmur something in the redhead's ear. Whatever he said made her laugh, and the unexpected flash of his smile caught Billie in the heart like a flaming poker. He was talking to the woman like he'd talked with *her*. Intimate, seductive, his mask melting into warm pleasure. His hand disappeared behind the client's back. Probably on her skinny ass, Billie thought bitterly. In response, the woman nudged him against the nearest wall, set his arms around her waist, and rose on tiptoe to kiss him.

At the last second, Adrian smoothly turned his face and her lips landed on his cheek. While Billie stared in openmouthed dismay, his lashes raised and his gaze locked on hers from across the room.

Immediately his head jerked up and he stared back at her.

Billie couldn't breathe.

Even from where she stood, she could see the color flood Adrian's cheeks, and her own face burned, some sort of misguided, sympathetic reaction to his obvious discomfort.

Seconds ticked by as they watched each other, astonishment melting into longing, and then into hopeless realization.

Joe reappeared at her side with her champagne and chose that prime, painful instant to brush his lips against her temple. "You look so damn sexy standing here all by yourself. Sure I can't persuade you to hang around tonight, sugar?"

Across the room, Adrian's black gaze bore into her, taking in Joe's brawny arm sliding around her waist, the way his mouth hovered at her ear, too intimate. Billie flinched away from Joe's audacious touch, but the look on Adrian's face showed no understanding. His attention shifted back to the redhead in his arms, and that smooth, emotionless façade fell back into place. The face of the man who'd greeted her the first time she stepped foot in Avalon weeks ago. A stranger.

His hands slid up his client's spine, bared by her skimpy black dress, and he kissed her hard, his hands cupping her pale neck beneath her hair. As though he wanted Billie to watch. As though to say, *See how I can hurt you. See what I am.*

Now there was no denying it. Adrian was a prostitute. Billie, a fool.

"I have to go," she told Joe abruptly, moving from his unwelcome embrace. "Thank you for your time."

"What about your article?" Confusion flushed his features and stole his hayseed accent. "You hardly asked me anything. I can tell you whatever you want to know about this place."

"I have all the information I need." All the information she'd ever need when it came to heartache and bad decisions. "Good-bye, Joe. And please, thank Azure for me. I won't be back."

She darted through the crowd to the entrance, where she waited with her heart drumming while the well-favored butler retrieved her silk wrap and swung open the door for her.

"Billie." An infuriatingly familiar male voice rose over the steady din of chatter behind her, but she didn't stop. "Billie, wait."

"Go to hell," she muttered, her heels tapping out her rage in hard staccato against the steps.

She shooed off a valet and headed down the sidewalk, unsure of her direction, knowing only that she wanted to get away from Avalon. Adrian's voice drew closer. Damn his long legs. Damn her strappy, too-high sandals. She paused, hopped on one foot to remove one shoe, then the other. Then she sprinted, mindless of the punishing concrete, weaving between pedestrians, the warm wind shaking free her carefully styled chignon.

Despite her mad dash, Adrian caught up with her a block from Avalon. Grasping her arm, he swung her around to look into her hot face.

"Don't touch me." Panting, she shook off his hand, but he captured her wrist. She didn't know she was crying until she heard her own voice, choked and raw, pierce the night. "I thought I could handle it. Azure sent—she said—damn it! I thought I could still get the answers you wouldn't give me about Avalon, about you, but it was foolish of me. Let go of me, Adrian. You don't do relationships, remember? You'd rather screw total strangers and have no one give a damn about you, your needs, your pleasure . . . you don't want love. You want an opponent, and I'm tired of playing."

Instead of releasing her, he drew her into the darkened doorway of a vacant boutique and pressed her against the brick siding. They were both panting, two runners fleeing the truth. Heat radiated from his body, through his clothes, through hers. He burned her alive.

"I'm losing my mind," he whispered into her hair. "And probably my job too."

Something in his words made her push on his chest to get a better look at his face. "What are you talking about?"

"I shouted your name across the entire party." A rueful smile tugged at his lips. "I blatantly abandoned a loyal customer in the middle of one of the most important events of the year to chase after you. What the hell were you doing there?"

A bittersweet wave washed through her anger. "Maybe you should ask Azure. That woman's a smart cookie. She's the one who invited me." Her voice quavered on a fresh wave of unshed tears. "At first I didn't know why, but now I see her plan. She knows about us, doesn't she, Adrian? I'll bet she warned you to stay away from me."

He hesitated, his eyes narrowed as realization flashed behind them. "She found out about the concert. She knows we've been seeing each other."

"How? How does she know?" She glared at him. "Did you tell her?"

Weariness seemed to press down his shoulders, and he closed his eyes. "A client saw us at the park. Not one of mine," he added when Billie made a sound of derision. "But a frequent customer at the club. I've told you before—nothing's sacred. Not even my personal life."

Despair rose in her throat like clawing fingers. "This isn't going to work. I'm going to get hurt. I already am." She tugged fruitlessly against his grasp. "Let go, damn it."

"God help me—I want to. Don't you know that?"

That was when she saw his intention, and everything in her screamed not to allow his kiss, that one taste of him would surely shatter her.

But it was too late to move. His face blocked out the night as his ravenous mouth opened over hers. He kissed her until she quit fighting him and desire weighted her limbs, until her knees crumpled, and then he held her up, pressed between the doorway and his hard body, one palm flattened on the bricks by her head, the other hugging her hips. He kissed her until the breath had long abandoned her lungs and she existed solely on sensation.

Then she grew aware of the unsteady tremble in his body, and realization washed through her, brought her back to consciousness. He was shaking. Emotions stretched to the limit. Passions unleashed . . . because of her.

The sandals still clutched in her hand hit the ground.

"Don't," she said weakly when his mouth slid down the side of her neck. The damp flicker of his tongue against her sensitive skin made her shudder. "Don't make this harder for me than it already is."

He raised his head, his breath rushing between them. "You want me to let you go, Billie?"

No. "Yes. And don't you dare try to dicker with me. I won't owe you a thing."

"But you will." His palm slid down to cup her breast through the thin, silky bodice of her dress. "There's always a price."

Billie groaned, but he swallowed the protest when he lowered his head and kissed her again, more gently this time, his tongue slipping between her teeth to caress and incite. She melted into him, but common sense assailed her when he let her up for air.

"I can't do this, Adrian. I *won't.*"

"Why not, when it may solve the problem?" He dipped his knees, aligned his hips against hers and slowly straightened, dragging his erection against her in a way that made her groan again, with desire this time. "A favor for a favor. Come back to Avalon. As a client. My client."

His words sank in, and chilled understanding settled over her, stiffening her in his embrace. "Why? So you can prove Azure wrong?"

"This has nothing to do with Azure."

"It has everything to do with Azure," Billie said bitterly. "She doesn't want you involved with me, and you know it. You're the jewel in her crown. She invited me so I could see you at work, with another woman. To show me . . ." *What you really are. Lost in a world where I don't belong.*

"God—I should've never come to that party." She shook her head and slipped from his arms, needing space to breathe. She could smell his skin, cedar and passion. It soaked her senses, made it hard to think. "That woman you were with . . . Did you have sex with her tonight?"

"No."

"But you planned to."

He gazed back at her, unwavering. "Not quite. She's a voyeur."

"Please." Billie slumped against the wall. "Spare me the soulless details."

"Why? You want to ask me what I was doing with her. Do you know about voyeurs, Billie?"

"I know enough to be disturbed."

"But this one's different." He stepped closer and circled his hands around her neck, thumbs brushing sinuously against her collarbones. "A voyeur likes to watch other people's pleasure. The woman I was with tonight likes to watch her companion pleasure himself."

"It sounds humiliating," she muttered.

"It can be." He leaned forward and his lips feathered over her eyebrow. "Every aspect of my work has that potential. But I let my fantasies pull me out of the humiliation." His lashes brushed a butterfly's kiss against her cheek. "Ask me who I was going to think about tonight, when I was jacking off for the benefit of a stranger.

Ask me who I was going to think about to get through the degradation and take me to a place of incredible pleasure."

"Stop it." She shoved aside the provocative possibilities and narrowed her gaze at him. "Let's be straight with each other, shall we?"

He sighed and stepped back, weight on one foot, a posture of weariness. "All right."

"It's apparent you want me."

"Yes."

"And you know how I feel about you."

The hard lines of his face softened almost imperceptibly. "Yes."

"What I *don't* understand is why I have to come to Avalon to make love with you when you could take me home with you right now."

It rang in the air between them, the truth only one of them could speak.

When he didn't answer, she glared at him in accusation. "You want to turn me into your client because it's the only way you'll be comfortable being intimate with me. You can't stand the idea of a real relationship outside of Avalon. It scares you."

His expression blackened. "Be careful, Billie. You don't know me as well as you think."

"I know you enough to be hurt by you," she retorted. "I know you enough to see that you're confused about me, and that maybe you want something more from me than you get from your customers."

"Oh, really?" His arm snaked around her waist and pulled her up against him. "I know a few things about you too, Billie. You think you're above coming to Avalon as a client. You're too high and mighty. The women who pay for sex are desperate, right? Lonely. Unsatisfied with the real world. And you think you're not?"

"I'm not." She shoved against him, but he only tightened his embrace, reached beneath the short hem of her dress and slid under her panties, absorbing her struggle until his fingers made contact with the wet, hot evidence that she couldn't hate him no matter how she tried.

"You're the most desperately lonely woman I know, Billie Cort. If I put your name in the appointment book, you couldn't stay away."

"Try me, you egotistical bastard."

They stared at each other, both breathless, as his finger searched, probed, found the entrance to her body, and brought her to her toes with a single, well-aimed stroke. Then he dipped his head and caught her mouth, angry, bruising.

The instant she stiffened in alarm, the kiss changed. Slowing. Melting into languid gentleness as his finger thrust rhythmically inside her. Switching tactics.

Defeated by desire, Billie slid back against the brick wall. Her hands crept over his shoulders, across the smooth material of his jacket, reading the shift of muscles beneath. He too was sweating from the chase, from tumultuous emotion. She wanted to rip away his clothing, feel his damp skin, the result of his exertion, the proof that he hadn't wanted to let her get away.

They flowed together in the shadows, passion mounting between them, connected by turmoil and the sinuous thrust of his finger inside her. She was going to come. There, in public, on a city street, shoved up against a cold brick wall with a man's hand between her legs. Nothing had ever been this degrading—or exciting. She pressed her open mouth to his shoulder to muffle her cry as the climax racked her with violent shudders.

Somewhere beyond the doorway where they stood, a group of people approached on the sidewalk, laughing, chatting, breaking the spell and spilling Billie from her unbidden ride to ecstasy.

Reality returned with all its twisted vehemence.

Adrian's hand went still against her heated flesh and he moved around to shield her with his body until the pedestrians passed. When the voices faded, he gently withdrew from her, smoothed down her dress, stepped back. The lines of his posture straightened, and Billie could read his utter withdrawal, not just physically, but emotionally.

In a sudden fit of anger and desperation, she shoved him back against the opposite wall, a feral assault that surprised both of them. It felt good to strike out, and Billie wasn't done. She anchored herself before him, her posture threatening, fingers curled into fists at her sides.

Adrian didn't push her away. He tucked his hands behind his back and watched her in silence, as if daring her to take it further.

She rose to the challenge, gliding over her anger with self-control born out of nowhere. "So far we've established the kinds of things your clients like, and that I'm to be one of the elite few, right, Adrian?"

Her fists unknotted and she let her palms sweep between his lapels, down the front of his damp linen shirt. His abdomen was rock hard beneath her hands when she yanked his shirttails from his pants and slid beneath to touch damp, bare skin. "I can tell you right now what I want from you. I want the reins. I want control."

His stomach contracted beneath her fingers. A shaky rush of breath slipped between his teeth and he shivered hard, but didn't speak.

"Can you give me that, Adrian? Can you give up your precious control? I'll pay you. A thousand bucks an hour—what do you say? Give me the control." Her teeth closed around his earlobe, tongue flicking. "Or are you too scared you'll never get it back?"

His only answer was resolute silence.

She slid her hand lower to press against the granite evidence of his need. Her palm curved around his erection, stroked with enough pressure that she could feel the quickening throb of blood through the material of his pants. "Could we pretend, just for one night, while I'm paying you my hard-earned dollars, that you have no will of your own when it comes to me? I'm sure you've done it with other clients."

"Billie," he hissed finally, a sound of agony and delight as his palms flattened against the wall behind him, hips thrusting into her relentless caress. His pretense at impassivity fell away, exposing the man beneath as hungry, needful, and just as desperate as she.

Billie wasn't finished. "Will you let me tie you up? Touch you and tease you and taste you until you beg me to finish it? I could one-up your redheaded voyeur when it comes to doling out humiliation. And you'd let me, I'm certain, for the right fee. Everyone has his price, right, Adrian? How much money would it take to get you to admit that you're falling for me? Because I know—"

Tears choked off her words and she shook her head, scrambled to regain equilibrium. "I know what a talented actor you are, and I believe, for the right price, you would admit to falling in love with me. You would relinquish all the wonderful control you've wielded in our short-but-sweet relationship."

"Damn the money," he gritted. "You know it's not about that."

"It's all about that. You've sold your soul for it a million times."

He didn't argue.

For a thick, silent moment, she continued to rub him in firm strokes, reveling in the steeliness beneath her palm, the harsh, uneven breaths that heaved from his chest. Some feminine instinct told her if she kept on, goading him with provocative words, massaging him in this semipublic place with their defenses lying shattered at their feet, she would bring him to orgasm.

And then what?

She would have stopped, but then he came to life, his features steely as he shoved aside her hand.

"Here," he said roughly, jerking open his pants to free his erection. "If you're going to jack me off in public, do it right."

"How's this?" she snapped, and wrapping her fingers around him, pumped his erection, hating him, hating herself. "Better?"

He didn't answer, only closed his eyes, the muscles working in his jaw.

Driven by rage, Billie quickened the rhythm of her caress, watching his face, her heart pounding, dirgelike, one beat to every stutter of the frantic pulse beneath her hand.

More pedestrians passed by the shadowed doorway. Billie didn't know if anyone saw the lurid display, and Adrian didn't seem to care. He widened his stance and let his head drop back against the wall, the shadows slashing across his features like strips of a mask.

When he came, he bit back a cry and clenched his fists against his eyes, hiding his vulnerability, shutting her out, even as he spilled himself in her fingers.

The scent of his release filled the air between them, and instead of feeling triumphant, Billie was ashamed. There was no tenderness in what they'd done. They'd humiliated each other.

The anger trickled away, replaced with broken defeat. Releasing him, she straightened and stepped back, leaned against the wall behind her, forcing her raging pulse to calm.

Adrian didn't move for a long, long time. Then he cleared his throat, withdrew a handkerchief from inside his jacket, and handed it to her. "I deserved all that and more," he said quietly, fastening his pants. "I'm every bit the bastard you think I am—although it's not just me you're angry with. You're mad at yourself for being foolish enough to invest feelings in some glorified female pimp's idea of the perfect man . . . aren't you?"

She opened her mouth to protest, but he shook his head.

"I share the blame. This is what you truly wanted to hear from me, and I admit it. I'm nothing. I have nothing of value to give you. No heart, not an ounce of love in me. It's all been fucked away."

"Shut up," she whispered, leaning her head back against the hard brick rather than look at him. "Shut up, Adrian. You're a liar."

"I'm that too. Everything low and base and aberrant is right here." To her utter astonishment, he reached out and caught her hand, pressed it to his thundering heart. "I feel nothing for you. I don't love you. I don't want you. That's what you really want me to say. I can do that for you."

In the place where her anger had burned came a spiraling, potent sadness. "Let me go, Adrian."

He didn't.

When she lifted her head to meet his gaze, his eyes were closed, lashes like inky brushstrokes on his cheeks. His palms came up to cup the sides of her neck, and with a shaky sigh, he rested his forehead against hers.

"I'll let you go, Billie." His words poured against her lips, husky, raw. "I always keep my end of a deal. In exchange, you'll come to Avalon as a client. Tomorrow. This week. Walk through those doors and send for me. I'll be whatever you want. I'll take you up to my room and turn you inside out. I'll taste and touch and fuck you until you scream. And if you want control, it's yours. A favor for a favor."

She clung to him to keep from collapsing, torn between tears and wild, wayward laughter. The scenario was unreal. And the only argument she could think of was a frail one, easily shot down. "Azure would never allow—"

"It's as good as done. I'll put you in the book myself. Maria will call you with the date, and I'll keep my distance from you until then." His lips brushed her ear. "Please, Billie. Let's end this before it kills us both. Say yes."

The truth wrapped itself around her. *You're hopelessly in love with this man, aren't you, Billie Cort?*

"Yes," Billie said, squeezing her eyes closed. "God help me, yes."

CHAPTER FIFTEEN

Adrian walked Billie back to the club and waited with her while the valet hailed her a cab. Neither of them spoke; she clutched her shawl, gaze fixed on the sidewalk, but he could read the misery etched in her profile.

He was responsible for it. For so much of the unhappiness around him. He'd hurt Lucien. And his own family—*Jesus*. Without their knowledge, he'd sullied their faith in him, their honor, disrupted the track record of generations of honorable, upstanding Antolis. If his parents knew, it would destroy them.

Who else would he wound before all was said and done? Himself, most assuredly. It had already happened. He felt betrayed by the smooth mannequin he'd become. It hadn't been a strong enough fortress, and now it crumbled around him, leaving him raw, a stranger to himself.

And now *this* . . . this deep, encompassing unhappiness he experienced, standing in somber silence next to Billie, was born of the knowledge that one night with her wouldn't be enough. Yet it was all he'd take, and no more, because he didn't deserve her. She sure as hell didn't deserve the futility he could offer—empty promises, paths leading to dead ends . . . everything he had to give, all of it, incomplete. *He* was incomplete. Eight years at Avalon had whirled away, passed in some sort of suspended bubble, where life hadn't touched him and he hadn't touched anyone, not truly, until Lucien died. Until Billie.

The grinding sound of wet pavement under tires brought him back to the humid, rain-soaked night, and he automatically took Billie's elbow as the valet opened the cab's rear door for her.

Her gaze darted to his for a split second, and he read the reticence in her face. "Adrian . . ."

She wanted to back out, to run.

He would let her. Soon.

"Maria will call you with the time," he said in a low, firm voice. "Keep your appointment, Billie. I'll be waiting."

M y God, Adrian. I'm simply speechless." Azure paced behind her desk, fingertips steepled and pressed to her forehead as if deeply in prayer, while Adrian sat on the opposite side and watched her with distant fascination.

"What would possess you to act so carelessly? Finola Casselberry has spent a fortune within these walls—and you flagrantly abandoned her in the middle of the most important function of the summer. And why?" Her voice rose in pitch, shrill with outrage. "To chase after some ridiculous girl who means nothing? She's nothing, Adrian!"

He lifted his head and stared at the woman with the silken fall of black hair, the satin-pale skin, the soulless blue eyes that stripped him and left him with nothing as a weapon but truth. "You're wrong, Azure. She's everything. *Everything.* But how would you know? You wouldn't know love if it threw itself in your path and screamed your name."

Her blue eyes flashed fire. "So it's love now, is it? You actually think you're in love with this woman?"

"I don't think," he said wearily. "I know."

Azure laughed and sagged against her desk, hand clasped against her chest as though her amusement stole her breath. "Oh God, Adrian, that's rich. Do go on. You're in love with this silly little hometown reporter, and—let me guess. She's going to save you from yourself with her wholesomeness and innocence. You'll leave Avalon, get married, buy a Cape Cod with a picket fence and have two-point-five children. Leave all this debauchery and iniquity behind you, no worse for the wear after years of fucking for cash."

Adrian forced his fingers to unclench and folded them in his lap, maintaining a placid exterior. "I hadn't thought that far, but you do have a way of making the unlikely seem sort of appealing."

Her mirth fell away like a mask peeled from her features. "Do consider, Adrian. You're not the person you were when you first walked through these doors eight years ago, and a man like you doesn't ever go backward. I know. I've seen it over and over in this business. You make a living fulfilling fantasies, and in the process you've seen the truth in a woman's soul. Trust me, if you don't shatter her heart, she'll surely crush yours. Because if she's as pure and undriven as you believe, she'll never be able to live with the fact that you whored yourself night after night with countless, faceless women."

Battered by a sudden surge of virulent hatred, Adrian clenched his jaw and looked away from her pale, hard features. Beneath that flawless cosmetic shell dwelled a monster—one who spoke a truth he couldn't abide.

He drew a breath, exhaled, willed his violent pulse to even out and his emotions to settle. When he could speak again, he stood and straightened the shirtsleeves inside his jacket cuffs to occupy his trembling fingers. "You say nothing I haven't already considered, Azure, but thank you for your insight. Believe it or not, I realize the futility of the relationship between Ms. Cort and me, and I know what needs to be done to end it."

Azure hesitated, her eyes narrowing. "What?"

"I've made arrangements to entertain her as a client here."

Stunned disbelief flickered across her features. "You want to make her a client—and she *agreed*?"

He merely looked at her in placid silence.

A slow smile crept across her red lips. "Ah, Ad. You haven't yet taken your precious Ms. Cort to heaven and back, have you? *Have* you? And you think . . . you think—"

She shook her head and burst into laughter again, a cruel, sharp sound, meant to debase and wound. "Adrian—my God, I hadn't thought a single naïve bone was left in your beautiful body, but I was utterly mistaken! You really think if you spend one night with this woman, at Avalon, where you feel safe, where you can fuck all the confusion and passion out of your system—that you'll get your life back and be rid of her?"

"I mean to spend one night with this woman to decide if my desire to leave Avalon is as genuine as it now appears to be," he said with slow precision.

She paused to regroup, her features shifting from darkness to light and back, as though undecided on which mask to don.

The duel continued.

"Client or no, if she walks through those doors again, your employment will be utterly compromised."

"If you're going to fire me, Azure, do it now, because she's already in Maria's appointment book for Tuesday night."

"Cancel her," she snapped.

"No."

"I hope she's worth it. You may find yourself a jobless whore."

Adrian sighed and turned toward the door. "God, you're hateful. A great opponent. Some sick part of me will miss you, I do have to admit."

"Adrian!"

The piercing cry paused him at the threshold. "What," he said, without turning around.

Desperation wavered in the air behind him. "You're placing me in a terrible position, my darling."

"Her money spends as easily as Finola Casselberry's, Azure."

"Then she will pay double."

He waited, his gaze fixed on the Manet original showcased in a heavy gilded frame on the opposite wall. "Anything else?"

"If you entertain Billie Cort as a client on Tuesday night, it will be for the last time."

"Yes," he said, hearing the double meaning behind her words. "I know." And left the office, closing the door gently behind him.

It's pure sex, Billie told herself four days later as she paused outside Avalon and stared at the red door. *You've already been intimate with him. It won't be a dramatically different experience.* She scowled at the rationalization, unable to fool herself even for the sake of pride. Of course it would be dramatically different. She was in love with him, had admitted it to herself, and even if she'd wanted to turn away, she couldn't.

Taking a deep breath, Billie reached for the brass doorbell, then changed her mind for the third time and glanced nervously toward the street. An elderly woman, on a rainy evening stroll with a miniature terrier trotting beside her, gave her a solid visual scouring as she quickened her steps and hurried by.

For an instant Billie froze. Then she remembered. Avalon looked like any other D.C. town house-mansion. Nothing about it advertised that it was a business, though the neighbors more than likely whispered. Adrian was right. Nothing in the world was truly sacred.

Resisting the urge to offer an offensive gesture to the old woman's back, Billie rang the doorbell.

The butler, a different man from the one at the party a few nights ago, greeted her with a warm smile. "Yes?"

"I'm Billie Cort," she told him, spine straight, shoulders level. "I have an appointment."

"Come in." He stepped back and let her into the cool confines of the women's club. "May I take your coat?"

"That won't be necessary." She clung to it, needing the protection. Silence hung like a mantle over the deserted lobby. Outside, a distant rumble of thunder promised more rainfall after a steady seventy-two hours of late summer drizzle.

"So you decided to keep your appointment after all." Azure's disembodied purr floated over the room. Billie couldn't see her right away, then she focused on the sweeping staircase and found the club owner gliding down the steps, her trademark white duster billowing out behind her like fingers of smoke.

"Adrian will be so pleased." Azure approached Billie with a Cheshire cat smile. "He was quite insistent about squeezing you into the schedule."

"He told you?" Billie said uncertainly.

"He told me. And what he didn't say, I already knew."

"I was certain you'd forbid it."

Azure's smile lost its edge of satisfaction. "I did forbid it, but he's quite single-minded about you, even at the risk of losing his position here."

Billie's temper surged. "You would fire him for this? Is it so taboo for your employees to have relationships?"

Azure's laughter was as soft and magical as the ringing of a tiny bell. "Is that what you think you have with Adrian? A relationship?"

Billie stared back at her, unblinking. "I know we do."

They glared at each other. Then to Billie's surprise, the other woman's gaze darted aside and she moved toward a small table in the sitting area, her graceful hands drawn to the erotic bronze statue Billie had noticed there on her first visit.

"You're beautiful, bright, and sexy, Ms. Cort. A pleasant distraction to Adrian, no question. The first in many years. The last one was a bourgeois girl from a nouveau riche background who ran for home when she found out his truth. Since then he's reveled in the company of the wealthiest, most cultured and educated women in the world. I'm quite certain his definition of a relationship is different than yours. I'd keep that in mind if I were you."

Billie's eyes narrowed. "Is that a warning?"

Azure shrugged, caressing the sculpture as though it were a living thing. "Your confidence is astounding. You're terribly determined to pursue pleasure with a man still under suspicion for murder."

"He hasn't been charged."

"Thankfully, no."

"He says he didn't kill Lucien. I believe him."

Azure abandoned the sculpture and circled her slowly, like a panther examining potential prey. "Will you also believe him when he tells you he's in love with you?"

Billie's stockpile of retorts dissolved and scattered. "Should I believe him if he says such a thing?"

"He'll say it before the night's through. He believes it. He's utterly convinced, in fact." Azure paused in front of her and took Billie's hand in her cool, manicured fingers. "But I know Adrian, Ms. Cort. I know him better than he knows himself. If you're as intelligent as I think, you'll back away and give him time to examine his true desires. He's so busy fulfilling everyone else's, he has no idea what he wants."

"I've been under the impression that he wanted me," Billie said coldly, "or I wouldn't be here."

"For tonight, there's no question." Azure patted her hand, a humoring gesture, then glided back toward the reception desk and pushed a button beside the phone. "He'll come for you now. Are you ready?"

Billie drew a slow, shaky breath. Who was ever truly prepared for her first night at Avalon? "Absolutely."

Azure merely smiled and turned her graceful profile to wait for Adrian's appearance at the top of the stairs.

When he paused at the rail, the world disappeared for Billie. Azure, Avalon, the scent of coconut and sensuality, the sultry flicker of candlelight that gilded Adrian's solemn features. Only the man remained, his dark eyes unreadable from such a distance, yet their heat was tangible on Billie's skin.

He moved. Between one breath and the next, he stood before her, his hand extended, ready to lead her away. She glanced down at those fingers. The promise of ecstasy hung thick in the air between them, and suddenly she was afraid of his hands. Hands that could incite the most excruciating response with a few choreographed caresses. Hands that would crush her heart, as he'd threatened, to dust.

"Welcome to Avalon, Billie," Adrian said, softly enough that the air hardly stirred around him. "Will you come with me?"

* * *

Upstairs, he paused for Billie to enter the room before him, then followed her inside and silently closed the door. Candles flickered on every table, their flames casting shadows that danced like frantic spirits on the ceiling and walls.

He stopped behind her, close enough that she felt the soft kiss of his breath against the nape of her neck. Then his fingers slid the damp raincoat from her shoulders.

Billie closed her eyes as cool air brushed her bare arms. She should have worn sleeves, but the periwinkle dress made the warm highlights in her hair a little brighter; her green eyes a little greener. Tonight she had dressed for him, craving the feel of his appreciative gaze on her body. One last night. A fleeting pipe dream laid to rest.

She listened to the sounds of his movements as he opened a closet door, hung her coat, and closed it again with a quiet click.

"What's your pleasure?" he asked from across the room.

She met his eyes and leaned to remove first one pump from her foot, then the other. "You."

He watched her, the heat from his gaze lending inexplicable eroticism to the simple task of taking off a pair of shoes. It was only when she set the pumps by the bed and straightened that he moved to the sitting area, where a crystal ice bucket cradled a bottle of champagne.

Billie crept closer, her attention fixed on his hands as he withdrew the bottle and wiped it with a towel. Skillfully he released the cork with a quiet pop and leaned to the crystal flutes sitting on the occasional table.

He was dressed sedately in black pants and a black turtleneck. His shoulders were wide, his recently trimmed hair dark and thick, as black as his attire. When he glanced at her, his gaze swallowed the light. Then he turned his attention to the task at hand, and the sound of champagne felt like fingers trickling across Billie's senses.

"I assume you like champagne," he said, extending one of the stem glasses to her.

She nodded and took it from him, painfully aware of his ebony observation as she tilted the glass to her lips. The beverage foamed on her tongue, a bubbling, cold caress, before she swallowed it and blinked in relief. Her throat was desert dry, but everywhere else she was damp. Sheer nerves. Undiluted anticipation.

"What happens next?" she asked when she'd emptied her glass.

Adrian took it from her and refilled it. "I leave you alone long enough for you to pull yourself together." He set the flute in her hand again, stroked a single, burning finger down her bare arm, and started across the room toward the bathroom.

She followed him a few steps. "Do I seem nervous?"

"Yes."

"Where are you going?"

"To draw a bath." His voice faded as he disappeared around the corner.

"A bath," she muttered, perplexed. Then her eyes opened wide. A bath. *Oh God*. The Kouros. The special jets.

A good five minutes passed while she stood outside the bathroom door, listening to the splash of water and the gentle hum of a whirlpool motor. The champagne seeped through her body, chased by a rush of dizzying warmth. She glanced back at the bottle sitting on the table and recognized the label. The best champagne. The best lover. The most expensive night of her life, because she would pay with her soul.

Inside the bathroom, the rhythmic rush of water abruptly ceased.

When Adrian reappeared in the doorway, she set down her glass and faced him. "You're going to put me in that extraordinary bathtub and show me more pleasure than I've ever known in my life, aren't you?"

"To begin with."

"And then?"

"Then I'm going to take you to bed and make you come so many times, you beg me to stop. And then I'm going to make you come again."

Her head tilted as she considered him. "And will it be making love? Or fucking?"

His silence was all the answer she needed.

"May I be totally honest with you, Adrian?"

"When have you ever failed to be?" He took a few steps toward her, then stopped. "What is it?"

"I'm terrified."

His expression remained placid except for a slight crease between his brows. "I see."

Flustered, she went on. "I wanted this, I thought, more than anything. I know it will lay this thing between us to rest. I even told myself I could use the experience to finish the article, to give it an edge no *Illicit* articles ever had. But looking at you now, I know myself too well." She tried to swallow the lump rising in her throat and failed. "I know I won't be able to write about this night. I could never do it justice. Worse—I'm afraid I'll forget the precious details in time. Fragments of it will float away, and I'll miss—"

"Billie," he said softly. A flicker of something crossed his features. Humor, maybe. Tenderness. Confusion.

"People like me don't do this sort of thing, Adrian."

"People like you do it every day. They do it with me."

Her heart plummeted. "I wanted it to be different with us."

"It has been." He moved toward her and drew her into his arms, smoothed back the dark strands that escaped her bun. His scent rose with his body heat, soap and musk and faded champagne, to feed her senses. While he held her face and studied her with excruciating diligence, she clutched his wrists, closed her eyes, and waited for the touch of his mouth.

It came, not on her lips, but on her brow. The left, then the right. Soft, patient flutters over her lashes, her nose and cheeks.

Drowsily she said, "Azure told me something when I arrived here tonight. She said—"

"Azure says a lot of things," he murmured, nuzzling her jaw.

Her fingers clung to his shoulders. "Are you saying I shouldn't believe what she tells me about you?"

He drew back to meet her gaze. "What did she say?"

"She said . . . you think you're in love with me, but that it's a mistake."

He didn't admit or deny it. He only withdrew and went to snatch his champagne from a small console beneath an Impressionistic painting, the subtle tightening in his posture revealing his indignation. A wry smile twisted his mouth behind the glass as he tipped it to his lips and drained it dry.

Abandoned where she stood, Billie felt unprotected, foolish, uncertain of the man standing before her.

"What's your real first name?" she said, desperate for something, anything to remind her that he was living, breathing, caring.

"It's not important."

Another strand of hope unraveled from around her heart. "It is to me. I want to know who I'm sharing my body with."

He set the glass down and returned to her, his feet silent on the plush ivory carpet. "You tell yourself that, and maybe it buys you a modicum of propriety. But the truth is you don't know me outside of what I want you to know. And still you're here, and you desire me, and I desire you. Names don't matter. Pleasure matters. This."

He reached out and touched her breast, lightly stroking his fingers over the tip until it hardened and she shuddered. "Sex with a stranger. You can't rationalize it or justify it, but you can enjoy it. And I promise you will."

Despite the scripted flavor of his statement, it was the hollow, aching truth—his truth, not hers.

He would drive that fact home again and again in the next few hours. He would devalue the love they made in this room by setting a price on it. He would make it easy for her to let go, just as he'd promised.

In that instant, Billie appraised the true value of her feelings for Adrian . . . and changed her mind.

She stepped back, gathered courage around her like bricks to build a hasty, lopsided barrier between them. "Thank you," she said, holding his gaze as confusion clouded its black clarity. "But it seems I can't do this after all."

The only sign of emotion on his face was a slight upward nudge of an eyebrow. "Oh?"

"Yes."

"Why not?"

"Because . . ." She twisted her hands together, a mindless prayer for strength. "Because of how I feel for you. I won't cheapen it by buying what you sell to strangers. I'm not a stranger. I'm the woman who's fallen for you."

The spoken truth shattered the air into crystalline shards.

She paused, cursing the telltale tremble that would quake her words. "Walking away from you with a broken heart is easier to handle than selling my soul to make love with you. I'm sorry, Adrian. I might be lonely, and naïve, and all the things you think about me. But I'm also true to myself, and I won't denigrate my feelings for you. They're much too precious in a world that offers so little love."

Without waiting for his response, she turned and retrieved her shoes, slipped them on her feet, then walked with chin erect to the closet, where she withdrew her coat and put it on.

"My purse," she said in a low, even voice.

He hadn't yet moved from where she'd left him. Wordlessly, he pointed to a console near the fireplace. She crossed to pick up the leather handbag, then glanced back at him.

His face was impassive. No sign of the man who'd touched her body, mind, and heart while swaying in a hammock in the haunted woods of suburbia.

He said, "I'm curious about something."

"What?"

"About why you've chosen me to love. Why? How can you be so sure of me?"

She swallowed. "I'm not sure of anything. But my heart won't listen to reason. And I'm quite certain you've known that about me from the beginning, since you seem to know *me* so well."

He didn't respond. His dark eyes watched her, betraying nothing but a strange sparkle she didn't understand. Triumph, maybe? He'd conquered her. Not much of a victory, but another notch on his belt, anyway. He'd won the game of cat and mouse.

Billie started to turn for the door, and just as suddenly, Adrian moved. It startled her. While she clutched her purse, the only protection against his dark, mesmeric force, he approached her, his gaze hot on her face.

"And what do I owe you for the gift of your love, Ms. Cort?"

"Nothing." Tears thickened her voice. "You owe me nothing. It's my mistake."

"One that has benefited me." He reached out and fingered the lapel of her coat, not touching her skin, but Billie shivered as though he had. "Anything of value must be repaid, Billie. I insist. A favor for a favor. What do you want in exchange?"

She looked away, tears clinging to her lashes, not yet plump enough to trickle down her cheeks. "I don't know, Adrian. Nothing."

"Something."

Her gaze shot back to his. *Admit your feelings for me.*

He waited, as though he knew what she would ask.

In the end, she drew a trembling breath and said, "Your name."

A frown creased his forehead. "That's all? Are you sure?"

She nodded. "I just want to know who you are."

He lifted his fingertips to her face and let them trail against her cheek, his gaze following the path of his caress. "It's Christopher," he said in that same easy, soft tone that hardly rent the thick silence.

Christopher.

"Christopher Antoli?"

"That's right."

Billie's face crumpled under the urge to cry, and quickly she righted the reaction, sucking in a deep, healing breath even as she stepped back from his tender touch. "Okay, then. We're even. That's all I wanted." She turned and grasped the doorknob, her pulse so heavy it stirred waves of weakness through her limbs.

"I don't know if this matters to you," his voice came quietly behind her, "but I would've never allowed you pay for this night, Billie. I already took care of it with Maria."

A sad smile touched her lips. Something deep within her had already known, but hearing him say it stood as a bittersweet send-off.

"I hope you find your place in this world, Christopher," she told him without turning around. "I don't think Avalon is it." And before the deluge of tears broke, she slipped out the door with her dignity somehow intact.

CHAPTER SIXTEEN

For a long time after the door shut behind Billie, Christopher Antoli stood in the middle of the room, listening to the static clamor of his own heart.

A slow ache had begun to stir in its general region, a sense of emptiness that wiped out every stronghold he'd built around himself in preparation for this night.

The silence around him was keen, agonizing. He moved out of sheer need to break its thickness, systematically picked up a champagne flute and set it in the sink of the wet bar, straightened an already smooth duvet, returning order to a room sterile and uncluttered.

In the bathroom, he released the drain on the tub and stood watching the scented, steaming water seep away, waiting for the knock on the door that would announce Azure's arrival, and the advent of his subtle torture under her smug regard.

At last it came . . . a soft, unassuming tap.

Wiping his hands on his thighs, he approached the door and opened it, then stepped back to allow her entrance.

She'd changed outfits, from trademark white to a black, form-fitting pantsuit. He knew the look. She cloaked herself in darkness whenever she ventured out to prowl the city in search of new companions for Avalon.

Her hair hung silky and gleaming behind her shoulders, untethered by clasp or band. A smirk curved her lips, as though she couldn't contain her triumph long enough to stand before him with the solemn air of chastisement he'd half expected.

"Your client has left prematurely. Tell me, Ad, did you fail to perform with her too?"

"Yes." His tone was emotionless as he moved to gather his things. His life at Avalon was over. He'd known it the minute Azure consented to allow Billie's name in the appointment book. Opening the closet door in the bathroom, he removed a leather duffel bag and returned to set it on the bed. Nothing belonged to him in this room, save two bureau drawers filled with fresh clothes and a few garments hanging in the closet.

Behind him, Azure watched, her gaze searing him with contemptuous glee.

"I'm afraid that's two dissatisfied clients in a week. Make that three, including Finola Casselberry at the party, when you blatantly abandoned her to pursue your dear Ms. Cort." Her tone tightened. "I hope the reporter's worth it, Adrian. You realize she's cost you your position here at Avalon."

He continued to pack without responding, as though she weren't skulking behind him with fangs bared.

"Did you hear me?" Irritation snapped through her words. "I'm releasing you."

"I heard you, Azure."

He headed back into the bathroom, grabbed a few toiletries, and stuck them in the duffel. Then he zipped it, moved around her, and retrieved his shoes, all in excruciating silence that vibrated with Azure's mounting rage.

When he sat on a wingback chair to put them on, she approached him, her exotic scent rising off her like radiant heat. It reminded him of sex and humiliation.

A long white envelope floated into his view from between her manicured fingers, and he hesitated, let his attention rest on the familiar handwriting for a moment before recognition sank in. Then his spine slowly straightened and he lifted his gaze to hers.

And knew. Instantly.

"This came a short time ago," Azure said, watching his face with narrowed eyes. "I'm afraid it must have gotten lost in the mail. You know how unreliable the postal service can be on our block."

Swallowing the knot in his throat, Christopher took it from her fingers and stared at the postmark. It was dated one day after Luke's suicide.

Lying bitch.

He clenched his jaw and met her gaze squarely. "Thanks."

The acknowledgment hung in the air, an icy, gritted dismissal. Her pleasure faded.

"That's all you're going to say?"

"I'll read it in private."

"As you wish." She gave a careless shrug and started toward the door. "Don't you want to know whether I contacted the police and shared the letter with them?"

His fingers tightened on the envelope. "Tell me, Azure. Did you contact the police and share the letter with them?"

"Of course, darling. Failure to do so would be withholding evidence." Her expression melted into one of benevolent tenderness. "You're utterly off the hook."

Lips tight with rage, he managed a curt nod and rose to tuck the letter into the duffel. Then he paused and cast her a look of sheer disdain. "Anything else?"

"You can't have that letter, Ad, even though it stands as monumental proof of your impressive ability to devastate everyone around you. But that's the original copy. Leave it on the bedside table so I can deliver it into the proper hands. If you want a photocopy for posterity, let Maria know before you leave." She opened the door, her graceful fingers lingering on the knob. "I'm sorry it's ending this way, Adrian. You must know that."

"My name is Christopher," he said, and slid into his jacket. When he looked up again, she was gone, a wisp of shadow, a bad memory.

Christopher waited until he was certain he was utterly alone before he allowed himself to breathe. Then with shaking hands, he withdrew the envelope, pulled out Lucien's letter, and began to read.

H old your horses!" Billie muttered, juggling two bags of groceries as she blindly searched for her cell phone.

Somewhere in the depths of her purse it rang with cheerful insistence, and she cursed it as she dug through the crowded pockets. Her fingers closed around the phone but then her purse strap slid off her shoulder to the crook of her arm and one of her three bags of groceries hit the ground.

Cursing, she set down the groceries in the hallway, snatched up the keys and jammed the right one into the dead bolt. Her mood, already as gray as the rain clouds choking the afternoon skies outside, darkened an additional three shades of gloom. She picked up the bags again and shouldered her way into the apartment. The shrill, unrelenting demand of the phone pulled at the wayward hope that refused to die in her heart. No one was so important that she had to kill herself to get to the phone, not even . . .

Well, no one was that important.

She forced herself to calm as she kicked the door closed behind her and set down the bags in the kitchenette. She would not kill herself to locate that damn cell phone. There was no need to rush.

It wouldn't be Adrian. Christopher. Whoever the hell he was.

Pacing her steps with studied decorum, she set her purse on the counter, found the bloody thing and studied the number on the screen. It was a Maryland area code. "Hello?"

"I'm trying to reach Billie Cort," a woman's clipped voice said. "Do I have the right number?"

Ever wary of being trapped by a solicitor, Billie hesitated. "Who's calling?"

"This is Rosalie Baxter."

Billie drew a blank. Then her heart tripped and thudded in her chest, and she eased herself down to the padded bench beside the telephone. Not Adrian.

But his *sister*?

"Yes, hello, Rosalie," she said finally, breathless from exertion and surprise. "You've got the right number."

"How are you?" The other woman's question was laden with a heavy emotion Billie couldn't identify.

"I'm fine, Rosalie. How about you?"

"I'm—well, I stole your number from Chris's cell phone the last time I saw him because I knew I could check on him through you, you know, when we don't hear from him for a while."

"I see." Billie hesitated, unsure of what to say next. Before she could scramble for polite conversation, or even entertain why Adrian's sister was calling in the first place, Rosalie rushed on.

"I'm sorry to bother you like this, Billie, but have you seen Chris?

We haven't heard from him since the night you came for dinner, and I'm starting to get worried."

Chris Antoli. Chris Antoli. The name played like a singsong rhyme in her mind. She straightened and pushed her hair back from her face, a frown knitting her brows. "Truthfully, I haven't seen . . . Chris, uh—in a couple of weeks. He and I . . . we—"

"You didn't break up." Immediately the concern in Rosalie's tone shifted to brittle disapproval. "Did you break up? What happened? Why would you break up? Who did it, you or him?"

"It just didn't work out."

The other woman made some derogatory remark in Italian. "He did it, then."

Billie closed her eyes and swallowed against the lump rising in her throat. "You know how these things go."

"With my brother, yes, all too well." Rosalie sighed. "I'm sorry, Billie. I thought you were good for him, you know? He just seemed happy with you."

"He wasn't." It came out more sharply than she'd intended, so she quickly added, "And truthfully, Rosalie, I don't think it had anything to do with me."

"Yeah, I know. He's too closed off, too secretive, but something's wrong in his life and we all know it. He thinks he can hide it, but his family—we know."

Not well enough. Billie rubbed her left temple, where an ache had begun to tighten in spiraling circles. "He's lucky to have you."

"Yeah, well, damn him. I've left fifty messages on his cell phone and with his hoity-toity answering service and he hasn't returned a single one. But if you two are having trouble . . . that might explain it. Maybe his heart is broken over you."

"Doubtful," Billie said wryly. "But thanks for trying."

Rosalie released a little huff of mirthless laughter. "I ought to strangle him. But it's not like him to be out of touch so long. Maybe I'll drive out and check on him tonight." She paused, then groaned. "*Dio*—Sophie has cheerleading practice until seven, and David's out of town."

Billie braced herself and winced, innately knowing what would come next.

"Billie, what kind of terms are you on with Chris?"

"I haven't seen or talked to him in a while," she said, dread lodged in her chest. "I have a publication deadline tomorrow morning so I've been incredibly busy, and I'm sure he is too. He could be out of town."

"He could be, except he always leaves Rudy with us when he goes away." Rosalie drew a breath. "So would you say you parted on good terms?"

"Civil," Billie allowed, eyes closed.

"So if you, for example, knocked on his door—"

"He wouldn't slam it in my face." She muffled a deep, weary sigh. "You want me to drive over to his apartment and make sure he's okay."

It must have sounded more like an offer than an observation, because Rosalie exclaimed, "Oh, you sweet—thank you, Billie! You're such a good girl. My brother's an idiot, yes? When you get there, look him in the eye and smack his beautiful face *twice*. Once for me, for scaring his poor sister to death, and once for yourself, for spitting in God's eye when He would send such a beautiful girl to that undeserving . . . *sciocco*! You're a jewel, and Zio should know it."

Billie laughed in spite of herself. "Thank you for the kind words, Rosalie. I'll give him your message and I'm sure he'll call you right away."

When she hung up the phone, she sat and stared at it, her heart banging out a frantic rhythm. She had just agreed to see Adrian again, to hear his voice, to step foot—even briefly—in his world again, where she wasn't welcome and didn't belong.

"*Sciocco*," she muttered, closing her eyes as she recalled Rosalie's fervent proclamation.

It meant *fool*.

First she called his cell phone, to no avail, then his private room number at Avalon, her pulse doing backflips while she let it ring once, twice, three times.

A husky male voice finally answered, "Jean-Pierre."

Billie paused. "I'm sorry—I was trying to reach Adrian's room."

"You did not misdial," Jean-Pierre told her in a clipped Parisian accent. "Adrian can no longer be reached here." He paused. "How did you get this number?"

She straightened on the bench and clutched the cell phone against her cheek. "He gave it to me. Is he . . . has he left Avalon?"

"I'm afraid I cannot answer that. Is there anything else?"

"No. *Merci*," she added tartly, and hung up the phone.

Darkness had fallen by the time she reached Adrian's condominium building on Connecticut Avenue. She circled the high-rise, looking for a parking spot along the car-lined side streets, and was relieved to see Adrian's navy blue BMW parallel-parked near the rear of the building. It didn't guarantee he was home, but something inside her clung to the hope that she'd find him holed up in his luxury condo. Maybe he was taking a good, hard look at the real world for the first time in eight years.

An odd tugging in her heart told her if that were the case, then he was suffering, even more than she had been over the last two weeks.

She didn't have to cajole or bribe to get into the building. The pudgy, red-coated doorman from weeks before was absent. A well-dressed woman coming out the glass door held it for Billie when she approached, giving her tank top and khaki shorts a cursory glance as Billie thanked her and headed into the complex.

The lobby was deserted. She headed straight for the elevators, pressed the button, and waited, heart pounding, every sense sharpened to the plush environment around her. Classical music drifted from somewhere down the chandeliered hall beyond the elevators. The sound of female laughter muffled behind walls floated on the air, and the faint fragrance of incense drifted around her.

After a moment, the brass-paneled doors slid open and she stepped into the empty elevator, her fingers shaking as she reached to push the button for the fourteenth floor.

What would she say to Adrian if he actually answered her knock? She envisioned herself relaying Rosalie's terse message, then turning on her heel and marching away without another word, head held high.

He might let her too. A wry smile curved her lips. It would be so like him to do the unexpected, and not necessarily the most courteous thing.

Then again, what if he flung open the door, grabbed her arm, and hauled her against him, swallowing her words with his kiss before she could utter them?

"Stop it, Billie." The sharp sound of her own voice bouncing off the mirrored walls startled her out of her romantic musings. Damn it—the man was no good for her, and she, all wrong for him. Despite the lovely potential that had seemingly lurked around every corner of their brief relationship, they had nothing to offer each other. If they had . . . if the chance for love had truly been present, she'd be with him now instead of in this elevator, throat dry with dread and anticipation. Fate wasn't so cruel that it would dangle this man before her, this *impossible* man, as her one and only chance at true love . . . was it?

The doors opened onto an empty, silent hallway. Drawing a deep breath, she stepped out, arms clasped tightly over her chest, and started in the direction of Adrian's apartment.

She paused outside his door and listened. No sound came from within. She knocked firmly, then waited, her gaze drifting to the Chippendale console across from his apartment. A lush fern had replaced the elaborate bouquet she remembered from before. Even a simple plant looked expensive in this exclusive building.

As Billie had feared, Adrian didn't answer his door. A niggling concern tugged at her conscience, and she knocked again.

No answer.

Her fingers strayed to the brass knob, hesitated, then grasped it and twisted.

The door clicked open.

Holding her breath, she edged it ajar, just enough to peek around it. The foyer was dim, the kitchen lights off. Pushing the door open wider, Billie crept over the threshold, took a few more tentative steps, and glanced into the living room.

The elegant room was a mess. Newspapers lay scattered on the sofa and coffee table. Clothing—a hodgepodge of T-shirts, running shorts, jeans, socks—spilled from a laundry basket on the floor in front of the grandfather clock. A pair of tennis shoes had been abandoned in the middle of the carpet, kicked off with the laces still tied. An open pizza box sat on a leather armchair, its contents hardly touched and already yellowed from sitting too long.

Lined up in an odd, precise pattern on the nearby occasional table were six import beer bottles, six Budweiser cans, a half-empty fifth of bourbon and an assortment of drained shot glasses.

Her eyebrows crept up. It looked like Adrian had recently embarked on a one-man bender.

She slowly crossed the room, her attention fixed on the gentle flutter of the gauzy curtains covering the balcony doors. One panel flipped aside, tossed by the night breeze, and finally offered her a glimpse of the man she sought. He was sitting astride the balustrade, his attention focused downward.

Billie froze, every muscle in her body tightened in alarm. "Adrian—" she choked. *"Don't!"*

His head turned sharply, but she couldn't read the expression in his dark eyes before Rudy appeared from behind the curtains and bounded toward her with a startled, ferocious bark.

Frantic, Billie backed up and held out her hands to the exuberant Labrador, who had recognized her as someone familiar and fun to play with.

"Hi, Rudy," she said in a shaky voice, and he dragged his slobbery tongue across her hand. He trotted back toward the balcony with one last plaintive look in her direction, as though to coerce her to join him.

Trembling, Billie approached the curtains again, brushed them aside and stepped out into the balmy night.

Adrian shifted to look at her without moving from his precarious perch. The wind tossed his dark hair, plastering his long-sleeved T-shirt to his body. He wore faded gray sweatpants and no shoes. His unshaven face was pale, his eyes circled with shadows.

Still, a wayward smile played around his mouth, that old, familiar amusement that seemed to creep across his features so often when he regarded her. "Sorry about the overzealous welcome wagon. Are you okay?"

"I'm fine." She lifted her chin, cheeks burning. "Are *you?*"

His smile twisted. "Have you come to talk me down from the

proverbial ledge?" The soft slur of his words confirmed he was at least mildly intoxicated.

"Adrian—"

"It's Chris," he interrupted, the humor fleeing his expression. "My name is Chris."

"Okay." She took another step toward him, one eye on Rudy, who watched her with his tongue hanging out of his mouth. "Chris, what are you doing up there?"

"Seeing the world through Luke's eyes." He turned back toward the glittering sea of lights sprawled beyond the balcony. "And looking for Rudy's banana while I'm at it."

Billie gulped in a breath, heartbeat slowing. "His banana?"

"A stuffed toy. He likes to throw it off the balcony, and inevitably I have to run down and get it." He glanced at his dog. "Something's not quite right with that scenario, Rudy."

The dog panted and licked his chops.

"Will you please come down from there?" Billie demanded. "You're making me nervous."

Instead of doing as she asked, he motioned to her. "C'mere."

With slow, careful steps, she approached the balustrade and peered over, one hand resting close to his hip, ready to grab in case he slid forward.

"Look," he murmured.

A million sparkling lights shimmered across the surface of the city, a landscape deceptively glamorous, and one that had yielded so much pain for Lucien DeChambeau. It was beautiful and haunting in its significance. It was the last thing Lucien had seen before he died.

Billie glanced up at Adrian's profile. "What am I looking for?"

"Rudy's banana."

But the hollowness of his reply told her that his attention wasn't on the dog's toy. For a silent moment they stared down at the concrete, at the spot where Lucien had died. Then anger curled around the edges of Billie's anxiety and she cast Adrian a narrowed look of reproof.

"When I saw you up here, I thought you were planning to jump."

His lips curved upward. "And upstage Luke's dramatic exit? Never." He lifted his head and blinked as though to focus his eyes. "Disappointed?"

She didn't reply. The breeze lifted wisps of hair that had escaped from her ponytail and drifted them across her lips in feathery caresses.

"I don't see the toy," Adrian finally said. "Do you?"

"No. I'm not looking for the damn banana. I'm here to check on you."

"I'm more than okay." Moving suddenly, he swung his leg back toward the safety of the balcony and landed with impossible grace, one hand braced on the ledge to balance himself when he might have swayed. "*Sono libero*. I'm free."

The scent of alcohol drifted to Billie's senses, and she backed up. She'd seen Adrian a lot of different ways: smooth, manipulative, infuriated, impassioned, tender . . . but drunk and speaking Italian was not on the list, and the way his gaze skimmed her, head to foot and back, clobbered her equilibrium.

"So tell me, why are you *really* here?" He moved toward her like a sleek, if somewhat intoxicated, panther. "To dig up more dirt for your scintillating article on the life of a gigolo?"

"No. I—"

"You've come to the wrong place," he said bitterly, and swerved around her to enter the living room with Rudy at his heels.

She followed, paused to watch him examine the collection of

empty beer bottles and cans he'd arranged on the table. He picked up a can, squinted at it, shook it. "Azure fired me."

"Why?" Billie asked.

Laughter rumbled in his chest, a mirthless sound of derision. "Failure to perform. So now I'm an unemployed whore, although not destitute yet. I never was one to squander my money on the high life."

She didn't know what to say. She closed the French doors behind her, rearranged the curtain panels, then turned to face him. Adrian had collapsed on a plaid armchair, slouched down so that the back cushion caught his neck, one arm flung over his eyes.

"Did you hear me? You can finish the article, Billie. Just say I self-destructed." His throat moved as he swallowed in an obvious bid to maintain control over his emotions. "Stories like mine never have a happy ending."

She said nothing, just watched him, a blur of high-speed thoughts darting through her mind. Part of her wanted to flee, to leave this man she didn't understand and couldn't reach. Part of her toppled a little further into love and wanted to touch him, hold him, battle away the demons of his past—something only he could do himself.

Right now it looked like the demons were winning the war.

Inhaling strength and poise, she said, "When was the last time you had something to eat?"

"I'm not hungry." He spoke from behind his arm, only the lower half of his face visible. Several days' growth of beard darkened the too-angular lines of his jaw.

"You've been drinking."

His mouth quirked. "What gave me away?"

"You need something to absorb all the booze flowing through

your veins." She started toward the kitchen. "Let me at least fix you something to eat."

As she passed him, his hand shot out and caught her wrist. His grip was ruthless, and Billie winced as he pulled her back to stand in front of him.

His eyes narrowed to black slits as he stared up at her. He didn't lift his head or shift his lax position, but danger lurked about him. Desperation rendered him utterly unpredictable. And still she wanted him, with a wild, ferocious hunger that warred with every commonsensical intention she harbored.

"You want to do something for me, Billie? I can think of a few things that would make me feel better right now, and food isn't one of them."

"Go to hell."

He didn't release her. Under his cruel, silent direction, she sank to her knees before him, one hand trying in vain to pry his bruising fingers from her wrist. "Damn it, Adrian—you're hurting me!"

"But that's what you expect, isn't it? Why else would you keep coming back for more?" His grip loosened, though not enough to free her, and the fingers encircling her wrist trembled. "You know what I am, what I have to offer you. Nothing but pain. What's wrong with you? Afraid to admit you have the same dark, twisted desires as everyone else?"

"Nothing's wrong with me, you son of a bitch." Anger choked her words even as a sick feeling crept through her, a fear that he'd stumbled upon something secret within her she was unaware of. Twisted desire—yes. For him. Twisted because he didn't want it, and she couldn't stop the sentiment from growing inside her, insistent and uninvited.

"I'm not here because I want to be," she gritted. "Your sister's worried sick about you and she called me to ask if I knew where you were."

Adrian released her and sat up. "Rosalie called you?"

"That's right." Rubbing her wrist, she got to her feet with as much grace as her trembling legs would allow. "She's been calling you for days. She couldn't get away to drive into the District and check on you, so she asked me to do it for her. And I foolishly agreed."

What little color remained in his cheeks drained away.

"I came only for your sister's sake," she repeated in a blind, stumbling attempt to convince herself. "And now I see you're just fine. Enough to be cruel and ugly." Her breath hitched under the urge to weep as she backed toward the foyer. "I'm leaving now. Call her, please, and let her know you're okay."

Billie made it as far as the door and opened it before Adrian's hand emerged from behind her and slammed it closed again. She hadn't thought an intoxicated man could move so quickly.

His electric presence behind her sent a shimmering wave of awareness up her spine. Drawing a breath for strength, she slowly faced him. His eyes were bleak. He looked like he hadn't slept in days, and she tried not to care. She tried not to wonder what the hell had happened to create this ghost, a shell of the vibrant force she'd known mere weeks ago.

"I'm such a bastard," he said softly.

"Yes. You are. And I'm leaving."

He stepped back in capitulation, his hand dropping to his side. Billie started to turn, but then he said, "Wait . . ."

"What?" she snapped, too aware of his plaintive caress hovering just short of her elbow. If he touched her with any of the need already written in his face, she'd fold. "You're drunk and ornery, and I've got a million better things to do than spar with you."

He straightened, a frown darkening his face. "Like what?"

"Like working to meet tomorrow's print deadline. I do have a life, despite what you think. My world does exist without you in it."

He studied her with such intense concentration, Billie wanted to squirm. But she raised her chin and met his searching stare head-on, waiting for his delayed rejoinder while misplaced excitement left a damp burning between her legs.

After a moment of excruciating silence, Adrian reached past her shoulder and turned the dead bolt on the door, locking them in.

The resounding click shuttered through her, as did the intent in his face.

"You can't keep me here."

"No, I can't."

"What do you want?"

He stepped impossibly closer, and the warm, familiar scent of his skin, mixed with the lingering smell of liquor, assailed her senses.

"You," he said starkly. "And not seeing you for the past two weeks has only made you seem like an unreachable fantasy. I can't eat, I can't sleep. I can't remember what my life was like before you were in it." His voice dropped, the words dredged up from some deep well of despondency within him. "I can't remember what my life was like before I became a stranger to everyone and everything that used to feel right, and good, and valuable to me."

She shook her head in denial of the sentiment his words stirred, searched for resolve, and found it had abandoned her, replaced by the urge to cry. "But you'll break my heart, Adrian. You already have."

"I know." He looked away, as though he couldn't bear to see her reaction. "I've hurt everyone who loves me. You. Luke. My family, even though they don't know how I've betrayed their honor. It would devastate them." He dropped his head and rubbed the heels of his hands against his eyes. "I hurt everyone who gets too close, and I don't know who I am anymore. The man I was raised to be would never damage the people who care for him, would never sell his soul to—" He stopped and pressed his lips together as though to thwart the flow of desperation pouring through them.

Billie swallowed. "So you're an ogre. Inhuman. Blackhearted. What reason, then, can you give me to stay here with you, even for a few hours?"

"Out of pity." He laughed, but it was a desperate sound, the misplaced humor of a man grasping at threads of a life fast unraveling. Tears trickled down his cheeks and he swiped at them, staring at the palm of his hand as though the moisture he'd wiped from his face was something utterly foreign. When he looked at her again, there was little of the old veneer left, the features behind it made all the more naked with pain.

"Please, Billie. Indulge me. Stay for a few hours and let me pretend I haven't damaged our relationship beyond repair."

Billie didn't trust herself to answer. She stood in stunned silence and cursed him for his barefaced anguish, for choosing this moment to let her see beneath the façade. She cursed herself for falling for such a broken man.

But when he started to move away, her hands reached of their own accord and made contact with the front of his shirt, worn cotton, warm from the heat of his body, and she wrapped her fingers in the soft material and tugged him to her.

He came without hesitation, one step, then two, and when he stood so closely that her nose brushed the base of his throat, his hand slipped between their bodies and closed gently around her wrist to caress it.

"I was too rough. I hurt you."

Yes. A million times over.

"I'm so sorry, Billie," he whispered. "Please believe me. I'm sorry for everything." He buried his face in her hair and his hands came up to caress the strands, dislodging them from the elastic band of her ponytail, clinging to her in a way that spoke of need and anguish.

Everything warm and tender within her responded with slow-melting compassion. She slid her arms around his waist, palms gliding over his back, reading the shudder of his lean body without fully understanding the depth of his injury, only that it was self-inflicted and too grave now to deny. "What's happened to you, Adrian?"

"Christopher," he whispered against the curve of her neck.

She sighed. "It's going to take me a while to get used to it. I don't know Christopher. I've never met him."

"Then maybe it's time," he said.

CHAPTER SEVENTEEN

Wading through a Bourbon-induced fog, he told her the story of his dark descent into Avalon, while intermittent tremors of exhaustion and grief shook his frame and quavered his words. God, he was cold, down to his very soul, and recalling the past he'd so skillfully shoved beneath layers of concrete restraint chilled him all the more.

But Billie gently prompted him whenever he faltered, and in the end he told her everything. Sitting a modest distance from her on the sofa, he recounted how he'd landed a soccer scholarship to St. Michael University right out of high school, and how binding his parents' pride had seemed to an eighteen-year-old so unsure of his destiny. Neither Franco nor Sophia Antoli had a college degree, and with their youngest and only boy, they had always pushed the hardest.

Initially, the pressure and coaching appeared to pay off. Christopher had his choice of colleges, and he chose nearby St. Michael to stay close to home. At first it was idyllic.

"But I blew out my knee my sophomore year during a tournament, had surgery, and lost the scholarship," he told Billie. "My parents fell into that limbo income bracket where they couldn't afford to pay my tuition, but they made too much money to receive the financial aid I'd need. They offered me a place to live, but they couldn't pay for my classes. I started looking for a job. Luke was my roommate at the time, and he was already tending bar at Avalon. Good ol' Luke to the rescue. He had all the answers."

He smiled at Billie's deep, intent frown and shook his head. "He and Azure hardly had to persuade me to come aboard. Getting paid for sex with the most beautiful women in the world was something miraculous to a kid barely twenty. I thought I was in heaven. A thousand bucks a night sometimes. It seemed like so much money. So much pleasure. It was a drug."

With a sigh, Billie reached for his hand resting on the sofa between them. The suspicion had long ago left her features, and tender concern softened her green eyes to the dappled shade of forest moss. "So you worked your way through college in Azure's club, and never told your parents."

"I never told them. It would kill them."

"It nearly killed you," she pointed out. "Look at you. Why didn't you just leave Avalon after you graduated? Walk away?"

"I never had a reason." His fingers closed around hers, thumb whisking across her knuckles in restless sweeps. "Then I met you, and Luke died. The night you left me at Avalon, I found out he had written a suicide note, but he'd sent it to Azure through the mail. Why he chose her as the recipient instead of me, I don't know. I'll never know. All these weeks she kept the note from me. I had no idea it even existed."

Billie's face paled. "But that's so cruel! Why would she do such a thing?"

"Some sort of bid for control. When she knew I would leave Avalon, she showed it to me—the final straw."

Billie sat up. "She could get into a lot of trouble for that, Christopher. Do the authorities know?"

"They knew. She was just enough of a bitch to let me drift in the wind for a few days before she told them. Money exchanged hands and bought her some time, no doubt. That's why they stopped questioning me with no explanation."

"And what did the letter say? Will you tell me?"

He studied her face with bleary eyes. She was the only person he could trust, *wanted* to trust. No one could hurt him more than he'd hurt himself, not even this woman, who'd stood as the catalyst for his complete undoing.

Absently caressing her slender fingers, he said, "Luke couldn't live with what he'd become. He blamed himself for dragging me into Avalon, for ruining both our lives. But what he didn't understand was that I went willingly. I was a grown man, I made my own decisions, and when things went wrong in my life, it was because of those decisions. He wasn't to blame, but he felt he was, and I had no idea how deeply he bore that responsibility until I read his letter."

His eyes met hers again, stinging with the release of a weighty truth. "But that's not all. I told you before, he thought he loved me, in a way that disturbed me and twisted our friendship. And he was right to think I wouldn't have hung around to deal with it. I was repulsed by his attraction to me, by his drug worship and his sordid little penchants—me, no less a whore than he was."

He laughed, short and humorless. It was either that or cry, and something in him feared if he started he'd never stop. "I rejected him and closed him out, right when I was all he had left. My timing was impeccable. He spent the last hours of his existence in my home with no friends, no love, no purpose. The whisperings at Avalon weren't all wrong, Billie. In a sense, I did help him over that balcony."

She edged closer to him and reached to stroke his cheek. "No, Chris. It's no one's fault. Look what blaming yourself is doing to you. I'm certain Luke wouldn't want this. He wouldn't have expected you to come undone too. You and he stand equally mistaken: Luke, for taking sole responsibility for bringing you to Avalon, and you, for blaming yourself over his death. There are too many shades of gray in this story, and no one's truly at fault."

He looked away from her face, knowing the understanding in her green eyes would shatter him. "You believe wholeheartedly in the goodness of people, don't you, Billie? It's one of the things that made me want you, from the moment we first spoke. I wanted what you have by nature. Guilelessness. But I gave mine away, and there's no going back."

She started to reply in her sweet, hopeful way, maybe a loving reassurance, something he didn't merit, and he stopped her with a shake of his head.

"Please, let me finish. There's so much— I— Christ, Billie. For the last few weeks, my relationship with you has been the only thing of value in my world, and though you're still here out of sympathy, I know I've hurt you." His eyelids slid closed and he sighed. "I hate myself for it. I've ruined what we had."

"Well," she said quietly, "you certainly did your damnedest. But right now I can't measure the damage. I've missed you too much these past two weeks, and I was glad Rosalie gave me the excuse to see you again. I'm not here out of pity, Chris. I might have a soft heart, but believe me, it's not that soft."

He opened his eyes to read her expression, and found remnants of anger warring with compassion in her features as she grasped his other hand.

"You're one man I'll never feel sorry for, not even now, when you've made an utter mess of your life and you're drowning in the consequences. I can hate you, rail at you, be confounded and angered by you, and I am. All of the above. But I don't pity you."

"Then why haven't you left?" he whispered, watching her with unqualified confusion and a spark of hope.

"Haven't you heard anything I've said?" She released his hands and clasped his face between her palms. "I'm waiting for you to make it right between us again. Make it right, Christopher. Give me a reason to stay."

Billie watched his face, the fathomless eyes gone darker with anguish and uncertainty, the flush of awareness seeping into his cheeks, and knew she had stepped across the final boundary that separated them . . . and that it might be the biggest mistake of her life.

It only took a moment for her to realize he couldn't speak. The same piquant emotions squeezing her throat had constricted his own. He was vulnerable at last, and when his hands covered hers and held them to his fevered face, he was needful too and as hungry for her touch as she was to give it.

He drew her back with him against the cushions, the same cushions where, weeks before, he'd broken down every preconception she had about pleasure and sex and desire. She wanted to do the same for him, but it felt wrong. There were no guarantees between them now, any more than there had been that night. Just the danger of heartbreak.

So Billie did what any confused, impassioned woman would do. She kissed him. She started by brushing her lips against his, once, twice, feeling his mouth soften under hers in response. For countless moments it was the only movement between them: long, slow, gentle kisses, beneath which an inexorable desire began to build, part lust, part tenderness, fed with hunger for the taste of each other.

Even as her excitement grew, she knew there'd be no fervent coupling between them tonight. He was more exhausted than he'd admit, and still intoxicated, and what he truly needed was to sleep. She would stay just long enough to see him into rest. She would ful- fill her own helpless need to lie alongside him and feel the warm, hard length of his body . . . and then she'd leave him to finish his recovery on his own.

Tentatively, his hand tugged the tank top free of her shorts and crept beneath to rest on her bare skin with an unassuming, gentle pressure. Waiting for her to make the next move.

"Billie," he whispered against her lips. "Take me out of this night."

"I want to." She drew back to meet his eyes. "Tell me how."

"I only know one way," he said roughly. "Put your hands on me. Your mouth. Your tongue. Get on top of me and fuck me."

The words sliced the air between them, so raw and shameful, she couldn't respond for a moment. In the heavy, expectant silence, a faint tinge of color seeped into his cheeks. Shame. Billie instantly recognized it and grasped his face in her hands, kissing his lips, his chin. Soothing away his degradation.

Christopher didn't speak, only swallowed and covered her hands with his, holding them to his cheeks.

"Show me your bedroom," she said finally, her throat tight with sympathy and sadness.

He got to his feet and grasped her hand to help her up. With her fingers laced through his, he paused by the grandfather clock to address Rudy, who gazed back at his master with somber brown eyes.

"*Soggiorno,*" he told the dog, and Rudy's tail thump-thumped on the carpet.

"Rudy speaks Italian?"

"And a little Spanish."

Billie smiled to herself as Christopher led her down the hall. "Does he sleep in your room?"

"Not tonight." They rounded the corner and stopped for him to throw open a set of double doors. Then he stepped aside and allowed her to enter the bedroom before him.

In silence, Billie took in the queen-sized cherry bed and its accompanying furnishings. At the foot of the unmade bed, a weathered travel trunk held a stack of hardback books and a folded chenille blanket. Beyond that, two large windows flanked a sitting area containing a plaid loveseat and a leather club chair. Books were scattered everywhere, piled on the bedside table, the loveseat, spilling from the ottoman by the chair. He was obviously a voracious reader, something that didn't surprise her.

Soft light spilled from a brass floor lamp to her left and two table lamps behind her. The golden glow played across Christopher's features and gilded his complexion as he watched her from the doorway.

The man fit the furnishings, Billie mused as she ran her fingertips across a copy of Henry James's *The Bostonians* lying open and facedown on the night table.

Her eyes flickered over the bed's rumpled sheets as she kicked off her tennis shoes, resolve wedging itself before impatient desire. Ever aware of his searing regard and the wash of heat it poured over her, she unfastened her shorts, let them slide down her legs, and tossed them on the ottoman. Then she crooked a finger at him. "Come here."

Christopher straightened from the doorjamb and crossed to

where she stood. He waited before her in silence, the only sign of puzzlement the slight furrow between his brows.

"Hold up your arms," she instructed, and when he lifted them, she caught the hem of his T-shirt and drew it up and over his head in one strong sweep, leaving his raven hair ruffled, his lean cheeks flushed.

He reached for her, but she evaded his touch.

"Now your sweatpants." Moving with excruciating care, she slipped her fingers between the drawstring waistband of his jersey bottoms and his hard, flat stomach, the soft trail of hair there tickling her knuckles as she found the strings and tugged them loose. His pants slackened on his hips, and he said nothing as she tugged them down and let them fall in a puddle at his ankles. With a single step, he freed himself and kicked the garment aside.

Billie wanted nothing more than to drink in the sight of his smooth, hard-muscled physique clad only in a pair of white boxer-briefs, but she averted her gaze and led him by the hand to the bed, where she held back the sheet for him.

For the first time, genuine humor played around his mouth. "Tucking me in?" he asked.

"And myself with you, just for a little while."

After a surprised hesitation, he climbed beneath the sheet and scooted over, and she followed, waiting until he'd situated a pillow behind his head before she stretched out on the mattress beside him.

"Closer," he murmured.

She aligned herself against him and her cheek found his chest, the place where the skin was warm and stretched tight over muscle, beneath which his heart beat firm and steady. Her arm encircled his waist, and when she was comfortable, she released a deep, contented sigh.

"I don't know how I'm supposed to act," he spoke against her hair as he stroked her arm, bared by the sleeveless tank.

"Happens to the best of us," she said drowsily.

Beneath the sheet their legs tangled, naked skin sliding together, sleek against hirsute.

His fingers settled at the curve of her backside, his touch warm through the thin silk of her panties. Above her, he shifted his head to meet her gaze. "What happens now?"

"Now you sleep," she whispered.

His mouth quirked. "I suppose I deserve this, to have the woman I desire take me to bed to . . . sleep."

"You're drunk." She reached up, found his cheek, and brushed her fingers through his tousled hair. "Close your eyes."

His chest rose beneath her temple as he drew in a breath, released it in a slow, heavy sigh. His lashes lowered, opened again, and then slid closed.

Gradually Billie felt the tension seep out of his body, and soon his breathing came deep and even.

She nestled her cheek against him, reveling in the sexy scent of his skin: faded soap, laundry detergent, and something else deliciously, wholly male. Desire thrummed as forcefully through her veins as the blood that carried it.

She could teach him a thing or two about making love, no question. Show him the difference between sex born of love and mere copulation.

But not now. Now he slept, and after a moment, without meaning to, she followed.

Somewhere in the night, Christopher stirred awake. A blinding light pierced his eyelids. He held up a hand to block the glare before he realized it was only the dimmed light spilling from the bathroom.

God almighty. To his pounding eyes, the glow seemed as intensely bright and relentless as a spotlight, and he turned to bury his face in the pillow, wondering how the hell he'd slept through it in the first place.

Ah, yes. Beer, then beer, then more beer. Then whiskey.

Then Billie.

The scent of soft, warm female filled his senses and he shifted his head, squinting against his rumba-rhythm headache to look at the woman sleeping next to him.

Her face was turned slightly away from him, dark hair puddled on the pillow like a halo. He could only see the curve of her cheek, the fringe of her lashes, tipped gold by the glow pouring through the bathroom door.

A strand of hair threaded through the small silver hoop in her earlobe and curled against her cheek. Her breasts rose and fell beneath the thin white tank top with an almost imperceptible motion. She slept as silent and motionless as if she were under an enchanted spell.

He braced himself on an elbow to get a better look at her and held his breath, momentarily forgetting the pain behind his eyes. There was something excruciatingly intimate about watching a woman sleep, especially this woman. Because even with a vicious hangover battering his system, all he could do was stare at her, wanting and needful, while desire quickened the flow of blood in his veins.

She'd stayed and held him through the storm, wrapped her warmth and comfort around him . . . and for that alone he cherished her, but there were so many more reasons he'd fallen in love with her.

As if sensing his regard, Billie stirred and turned her face toward him, dark lashes fluttering. Her lips parted, expelled a sigh. One hand brushed at her nose, then flopped onto the pillow beside her, palm up, and she settled back into stillness.

Christopher let his gaze slide down to her lips and imagined them curved in humor. It had sucker-punched him in his solar plexus the first time he heard her laugh . . . and since then, she'd hardly smiled at all, and laughed even less. He'd seen far more confusion and unhappiness in her features in the time they'd known each other, and the burning compulsion to banish the foundering past, to bring her to a place of joy, reared up within him.

Make it right, Christopher, she'd said. *Give me a reason to stay.*

He loved her. He wanted to wake her up and tell her, show her in the only way he knew how.

In the end, though, his hammering headache demanded a return to sleep. Settling back against the pillow, still half drunk on liquor and the scent of her skin, he laid his hand in hers, closed his eyes . . . and smiled when her fingers curled around his in response.

Billie awoke with a start, wide-eyed and instantly alert. The cheerful morning sun glowed beyond Christopher's bedroom window.

Oh God, what had she done?

She'd only meant to close her eyes for a moment; instead she'd slept through the night, and the three articles she owed Nora for the upcoming issue of *Illicit* still needed last-minute polishing. Nora would kill her if she overran this morning's deadline.

Beside her, Christopher was still positioned on his back, sheet slung low across his bare stomach, one tanned arm flung above his head, as though he hadn't stirred even once during the night.

Sleep of the dead—or the drunken. A fresh wave of consternation swept over her at the memory of last night's strange unfolding, and she slid from beneath the sheets, careful not to wake him.

As she stepped into her shorts and fastened them, her gaze

drifted back to him. Desire dried her throat. All she wanted was to forget *Illicit*, forget her obligations, climb back into bed with him, run her hands over his bare chest, kiss his delectable mouth . . . and he wouldn't push her away. Deep in her feminine soul, she knew how he'd wanted and needed her last night, and that nothing, not even the dissolution of the alcohol's effects, would change that now.

Wake him.

Briefly, thoughts of deadlines and rushing home to dress for work faded away. Heart thudding with indecision, Billie moved in silence around to his side of the bed and gazed down at his face.

In repose, his features were seraphic. His lashes lay like ashy shadows on his cheeks; the untold stress of the last few days had worn lines in his complexion. Even in rest, a frown left two shallow creases between his brows. His fingers still rested on his stomach, tanned against the stark white linen; they twitched once, and his dark head shifted slightly on the pillow.

She wondered what he was dreaming.

Easing down on the mattress, she studied his hand, the long fingers that had plied and caressed her body with such skill, the broad wrist and smooth skin. Veins stood in rigid road maps along his forearm. The inside of his biceps was a little paler than the rest of him.

There was so much she didn't know about him . . . like how he would taste there, in that fair-skinned, vulnerable place where she so wanted to press her lips.

A soft ticking drew her drugged regard from his body, and she glanced at the alarm clock sitting on the granite-topped night table. God, now she really was late.

As she rose to turn off the alarm, Christopher stirred and rolled to his side, reaching for her hand. "Where are you going?" he murmured, voice husky and sleep-slurred.

"I have to go home and get ready for work," she whispered. "Don't wake up."

His lashes never lifted. He settled back against the pillow with a deep sigh, and the veil of unconsciousness softened his features again.

Unable to help herself, Billie leaned down and kissed his mouth, letting her lips linger for a sublimely sweet, breathless instant.

Loving Christopher Antoli, she reminded herself, was like waltzing on quicksand.

Tiptoeing out the bedroom door with tennis shoes in hand, she glanced back at his sleeping form and heaved a sigh of regret. For the mistakes she'd made. For the mistakes he'd made. As much as she wanted it, how could their relationship grow from the muddied place it had begun?

CHAPTER EIGHTEEN

It was gone.

The thumb drive containing Adrian's interview was gone!

Frantic, Billie ruffled through the loose reports and documents on her desk, then dug into the desk drawers, yanking out folders, notebooks, paper supplies. A glint of lime green caught her eye and her pulse leaped. Lifting out a file filled with interview notes, she snatched up the thumb drive. When she plugged it into her computer, it read "Women over Thirty Dating Interviews."

Wrong thumb drive.

Her heart plummeted . . . and a sick, clairvoyant like suspicion gnawed at the edge of her mind.

Pulse racing, she picked up the phone and buzzed her editor's office.

"Nora Richmond."

"If I come down there right now, you're going to reassure me that you know nothing about the disappearance of a thumb drive off my desk, right, Nora?"

Silence. "Come to my office," Nora said finally. "We need to talk."

The trek from Billie's desk to the editor's door took a century and drained every last ounce of strength from her body. Her darkest desires were on that little piece of plastic. She felt as though she'd been marched onto a platform and stripped naked.

Stepping into the sleek, contemporary office, she closed the door gingerly behind her, panic widening her eyes as she sought to read the truth on Nora's face. "Did you take my article about Adrian?"

Nora squinted at her from behind a mug of steaming herbal tea. She'd been trying to kick her caffeine habit for the past week and was crankier than a junkie on the wagon. After a hesitation, she wheeled back on her chair, opened a desk drawer, and slid the incriminating evidence across the desk toward Billie. "I had a feeling you'd be angry."

Hysterical laughter threaded with relief bubbled in Billie's throat as she reached for the thumb drive. "It's a total invasion of privacy."

"An inadvertent one, and I'll explain that in a minute. First, I don't understand why you lied and told me the article was incomplete and that you had no interest in finishing it."

"It wasn't intended for anyone's eyes but my own. I erased it off my hard drive. For all intents and purposes, it was gone, except for that damn flash drive." Tension banded the muscles in her neck, and a relentless throbbing began behind her left temple. "You read it?"

"Of course I read it. It's brilliant." Nora stood and braced nail-bitten fingertips on the desk blotter. "I don't normally snoop through your work, Billie, but as usual you ran late this morning, and I had a deadline! I sent one of the interns into your office to find the articles you were supposed to deliver to me at nine o'clock. Your hard drive was clean except for the dating article, but she finally came back with three thumb drives. Lo and behold, I stumbled across the finest, most provocative writing I've ever seen you produce." Her frown deepened. "And speaking on a strictly personal basis, I made a few assumptions based on what I read."

Billie swallowed her anger and crossed her arms across her breasts, flipping the piece of plastic end to end between her fingers. "So now you know."

It shouldn't matter. There was no shame in loving Christopher. The shame lay in using him for his favors—paying him, but denigrating him all the same—as Nora had once done.

"Are you still seeing him?" the editor demanded.

"Yes. No. I don't know." Billie glared at her, restless and incensed. "It's certainly none of your business."

"What's that supposed to mean?" Nora found her chair and sat again, an expression of insult and confusion darkening her hawkish features. "Why is this such a secret, Billie? You obviously love this man. You always tell me about these things. I thought we were friends. So what have I done lately to make you think you can't talk to me anymore?"

Billie could hardly stand to meet her eyes. "Oh, come on, Nora! Think about it. Why would I talk to you about falling in love with Adrian? I know you paid him for his services, long before I ever met him."

Nora sat back, slack-jawed. "Where the hell did you come up with that?"

Billie searched her mind and couldn't pinpoint an exact source. "You alluded to it."

"Oh, for crying out loud." The editor took another gulp of herbal tea, tossing it back like whiskey, then set the mug on the desk hard enough to slosh the dregs in the bottom. "I visited Avalon twice. Two parties, on someone else's tailcoats. Window-shopping only. No sex. No fun and games. You think I'd pay Azure's fees? She gives new meaning to the old term *whorehouse prices*."

"But you said . . . You told me . . ."

"I might have name-dropped, but I didn't say I slept with any of those men. For heaven's sake, Billie, only the wealthiest women can play that field. Although I do believe you've now single-handedly rendered that law null and void."

Billie covered her face with her fingers, a sick relief adding to the heat burning her cheeks. "Oh, Nora. I thought . . . I mean, you talked about Adrian like you and he—"

"It wasn't for lack of trying, of course. But even if I'd had the money, it was impossible to land an appointment with him. As you now know, he was like a god in that place. When I thought of asking Azure to let us interview one of her boys, I thought, who better than the very best?" Nora smirked. "I'll bet she's kicking herself in her svelte backside right about now for letting him slip through her fingers."

"He didn't quit," Billie said with a tired sigh. "She fired him before he could."

"You should have put that in the article. It ended with too many unanswered questions."

"Why would it matter?"

"Readers will want to know."

"That article's not intended for publication, Nora," Billie said sternly, her fingers tightening on the thumb drive as though she could squeeze its secrets back into safekeeping.

Nora's penciled brows arched up. "Too late."

Even the air molecules seemed to pause. Then Billie remembered to breathe, and her heart remembered to pump, and pump, and pump, until it lurched with sheer, frigid panic, a wild thing behind her breast. She closed her eyes. "Please tell me you didn't publish that article."

"Don't be ridiculous! How could I not? It's incredible! I can't wait for the buzz it'll stir in this town. You're going to be famous, Billie Cort," she added with a broad smile.

So her name was on the article too. *How to Betray the Man You Love, by Billie Cort.* "But—who edited it for privacy?"

"I removed anything that could expose Adrian's identity."

Trembling, Billie clasped a clammy hand to her pounding throat. "You took out all the names?"

"Everybody's except Luke DeChambeau's. His suicide is public record, of course, and proof that the piece isn't some tabloid-quality fairy tale we made up for ratings. Truth is a hell of a lot more provocative than fiction, isn't it?"

Billie's legs wobbled beneath her; even her insides seemed to liquefy and dissolve. "But you can't publish Luke's name. You can't—"

"I can. The layout's already left graphic design."

Faint rumblings in Billie's subconscious signified the advent of the world's collapse around her. "The—printer has it?"

Nora glanced at her watch. "The first pages are coming off the press as we speak. But why are you so frantic? No one's going to know who Adrian is. I know how to damage-proof these articles, Billie. I've done it for years. Who would possibly draw a correlation between Lucian DeChambeau and—"

"The Antolis." Billie backed toward the door. "They knew Luke DeChambeau. They know my name. When Rosalie reads that issue, she'll know. I have to warn Chris."

"The Antolis? Rosalie? Who's Chris?" Nora yelled after her as Billie flung open the door and sprinted into the hall.

But Billie didn't stay to explain. She didn't see the startled faces of the office workers she shoved past, or feel the perspiration mist her hairline and trickle between her breasts. The buzzing in her ears had blackened out every sensory detail of the world around her, until the only visible path before her led directly to Christopher Antoli's door.

When the apartment door swung open, a jolt of electricity galvanized Billie's already quivering nerves.

The mere sight of him stole the purpose from the forefront of her resolve and replaced it with hot, shivery delight. She stared—the hungry female in her couldn't help it.

Gone was the desperate, tousled man from the night before. The one who stood in his place was freshly showered, wet hair combed back from his face, dressed in a crisp white T-shirt and faded jeans. Relaxed. Rested. Welcoming. Even the sight of his bare feet acted like an aphrodisiac on her flustered senses.

A smile had softened Christopher's features when he opened the door and found her there, an expression of sheer pleasure and something suspiciously close to relief. Now he stepped back to let her into the foyer, dark eyes sparkling and trained on her face. "Good morning."

At the same time Billie opened her mouth to reply, the scent of soap and woodsy aftershave slammed into her, and the words died in her throat.

God help her. This was going to be devastating.

"You look beautiful," he added, when it became apparent she wasn't going to speak. "I like the dress. Very professional." He took a single step forward and started to reach for her, but then their eyes locked, and he paused.

"I can't stay," she blurted, a surge of self-disgust snapping the tail of her declaration.

Her dismay spiraled deeper as the pleasure fled his features.

Christopher might have left Avalon behind, but he still knew how to read a woman, and Billie sensed the slow realization creeping through his mind as his gaze swept an inventory of her face, her posture, her body language—arms clasped tightly across her waist, a barrier against him.

Confusion dimmed the warmth in his eyes. The same vulnerability of last night, the same hurt and bewilderment. Just a glimpse. Then it was gone.

Enthusiasm now coolly under wraps, he moved around her and closed the door. "I wondered about you when I woke up. I looked for a note, but you didn't leave one."

"I was late for work. I hadn't intended to spend the night, but then I fell asleep . . ." Billie swallowed and tried not to notice the slightly paler skin of his fresh-shaved jaw. "How do you feel?"

"Much better, thank you." The words carried a deeper import than the usual perfunctory response. He nodded toward the kitchen. "Can you stay long enough for a cup of coffee?"

Something to hide behind while she brought the world crashing down on his head. "Okay."

Neither of them moved right away. Their gazes clung, a silent conversation unfurling between them, comprised of questions too painful to answer.

Unable to bear her guilt another second, Billie swallowed the lump in her throat and grasped his hand. His fingers curled around hers, and after a hesitation, Christopher drew her close to him and leaned to brush a soft, tentative kiss across her lips.

It wasn't enough. With a hunger born of long-restrained desire, of broken hope and the inevitable grief to come, Billie surged against him, snaked her arms around his ribs to meet at the long sweep of his spine, and let her lips open beneath the warm, sweet pressure of his mouth.

"You came back," he whispered, and with trembling despair, she realized he'd been waiting, unsure, unsettled by the lingering promises of last night and the uncertainty of today.

They stood in the foyer like that, wrapped around each other, reassuring with tongue, hands, and the urgent sway of man into woman, until a panting Rudy materialized at their feet and wedged his ninety-pound body between them.

Christopher gave a shaky laugh. "Coffee," he said, as though suddenly remembering. "If you still want it."

"Yes." She drew in a deep breath and averted her gaze. "We need to talk, Chris."

In the kitchen, she seated herself at the tiny café table and watched with a trudging pulse as he retrieved two mugs from a cabinet and poured the hot, fragrant liquid that had been brewing in an espresso machine near the stove.

He was poignantly oblivious to the approaching storm, this man she loved. And though she knew it wasn't truly her fault Nora had published the exposé, Billie felt as though she alone wielded the weapon that would unravel the finely woven threads of his well-being . . . fragile threads he'd clung to last night. Strands of his dignity that she'd once sought to help him lace back together.

Setting a steaming mug on the table before her, he paused beside her and laid a gentle palm on the crown of her head. "What's on your mind?"

Billie swallowed, the truth tap-dancing on her lips. "Last night, to start."

"Ah, last night." He seemed to mull over the memory while he seated himself across from her, fingers embracing his coffee cup on the table in front of him. The steam curled a caress beneath his chin as he watched her with speculative concern. "I may have been intoxicated, but believe me, I remember."

"You know I stayed," she choked, her fists clenched in her lap. "All night. I slept beside you."

"Yes." His gaze drifted to her lips, lashes disguising his sentiments. "Thank you. Apparently I needed it."

She bit her bottom lip and stared at her coffee.

"Billie." He slid aside his mug. "What's wrong?"

The realization hit her then: she couldn't do this. She couldn't break the news to him now, not while he sat so patient and attentive across from her, his consideration focused on *her* feelings.

And *his*—Billie smothered the desire to weep. His feelings would be pulverized when she was through.

But it could wait, couldn't it? The October edition of *Illicit* wouldn't be released for another week. She could tell him about the article in a few days, after she'd scrubbed the scent of him from her skin, the memory of his warmth and tenderness from her mind.

Still, she'd never be able to accept the fact that she, Billie Cort, had somehow managed to transform Adrian of Avalon into Chris Antoli, a beautiful, vulnerable, and—*God!*—maybe even enamored, man. She'd made him feel safe again. Safe enough to care for her. He thought the hurdles were behind them, yet the black mountain looming before them was insurmountable.

Looking at the frown darkening his features, she found herself incapable of divulging the truth.

"Nothing's wrong, other than I've been neglecting my job. I have deadlines, which I actually missed this morning, because I was here, sleeping in your bed. I . . ." She drew a breath, ever aware that her falsity froze her features and probably screamed its presence to him. "I don't even know why I'm here, really." Her gaze skittered away. "I just wanted to make sure you were all right."

"I'm all right," he said, his dark eyes searching her face.

"I'm glad." Pushing back her chair, Billie stood. "Thanks for the coffee. I have to go."

Christopher didn't move. "Please don't."

"But I have errands. I have to pick up my dry cleaning."

"They'll be open all day," he said, then added softly, "coward."

The air around them seemed to pop and sizzle, like the single drop of water that, in the silence, slid from the coffeemaker and boiled itself on the still-scorching hot plate.

Restive, Billie hugged herself and unconsciously sought to rub heat into her arms, bared by the chestnut sleeveless dress. She knew how to reject a lover. She'd done it before, swift and merciless to put the guilt behind her. No matter how much it stung, she knew how to cut ties with a man, no hesitation.

Any man except this one.

"Last night was a mistake," she said in a defeated voice. "Thank God nothing happened between us."

"Oh, I wouldn't say nothing happened." His mouth curved up, that old provocative smile, telling Billie she'd already lost control of the situation. "I came to some monumental conclusions somewhere in the night."

She lifted a hand to stop him. "Please— I just— I shouldn't have stayed. I never intended—"

"So why did you?"

"I was afraid you'd hurt yourself."

"Liar. You stayed because you couldn't help yourself. You stayed because you love me."

"That's— I—"

"Billie."

She closed her eyes, broken. Before she could move, think, react to this wild, electrifying moment, he reached out and grasped her wrist, leading her around the table to his side. "Come here."

Numb, she followed his direction, then dropped to his lap at his urging, eyes wide and fixed on his face.

He fingered a strand of hair that had escaped from the bun at the nape of her neck and tucked it behind her ear, the feathery touch raising chill bumps on her arms. "You stayed because you know, despite the despicable bastard I've shown myself to be, that I love you too."

Billie's heart stumbled in her chest. The brightly lit kitchen faded around them, the hard heat of his muscular thighs beneath her bottom, the scent of coffee and delectable male—details tunneling to nothing until all that remained were Christopher's piercing, watchful eyes.

He loved her.

Throat dry, she clenched her jaw and looked away from his painfully beautiful face. "How am I supposed to respond to that?"

"I don't know. Let's try it again and see if anything comes to mind." His thumb brushed her chin, then her bottom lip, a fleeting caress, drawing her attention back to him. "I love you, Billie."

The reiteration slammed into her like a steel wrecking ball. She shot from his lap and turned away, trapped by disbelief and utter dismay. She'd waited so long to hear the words. She'd so desperately wanted his love—and now . . . now . . . the weight of his heart in her hands was too great to bear. Tears welled in her eyes, too long pent up.

Behind her, the iron legs of Christopher's chair scraped the tile floor. His touch came at the small of her back, his voice at her ear, low and direct. "Still can't think of a response? Tell me, then. What does a woman want to hear from the man who loves her? Teach me, Billie. All I know are scripted lies."

A sob, sudden and unbidden, rose in her throat. "Have you ever used those lies on me?"

He didn't hesitate. "Yes."

"And now you're asking me what I want to hear from you? You expect me to believe what you say?" The anger she'd harbored toward herself exploded inside her chest. Whirling to face him, she snapped, "Hell, I don't know. Choose something from your broad repertoire. Impress me. And then I really do have to go."

He never flinched under her vehemence. "Why are you doing this?"

The bewilderment in his expression couldn't possibly be a lie. Nor the ardor. And oh, Billie hated him for it. Hated him for coming clean so very late in the game, almost as much as she abhorred herself.

Just tell him about the article and be done with it. The Adrian she'd once known would have offered *her* such devastating truth without blinking. But Christopher was someone else. A sweet, beguiling stranger.

Weeks of frustration and heartache—and a silky, curling thrill too deadly to acknowledge—welled within her, pushing aside her misplaced ire, swelling the tears on her lashes until they spilled down her cheeks. "But if I stay, you know what'll happen."

He seemed to recognize the momentary falter in her belligerence and his hand immediately grasped hers. Never taking his gaze from her face, he led her from the kitchen, his movements calm and intentional. "Tell me what you think will happen, Billie."

"We'll end up in bed."

"Seems we already crossed that bridge," he said, and leaned to turn on a living room lamp.

They reached the sofa, where she refused to sit. The urge to weep made it hard to breathe. "But this time will be different. We'll have sex."

"Yes," he said, wiping his thumbs over the tears escaping down her cheeks. "That's what people do when they love each other."

Billie shook her head, swallowed, tried to speak. A sob escaped her, then another, and another, ripped from her deepest conscience, until her shoulders shook and her head dropped beneath the weight of despair.

As she cried, Christopher drew her against him, cradled her head and pressed her cheek to his chest, where his heart beat steady. His fragile heart—as tenuous as her own. He would feel so betrayed when it was over. He would try not to hate her, and he would fail.

She cried until her insides felt hot and empty, until her feet hurt from standing in chic pumps, and beneath her cheek his T-shirt was soaked translucent from her tears.

"I n-need a t-tissue," she managed finally, shuddering with intermittent vestiges of grief as she sank down on the sofa.

"Don't go away." He left her sitting there and disappeared down the hallway, then returned with a box of Kleenex. Kneeling before her, he removed her shoes with solicitous care and set them neatly aside, then waited while she blew her nose and wiped the smeared mascara from her face.

When she was done, he eased up on the sofa beside her and curled a finger beneath her chin, tilting it to examine her swollen eyes. "I don't know why you're crying, only that it has to do with me. Usually I'm more than a little aware of the damage I've caused, but this time I don't understand. Make me understand."

She shook her head, squeezing her eyes closed to yet another opportunity for confession.

Christopher sighed, waited, and when she still didn't speak, he pulled her closer and pressed his lips to her hair, the warm comfort of his body soaking into her. "If you really feel compelled to leave, I won't try to stop you. But first . . . tell me you know I love you, that no woman has ever touched me like you have. Tell me I haven't failed in this one thing, Billie. Even if it's all you leave me with."

Billie couldn't contain the cry surging in her throat any more than she could stop the inexorable passage of time, counted off by the soft tick-tock of the grandfather clock nearby. Her arms slid up between them and around his neck, clinging, her eyelids lifting to find his gaze filled with uncertainty and need. Oh, the agony of this. How could such wild confusion and delight exist in the same moment?

"I believe you," she whispered, turning her cheek into the gentle caress of his palm. "I believe you love me."

"Billie . . ." Before she could move, think, draw a breath, his mouth covered hers, and she was instantly, utterly lost.

CHAPTER NINETEEN

Desire exploded in every cell of Billie's body and blasted away her common sense as she melted against him, trembling lips parting under his, at once ravenous and suppliant. Flavored with the remnants of coffee and the salt of her tears, the kiss was ambrosia and aphrodisiac both, a tantalizing hint of pleasures waiting to be explored.

"Chris," she whispered. "I want you so much."

"Then take what you want." His smile blossomed against her lips, a fleeting manifestation of joy, and then he slid one arm beneath her knees and hauled her onto his lap, impossibly close, not close enough.

The faint fragrance of laundry detergent and sultry hot skin suffused her senses. Agitated by the barriers of their clothing, she twined herself around him the way ivy wreathes the oak, and rubbed her temple against the feathery softness of his hair. Her fingers guided his roaming hands to her breasts, left him there to take his fill, and moved to stroke the smooth nape of his neck, dipping inside his T-shirt collar in search of muscle and sleek heat.

With a groan, Christopher hugged her and buried his face

against her breasts, his warm, moist breath bathing her through the linen of her dress. "You feel so good, Billie. I need you so much."

She nipped at the tender skin on the side of his throat, took from him a trace of salt and faded aftershave before she nosed up to touch his ear. Her lips closed around his earlobe and she drew it into her mouth, and sucked until he shivered and his fingers dug helplessly into her back.

"Christ . . ." The single word hissed into the silence, prayer and oath and completely void of pretense. It fanned Billie's excitement and drove her to mesh herself with this beautiful man who'd been part tormenter, part lover, and now, at last, the fulfillment of her heart's desire.

"Kiss me," he gritted, palms moving up to clasp the sides of her head. And because he sounded as desperate as she felt, she acquiesced without hesitation, and moaned into his mouth when it opened hotly beneath hers.

Oh, the sweet torture of the age-old ritual unfolding between them—the blind, searching crush of lips, the seesaw of strident breaths, the lift and thrust and retreat of male into female—all leading to one elemental act that Billie could no longer live without.

Darkness and dread slid away. Nothing mattered anymore except the restless shift of Christopher's muscles beneath her hands and the growing fervor of the kiss they shared, until it seemed they sustained each other on breath and carnal hunger alone.

"I've wanted this a long, long time," he whispered. "Since the beginning. I've wasted so much time . . ."

"Shh." She laid a soothing palm to his chest. "Your heart is beating like a runaway train." Her fingertips trickled along the smooth brown hollow of his throat. "And here . . . I feel it here, as though it could jump out of your skin."

"And here." He pushed her hand down between their bodies and led her fingers to cup his erection through his jeans. Even with the thick denim as a barrier, Billie felt the throb of blood racing and swelling him, and her eyelids slid closed with the sheer sensuality of the moment.

Their only exchange after that was the sound of their breathing, hers a sporadic release, his escaping in sharp pants. Christopher lifted Billie free of his body as though she weighed nothing and turned her to straddle his lap, tugging the hem of her dress up over her hips when it impeded her movements.

Her knees settled to bracket his thighs, hands twisting in his T-shirt, clinging in preparation for the sinuous ride. Instantly his hips pushed up and she sank down, again, again, control lost, swaying and grinding against his straining erection, as though no clothes existed between them, as though he could thrust through his jeans and the lace of her panties and burrow his way to her very heart.

Breathy sounds of pleasure and desperation tore from their throats. The pressure was unbearable, yet not enough. He could delve so deep inside her there'd be no beginning or end to their bodies, and it wouldn't be enough.

"Billie." He grasped her waist to still her against him. "Wait."

She understood. The violent shudder of his body told her that the rhythmic rub of sex against sex could only offer a premature finish to the naked union they both craved.

Parting, they took in each other's hot, sleepy eyes and flushed cheeks and swollen mouths, and exchanged smiles born of the joy and uncertainty of first-time lovers.

Then Christopher's lips returned to hers, slowing, his grasp loosening from its concrete hold on her ribs to glide and stroke, breasts, arms, shoulders, molding her into a malleable, languid form under his hands. An artist working his creation.

Billie tried not to protest his slowed pace. He was the finest lover, but it wasn't his practiced skill that propelled her to the height of arousal. Rather it was the loss of his control, and the revelation of his fragile human heart in the face of a woman's love.

Man or mirage, he understood her so well, her needs, her urges, and deepest secret desires. It had always been this way, as though his black, black gaze could pierce straight to the core of her feminine soul and read what simmered there. Wild desire . . . and the desperate need to be loved for every part that constituted Billie Cort. The girl, the woman, the myriad misplaced puzzle pieces that his love could set right.

"You're everything to me," he murmured, nuzzling his nose against the sensitive skin behind her ear. "Making love to you won't be enough, Billie. I want more. I want everything."

"We have forever," she replied, and buried her face against his shoulder when the dark truth tapped a chilled, bony finger at the base of her conscience.

But they did have this moment, damn it. And if it was all Billie could cling to, she planned to show him what making love was truly all about so that neither of them would ever forget.

Shifting away from the cushions, Christopher slid down on the sofa's expanse and took her with him, letting her weight guide him until they lay prone, Billie on top, breasts crushed against the hard wall of his chest.

His fingers inched her dress up higher until it wadded around her waist, leaving only her panties to shield her. Instinctively her hips moved against him again, seeking his hardness, offering a sultry invitation. Christopher let his knees fall open so that she slid between them to find brief succor once more against the hard ridge of flesh rising beneath his jeans.

And it was right to do this, to fall into him, to be absorbed in his beauty and need and passion, away from the pain of reality.

"I want you inside me," Billie whispered against his ear. "Don't make me wait." Her tongue swirled there, in the wake of her heated words, until he shuddered and his breath came quick and shallow.

Impatient now, his palms slid inside the elastic of her panties to cup her bottom, fingers bracketing strained, tensile muscle, then easing down to tease the feminine chasm that waited, wet and wanting, for his entry.

Billie's back arched in response to the fluttering caress.

"Ah, Billie," he said, his eyes heavy-lidded as he stared up at her. "I feel like I'm touching you for the first time. Like the past never happened, like I never knew all the soft and hard and wanting places on a woman's body until now. I never knew what it was to want like this. I could go crazy from it."

She swallowed thickly, her excitement climbing with each circular dip of his fingertips as they teased but never quite penetrated. "I love you, Christopher."

"Then make love with me." He shifted his head on the cushion, hands returning to her hips to draw her more snugly into his body. "Show me how, Billie."

Gladness seized the reply in her throat. She pressed her lips to his with unrestrained passion, sinking her fingers into his hair to hold him, and sealed her fate.

When they parted to draw breath, she got to her feet and extended her hand. He took it and let her lead him past the blinding sun spotlighting the balcony, past Rudy, who raised his head just long enough to watch them move by, and into the cool, dim bedroom, where mint green walls swallowed them in silence.

They paused in the middle of the room, and when Christopher grasped her shoulders and turned her toward the closet, Billie found herself gazing in the mirrored bifold doors at a snapshot of two lovers treading in the eye of a swirling storm.

Christopher's reflection stared back at her, dark, solemn, waiting. And she: wide-eyed. Pale. Wanting. The picture seared itself into her memory forever.

"I want to see you." Her voice trembled. "With nothing between us. Take off your clothes."

In reply he reached behind his head, grabbed a handful of his T-shirt and drew it up and off in one strong sweep.

His hands went to his button fly, his lashes shielding the fire in his gaze as he glanced down and slipped the buttons swiftly through their holes. The jeans slackened on his hips and he pushed them down, took his boxer-briefs with them, stepped free and kicked the clothing aside.

Billie held her breath, the only sound in the room the thud of her own hammering pulse. She had tasted his mouth and skin and manhood, swallowed his essence, held his head as he suckled her naked breasts, taken his fingers and tongue inside her . . . and yet none of it had been as telling or intimate as this moment.

He was lean and sinewy without being bulky, every muscle sculpted by an ethereal hand. The epitome of male beauty . . . and he wanted her. His body said so. His eyes burned it into her soul.

"Oh," she said at last, her gaze volleying between his body and his reflection in the mirror to examine each delectable side of his physique. "I'm speechless."

Amusement softened the stern lines of his face. "Turn around."

She did as he directed, and felt his hands rest on her shoulders, his lips brush the nape of her neck. The pins slid from her hair. Her bun loosened and uncoiled, tumbling free. Against her back his naked body radiated heat. She stared ahead at their reflection, watching him, the fine curve of his brow, his dark lashes and sensual mouth, the rise of his bare shoulders behind her, the way his blunt-tipped fingers curled against her hip. His hand slid around to her stomach, rubbing in slow, sinuous circles as he dipped his head and caught her right earlobe between his teeth.

Billie tilted her head to the left to give him better access, shivering as his warm breath sent chills along her sensitized skin.

His mouth grazed and nipped at the tendon on the side of her neck. The circular stroke of his hand moved lower, until it rested at the juncture of her thighs. Rubbing, rubbing, sliding desire-dampened silk against her yearning flesh, while behind her, his erection burned and prodded.

The slide of her zipper sang in the silence, and the radiant warmth of his body seeped into her naked back. When Christopher slipped the dress from her shoulders, released her bra and bared her breasts, goose bumps spread anew over her skin, tightening her nipples until they ached.

Watching her reflection, he caught her wrists, brought them behind her back, and held them captive with one hand, the motion jutting her breasts forward. "You're beautiful."

"Thank you." Her words shook. "But don't compare me to the women you've seen."

"There's no comparison." His free hand captured her chin and forced her to face the mirror. "When I look at you," he said against her cheek, "I see the beauty of a life I never should've left behind."

Instant reality whipped out to sting her, but she shook it aside. *Don't think, Billie. Just feel. Feel.*

Behind her, his erection brushed against her captive palms. Her fingers curled around him, blindly reading his tumescence, but then he stepped to the side, out of her reach, and cupped her breast with a gentle hand. Capturing her nipple with thumb and forefinger, he enticed her with tugs and flicks, like the soft, sinuous workings of a mouth, until she cried out in divine frustration. He released her wrists and shoved the wrinkled dress to her feet, then delved inside her panties, feeling for her wetness as his black, sleepy eyes stared at their mirrored image.

Pleasure coiled tight in Billie's muscles and stripped her inhibitions. She didn't like to look at her naked reflection. The mirror at home showed a lonely girl locked in a thirty-three-year-old, less-than-perfect body. But the woman in this mirror was oddly beautiful, flushed, trembling, her dark hair wild against her shoulders. Christopher's easy worship lit a flickering flame inside her, and she glowed with the luminescence of a woman adored.

He watched too, mesmerized, his fingertips circling, circling, slippery wet and unerring as they sought entrance to her body. He slid one finger inside her, then two, testing her. *How much can you take?*

Until her head dropped back and she uttered a half-human cry. *Enough.*

Then it wasn't enough. She wanted him inside her. More than his fingers. More than the slow, measured thrust he now offered, the heel of his hand brushing her swollen flesh with each deliberate rotation.

Desire weighted her eyelids and she struggled to keep them open and trained on that dark hand buried inside her panties. To oblige her, he tugged the lacy bikinis down to her thighs, baring her to both their gazes.

The short, harsh breaths that escaped her escalated into whimpers. She turned her face sharply aside, riding the edge of orgasm, every muscle tight and quivering.

"I'm going to come," she whispered, her fingers digging into his forearm as it flexed with the thrust of his hand.

"Open your eyes." Christopher's voice came rough, feral against her neck. "Watch yourself, Billie." His fingers spun magic inside her body, dancing against that electric place deep within her.

In the back of her frenzied mind, Billie saw the explosion before she felt it. Wide-eyed, she stared back into the mirror and watched the stranger there as the shudders began. They started small, radiating out like ripples from the point of a pebble's impact, coasting with the pitch of her cry as it built in her throat and burst forth.

"Oh, oh, oh!" The tidal wave of pleasure swept her consciousness far out to sea, where a riptide caught it and held it, suspended, until she drowned in it. The strength dissolved from her knees and Christopher held her upright, his mouth at her ear, whispering, his hand playing the rhythm, playing her body, relentless, until all she knew was wet, hot, thrusting ecstasy.

When the surge ebbed away, he turned her, limp and drained, in his arms, and whisked her panties to her feet. His erection brushed her stomach, so hot and hard it stirred her from hypnotic stupor. Immediately her fingers went to it, caressed the firm, fiery head, slid around the drop of moisture that had gathered there. While she touched him with hands that still trembled, he kissed her mouth, drew out her tongue and suckled it, stealing her breath. Then pleasure seemed to get the best of him and his head listed to the side, eyes closed, captive beneath her rhythmic touch.

"Ah, Billie. That's so good . . ." Abruptly he made a violent noise in his throat and jerked her fingers from his flesh. "Too fast," he said breathlessly. "Where's my control?"

Encouraged, her hand slipped down again and sought him, a fresh wave of heat flooding her cheeks when she found him impossibly harder, like satin-covered stone. It throbbed in her fingers, a rhythm of warning. "You feel like you could burst."

"I might, if you keep that up." Backing away, he caught her hand and led her to the four-poster. "This is my bed," he said, his voice low and strangely hollow. "You're the only woman I want here"—he guided her hand to his heart—"and here."

Quicksilver joy stole her reply. Holding tight to his hand, she climbed into the bed, where the soft linen was cool against her feverish skin. Christopher paused long enough to retrieve a condom packet from the night table drawer, then followed her, graceful, sinewy, exquisite. Hers.

Kneeling before her, he caught her chin, his thumb stroking her bottom lip, then inside it, against her teeth.

"Billie," he said, his words thick with want, "put your hands on me again."

But the frantic push toward sexual union had stilled within her, smoothing into sultry need that fed itself on sweet, torturous delay. She closed her lips around his thumb and drew it into her mouth, flicking her tongue over the short, smooth nail the way she'd caressed his erection in the woods at Rock Creek Park. When she released his thumb, she looked up at him. "More."

In wordless reply he offered his palm, and she kissed the center where the skin was tough, tasting salt and heat. Her lips moved to his wrist, and her tongue traced the rigid veins that throbbed with the ferocity of his pulse. There his skin was soft beneath her lips, vulnerable. Farther up, his muscles were tightly strung, and she sank her teeth gently into his biceps, her fingers brushing the soft hair beneath his arm.

When she reached his shoulder, she trailed a line of slow kisses to the base of his throat, which moved as he swallowed and said, "My God."

Billie drew back and met his hot, piercing eyes. "Where else?"

Sliding down on an elbow beside her, he slipped a hand beneath the heavy hair at the back of her neck and pulled her forward to meet his lips. It was a moist, openmouthed kiss, tongues sparring, rapid breaths exchanged.

But she wasn't yet done. With a gentle palm to his chest, she pressed him back against the pillows, and when he acquiesced, folding an arm beneath his head to watch her, she shifted to kneel beside him.

Her breath caught and held as she skimmed a single fingertip down his throat, over his hard-muscled torso, to the tough, flat terrain of his abdomen. The muscles there contracted when she dipped into his navel and followed the faint path of hair that encircled it and trailed to his groin. His cock jutted from the dark thatch, surging slightly with every beat of his heart.

"Chris Antoli is beautiful," she said softly. "I'm so happy to know him at last."

His throat moved, but he didn't speak, just watched her with suspiciously bright eyes.

Swallowing the lump of emotion in her own throat, she wrapped her fingers around his shaft, stroked him, counted the rhythmic throb of his pulse as she leaned to kiss the engorged tip of his arousal. But there were other parts of him she didn't yet know, and she wanted to learn all of him before these euphoric, fleeting moments dissolved into cool reality.

Moving to kneel between his legs, she nudged them farther apart, slid a hand up the inside of each muscled thigh, and gently cupped his testicles. They too seemed to throb in her palm, and she studied them, their resilient texture, so at odds with the concrete solidity of his penis. Tucking her hair behind her ears, she leaned forward, skimmed her lips along the taut, hair-roughened skin of his inner thigh, and then carefully drew the soft orbs into her mouth, first one side, then the other. Suckling. Stroking with her tongue. Testing their weight. Marveling at the physical beauty of a man, this man. His taste. His texture. His rising passion.

Christopher was silent, watching her with heavy-lidded eyes, his quickened breaths escaping between slightly parted lips.

While she tongued him, Billie reached up and closed her fingers around his steely erection, and found it so hot and hard, it burned her palm. Her other hand slid under his buttocks, paused to explore the firm anatomy of him, to read the restless shift of muscle as his hips thrust hard and instinctive into the cradle of her touch, into the suckling heat of her mouth. Lifting her head, she touched a careful fingertip to the stretch of tender skin beneath his testicles, and smiled when at last a soft sound rumbled in his throat and he let his head drop to the pillow.

"Please," he said.

"Please what? Please stop?"

He groaned, one knee falling wide to grant her access.

She'd never touched a man so intimately. Her heart pounded with the recklessness of it, with the power of giving such personal pleasure.

His body was on fire, and yet chill bumps raised the fine hairs on his torso, and he shuddered.

Breathing erratically, she tightened her right hand on his erection, gave it a slow pump, down to the base and up to the head now pearled with seminal fluid. At the same time, she leaned to close her mouth around his testicles again, to suckle and lick and stroke.

A series of hard shudders vibrated through Christopher, warnings of an impending orgasm. "Not yet," he whispered, a tormented plea. "Please. Not yet."

Quickly releasing him, Billie crawled up his body and into his desperate embrace.

He rolled her beneath him, damp body arching into her, mouth hungry and searching as it opened over hers. "What are you doing to me?" he groaned against her lips, his voice feverish and hoarse. "Whatever it is, don't stop. Don't ever stop touching me. Don't ever stop loving me . . ."

"I can't stop," she replied, her words shaken as she clutched his hair and stared up into his eyes. "I don't know how."

His hand blindly fumbled for the condom on the bedside table, knocking over the brass lamp with a resounding crash, but neither of them looked to measure the damage. Trembling, Christopher knelt in the middle of the bed, ripped into the packet, and together they rolled the condom over his erection. Then easing back against the pillows, he drew Billie toward him until she straddled him and her knees sank into the soft give of the mattress.

Need rushed between them, beaded their skin with perspiration as she held his head against her heart and his lips found her nipple, pulling, sucking, sending jolts of pleasure to the aching place that rode the tip of him.

"Take me inside you." His fingers dug into her hip while the other grasped her hand and led it to him. Together they found the slick, hot portal where her body opened for him, and with a sharp inhalation, Christopher thrust up inside her.

Instantly it was more pleasure than Billie could stand. The idea that they'd only just begun nearly frightened her. A climax from this—the kind only Christopher could give her—would kill her.

"Chris," she said, "oh, please," as he held her waist and moved her up and down his shaft. It became a sobbing chant, as rhythmic as the undulation of his body under her; it went on and on until the second orgasm shook through her, and then a third. One spasm rolled into the next, until ecstasy and lust melded into sweet pain, no longer divisible.

Christopher lunged upright and buried his face between her breasts, his breath coming in ragged pants against her skin. The muscles in his arms bunched beneath her fingers each time he lifted and lowered her, and Billie's head fell back, her body a vessel for him, floating above him, floating in rapture.

She cried out in protest when he abruptly unseated her. "Wait," he hissed, holding her at arm's length with shaking hands. "Wait."

But primitive need pushed them back together, and Billie didn't want his skill, his iron restraint, his go-all-night control. She regained her position and wrapped her legs around his waist, so open to him that he slid inside her as though they'd never parted.

"Let go," she whispered. "For once. Let me do the work. Let me do it all."

"Billie." The strangled word wrenched from his throat, and he finally surrendered. Bracing his hands behind him for leverage, he clenched the sheets in desperate handfuls and arched into her like a wild horse bucking its breaker.

Billie clung to his damp shoulders with every ounce of strength she owned. "I love you," she whispered, seeing the gradual loss of focus in his dusky eyes as his climax began to crest. "I love you, Chris."

The passionate declaration seemed to shove him into oblivion. His features tightened with the agony of pleasure too great to be borne.

As the shudders took him, she covered his open mouth with her own and rode him through his orgasm, absorbing the violent shake of his body, the hoarse sounds of ecstasy, his complete vulnerability as his ejaculation jetted in scalding rushes from him.

And for that sweet, surreal instant, Billie Cort felt like the most powerful woman in the world, the only one who'd ever truly known Christopher Antoli, heart, body, and soul.

CHAPTER TWENTY

With the gradual return of sanity came the serpentine shadows of dread that passion had held at bay. Darkness snaked around them, stealing Billie's peace while Christopher remained blissfully, fleetingly unaware.

She tried to shake off the creeping truth, grasped at a few more precious minutes of peace and euphoria, and failed. She had to tell him about the article. She had to warn him.

Somewhere in the spacious condominium, an air-conditioning unit kicked on and flooded the room with a chilled draft. Billie shivered and curled closer to Christopher's still-damp body, aching deep in her soul.

There's an article, Chris. About you. Neon arrows pointing down at your head couldn't make your identity more obvious. If your family sees the issue, they'll know. They'll know how you sold your soul and lost your honor and identity for all those years. Lucien's name will tell them . . . and the words are mine.

She groped for his hand and laced their fingers together against his flat stomach, loving him, hating herself for her recklessness.

Christopher lay in replete, easy silence, eyes half closed. In the living room, the grandfather clock softly bonged the hour of one. Rudy's claws clicked on the wooden floor out in the hallway, but he didn't invade their intimacy with his sweet, mournful presence. The sighing huff and thud indicated his heavy collapse at the bedroom's threshold.

When Billie at last tried to shift and meet Christopher's eyes, he held her tight. "Don't . . . move. Don't go tearing off. Lie here with me. Rest."

A sigh shuddered from her lips and she tried to relax against his chest. She couldn't control the trembling that rippled through her, and didn't trust herself to speak.

Seconds ticked by. Dread tightened her chest, closed her throat, ached in the marrow of her bones like a pervading cancer.

When at last her heart thudded heavily enough for him to read its death-march rhythm against his own chest, Christopher stirred and glanced down at her. "What's wrong?"

She didn't answer. He rose over her and pressed her against the pillows to study her. "What is it? What's wrong, Billie?"

She blinked back a hot rush of tears. "I wanted to tell you before. It's why I came here in the first place. But you see, I'm too in love with you." She didn't care that it came out sounding raw, or that her every vulnerable emotion was written on her face. "I don't want this to end."

He didn't reassure her or question her or demand the reason for her unruly emotions. He just stroked her face, his lashes raising and lowering as his eyes searched her features.

At last she drew a breath and retrieved the truth from beneath viscous layers of remorse. "I overslept this morning with you, and missed my deadline at *Illicit*. I owed my editor three stories by nine o'clock, and of course I was completely late getting to the office." A sigh escaped her lips, and she closed her eyes. "In the process of searching my desk for the articles this morning, Nora came across the thumb drive I'd saved your article on. She read it. Then she pulled up some of my notes, shifted things around, edited the article, and sent it off to the printer under my name. All before I could get there and stop her."

His fingers slid from her jaw and he shifted his weight to both elbows, his frown focused on his hands. "Did you use my real name in the article?"

"No. I told you I would never betray your trust."

The tension drained from his shoulders and his dark head dropped.

"But Nora used Luke's real name in the article," she added low. "She added details about Luke DeChambeau jumping from your balcony. Adrian's balcony. Adrian with the dark hair and eyes, who came from a big, loving Italian family and grew up in Bethesda."

Christopher lifted his head and met her gaze. She couldn't read his face, couldn't measure the damage. Adrian's mask looked back at her, remote and steely.

The sheets rustled and a cool draft of air shivered over her naked skin as he sat up on the side of the mattress. "Do you have the thumb drive with you?" he asked, his voice low and even. "I'd like to see what truths Ms. Richmond had to work with."

"It's in my purse."

"I'll wait."

Painfully aware of her nakedness, Billie climbed from beneath the sheet, grabbed his T-shirt off the floor, and put it on, pulling it down over her breasts as she headed toward the living room. The sofa cushions were still rumpled from their lovemaking, and the sight of the disarray loosened the flow of tears that had built in her chest. Thirty minutes ago on this sofa, they'd been totally immersed in each other, wrapped in love and lust and perhaps for the first time, honest emotion.

That was all over now.

When she returned to the bedroom with the thumb drive, Christopher had pulled on his jeans without bothering to button them. Wordlessly he extended his hand to her, palm up. She laid the small plastic piece in his grasp, and avoided his eyes when he moved by her toward the room that held the computer.

Down the hall, a door clicked shut. He wanted privacy. He wanted distance from her.

Bereft, she closed herself into the bathroom and washed up, unable to meet her own reflection in the mirror. His belongings were scattered over the granite countertop: a Mason Pearson hairbrush, an amber bottle of some expensive aftershave, a tube of toothpaste beside a still-damp electric toothbrush. An unbearably intimate display of his personal effects. She used the burgundy hand towel to dry her face and paused to inhale his scent buried deep in the plush terrycloth threads. It was on her skin, the fragrance of his passion.

When Billie reemerged, she searched for her panties through tear-blurred eyes and put them on, her grief sitting like lead in her chest.

Her dress was a wadded mass of wrinkles. Holding it up, she stared at it in dismay and wondered what to do. Damn it, she wouldn't suffer wearing it through the lobby on some sick adolescent walk of shame.

Retrieving a pair of Christopher's khaki shorts folded in a nearby laundry basket, she pulled them up over her hips and rolled down the waistband's excess material to keep the shorts from puddling to the floor. She would just have to go barefoot and carry her pumps under her arm, chin held high, not making eye contact with any passersby . . . if Christopher told her to get out after reading the article.

Which, undoubtedly, he would.

Billie gingerly opened the first door to the left and found him in a smaller bedroom, seated at a maple desk that faced the door, his attention fixed on the computer monitor in front of him while its blue glow washed the life from his stern features.

Everything commonsensical within her shouted that he didn't want her intrusion, but she couldn't just leave without saying something, without expressing how much she loved him, how regretful she felt.

For a torturous eternity she hovered in that doorway and watched the frown lines deepen between his brows as he stared at the computer, his elbows propped on the desk, hands fisted together against his lips.

She never loved him more than at that moment, when he was slipping away from her, a mile for every traitorous word he read.

Finally he drew a breath and looked over the monitor at her. No emotion played on his features, just that glassy impassivity she recognized so well. "May I keep the thumb drive?"

"Of course." She shifted her weight away from the doorjamb, arms tucked tightly around her waist.

He ejected the thumb drive, set it aside, rose, and tucked the rolling chair beneath the desk. Perfectly contained, an Avalon automaton . . . until he wrapped a hand around the back of his neck, as though it hurt him. As though he were wounded.

She swallowed. "I don't know what to say."

"There's nothing to say." He brought his hands over his face, dark head bowed as if in prayer. Seconds passed. Then his palms slid away and he looked at her, flushed, blinking, like a man awakened from a nightmare. "Luke's family will be devastated by this."

"Oh God. I know. I—"

"My sister has a subscription to *Illicit*, Billie. Want to know what's really ironic? I'm the one who bought it for her, for Christmas last year. *Illicit* and *Cosmopolitan* and *People*. She reads all that stuff."

"Chris." She started toward him, but he stopped her with a shake of his head.

"Please . . . don't talk."

Silence fell between them, so crowded with anguished sentiment that no room remained for spoken words. Then his troubled gaze focused on her figure. "I see you found something to wear home."

She took a step back as he approached, inexplicable shame climbing up her neck at the blank observation. "My dress—"

"You can keep the clothes, of course." So composed. So polite. "Toiletries, towels, whatever you need are in the bathroom vanity."

"I already used them."

He paused before her. "Did you drive, or do you want me to call a cab?"

"I drove." She swallowed. "Thank you."

Two polite strangers, mere minutes after engaging in the most personal act of all. An awkwardness Christopher had been well acquainted with as Adrian of Avalon. If he'd addressed her as "Ms. Cort" it wouldn't have surprised her. But he didn't. He didn't address her as anything. He looked right through her.

A hollow yearning nestled deep in Billie's stomach. The universe stretched between them now, and she knew better than to reach for him. His stony features told her he didn't want the touch of hands, words, or sympathy.

"Do you have all your belongings?" he asked.

Everything but her heart. She nodded, stricken.

"Then you'll forgive me if I don't accompany you down in the elevator. I have to get ready for the repercussions of this—I have to think of the least destructive way to approach the people this will hurt." He paused. "I don't think there is one, do you?"

Restive, she ducked her head to meet his eyes. Their love affair couldn't end like this, in such a chilled stall of emotion. Billie wouldn't allow it. Straightening her spine, she said, "Chris, you have to know how much today meant to me. How much *you* mean to me. Making love with you—I felt—"

"You felt guilty," he said, staring at some distant point over her head. "I understand. All along you knew about the article, and yet you couldn't bring yourself to spit it out. But you should've told me before I put my hands on you, Billie. Before I let down my guard."

"Don't you think I know that?" She twisted her hands together to keep from reaching out to him. "I tried to tell you."

"You didn't try hard enough."

A fresh wave of heat flooded her face and confirmed the truth of his words. "Would it have changed what happened between us?"

His attention shifted to her face, features tight with insult and anger. "I can't answer that. I can't even think right now."

"Chris—"

"You want me to accept your apology for something that technically wasn't your doing, right? Then you can walk out of here redeemed, wearing your regret like the uniquely kind-hearted exposé reporter you are. But when that magazine hits the stands, Billie, you'll forget your remorse. *Illicit*'s going to make a vulgar amount of money at the expense of everyone who loved Luke. His family. *My* family. Me. Nora knows it, and you know it. You knew it when you walked in here this morning."

She shook her head and covered her face with her hands, her

blood gone icy in her veins. She'd expected his dismay, his hurt—but this derision—she hadn't been prepared, and she didn't know how to defend herself.

In the wake of her wordlessness, he moved back toward the desk and swiped up the incriminating thumb drive. "You know what kind of ball-busting editor Nora Richmond is. She headed up sleazy tabloids for a decade before she ever hopped on the *Illicit* luxury liner. You *knew* this. You knew it was a risk to leave anything as personal as that article and all its notes in a place where she had easy access. So don't you suppose, in the farthest reaches of your subconscious, that maybe you hoped she'd find it?"

"No!"

His lips curled. "Not even a little bit?"

His contempt sliced through her like razor wire. "Christopher—what could I possibly gain from hurting you this way?"

"I think we just covered that." He turned the thumb drive in contemplative and caressing fingers, then abruptly dropped it in the trash can beside the desk. "You should go."

Anguish and indignation jockeyed for position in the sunken place where her heart had crumbled. "I'm not finished! If you think this was intentional, then you really have no idea who I am at all. How could you possibly love me and in the same space, think me capable of such spite? You don't love me. You don't love anyone. All the . . . the things you said when we were in bed . . . they're just . . ."

Tears sprang to her eyes and she shook her head, coming apart despite her effort to contain her emotions. "It's a scary thing to be vulnerable like this, isn't it? To be out in the real world where people have real feelings, and real love is just as available to you as the sick emotional games you've become so comfortable playing?" She stepped toward him and jabbed a hard finger in the center of his bare chest, beyond humiliation, beyond pride. "I want to know why you bothered to leave Avalon, *Adrian*, when it's so obviously where you belong?"

He stilled, and with him, the world. "I fell in love," he said softly.

The unarguable hopelessness of their relationship crashed through Billie, and suddenly she couldn't get out of there fast enough. She started to turn away, but he caught her elbow and jerked her back to face him. They were both panting, Billie's breath leaving her in short, furious sobs.

Myriad shadowed emotions played across his features as he stared into her face, fingers tight on her arm. Even amid the dark anguish of the moment, wayward passion simmered between them, hot and sparking to ignite.

"No more," he said wearily. "Let's put this to rest. Go home . . . and let me pick up the pieces of the mess I've made. I don't know what I'm going to say to my family, to Luke's. I don't know how . . ." He stopped and looked away, his throat working. When his eyes drifted back to her, they were filled with despair. "But I'll leave you with this. Think what you want about me, Billie. You're the only part of my life that hasn't been a lie."

Grief choked any response she might have made, and she closed her eyes, hot tears pooling and trickling down her cheeks.

He moved past her to the bedroom and left Billie standing alone in the midst of their shattered beginning, the slight stirring of air currents between them his parting caress.

Christopher found Rosalie in the backyard, raking leaves that floated to the ground as quickly as she could scrape them into piles.

She was humming "It Was a Very Good Year," sweetly off-tune and with the passion of one unaware of being observed.

Wordlessly, he grabbed a plastic bag and began filling it, clearing three large, sweet-smelling mounds near the flagstone patio before she glanced back toward the house and noticed his presence.

"Oh my God!" She clutched her heart as the rake fell from her hand. "Christopher! You scared me to death! Where have you been?"

She approached him, her stodgy legs strong and determined in faded jeans as she strode across the grass to glare up at him. "I don't know whether to hug you or slap you silly."

He gazed into her frustrated, velvet-brown eyes. Despite his roiling anguish, humor tugged at his mouth. "I'm sorry."

If at all possible, her frown deepened. "So no explanation for your sister? You always have excuses, Zio. What is it this time? Why the disappearing act?"

Glancing around the yard, he folded his arms across his heavy, thudding heart. "When do the kids get home?"

"Not until three thirty. Why?"

"Do you have time for a cup of coffee?"

"Of course." She paused to shuck off her man-sized gardening gloves and nodded toward the house. "Come in, then. And I expect a full explanation as to why you fell off the face of the earth."

For the second time that day, Christopher called upon finely honed emotional control. The first time was to distance himself from Billie. Now it would help him lay out the truth—*Adrian's* truth—for his sister. He spoke in measured tones as his fingers turned the coffee cup around and around in its saucer, voice soft and even, heartbeat and nerves firing like a slow-measured metronome under Adrian's intense will. The only thing he failed to do was look into Rosalie's eyes. If he had, if he'd seen the big, liquid tears he knew had gathered on her dark lashes, it would have broken him.

It took forty-five minutes to condense eight years of impropriety into a single, sordid tale. Through all of it, Rosalie sat across from him in silence, unmoving, her coffee gone cold in its pretty porcelain cup.

When he was done, silence filled the space between them, thick with consternation and anger and grief—whether his or hers, he didn't know.

"And Billie knew all the while?" Rosalie's words shattered the brittle quiet, uncharacteristically subdued with shock. "She knew what you were all this time? What you did at that place?"

"Yes." And had loved him in spite of it. *Christ.*

"Was she your customer?" She stumbled on the question, her voice hushed, as though the idea was too heinous to verbalize.

"No." He met her gaze and flinched at the pain he saw in her chubby face. The same pain that had been in Billie's features right before she'd walked out of his life.

His initial anger and sense of betrayal over the article seemed inconsequential now to the hole Billie's absence created in his world. In his deepest heart he knew she hadn't meant to hurt him. He'd been far more deliberate in the way he retaliated. He'd caused her far more pain, and worse, he'd done it on purpose.

Because he was afraid. Because his soul was wide open to any damage, deliberate or accidental, she might inflict. Because . . . "God help me." He scrubbed his hands over his face. "I love her."

"Yeah? You've got a funny way of showing it." Rosalie shoved aside her cup, her fingers playing with the edge of the paper napkins she'd set between them. "As for her—she must be some kind of saint, or nutcase, that she could love a—a—"

"Please." He bowed his head, rubbing the space between his brows with trembling fingers.

Rosalie shoved back from the table and stood, her shoulders stiff as she set her cup in the sink and ran the water. "You have to tell the DeChambeaus."

"I've written them a letter. They would never agree to see me."

"They'll never speak to you again. They'll want to forget you ever existed in Luke's life."

"I know, Rosie." He swallowed and stared at her back.

"The kids will be home soon," she said without turning around.

Christopher's cue to leave. This subdued, hollow response from his volatile sister was far more punitive than any screeching explosion she could have subjected him to. Woodenly, he got to his feet, pushed in his chair, and moved to set his cup and saucer on the counter by her elbow.

"I'll be at my apartment tonight," he said. "I'll answer the phone."

"What makes you think I'd want to talk to you?" She turned off the spigot and looked at him, plump tears pooling on her eyelids. "I feel so betrayed, Chris. On behalf of our family, I feel shamed and confused and wounded. I don't understand where we went wrong with you that your path would go so far away from God and love and integrity. We loved you too much, maybe. Made it too easy for you, that you could bruise your own soul like this. Is that it? Tell me, where did we go wrong?"

"I'm the only one who went wrong, Rosie. It's not your fault, or Mama and Papa's. Just mine. And then my refusal to see my life for what it had become."

He started to reach for her, then thought better and clenched his hands at his sides. "But then Billie came along and halted me in my tracks, first with her relentless questions, then with her love, and— hell, she's exposed me to the world with this damn article. My life is ruined. My worst fears realized, and . . . I love her for it. *I love her.*" Hearing himself say the words filled him with a misplaced peace that burned in his chest, a fragile fire. "I don't deserve her."

"No, you don't." Rosalie wiped her hands and leaned a forearm on the counter, her frown easing just slightly. "You want this woman? This reporter?"

He didn't hesitate. "Yes."

"Then you'd better get your act together, Christopher. Make it so you do deserve her. Make it right so you deserve love all the way around, from Billie, from your family, and from yourself. *Get honest.*"

Christopher didn't reply. He couldn't. He reached out and closed his hand around hers, and she didn't recoil as he'd feared.

A tear rolled down her cheek and she wiped it on her shoulder as though it were an inconsequential mote of dust. "This information doesn't go out of this room, you hear me? Mama and Papa—it would kill them. I'm the only one who needs to know. God—it reads like a soap opera, and a shabby one at that."

After casting him one last searing, derisive glance, she stood on tiptoe, grabbed his jaw with both hands and pulled him down to kiss each cheek. Then she stepped back, and with an expression fierce with pain and passion, smacked him clean across the face, so hard his head snapped to the side.

Christopher heard bells.

"That's for keeping secrets from the people who love you, you foolish man. And for selling your soul in the gutter. You'd do well to make your confession to Padre Rosetti. And not through some private screen in a dark booth. Face-to-face. Or have you given up the Church too?"

Jaw stinging, he managed a smile and leaned to press his lips against her furrowed forehead. "*Ti amo*, my sister."

"Yeah, yeah." She wiped the heels of her hands against her eyes. "The kids are almost home, and if they see you here without Rudy they'll disown you."

"I'm going." He paused at the kitchen door and looked back at her, eyes moist with welling gratitude and regret. "Please forgive me, Rosie."

A single sob shook her shoulders, then it was gone and she waved him off. "Forgive yourself, *idiota*. And come on Sunday for dinner. Bring Billie, if you haven't already run her off."

Ah, Billie, he thought, prayer and lament both. *If only I could turn back time.*

*I*llicit's October issue was the best-selling edition in the magazine's history. A hollow victory for Billie, who sat in the weekly staff meeting with her head in her hands, hardly able to meet Nora's gaze across the conference table.

She hadn't heard from Christopher since that awful day over a week ago, nor had she tried to call him. If he'd had a miraculous change of heart and attempted to reach her, she wouldn't know. Her answering machine remained in disrepair, and when the phone did ring, she jumped, but she didn't answer it. Her single wild rebellion against the world.

Part of her didn't want to hear his voice if he still cared enough to call.

Part of her wanted to throw herself at him and beg him to come back, like a child in the throes of a violent tantrum.

Think whatever you want about me, Billie. You were the only part of my life that wasn't a lie.

Yes, he'd said it, sent her into a tailspin of confusion and grief and another incongruent emotion that felt steady like . . . joy. Because she'd seen the conflict beneath his anger in the instant before she fled his home, his painful uncertainty.

She was the certain one now. Certain that if she didn't get away, she'd beg him to keep her. Then he'd have her pride along with her heart, and for God's sake, she needed to keep something.

Christopher didn't try her cell phone or show up at her apartment, either, and after ten days of holding her breath and ten nights of lying awake with her dry gaze fixed on the ceiling, she made a decision.

The next day, she cancelled her apartment lease. Then she typed a two weeks' notice of resignation, and with tears streaming down her cheeks, set it on Nora's desk.

CHAPTER TWENTY-ONE

Nora reacted with typical indignation, as though Billie's resignation were a personal affront. "You're doing this on purpose. To get back at me for publishing that article on Adrian without your permission. My God, Billie, it was shitty of me in a personal sense, I'll admit it. But the magazine has to come first. I wasn't thinking about your romance with this guy. I didn't know it would affect *you*, that it would ruin—"

"This has nothing to do with Adrian," Billie said, defeated.

"Then what is it? Do you need a steadier assignment? Your own column? Anything you want, I'll arrange it. Just—"

"I need to start over, Nora." Her eyes welled up. Damn it. She never used to cry. "There's nothing here for me anymore. I'm moving to Atlanta. Or farther south. Some place far, far away from D.C."

"You're running away," Nora pointed out. "Throwing away an incredibly promising career for nothing. You're acting like a lovesick fool who's letting her broken heart call all the shots."

Billie glared at her. "Fine. I *am* a lovesick fool. And yes, my heart's calling the shots on this one. It's taking me away from here, where I can forget about Adrian, and *Illicit*, and everything that smacks of the last few weeks, and my dull, depressing life before them."

"It was only dull because you don't know how to relax and live, Billie. You should be more like me," Nora said, despicably self-righteous as always. "I let the body call the shots. I see a man I want, and I grab him. Pure sex, no heart involvement."

"Yeah?" Billie's eyebrows shot up. "That's what it was with Adrian. Pure sex, no heart involvement. Until I fell for him like a block of concrete out a fifty-story window. Trust me on this, Nora. You need to be careful. Your carefree field-play is going to bite you in the ass one of these days."

"And you won't be here to crow about it. Think of all the I-told-you-sos you'll be missing." Nora fiddled with a pen on the desk, then restlessly flipped it aside. "You big chicken. Running away never solves anything. You're throwing away a potential million-dollar career, and don't expect me to support your foolish decision. And if you think I'm going to feel guilty over this, you're dead wrong." Then she shooed Billie from her office, but not quite in time to hide the glimmer of tears in her eyes.

The movers spent the chilly, rainy afternoon hauling most of Billie's belongings down to an orange truck parked in front of her apartment building. While they came and went, she jogged down the street to the neighborhood deli and returned with dinner for the four men, excluding herself. Nothing tasted good anymore, and she'd been too preoccupied with packing up her old life to even think about food. As a result, her jeans bagged in the rear and she had to cinch her belt another notch. There was no one to scold her. No one to worry about her. No one to love.

When she returned, the movers, a ruddy, amiable crew, grabbed their hoagies from her hands with ravenous enthusiasm and sat down in the middle of the box-strewn living room to eat.

Billie wandered listlessly through the apartment and double-checked to make sure she hadn't left anything unpacked, then stood at her curtainless bedroom window and peered through the blinds at Connecticut Avenue.

Somewhere out there, in the big, wide world, Christopher was building a new life. Had his family disowned him? She thought of Rosalie and her capricious Italian passions. The woman loved her brother blindly, and Christopher's truth would bruise her, perhaps, more than anyone else.

Had he withstood the anguish of it all? Had he fled Washington? Was he as big a coward as Billie?

Footsteps thudded on the parquet floor behind her. "Ms. Cort?" Hugh, the foreman of the moving crew, hovered in the doorway, wiping his big hands on a paper napkin. "We're 'bout done with supper, then we're going to empty out the living room. Anything you need that doesn't go in the truck?"

She shook her head. "Take it all, Hugh." Turning back to the window, she gave the busy avenue one last look, and her bleary gaze focused on a gleaming navy blue BMW parked across the street.

Immediately her heart bounded behind her breast. Then she scowled. How ridiculous. Christopher was gone. Done with Avalon. Done with her.

In the living room, the movers returned to their task. Heavy boots clomped out the door, low voices fading down the hallway as they disappeared with another load of boxes.

With a sigh, Billie let the shade drop and turned around.

And found Christopher Antoli filling the bedroom doorway.

"Hi," he said, his dark gaze fixed on her face as though she were the only other person alive.

She forgot how to breathe. Nothing moved. Then he shifted and his car keys jangled in his fingers. "I thought you might have already left town."

"That's the idea." She found her voice, hoarse with shock.

"I guess I was nearly too late."

"Nearly." *Breathe, Billie. Breathe.*

His throat moved as he swallowed. "I tried to call you several times. It went straight to voice mail."

Billie filled her lungs with a steadying breath and recovered. "On purpose. I didn't want you calling me at your usual time, some ungodly hour of the night."

Amusement tugged at the corner of his mouth. "I've been trying to keep more regular hours."

"It's about time."

Christopher bit his lip and studied her across the ten feet that separated them. "I just wanted you to understand that my silence hasn't been deliberate. I came by several times in the last couple of weeks, but you weren't home. Today I went by *Illicit*'s office, and when the receptionist told me you'd quit, I tracked down Nora Richmond. Her secretary didn't look too kindly on me bulldozing into the editorial office, but Nora probably wouldn't have spoken to me otherwise."

Billie nodded. "You're right. Considering everything that's happened, she probably would have hightailed it in the opposite direction if she'd seen you coming."

But he'd trapped Nora in her office like a pinned rat, and the thought was supremely satisfying to Billie. She tried to picture the editor's stunned expression as Christopher Antoli burst into her plush quarters, all determination and dark charisma. Nora's fear would be palpable as violent scenarios of his vengeful motives flickered across her wary mind. Then, because Christopher was . . . well,

Christopher, she'd gradually forget about caution and alarm, and would most likely strike a pose, hand on one slim hip, head tilted, wide smile blazing charm across her features. *"Why, Adrian, what brings you to my humble little office?"*

Billie could envision it all, and the urge to laugh stirred within her for the first time in days. She might miss Nora. Just a little.

"She told me you'd moved," Christopher was saying, "but I decided to give it one last shot. You know"—he leaned a shoulder against the doorjamb, his key ring rhythmically circling his finger—"maybe sneak into your building while the doorman's back was turned and look in your mailbox."

No glib rejoinder came to mind. She felt behind her for the windowsill and leaned her hips against it, too weak to stand. The sight of him stole her most basic motor skills.

"So where are you going?" he asked in the wake of her silence.

She blinked. "Atlanta."

"What's in Atlanta?"

More loneliness . . . and the chance to get over you. "I won't know until I get there."

He wandered farther into the room, flushed from the cold, his masculine appeal so potent it fisted around her heart and squeezed away her breath. He looked less polished than usual. His jeans were faded in all the right places. His navy Georgetown Hoyas sweatshirt, though baggy and soft, did little to hide the breadth and strength of his shoulders. The drizzling rain had left sparkles in his dark hair.

Just a man.

Billie took shallow breaths to avoid being overwhelmed. Her emotions hovered on the edge of ruin, and if he said the wrong—or the right—thing, she'd dissolve.

"Atlanta's a long way from Washington." His shielded gaze

scanned the box spring and mattress, the boxes stacked in the far corner. "Are you running away, Billie?"

"Yes," she said without hesitation. "Absolutely."

Christopher nodded. "So am I."

Squeezing her fingers against the wooden sill, she asked, "Where to?"

"Virginia. I got a job in Roanoke. My condominium is on the market. I'm putting that useless degree of mine to work."

"And what will you do?"

"Social work," he said. "Something that matters."

She thought of him descending the marble stairs at Avalon, so poised and polished and sleek beneath the glow of a crystal chandelier. "The pay will be lousy."

"I don't give a damn about the money."

She stared at him, at a loss for what to say next. "You . . . you mean social work as in soup kitchens? Shelters?"

"Vocational rehab. I think I'll be good at helping people make new lives. I've learned a hell of a lot about starting over in the last few weeks. A lot about regret too and letting go."

"So have I." She averted her eyes from his painfully handsome face. "Christopher, why are you here?"

"For a lot of reasons." He twirled his keys, then clenched them in a fist. "I needed to see you again."

She straightened, focused on him again. "What purpose does it serve, beyond upsetting both of us?"

"I'm sorry." He took another step toward her. "I know it's selfish, but I needed to see your face. To know if I was right."

"About what?"

"About the fact that I struck out at you . . . unjustly. Harshly. That maybe I blew the one chance at happiness that's come my way in eight long years." Sadness imprinted itself in the downward curve of his mouth. "I needed to look into your eyes and be reminded of what I really want in this world. And now that I've looked, I see the pain I've caused. I never meant to hurt you or anyone else. Please believe me, Billie."

His gentle words stole another strip of decorum from her façade, tightening her throat until it ached. "You didn't do all the wounding, Chris. I hurt you too. The article—"

"Yes. The article." He moved closer, a muscle working in his jaw as his dark gaze swept her from head to toe and back. "It wasn't your fault."

"But—"

"I owe you my gratitude."

"Chris, for what? I made a mess of everything with my carelessness. I can't write for these damn seedy magazines anymore. People inevitably get hurt. And this time—I hurt myself. I'm so sorry for what happened."

"But you gave me the chance to set things right." His voice dropped as he approached with measured steps. "You gave me no choice but to do the right thing and come clean. After you left my apartment, I wrote a letter to the DeChambeaus. I know I'll never see them again. So much of my life died when Luke jumped off that balcony."

He stopped and stared past her shoulder at the gray world outside. "I also went to my sister's house and told her everything."

Tears stung Billie's eyes, welling faster than she could wipe them away. "Oh God. What did she say?"

He winced. "It was pretty ugly. She listened, and then she slapped the hell out of me." His hand drifted to his jaw and humor curved his lips. "Nothing like a good sisterly backhanding to put everything into perspective."

"She's a tough cookie," Billie said with a watery smile.

"That she is." He drew closer again, so subtly she was only faintly aware that his warm, particular scent now teased her senses. "Rosie said some other things too."

"Oh?" She pressed herself back against the window ledge, trapped by the invisible electricity radiating off his graceful body.

"She asked me if I want you." He paused, as if waiting for her to inquire what his response had been, but Billie only bit her lip and stared at him.

"I said yes." He stopped a foot away from her, his eyes more richly dark and fathomless than her dreams had rendered them. "'Make it so you do deserve her,' Rosie told me. 'Make it so you deserve love from all the people around you.'"

"She's right, of course," Billie said shakily.

"Rosalie's always right." His gaze glided over her hair, her face, down to her breasts, where it lingered as though he could read the nervous tick of her heart beneath her knit sweater. "And as for me, well . . ."

Billie strained forward, pulse wild in her veins, her attention rapt on his lips as she waited for the declaration that would set her cock-eyed existence right again.

"I know now that I can't live without the way you make me feel."

She tried to focus on him through the blur of tears. "How do I make you feel?"

"Forgiven. Whole. And in the end . . . desperate. I'll do anything for your love. Tell me what to do to win you back."

Oh God. She tried to reply, to swallow the sobs marching up her throat, and failed. Holding up a hand to keep him at bay, she choked, "Give me just a minute, okay? It's been a hard few weeks."

He stood there with his thumbs hooked in his front pockets and waited, watching her with loving regard while she struggled to regain equilibrium. The truth had always been in his eyes; she just hadn't known to look deeply enough. But now she knew. Even as Adrian, when everything about him was cloaked in secrecy, his heart had been the vibrant spark in the black depths of that gaze. And somewhere along the way, he'd given it to her.

"Let me touch you," he said softly. "Please."

"No." Billie flat-out wept as she held out a hand to stop him. "You had your chance to say all these things before I talked myself into living without you. It's too late."

"But my heart won't listen. I hate myself for saying the things I did, for accusing you of a cruelty that you're incapable of. I lie awake at night and everything in me hurts. My heart. My body. I miss your voice, your touch. Your smile. The lack of sleep's killing me."

The air between them vibrated with his sweet, plaintive words, so lush with emotion that she couldn't breathe through it. She groaned and pressed the heels of her hands against her eyes. "Please. You're going to screw up my plans."

"Ah, Billie, don't cry." He came forward and caught her wrists, pulling them gently from her face. "I don't mean to make you sad. I'll go. I'll disappear from your life if that's what you truly want."

"But there's a price, right? There's always a price." Her chest heaved from the struggle to cease her weeping. "What could you possibly want from me, when I feel like I have nothing left to give?"

"Just a kiss." With a mild tug, he brought her against his chest. "It might buy me a few hours of sleep. Yes, Billie? Will you leave me with that?"

In reply, her lashes fluttered closed and she tilted her face up for his taking, her fists clenched between their bodies.

With careful reverence, he cupped her jaw in his hands, and then his mouth brushed hers, warm, slow, gentle. He tasted like mint and heat and passion.

Her breath caught in her throat. His rushed out with her name.

"Billie. You're so soft," he murmured, his kiss a gossamer caress. "So damned soft. Your lips, skin, hair. Your feelings. Soft and sensitive." His mouth nuzzled hers, teasing, lighting and lifting, until she strained for a firmer taste. The silence was agony. Any minute, boots would thud down the hall and the movers would shatter the crystalline promise hanging in the air.

"Damn you," she whispered. "Damn you, Chris. Do you always get what you want?"

"Until I met you, I didn't know what I wanted." His tongue flicked over her bottom lip, dipped into her mouth just long enough to find hers. Then away again.

Billie moaned in frustration. "Kiss me."

"I will." He cupped her throat, holding her still for his delectation. "I'll do whatever you ask."

Liquid desire sluiced through her body and pooled in dark, aching places, taking her sadness with it. She wanted him naked, against her, inside her. He was a drug in her veins, a heady delight she couldn't live without. "Anything?"

"Anything you want . . . in exchange."

Billie was so enveloped in anticipating the hungry ravishing of his mouth, she didn't respond right away. Then the words sank in, and she opened her eyes.

And found his filled with tender humor.

"No . . ." She moaned and thunked a weary fist against his chest. "Come on."

"A favor for a favor." He slid a hand through her hair and brought her forehead against his throat. He was warm and sweet smelling and sexy and wonderful.

Torn between weak laughter and exasperation, she heaved a sigh. "Okay, let's hear it." Even as she spoke, her palms slipped beneath the banded hem of his sweatshirt to find the firm flesh of his back. "What is this, favor number five? What will I owe you?"

"Your forgiveness."

"You already have it."

He shivered beneath the featherlight stroke of her fingertips. "Then your promise."

She drew back to look into his eyes, found them dark and shining with tender gravity. "What promise is that, Christopher Antoli?"

"That you'll come back to me. Be with me. Fill the spot in my life that belongs to you." Pleasure weighted his lashes as her caress slid around to his muscled abdomen. "That feels so good. My God, I've been starved for you."

Enraptured by her power over him, she caressed his chest, tracing his ribs and the goose bumps that blanketed his skin in response, counting the fervent beats of his heart until his breath came in harsh rasps against her lips.

Then he jerked her hands from beneath his sweatshirt and hauled her up against him in a burst of fierce emotion. "I love you, Billie. Give me the chance to make you happy. To show you who I really am—the man who can't live without you. The man who deserves your heart."

Joy swept through her soul, wiping away weeks of gray, replacing it with love for this man, all sides of him. Shadow and light. Adrian. Christopher. Hers.

"I could be persuaded," she said huskily.

A provocative smile tipped his lips. "Tell me how."

"You can start by kissing me. Not a teasing touch, either. I mean down-and-dirty, lips and tongue—"

"I'll do more than that," he whispered, and opened his hot, hungry mouth over hers.

Then they were stumbling around the bedroom, tangled in each other and a slew of half-removed clothing, too ravenous for the contact of bare skin to take the time they deserved, but oh, Billie didn't care. She held his head between her palms and drank from his kiss like a woman parched, forgetting about the movers and the empty room and the throaty, desperate groans that escaped her lips with each sinuous dip of his tongue inside her mouth.

Walking her backward to the door, Christopher kicked it shut and pinned her against it, pelvis to pelvis, stalwart male to resilient female. He fumbled with her jeans, his fingers shaking too much—perhaps for the first time in his life—to undress a woman properly, until she finally pushed his hands away and loosened them for him. Her zipper followed, then his jeans. When she boldly reached inside his fly to wrap her fingers around his erection, he braced his palms on the door above her head and watched, his hips following the silky movement of her caress.

The terse, delicious moment passed in silence torn only by their strident breathing. Then Christopher gently dislodged Billie's touch and lifted her sweater above her breasts, pushed up his own sweatshirt, and dragged his naked chest against her nipples.

Again. Again. Again. Until Billie whimpered, every nerve crying out for more. Until Christopher shook with the enormity of his desire.

"No sheets on the bed," she managed when he swung her around in search of a place to land.

"I don't care." He swept her toward the forlorn queen-sized bed, and together they collapsed on the cold, bare mattress. Their bodies strained awkwardly, entangled, until he found his way between her bracketing thighs and arched against her, seeking heat and softness.

The bed frame squeaked and scooted a cadence along the naked floor without a rug to anchor it. Shoes hit the wooden floor, *thud,*

thud, thud, his loafers, her tennis shoes. Limbs meshed and hunger intensified, and bodies rose instinctively toward completion despite the too-many garments impeding them.

Braced on one strong arm, Christopher managed to get his jeans down around his thighs and then did the same for Billie, freeing one of her legs from her Levi's so that she could wrap it around his naked hips. Wreathed by her intimate embrace, he leaned to kiss her mouth, took his erection in hand and parted her soft folds with the swollen tip, graceful even in his trembling impatience.

Then he froze.

Her gaze searched his face. "What is it?"

"I don't have a condom," he said with a wry laugh. "Jesus, for the first time I'm ill-prepared."

Billie ran a hand through his tousled hair and twined it around her fingers, bracing herself for the answer to the looming question. "Have you been with anyone in the last few weeks?"

"Yes."

Her heart sank, even as a vague smile tugged at the corner of his mouth.

"You and only you," he murmured. "I don't want anyone else, Billie. And I don't want to share you."

"Then I'll go on the Pill. In the meantime . . . " She lifted her hips to press against him. "Are you willing to risk it?"

His answer came with a single slow thrust that filled her. He took in her cry, withdrew and sank into her again, and Billie cried out again, with joy, with pleasure, with the rightness of it. She arched against him, her palms gliding away from his ribs and over the satiny quilted mattress in search of something to anchor her. There was nothing, only the hard, hot body driving against her, the most solid thing in a life that felt utterly dreamlike.

Deeper. Deeper. She squirmed and bucked beneath him, nails

digging into his buttocks, needing more of him. He drove harder, perspiration slicking his belly, binding their skin.

Then Christopher found her hands, threaded his fingers through hers and drew her arms up in a wide arc over her head, pinning her. His breath came in soft pants, his body hovering in wait for her capitulation. Her thrust for his thrust. She moved, he moved, following her lead. In this way the frantic mating slid into a more sinuous rhythm, a dance of give and take. Making love, with no secrets between them, at last.

"I love you, Billie," he whispered.

Billie closed her eyes and pictured the ocean lapping at the sand, surging, taking pieces of land with its force, replenishing it in return. The waves crashed and she climaxed with a single, sharp cry.

When she opened her eyes, she found his gaze, black and fathomless, locked on hers.

Neither spoke. No sentiment could be as eloquently expressed as the ever-quickening exchange their bodies shared. He moved faster now, like a piston as he slid into her tight, welcoming heat, his breath rushing from his chest in harsh pants. The bed frame, lost without its head and footboard, squeaked and scooted a humble accompaniment. Down in the rain-slicked street, traffic zoomed by, brakes screeched. The sound of male voices rose faintly from the sidewalk. Somewhere in the hall outside the apartment, a door slammed.

Clinging to his graceful body, floating in the wake of her pleasure, Billie heard it all, the chorus of life beyond the measure of Christopher's erratic breathing, and she reveled in it, her senses electrified. Their love had a place in the world after all, and the binding power of their coupling made it more than sexual—it was a validation. Life spun around them, and they belonged together. Here, in this protected place. Out there, where no promises were made except the ones they carried in their hearts.

"I'm going to come," he whispered, lips against her ear. "Deep, deep inside you."

The urge to cry rose like fire in her chest and she choked it back, the tears burning her throat, the hot pulse of his ejaculation burning her tender, aroused flesh. Christopher shuddered with the force of his orgasm, struggled for silence and failed, granting grace to the sound of pleasure's power as he cried out her name.

When the storm passed he sagged against her, sought her lips and kissed her again with unbearable tenderness.

"Billie."

"Christopher."

"Come with me to Virginia."

"Oh, yes." A sob squeezed her reply and she reached up to encircle his head with her arms, drawing him down to her, tightening herself around him while they both trembled with the enormity of their emotions.

Male voices floated through the apartment, wood floors squeaking beneath heavy feet.

"Oh, my God—" Billie jerked alive beneath him. "The movers!"

"Uh, Ms. Cort?" Hugh called from the living room. "The company's going to have to send a smaller truck out here to pick up the rest of this stuff tomorrow morning. Rain's really coming down now." Pause. "Can you come out here and sign this form?"

"Okay," she sang in breathless reply, her panicked gaze locked on Christopher's sparkling one. "Just a minute."

They moved like two parked teenagers caught in squad-car headlights and scrambled to straighten their clothing, laughing under their breath and hopelessly driven to touch each other in the process.

When they were both decent, Christopher walked to the door and calmly opened it to three startled, whiskered faces.

"Oh," Hugh said, averting his eyes. "Sorry to interrupt."

"It's okay, Hugh." Billie wiped the dreamy pleasure from her face and stepped into the living room, catching Christopher's fingers in hers as she went. She signed the movers' form with her free hand, never relinquishing her hold on the man she loved. Never again. "Thanks, Hugh. You boys go on. Call it an evening."

"At least you've got your bed tonight," the burly man pointed out with a smile, and beside Billie came a rare, precious sound—Christopher's laughter. He drew her into the circle of his arms.

"Thank God," he said, hugging her tightly, "for small favors."

ABOUT THE AUTHOR

Jamie Disterhaupt has written romance since she was a teenager, and was first published in 2003 under the pseudonym **Shelby Reed**. Her contemporary stories are emotionally driven and contain unique premises that revolve around love and redemption. Jamie also writes paranormal romance and currently has several stories published with Ellora's Cave Publishing, Inc. She lives in Florida with her husband and writes full-time.